## T

## TIME WHEN ALL THINGS SEEMED POSSIBLE. . . .

KATE—Groomed to be a perfect wife and mother, she was a gleaming ornament to her successful husband. But one day she woke up to find the dream had become a nightmare, and the face in the mirror belonged to a stranger.

DOTTIE—The determined outsider, she wanted enough power so that no one could ever put her down again. She rose to fabulous heights and discovered too late that she was missing the one thing money couldn't buy.

ASHLEY—Named after Hemingway's boldest heroine, she was an exotic nonconformist who gave pleasure to her lovers and courage to her friends.

# THE END OF SUMMER

## Nancy Lamb

A DELL BOOK

Published by
Dell Publishing Co., Inc.
1 Dag Hammarskjold Plaza
New York, New York 10017



ISBN: 0-440-12372-0

Printed in the United States of America
First printing—November 1981

*For my family. All of them.*

## ACKNOWLEDGMENTS

Once again, my thanks to Terry Baker, Rita Gelman, and Elaine Markson.

Also, my appreciation to my medical consultants, Barbara Hanke, Rob Weber, Lisa Nicholas, and David J. Flesher.

Lastly, I thank my editor, Sandi Gelles-Cole, for sharing her expertise with me.

# PROLOGUE

Startled, she opened her eyes. The delicate light of false dawn had crept to the bed where she lay silent and alert. Unwilling to disturb the magic of the cool air as she inhaled its crisp freshness through the open windows that faced the mountains, she lay still and wondered if he was there. No, she decided. Gone until next time. She was alone.

Wrapped in the isolation of mourning, she moved slowly out of bed, dressing quietly and methodically in the dim gray light.

Walking barefoot to the kitchen, she prepared coffee and toasted a chunk of homemade bread in the oven. Then she moved to the terrace where she ate her simple breakfast. The rising of the sun, wild and sweet, cast elusive shadows across the hills, staining them with the color of the bluebell and primrose.

Inside the house once more, she made final preparations for this last journey, smiling sadly to herself as she pulled on her worn and soft boots. They would need resoling again soon, she mused absentmindedly.

Cradling a package carefully in her arm, Ashley squinted as she stepped out the door of the house into the bright, almost white light of the September sun. As if in a dream she no longer cared to remember, she walked slowly and resolutely to the stable that stood at the end of the path leading to the spring.

The house and stable, made of earth-colored adobe, blended naturally with the dull sandy red of the surrounding hills. The young woman also seemed an integral part of the land: The natural way in which she moved gave her an inherent dignity, a nobility of purpose that softened the austere beauty of her face.

Opening the heavy wooden door of the stable, she set her package down on the soft dirt near the tack room. Reaching up, she pulled the bridle and saddle from the rail and carried them outside. Then she called to her horse.

From the far side of the corral he approached, shining and sinewy, a magnificent black Arabian with a white star on his perfectly sloping forehead. Even he seemed to recognize the somber importance of the day, standing quite still as she slipped the bridle over his head.

Next came the blanket, hand-woven and thick with brightly colored stripes. Then, with a strong heave, she placed the saddle on his back and secured it.

Retrieving her package, she closed the door of the stable as she returned. With gentle care, she put the oblong container in the saddlebag, creating an awkward lump in the otherwise clean lines of the saddled horse.

Although he was a large animal, Ashley mounted him easily, her long legs moving over him with a strong fluid grace.

Then, turning toward the mountains in the distance, she began her journey. Riding slowly, she leaned over only once to touch the horse on its proud neck. Reaching up to adjust her beige cowboy hat so that it stayed securely on her head, she rested her hand on her thigh, moving naturally with the horse, as if she were an integral part of the animal.

After a long, twisting climb up the mountain, she reached the meadow. Brazen with wildflowers, the soft green grass stretched languidly before her to the trees on the far side.

"All right, Troika," she whispered as she nudged her

horse gently with the heels of her boots. He began to gallop slowly and gracefully, his crescent hooves working in perfect harmony.

Before entering the shade of the trees, Ashley pulled the horse to a stop. Turning to look down into the valley, in the far distance she could make out the speck of what was her house. Then she entered the silvery cool covering of the aspen that grew near the stream.

Hidden carefully in the shade of the ponderosa pine that towered triumphantly over the surrounding trees she reached, finally, the secret place where the wood lily grew.

Twisting her body so that she could touch the saddlebag behind her, she unbuckled the strap and lifted out the container. Carefully removing the lid and replacing it in the bag, she looked once at the contents.

A desolate sorrow passed briefly over the solemn fine lines of her face before she raised it to the sky and closed her eyes.

"Thank you," she murmured with an astonished gratitude.

Then she moved her arm and scattered some of the contents of the container over the lilies. Somber and gray, the ashes floated on the gentleness of the breeze, dancing with spectral purity to their final resting place.

As if she could not bear the sight another moment, she reined the horse suddenly and moved quickly through the trees back to the edge of the meadow. Pausing briefly, she looked to the mountains beyond, awesome in their splendor, then kicked her horse as she leaned forward and said, "Now."

Her midnight-black hair streaming behind her like the banner of a lost cause, she moved her hand back and forth as she rode, scattering the ashes to the wind, to the sun, to the everlasting memory of someone whom she had loved deeply and well.

Pulling Troika to a halt at the edge of the meadow, she returned the now-empty container to the saddlebag before leaning over and patting his neck once again. Bending forward in an awkward embrace, she rested for a short time. Then she began her slow descent down the rocky path that would lead her, finally, home.

She could see the smoke curling phantom gray above the trees long before the cabin came into view. She knew it must be her half-brother living there, but she did not know what to do. He was a stranger, this man, conceived in a secret summer passion long before her father had met her mother.

Vaguely frightened, she hadn't the slightest idea of what she should say, of how she should behave. Having just conducted her own private funeral service, Ashley was not prepared to become involved in a confused confrontation. So she made the decision to ride quietly past without stopping.

Bent over the table in the cabin, on which had been placed a fine piece of sandstone, Joseph Rosetta took the small strand of turquoise in his hand. Hearing the sound of the horse, he stopped his work, hoping it was not another poacher on the mountain.

He was standing in the doorway when Ashley entered the clearing that would take her past the cabin. Tall and lean, he had the dark skin and black hair of his Spanish and Indian maternal ancestors. The bones of his cheeks, high and broad, accentuated the straightness of his nose, the very slight slant of his eyes. But his eyes also revealed their father's blood: They were pure blue, the color of a mountain lake on a clear summer's day. Leaning on one arm against the door frame, he watched her approach.

Her heart pounding furiously, she smiled and nodded, carrying on with her decision to ride past. She would come to him tomorrow and tell him about Nana.

Joseph knew that his grandmother allowed strangers to ride on her land. What she did not allow was illegal hunting and fishing, and careless campers who might not extinguish their fires properly. This rider, he thought, obviously did not fall into any of those categories, since she was carrying no equipment. But there was something about her, something compelling, that made him move closer.

When he stepped out to the path, Ashley had no choice about reining in her horse.

"Hello," she said politely.

"Hello," he replied, his eyes searching out the details of this stranger.

"I'm sorry if I interrupted you," she began, groping for something to say.

"You're wearing my beads."

"What?"

"You're wearing my beads," he repeated.

Still not understanding what he meant, Ashley uttered a quick and puzzled "pardon me?"

"Your necklace." He spoke confidently. "I made it."

Ashley's hand moved involuntarily to her neck, grasping the delicate tendrils of turquoise that Nana had given her so many years ago. That first Christmas.

"The bracelet, too," he said, a simple statement of fact. "I made it for my grandmother."

Ashley looked down at him. It was obvious he had sensed her Anglo blood, even though her dark good looks might have fooled someone less observant. She came from the other world. The one he had entered briefly, then denied.

"Why are you wearing my grandmother's bracelet?" he asked, moving toward the edge of hostility.

Ashley spoke softly. "She gave it to me."

"She gave it to you?"

"How long have you been here?" she asked abruptly.

"Forever," he answered contemptuously.

"No. I mean . . . I mean, how long have you been at the cabin?"

"Here?"

"Yes."

"About a month this time."

"Then you don't know." A wistful kindness crept into her voice.

"Know what?"

"I'm sorry . . . sorry to tell you this."

"Nana?" he asked, his body stiffening as if he were waiting for a physical blow he had known all the time was coming.

"Nana . . . your grandmother . . . died three days ago."

There was no change in his expression to indicate that he had heard what she said.

Reaching down to touch him on his shoulder, Ashley gestured silently that she was sorry.

"She was a remarkable woman," he said quietly.

Ashley sucked in her breath, then whispered, "She was my grandmother, too."

For a long time he just stood there. Staring at her without a word or a gesture, he waited. Finally he spoke. "You are John Van Every's daughter?"

"Yes."

"My grandmother told me about you." He bowed his head in a silent indication of welcome, then said to her, very formally, "I would like to invite you in, but right now I must be alone."

"I understand."

"Are you staying at the house?"

"Yes."

"In a few days I'll come down. We can talk then."

"All right."

He reached out and took her hand. Looking directly into her eyes, he spoke in a manner that was distanced, yet true. "I am sorry for you. Sorry for your pain and your loss."

"Thank you," she responded awkwardly. "And I look forward to seeing you again soon."

"In a few days," he said with a solemn smile.

"Yes." Then she reined the horse toward the trail, never looking back at this stranger who was her brother.

When Ashley reached the last part of the trail she had a clear view of the house. She could distinguish Kate and Dottie sitting on the terrace. Seeing her, they waved broadly, then turned to walk down the path to the stable where they would meet.

It had not been necessary for Ashley to call her friends when Nana died. The wire services had picked up the story the following day, announcing to the world the death of a giant in her field.

Dottie had immediately canceled all appointments for the following week, and Kate arranged for someone to care for her children while she was gone. Then they took a flight to Santa Fe the next morning, arriving just after noon.

The house was unlocked and empty when they had arrived. Checking the stable and finding Ashley's horse gone, they assumed she was riding and settled on the terrace to wait for her.

Now, standing by the corral, they watched Ashley as she approached. They both recognized the tense language of her body—the language that spoke of holding herself together with the solitary strength of her will.

Relieved her friends were there, that she would not have to be alone through another haunted night, Ashley dismounted and greeted them with a flood of loving and warmth.

The three of them, the Troika they called themselves, had first met when they were ten years old.

For almost twenty years they had been close friends. And now, in their common grief, they experienced once again the special comfort of being together that long-term friendships create.

Kate took over immediately, her mothering instincts enveloping them as they returned to the house.

Once inside she spoke quietly. "Now just sit there and relax," Kate directed. "I'll get supper started. I bet you haven't eaten anything decent since Nana got sick."

In response Ashley nodded.

"And then," Dottie added, "we'll drink some champagne. Just like Nana wanted."

It was past midnight when they decided to go to bed. They had spent hours talking about Nana, about how Kate and Dottie had first met her in London, and the many acts of generosity and kindness she had directed toward them all over the years.

Tipsy from the champagne they had been drinking throughout the evening, they were tired and woozy.

"Before we go to bed," said Dottie as she stood, "one more toast to Nana."

Very formally, they raised their glasses. As they touched them gently, the sound of the crystal ringing became the passing bell tolled in honor of an extraordinary woman.

"To Nana," announced Kate. "To the elegance of her life."

"To Nana," echoed Ashley, her voice a profound lament against the backdrop of her anguish. "To my Nana." Then she whispered, choked, her quiet words a scream that rode on the desolation of the night. "I killed her."

# CHAPTER 1

The room was quiet. The special kind of quiet one hears when confronted with something that borders on the awesome. Ashley Van Every, dark and mysterious in her navy blue silk pajamas, was actually trying to hypnotize Dottie Langford.

"Relax now," intoned Ashley in her soothing husky voice. "Just relax. Your lids are getting heavy, getting heavy now. Very heavy. You are relaxed. Totally relaxed."

Dottie lay stretched out on the thick red and blue Persian carpet in front of the fire, moving with the words, drifting into their spell.

It was an astonishing sight. One that Kate Henderson would remember for the rest of her life. The room, even the feeling, was warm and tempting. Warm and tempting like brandy, she would think in later years. Golden and kind. It would become a pure sepia image captured forever on the selective film of her memory, of a time when the dream was innocent and the song was sweet. Three friends bound by the fierce loyalty born of adolescence survived and longings shared. It was all there that night. A melody that graced them with its fragrant cadence before the dream tarnished and the music died. Before it was bleached by a grown-up sun into a future filled with responsibility and choice and compromise.

Kate watched the magic of Ashley in action, warmed by the flames of the fire and excited by the power of her imagination. Her pastel-pink babydoll nightie—a sister in spirit to Dottie's yellow one—was an eloquent spokesman for the unsullied state of her seventeen-year-old body. She listened with wonder as Ashley told Dottie she was now a board. She lay there, her head resting on one chair and her feet on another, without any support at all for the remainder of her body. Stiff as a ruler she lay, just as Ashley commanded. Stiff, with glazed eyes open and silent lips slightly parted, just hanging precariously between two authentic Victorian side chairs as if she accomplished this feat as easily as she walked to the corner drugstore for a cherry phosphate.

Looking back on it, Kate thought that this was the first time she truly understood the confidence of Ashley's power. She knew who she was, in contrast to Kate, who was still searching for the magic formula—usually in the form of a boyfriend—that would make her whole. Dottie, too, knew who she was. And she had already vowed to change it.

"I'm going to be someone," she had sworn to Kate when she discovered that her parents were barred from being members of a club because they were Jewish. "I'm going to be powerful someday."

Kate knew even then that behind this chubby adolescent pledge there lurked a raw determination that left no doubt she would accomplish this goal. The effort alone lent her a kind of burnished grace from which a force and vitality quietly grew.

Eyeing her rigidly hypnotized friend, resembling nothing so much in the flickering light as a corpse laid out for a bizarre Irish wake, Kate whispered to Ashley, "What are you going to do now?" She made no attempt to conceal the anxiety in her voice.

"What do you mean?"

"Well . . . doesn't it scare you? What if you can't wake her up? What if she just stays like that?"

"Of course I can wake her up." Ashley spoke with a

quiet kind of authority that had never left her. "If you can close a door you can open it."

"But what if we get caught? What if the Langfords come home early and see her like that?" Kate squirmed uncomfortably.

Kate had always been like that, fearful of facing discord or coping with complexity. It was a fear honed over the ensuing years into a mask of competence behind which lived a frightened child: a child adept at tucking anxiety into the back of a jumbled mental closet, where apprehension and dread coexisted in the darkness of an uneasy truce.

Ashley managed to awaken Dottie with the technique of the nightclub hypnotist she had watched one evening years before when she had dinner with her parents.

That same night—the eve of their graduation from high school—they talked about how they had met so many years ago, as if their reminiscences would somehow give them strength to face a future much less secure than what they had known up to that time.

Dottie remembered her first day at The Jarrett Academy with something less than joy. It was the first time in her life she had ever heard the expression "show Jew." She also heard sniggering comments about how they had changed their name. It had originally been changed as a defense against Nazis. And now the irony was that they were still persecuted because of their name. She had been admitted to the school as a courtesy to the man Mr. Langford worked for. And it had not been easy being the first Jewish student in a school that had, until then, been the private reserve of well-bred Wasp society.

Powerless. That's what she felt, all dressed up in her navy blue gabardine jumper with the white uniform blouse. She remembered distinctly how she had gone to the bathroom. Somehow she had allowed her sash to become untied and the end of one side had taken the familiar dip into the toilet. Embarrassed, she was trying to blot the water from it with a paper towel when Ashley walked into the room.

"Here, I'll help you," she said sweetly, as if she encountered this situation every day. "I'm new here, too."

That was the beginning. It was the beginning of the friendship between Ashley and Dottie, and also of a kind of special gratitude toward her friend that Dottie would cling to for the rest of her life.

Two days later they struck up their friendship with Kate, and that very first weekend Ashley invited them both to her house for a slumber party. It was there, somewhere between the Cokes and the popcorn, that the Troika was born.

"I bought us a surprise this afternoon," Dottie announced ceremoniously on that graduation eve. "Follow me."

The three girls walked to the kitchen and watched as Dottie retrieved a bottle of champagne from the refrigerator. It was Taylor's New York State pink champagne, a bottle that would be the first of many that they would share through the coming years. Only the brand would change.

"To the Troika," they toasted. "To our friendship, and the class of fifty-six."

The night after the Troika graduation party Ashley raced up the four flights of stairs, taking them two at a time. Waiting for her at the top of the stairs was the only secret she had kept from her friends: Alexander Lain.

Seeing him, she felt shy all over again, remembering the measured cadence of her steps the very first time she had made this climb, six months earlier.

John Van Every could not have possibly imagined the consequences of taking his daughter along with him on a business dinner. He had invited Alexander out of courtesy to his younger colleague, because he had brought a major account into his investment banking firm. This was a coup of sorts, considering the fact that Alexander was only twenty-eight years old.

At this dinner, during which Ashley and Alexander recognized, then muted, their attraction, John Van Every discussed business and the future of this bright young man. The evening had been pleasant, courteous, and surreptitiously dynamic.

A week later, when Alexander called Mr. Van Every at home, Ashley informed him that her parents had gone to the country for the weekend. He took that opportunity to invite Ashley to dinner.

They had hardly tasted their meal. Ashley could not prevent herself from staring at him. He had straight, almost plain features and sandy blond hair. What prevented his being ordinary was the depth of his pale blue eyes, which harbored promises of intensity and discoveries of passion.

To the average eye Ashley might have been considered unattractive; or, at the very best, a young woman who had potential. Her hair, thick and black as the soul of midnight, hung loose and straight to the middle of her back. It was a style completely out of step with the fifties. She had distinctive high and wide cheekbones and a long nose with a hint of a bump on the bridge. It was her short upper lip and full mouth that prevented her looks from being hard. The quality she possessed upon which everyone agreed was "presence."

Secure as she was in herself, Ashley could not find the same comfort in her appearance. She simply did not fit, did not match her family. Her father's fair good looks and her mother's plain dignity offered no hint that they would give birth to such an exotic-looking daughter. She appeared almost Eurasian, with thick-lashed eyes that suggested an almond shape and smooth, creamy beige skin. In a decade in which to look cute was to look acceptable, Ashley Van Every was hopelessly out of sync.

Ashley did not quite understand the origin of her feelings of being unacceptably different. But she did understand that she had spent her life trying to please her father. No matter what she did, she always felt there was something wrong, something vaguely disapproving in his attitude toward her. It was as if she presented herself to him as a rose and his response would always be, "No, you don't understand. Roses are lovely, but what I really wanted was an orchid."

"You are so beautiful," Alexander Lain had said to her toward the end of dinner. "I've never met a girl with navy blue eyes."

"Most people think they're brown," she commented helplessly, enthralled by the electricity that was running between them.

Without artifice, without playing games, he asked, "Will you come home with me tonight?"

I wonder if he means what I think he means, she speculated. Until that time, Ashley—like most well-brought-up girls she knew—had been sacrificed on the virginal altar of generational convention. Reputations were taken as seriously as the communist threat, condemning most young women to the perpetual state of heavy petting and technical virginity.

But all convention sallied right out the window when confronted with the power of Alexander Lain. And Ashley's answer to his simple question had been a very quiet "yes."

As they climbed each flight of stairs inside the building on Fifty-eighth Street, Ashley expected him to stop at the top of each landing. Instead they climbed the distance, arriving breathless and excited at his apartment.

Once inside he took her shawl and draped it over the corner of the sofa. The apartment was lovely, although she hardly noticed. An eclectic combination of contemporary and antique furniture graced a room that was proportioned for another era. The ceiling was high with ornately carved molding all around. Three bow windows overlooked the Plaza fountain. On the dark-stained floor was a worn but fine Oriental carpet. A square carved oak table sat in front of the window, offering the diner the view of the fountain with an edge of Central Park as a backdrop.

"Would you like a cognac?" he asked quietly.

"No thank you," she answered formally. She could think of nothing to say. Instead she turned to him. He kissed her then, a kiss that was gentle and unprobing, yet exciting and erotic. Drifting, she reveled in the touch of his hands as they glided over her tall, strong body. Glided, caressed, conveying at once leisure and urgency. His hands skimmed her breasts and moved down to clutch her buttocks, pulling her hard against him.

"My god, what is that?" he asked, his lips buried in the nape of her neck. "Your ass is hard as a rock."

"It's my girdle," she answered with mild surprise, stepping back slightly from him.

"Do you always wear one?"

"Of course," she answered, shy with him for the first time. "Everyone does."

"Take it off," he said.

"What?"

"Take it off."

Not knowing how else to cope with the situation, she followed his directions, lifting up the black silk shantung skirt of her dress and grabbing the stayed binding of the girdle that bound her waist. Tugging, she slipped it past her hips, wiggling slightly to move it properly. Not bothering to unhook her stockings, she pulled them down with the girdle, leaning over gracefully as she slipped the rubberized combination off her feet.

Alexander bent over, expertly unhooked the stockings from the girdle, then held up the offending article of clothing.

"Never," he directed, "never again insult your body with one of these obscene contraptions."

Mute, she looked at him, having lost the power to speak some minutes earlier. She watched him walk over to the window and hesitate for a moment after he opened it. He took the girdle and tipped it to her as one would a glass of vintage wine, then turned and threw it out the window. Ashley imagined it floating leisurely to earth like a poor wounded pigeon in the throes of death, landing gently on the head of some unsuspecting lady as she crossed the street to join her husband for late supper at the Plaza.

Alexander never even looked back. Walking over to where Ashley was standing, he took her stunned face in his hands and whispered, his lips moving on hers as he spoke, "Let's go to bed."

They walked quietly into the adjoining bedroom. With her back to him, he reached out and unzipped her dress, slipping it easily off her smooth shoulders. Dressed in her underpants, bra and slip, she turned to him, shy, unsure, hesitant.

Unbuckling his trousers, he dropped them casually to the floor. Ashley was awed to see the horizontal bulge that protruded from behind the thin fabric of his shorts.

Suddenly naked in bed together, he kissed her, caressed her. And she followed him as she would an orchestra leader, taking her cues from him, enjoying, falling, feeling in ways that she never had before. On top of her, finally, he made certain she was ready.

When he tried to enter her, the tightness hindered him. More than that, it surprised him.

He leaned back and looked directly at her. "Why didn't you tell me?" he asked quietly.

"I didn't think it was necessary."

"Are you sure?" His hand caressed her brow with a gentle concern.

"Yes," she answered. "I'm sure."

He probed tentatively at first, barely entering, teasing, tantalizing. Each thrust went farther, until suddenly he was there, filling her. She thought then how wondrous, how lovely he could actually be inside her body.

They moved together, finding their own rhythm with which to explore their mutual paths of sensuality, of delight. When he withdrew from her, she was surprised. It did not seem complete. Reaching into the drawer of the table beside the bed, he picked up a foil-wrapped square, opening it with trembling hands. Placing the ring on the end of his distended penis, she watched with undisguised fascination as he unrolled it all the way down, encasing it in a semitransparent glove. Kissing her gently, ever so gently—knowing there was no need to explain, yet understanding that she was curious—he moved his hand down between her legs, touching her, opening her. She closed her eyes and gave up to the moment. Just as she was about to come, he entered her once again and they moved together in a passion she had only read about, only imagined in the safety of her own room, of her secretly erotic self.

The night after graduation she lay close in his arms once again, moving into his very center as he held her, his arms around her tight. Don't let this go, she thought, don't let go of this moment, this time. Don't ever let go.

The following evening, feeling rather silly, Ashley dressed for The Jarrett Academy graduation prom. Ashley had insisted on choosing her own dress, one that was met with disapproval when she brought it home. Mrs. Van Every reminded herself, however, that she had asked for it. She had not christened Ashley out of some southern reverence for *Gone with the Wind.* In an oblique act of courage and self-recognition, she named her daughter after Hemingway's Lady Brett, hoping that brave name would make Ashley less fearful of the world than she. It never occurred to her that her own examples of rigidity in the face of life's contradictions would be enough to set Ashley free.

Martha Reynolds Van Every, born of aristocratic New England stock, was a woman who blessed propriety whenever possible. She was the daughter of a Presbyterian missionary, and this proper code of conduct had been drummed into her since birth. Even though she was a painful captive of its insidious demands, she had sense and honesty enough to acknowledge the fault. And she wished something different for her daughter. Not too different, mind you. That could cause problems. Just different enough so that her only child would have courage where she, herself, had failed.

So when Ashley presented her with her dress for the prom, Mrs. Van Every was of two minds. She was pleased at her daughter's individuality of taste, yet fearful that the headmistress of Jarrett would disapprove.

It was a black gown of silk matte jersey, cut on the bias. Her mother went so far as to mention that a girdle should be worn with it—considering the clinginess of the fabric—that she didn't understand why her daughter had suddenly abandoned this necessary convention. Mr. Van Every suggested that a broach pinned at the bottom of the mildly plunging neckline might disguise the hint of cleavage that peeked out from the folds of the soft fabric. Neither parent was successful.

Kate's mother bought her gown for her. In pale blue tulle, it was an off-the-shoulder dress with a tight bodice that flowed into a full old-fashioned skirt that touched the floor. Her date, a boy she knew from her summers in Connecticut, brought her a wrist corsage of two gardenias tied prettily with silver ribbon. She knew the edges of the blossoms would be brown by the end of the evening, vaguely resembling her feelings for the boy. But she smiled prettily and put on the proper show of interest, gratitude, and delight, just as she had been taught to do. She was a well-bred young lady, a fact that she had never been allowed to forget.

Young ladies never offend if it can be avoided. They neither smoke nor curse; they cross their legs at the ankles and maintain a moderate tone of voice. They wear white gloves in the evening and hats to church . . . Anglican, of course. And they never—but never—indicate to an escort that they are anything except rapturously pleased with his company. That was the spun sugar and spice that young ladies of Kate's class were made of. And that, far too often, was Kate.

Mr. Langford, meaning only the best, bought his daughter a dress wholesale from a house in the garment district. It was expensive, well-made, well-designed, and entirely inappropriate for Dottie. Being blissfully ignorant of this fact, Dottie spent a happy evening decked out in a long red and white polka dot dress with a sailor collar edged in red satin and multitudinous gathers around her thickly emphasized waist. Layers of crinolines puffed the skirt out from her plump body, adding an awkward grace to her appearance when she whirled in an energetic lindy to the music of Lester Lanin himself. Her date, the son of a colleague of her father's, was a sophomore at Yale, enhancing her with an added status in the eyes of her classmates.

Ashley's escort was a boy she had met horseback riding in Central Park. She could hardly have invited Alexander Lain, although that was all she wanted.

But it was a pleasant enough evening for all three

girls. A last dance in commemoration of their youth, of the illusions of worlds to conquer and dreams to embrace. Much like the glittering lights that rained sparkles on them from the mirrored sphere over the dancers, the music and the song illuminated the uncomplicated loveliness of their lives.

The Troika decided to spend the week of July Fourth at the Langfords' Catskill cottage. All three enjoyed the undemanding and warm atmosphere of Dottie's family. It was relaxed and even earthy, something Kate and Ashley found wonderfully refreshing after the enforced propriety of their own lives.

Only Kate's mother objected. Although the Hendersons associated with the Langfords in a gracious stance of noblesse oblige at the various school functions they were compelled to attend, Mary Henderson firmly preferred that Kate stick closer to her own kind.

"Of course, your father and I certainly don't disapprove of people of the Jewish faith, Katherine," counseled Mrs. Henderson. "It's just that you must be careful with whom you associate."

"What do you mean?"

"We've always felt, your father and I, that it was best if you don't spend too much time with them, that's all. What if you were to meet a Jewish boy and fall in love?"

"I don't think that's something you have to worry about, Mother," replied Kate with an uncharacteristic tinge of sarcasm in her voice. "After all, I'm just going for a short visit."

"Things can happen, Katherine. We know that. We're your parents." She paused for a moment, shuddering inwardly at the stories her husband brought home from his medical practice, of girls—even nice young girls from good families—who got themselves into trouble. She sought the proper words for her daughter, words that would not appear too authoritatively intrusive. "If you were to marry a Jewish boy, for instance, it would most surely ruin your chances of ever becoming a member of the Junior League. Or of being a member of any good club, for that matter. And those things are important, whether you regard them as such right now or not. One day you'll care."

"Oh, Mother," she groaned, drawing out the words. That was the closest she could come to telling either of her parents that she thought they were hopelessly outdated. She wanted to scream at her mother, to tell her to stop interfering, that she was perfectly capable of looking after herself and forming her own opinions. But Kate had been borrowing thoughts from her mother for so long, she was not at all sure that she could, in truth, function without her. Thus, she allowed the moment to slide, as her mother knew she would. And Kate was left feeling angry and impotent. More than that, she was ashamed at her own lack of courage.

Ashley and Kate took the bus to the Catskills together, and they were met at the little station by the entire Langford family; Mr. and Mrs. Langford, Dottie, and Solomon, her twenty-five-year-old brother.

Both girls were delighted to be with Sol. They had missed his big-brother teasing since he had moved across town to the East Side and out of their sphere. He had been a favorite of Ashley's and Kate's since they had first met. He was one of those rare individuals whose life is made up of people who meet and love him, remaining forever loyal.

It was not so easy for his parents, however. For them—much as they adored him—their son represented a struggle. Because Solomon Langford was simply not that conventionally bright. He had a finely tuned instinct and an innate wisdom. But it was book-learning intelligence that eluded him so completely.

As if to compensate for this oversight, Sol was created enormous. Not fat. But tall, six foot six, with a perfectly proportioned body for his height—proportioned as a pro football player, yet still graceful. It was as if he had been set aside to join a new race of giants destined to rule over others by dint of size and exaggerated pituitary alone.

Yet, curled fragilely inside this huge man, was a gentleness that overwhelmed all other instincts, as if he were frightened of the physical power that he possessed. He was incapable of harming anyone, unless it was in defense of someone he loved. And even then he used only the force necessary to quell his victim. A stern look was usually sufficient.

Accompanying his ordinary mind was a radiating happiness and a sense of humor that was special to everyone who knew him. Even at the third-rate private school in which he struggled to earn his high school diploma, the teachers willingly tutored him when necessary, and friends were always available to help him pass another exam. He was a man to whom children flocked, jumping into his lap with complete trust, and a man to whom adults turned in time of trouble or celebration.

After high school, college attendance was clearly out of the question. Instead he got a job as a waiter in a restaurant in the East Seventies called Teddy's. It was one of the first sawdust-floored, dark-paneled restaurants that began to proliferate in the late fifties, a place where the aura pulled a crowd of people with careless money and leisurely evenings to spend.

After a year Sol was managing the restaurant, a position that surprised and pleased his parents. He could deal with anybody and was a definite magnet to patrons. He remembered everyone's name and handled difficult situations with ease. He knew when to send over a complimentary drink and when to ask someone to leave. He had at last found a valid place for himself, one where he could excel and one in which he delighted.

In short, Solomon Langford was a completely wise and lovable man. And the Troika, as a unit, adored him.

There was a party on the beach the evening of the Fourth. Sol had opted for a more intimate encounter with a girl who lived across the lake. But Dottie, Kate, and Ashley decided to attend, fully expecting to sing a few folk songs, drink a beer or two while they lit some fireworks, and be home by midnight.

That plan changed when Jason Feldman arrived around eleven with a group of waiters from one of the large hotels nearby. Finally released from their duties, for them the night had just begun. And they started with two large thermoses of French-Seventy-Fives that they had mixed with ingredients permanently liberated from the hotel.

Jason was the first one to notice Kate. Tiny and petite, there was an elfin quality about her, all the more enhanced by her pixie haircut. Her blue eyes shone and her skin had turned a pleasing pink after a day in the sun. That night she had worn a new outfit: pink toreadors and a matching angora sweater, with darker pink Capezios encasing her delicate feet. She looked like a modern angel, innocent and pleasing, when Jason offered her the first French-Seventy-Five she had ever tasted.

Still smarting from her mother's rebukes, Kate had been instantly attracted to him. He was a third-year law student at New York University, a fact that lent maturity as well as substance to his dark appeal. He spent an hour just talking to her, wooing her, which neither Ashley nor Dottie missed.

After finishing her fifth refreshing drink—"almost like lemonade," she had commented when she first tasted it—she rose unsteadily and took Jason's hand to go for a walk.

At one thirty in the morning, when the party was beginning to wane, Kate still had not returned. Dottie and Ashley were both concerned and did not want to return home without her. Nor did they want to interfere in a potential romance. And so they waited.

At two o'clock Jason appeared.

"Where's Kate?" asked Ashley as he sat down near the fire to warm himself.

"Over there," he replied casually, pointing in the direction of the woods that grew down to the edge of the lake.

"Is anything the matter?"

"Not that I know of," he said, picking up a marshmallow and jamming it on a stick to roast it over the coals. "She just didn't feel like rejoining the party, I guess." He smiled, speaking in the casual voice of one who knows better, and Ashley was quick to pick up the message.

Sensing that something was definitely wrong, she replied icily, "I'll just go and check then."

"I'll come with you," joined Dottie.

The two friends walked away from the party, pulling their sweaters tightly around them in defense against the cool night air that penetrated their bodies as soon as they left the warmth of the fire.

"Kate?" called Ashley when they entered the edge of the trees. "Kate?" she called louder. "Where are you?"

There was no answer. Walking farther into the woods, neither Dottie nor Ashley was willing to admit to the vague fear that accompanied them into the darkness. The shadows of the trees, cast from the clear light of a gibbous moon, became more ominous with every step they took. Threatening and grasping like the trees that reached out to grab Snow White as she fled through the forest, the branches scraped their arms and legs as they walked.

"Kate?" called Dottie, loud and intrusive in the silence of the night. "Kate?"

In reply they heard the muffled sounds of Kate's crying and followed them to a small clearing covered with pine needles and the hunched frail figure of their friend. She was sitting with her head resting on her knees, her arms clenched tightly around her legs. Her sobs were not loud. They were pitiful, pleading. Her entire demeanor spoke of desolation trapped in the spokes of her own sorrow.

"What is it?" asked Dottie, kneeling beside her, putting her face close to Kate's. "Tell us. Tell us what happened."

There was no answer. Instead, her tears increased—a barometer of the depth to which her convictions and dreams had been shattered. Ashley reached down and took Kate's hands. "Here. Stand up. We'll go home."

She pulled Kate's hands, and as she stood, the problem became evident. Her pink toreadors were hopelessly splotched with blood. Ugly dark stains marred the blatantly wrinkled fabric, bearing stark witness to foresaken illusions and abandoned hopes.

"Oh, Katie," crooned Ashley, putting her arms around her, rocking her gently. "It's all right. It really is. I promise."

"No it's not," she managed to utter between sobs. "It will never be the same."

Ashley made a simple decision.

"Sit down a minute, Kate. I want to talk to you."

Like a rag doll, Kate did as she was asked. Dottie sat down beside them, the three forming a moonlit triptych in the now-soothing shelter of trees.

"I want you to listen to me for a minute. Because I know what you're feeling and it isn't necessary."

Kate nodded silently.

"I know how you feel about being a virgin. We've been brought up to believe that it was the only way to go. Sex was beautiful just as long as it was sanctified by marriage. But that's not so. It's beautiful without it, too. I know."

Kate looked up at her sharply, then retreated into herself again. "But it wasn't beautiful for me. It was ugly. He just shoved it in."

"So it wasn't beautiful this time," continued Ashley. "But sometime it will be. And it won't make any difference if you've done it before."

"You're speaking heresy, you know," commented Dottie, not entirely without irony.

Ashley's spine stiffened. "No, I'm not. I'm speaking sense. It's time we learned to judge situations for ourselves. Without all the divine interpretations of our parents coloring everything we do." Ashley took Kate's face between her hands, forcing her attention. "I've had a lover for six months now, Kate. And it's been beautiful. I'm not ashamed, I'm not embarrassed. The only problem is the possibility of getting pregnant. And that's not a moral issue, it's a practical one."

"Why didn't you tell us?" asked Kate, more interested than she appeared.

"Because sometimes beauty can't be shared. But experience can. Knowledge can. Now I grant you, this wasn't the most pleasant initiation into sex. I would have wished something different for you. But it's not the experience that I think is bothering you. It's the fact that you won't be a virgin on your wedding night. And that's a crock of shit."

"Ashley!"

"Well, it is."

"She's right, Katie," added Dottie. "We're not little girls anymore."

"I'm afraid I still am," whispered Kate.

"Then it's time you grew up," said Ashley with a firm and convincing tone in her voice. "It's time."

Ashley stood up, bringing Kate with her. "So let's go home."

"How can I go home? Look at me. Maybe Dottie's parents will see me. Or Solomon."

Ashley took charge then. "All right. They're probably asleep. But it's not a long walk. You two stay here. I'll go back to the house and get another pair of slacks. It won't take long."

As she emerged from the woods, Ashley saw Jason sitting by the fire with the remnants of the party. He seemed quite at ease, a part of the group once again, just as Kate was already a part of his past.

As Ashley approached, the group suddenly burst into laughter, a carefree and delighted camaraderie that sailed on the winds of the summer night like a deep and deliberate insult.

Without really thinking, Ashley walked over to the thermos of French-Seventy-Fives, which sat innocently next to Jason. She picked it up. Without a word Ashley dumped the remainder of the sticky contents over his head. Then, dropping the thermos beside him, she turned and made her way back to the house through the moonlit and disillusioned night.

Kate's experience might have skimmed the clean shine of innocence off the edge of her summer. But Sol changed all that.

He came downstairs late the following morning. He was immediately concerned when he saw Kate sitting on the porch, coffee nestled in her hands. Her entire body, hunched over and defeated, spoke of a pain that had already grown silent within her.

"Hey . . . what's the matter, Kate?"

"Oh . . . a lot and nothing, I guess," she answered, staring out into the calm of the lake.

"Anything I can do?"

Kate looked up at him and smiled, grateful for his intrusion. "I wish there were."

"Well, there is," he said. "As soon as I get some breakfast, we'll go for a walk. Nothing like a walk in the woods. And I'll show you the secret place where the Watermelon Baby hangs out."

"The what?" she asked, not really caring, not able to concentrate.

"The Watermelon Baby. That's the creature, when Dot and I were little, that was supposed to be hiding in the woods, ready to snatch bad children away to his lair."

Kate looked at him, her eyes polished with tears. "Am I a bad child?" she asked.

He reached down to her, his huge beefy hand touching the side of her face, covering it protectively as it forced her to look at at him. "Never," he said. "You could never be a bad girl, Kate. It's just that everyone should know where the Watermelon Baby lives. So they can avoid him."

"Oh."

"So give me time for a bite, and we'll be off."

When he returned, he found Kate sitting exactly where he had left her.

"Ready?" he asked.

"I don't think I feel like going for a walk, Sol. It's awfully nice of you, but . . ."

"I said it was good for you. Scout's honor, Katie." He held up his hand in the V sign. "And I promise I'll protect you from the Watermelon Baby."

"Oh."

"That's not good enough. And besides," he coaxed, reaching out for her hand, "along the way, I'll tell you the names of all the flowers and trees. Birds, too." He leaned over and picked her up as easily as a child would catch hold of a rag doll. Cradling Kate in his arms, her legs draped over one arm, his other holding her carefully around her shoulders, he began to walk.

Kate squealed, in delight and shock, giving herself up to him, her lilting musical laughter resting briefly on the air before it faded into the pine scent of the woods.

When he reached the edge of the trees, he said, "I'm going to put you down now. Because you should feel how the ground is when you walk on it. Sometimes it's soft with moss or crunchy with pine needles and twigs. It makes walking in the woods better when you can feel it all over."

"Do you come here often?" she asked as she took his hand in hers.

"Since I was very little. I think everyone has to have a secret place where they go to feel different. No . . . to feel themselves. It's a retreat. Sometimes I've wished I could stay here forever. But I know I can't. Because then, this place, too, might become familiar and lose its magic. As it is, it's a place to be nourished."

They walked a long time in silence, comfortable and alert, listening to the special noises of the forest.

Finally Kate said, "Tell me about the Watermelon Baby."

"Oh." Sol smiled to himself, in silent homage to his childhood. "He has arms coming out of his ears and eyes in the back of his head. And his teeth are long and sharp and he's very very scary and wicked. He's . . ." Sol groped for the word, the feeling. "He's what everyone finds when they look behind the dream. The serpent in paradise, I guess."

"The loss of innocence?" asked Kate.

"Partly. But it's more than that. When Dot and I were little, we got very upset because our parents weren't accepted in certain places because they were Jewish."

"I know."

"Well, one day my father sat both of us down. And he told us that all our lives we'd have things like that. Not because we were Jewish, but because we were human. 'There's always a tiger to fight,' he said. 'And what is my tiger might be your pussy cat. We have to learn to fight, to grab it by the tail. And we have to respect each other's battles.' "

"I wonder when I'll meet my tiger . . . or Watermelon Baby," she mused.

Sol stopped and leaned over to whisper in her ear. "The secret is," he said, "to learn how to avoid the Watermelon Baby, even though you know he's there."

"How do you do that?" she asked, playing the game.

He took her head in his hands, raising her face to his. "Never toady to the Watermelon Baby," he counseled. "If you cower before him, you're his. Enduring is part of the secret. I know all about that." His eyes flooded with memories of his own struggle. "And the other secret is never to let go of your innocence."

"I think I've done that already," Kate said, her eyes wandering from his, shuddering inwardly at the thought of her tawdry initiation into sex.

"You're wrong, Kate. I know you're wrong." He forced her to look at him again. "You speak as though you've been tainted. That's nonsense. Nobody can take your innocence from you. You're the only one who can tarnish your dreams. And if you're feeling a little shaky about holding on to your innocence, I'll take care of it for you until you're ready to hang on to it again."

He knows, she thought with wonder. He knows what happened and he's telling me it's all right.

There, on a kinder bed of pine needles, Kate wept in his arms until she, too, was ready to return to her world whole.

Just before they emerged from the privacy of the trees, Sol leaned over and kissed her. The most gentle, loving kiss she would ever experience, she thought.

Ashley continued to see Alexander Lain as frequently as possible throughout the summer without arousing parental suspicions. It was a self-contained relationship, one that Ashley discussed very little with Dottie and Kate after her initial revelation. It was as if, by not sharing it, she could intensify the experience, hold on to it a moment longer.

She was a person who did not allow herself to fear endings. Understanding the inherent value of the moment, she drank lustily out of the cup of sensuality and warmth that Alexander offered her, enjoying every sip, never questioning how much remained. She did not yet understand how beautifully this instinct would serve her in later years.

And she did not yet understand the full measure of the gift Alexander gave her. The truth of the matter was he was the first person, besides Kate and Dottie, ever to validate her as a whole. The attitude conveyed to her by most of those close to her life was: "You're terrific. If only you'd change this or that, just imagine what you could be."

Her mother thought her "aggressive." Alexander thought her energetic and strong. Her father let her know that she had a long road to travel before she would ever achieve real femininity. "You're all woman," Alexander would tell her, covering her body with kisses.

The result of this validation by Alexander was an Ashley who blossomed into her own. It was a heady, erotic, self-actualizing experience. And, in the process, she fell in love.

There was only one problem that nagged at her.

"I don't know what I want to do. What I want to be," she would tell him. "Here I am going off to college in a month, and I don't know what I'm going to study."

"That will come, Ashley. Be tolerant with yourself," he would tell her. "It can take a long time, this process of finding oneself. Just don't look for it in the arms or mind or imagination of another person. It may take you a long time. But you'll get there."

"Do you think so?" she asked.

"I know so."

"How?"

"Because I've been there already. And look at me now. Ready to leave to live in Paris. What I wanted was to travel, to live in foreign countries. And I got it."

"Because you wanted it, you made it happen?"

"In a way."

"I'm going to miss you."

"I'll miss you, too," he said quietly. "I'm sorry that the timing is wrong, that I'm so much older than you."

"Ten years isn't so much."

"It is at this time in your life. You have a lot to do before you can come back to me." His voice was stronger than his conviction. He was suddenly feeling the loss of her, what it would mean in his life.

"Do you want me to come with you?"

Alexander turned to her, suddenly serious. "I know this may sound hurtful, but I don't. We'll have our time, Ashley. It will happen if we feel free enough not to own each other's life. I believe in will much more than I believe in fate. And if our wills are strong enough, we'll have our time." He paused. "We've had a lot already. More than I ever imagined we would have when I met you that first night."

"I know, but–"

"Sssh . . ." he said, putting his finger softly against her lips. "You're young yet. Although I have to admit that there are times when I'm convinced some ancient is living inside you." He paused for a moment, smiling. "You've got to have time to grow into your dreams. And that's a solitary trip. You'll know when you've found it."

"Oh, God, I'm going to miss you." Her body moved even farther in its closeness to his, pressing into it with a defiant wonder.

"No regrets?" he asked.

"None. We'll have more. I know it."

But there was one regret that she would only discover later, in measured and painful doses. Perhaps it was because she met the rare love in her life too soon, perhaps because fate played a stronger and more capricious hand than either she or Alexander imagined. But she would come to know that the feelings she experienced with Alexander—the joy and the intensity and the simple love—would be rare as the kiss of a unicorn. Most relationships with men would be pleasant but ordinary, kind but only mildly passionate. The rest—the ravenous desire, the enchantment and passion, the soaring and splendid warmth—would be entered most commonly in her heart's ledger under the column labeled Balance Due. And it would be this heading, and this sure knowledge that it once existed, that would compel her for the remainder of her life to search behind sunsets and beyond darkness for the answer that would total wholeness for her once again.

The prosaic quality of Dottie's life that summer contrasted directly with Ashley's and Kate's. Looking back on it, Dottie would always think of it as "my summer of carrots and celery." But even though she lost fifteen pounds, there were no boys in her life, a condition that she alternately bemoaned, then denied.

Sol would call her on the phone and tell her he had just met a terrific guy, one who was perfect for Dot.

"Not this time, Sol. But thanks," she would answer, wishing she had the courage to accept his invitation. But the plain fact was, boys frightened her.

"Oh, come on, Dottie, just this once."

"Listen, Sol," she would answer. "I'm in the middle of reading *Peyton Place* and, frankly, I can't imagine any boy I would meet who could be more interesting than that book."

There was a painful self-honesty about Dottie, one that would inhibit her, as well as serve her. It had to do with being needy. "I'm afraid I'll settle," she had once confessed to Kate.

"All or nothing at all?" Kate asked.

"Something like that."

Closer to the truth was the recognition of her own vulnerability. Time and time again she had witnessed people fall in love, or what they called love. Lacking Dottie's raw self-scrutiny, they reveled in their discovery. Dottie knew from the beginning that their elation was little more than relief and gratitude strung up on a banner of loneliness. And she refused to become one of them. Consequently, when she was not with her brother or her friends, she was usually alone.

"Aren't you seeing a little too much of Solomon Langford?" Mary Henderson asked her daughter in a suspiciously casual tone of voice.

"He has tickets for *The Diary of Anne Frank*," Kate answered on her way out to the theater with Sol.

"Last week it was *My Fair Lady*," Mrs. Henderson replied, moving in for one of those serious conversations that Kate abhorred.

"Look, Mother. He only has one night a week off, and it just so happens that we enjoy each other's company."

"Well, to be frank—since you seem to be avoiding the issue—I don't like it."

"I'm sorry."

"And while we're on the subject, I don't like you going over to Teddy's and hanging out in a bar for the evening."

"Mother, Sol takes care of me. You know that he wouldn't let anything happen to me. You know that."

"Of course I know that," answered Mrs. Henderson in a distinctly patronizing voice. She paused, trying to find words that would not antagonize her daughter any further. "But do you remember that conversation we had before you went to the Langfords' for the

Fourth of July? Solomon's being a nice young man doesn't change that at all. You mustn't forget that he's Jewish."

"Now, how could I possibly forget that?" asked Kate, her voice fluttering with the effort to stand up to her mother.

"Sarcasm won't get us anywhere, darling. It merely exacerbates the situation."

"What situation?"

"The one that I see building up. I can only say that I'm grateful you're going away to college soon. You'll meet lots of young men. Dartmouth is nearby. All the schools in Boston. You'll have a wonderful time." She was trying to be soothing and encouraging, a stance Kate knew well.

"Are you trying to tell me that you don't like the fact that Sol hasn't gone to college?"

"Well, now that you've brought it up, I do understand that he's not too bright."

With this Kate exploded. All her life she had found it easier to protect someone for whom she cared than to protect herself. It was the defense of her own self that left her weak and bewildered. She simply could not stand up to authority, could not tolerate the anxiety that confrontation generated.

"Well, now, you just listen to me," she said to her mother in an even, hard voice. "Sol is quite bright. He's just not the kind of bright that you approve of. He reads lots of books, he's literate, and most of all, he's the most extraordinarily kind man I've ever met. And I won't have you saying ugly things about him."

"Is that all you have to say for yourself?" asked Mrs. Henderson in exactly the same tone of voice that she had used on Kate when she was five years old.

"That's all I have to say for Sol," answered Kate as she turned and walked resolutely out the door.

* * *

Despite the surface rumbles of their lives, the Troika spent the remainder of the summer in a kind of extended holiday. With the Korean War finally behind them, like most of their generation—the Silent Generation they would later be christened—they casually rode a tide of ignorance in the sea of national and world affairs. The presidential race between Eisenhower and Stevenson was picking up momentum. And, following the Supreme Court decision of 1954, the first Negro student was admitted to the University of Alabama. But none of this wove much significance into the fabric of their lives. They lived their lives immersed in the surface of their own mirror images. It was not really depth that they lacked. It was simply that they had rarely been forced to explore any aspects of existence that contained a cutting edge of pain. Only Dottie, in the stories she had heard from her parents of fleeing Nazi Germany, had been introduced to that. But for the most part their lives were insular, protected, wrapped in the privileged gauze of wealth and expectation. It would eventually up the ante on the dues they would be forced to pay. But for that summer, innocence was a banquet at which they feasted with casual and ignorant indifference.

The Troika decided to have a going-away party for themselves. It would be the last night they would spend together before they all left for college.

Kate had chosen—or rather had had chosen for her by her mother—a junior college just outside Boston designed to bestow final and irrevocable touches of gloss on young women of background and means. She was pleased that she would be near Ashley, who would be attending Radcliffe. Dottie, in an act that indicated just how insecure she still was, stayed close to home by enrolling at New York University. She would be living in a dorm, of course. But she could dash home for a visit on a moment's notice.

The evening of their party they chose to go see

*Picnic* for the third time. And for the third time they clutched their own bodies in wonder at the vision of William Holden's magnetic confidence as he watched Kim Novak slither down the steps of sensuality into his waiting and all-encompassing arms.

"Oh, my God . . ." whispered Dottie to her friends in the darkened theater.

"Would you look at that . . ." gasped Kate.

Even Ashley, still aching from the experience of saying good-bye to Alexander, was enthralled by the magic.

After the movie they returned to Dottie's house where they would spend the night. Her parents were in the country, giving them the perfect opportunity for privacy.

Champagne was once again the drink. But this time, it was Korbel Brut, and too much of it was consumed. They were to face their last day at home secretly nurturing hangovers, a situation that none of them would remember kindly. And yet, the evening itself had been special.

They toasted that night to their futures. To their lives that they fervently believed would be strong and fine and true. They affirmed their past experiences and their future loyalties. For the last time they laughed and they sang together. They loved and they cried. Like newborn sea nymphs captured in the splendid ritual of confronting their destinies, they joined hands and danced, moving gracefully along the burnished edges of the gold coast of their dreams.

# CHAPTER 2

"Ashley? Is that you?" Kate's voice sounded excited yet shy over the long-distance connection.

"Kate?"

"I can barely hear you."

"There's a party going on in the dorm," explained Ashley. "I'm not sure what the occasion is, but we're having a good time."

"Ashley? I have a favor to ask you."

"Name it," she replied in her comfortably direct manner.

"Sol is coming to Boston for the weekend and I need a place to stay."

"With me, of course."

"Well, you know how this college is. They won't let me go anywhere unless the place I'm staying is chaperoned and all that. The *in loco parentis* stuff."

"Got it. Just be certain to be in before two."

"I will be. I'm meeting Sol at his hotel Friday as soon as I get there. Should I call you then?"

"Not unless it's convenient. Otherwise, just be here at two. I'll be waiting for you."

"Thanks, Ashley. And . . ."

"And?" she coaxed.

"Would you not mention this to your parents? I'd hate for them to tell mine." Her voice drifted off. "You know how it is."

"I'm not sure," replied Ashley. "We'll talk about it. But your secret is safe, my friend."

"Thanks."

"Don't mention it."

Kate could not stop thinking about her little deceit as she traveled on the train down to Boston. She hated lying to her parents, but she had reached the point where the lie was easier than the confrontation. She had told them that she was going to Boston to see Ashley for the weekend. And so it was just an omission, not really a lie. All the anxiety disappeared, however, when she saw Sol standing in the lobby of the hotel.

"Ah, Kate," he said as he enveloped her in his arms. "It's good to see you."

"It's good to see you," she said simply, reveling in the sense of relief that flooded her at being with him once again.

Throughout the summer they had seen each other. But for all Sol's instinctive knowledge about Kate, it was a chaste relationship. The most Sol ever did was kiss her good night. The same kiss that he offered her that afternoon in the woods: that of a gentle and loving man. He had never even taken her to his apartment, as if that act alone would be a betrayal of her.

Neither was prepared for the change that would take place after six weeks of communicating by letter and an occasional phone call. It was as if separation had injected a new eroticism into their feelings for each other.

And now, together in Boston, they could feel the difference, a difference that neither was willing to give words to. Instead, it was released in the way in which they held on to each other.

"Here," he said gruffly, "let me take your suitcase. We can leave it in my room and pick it up later. After dinner."

As soon as they were in the room alone, a rare awkwardness invaded the atmosphere. Both of them felt it, though neither was willing to admit it.

"Excuse me, please," said Kate quite formally. "I have to use the bathroom before we leave."

"Sure."

When she returned, he was sitting in the chair by the window, gazing out into an air shaft as if it were a new and fascinating view.

"Ready?" he asked heartily.

"Not yet," she replied quietly.

"What's the matter?"

She answered with a confused shrug of her shoulders.

"Come," he motioned to her. "Tell me."

She walked over to his chair, not really knowing what to do or say. Sitting on the arm of the chair, she looked at him without a word.

In a gesture that she would remember for the rest of her life, Sol reached up and cupped her face in his hands. There was a unique gentleness to it, a compassion and warmth so real that it radiated from him.

"You know, Kate," he said in a voice awash with honesty, "there's nothing in the world that you can't tell me."

Still, she said nothing.

"Is it your parents?" he asked plainly. "I've known for a long time that they don't like me."

Tears eased over the well of her eyes.

"If it's making you really uncomfortable, I'll take the next plane home." There was absolutely no artifice in his voice, no indication that he was playing a bluffing game.

"Oh, don't do that!" she said, putting her arms around him, burying herself in his shoulder.

And suddenly they were kissing, kissing in a new and dangerous way. For the first time Sol allowed his passion for Kate an avenue for expression, touching her, caressing her with an overwhelming desire that he had held in check too long. And each whisper of desire Kate returned.

Somehow, their being alone in a strange city allowed it. And when Sol stopped, leaned back to take a breath, Kate nodded "yes." Without consciously thinking about it, she knew this was what had been bothering her. She wanted Sol, wanted all of him. And for the first time there was nothing to stop her. Not even her own conscience.

Without a word they moved to the bed. Still fully clothed, they lay next to each other, kissing and touching as if they were the first people in the world to discover making love.

"Don't stop, Sol. Don't," said Kate, telling him it was, indeed, all right.

"I'm not sure you're ready," he said.

"I am."

"Then we'll undress and do it right." His voice was soft. He took her shoulders in his hands and spoke firmly. "I want you to understand something, Kate. We'll make love with each other. We'll do it in the light, because there is no shame to it." He paused a moment, making certain of what he wanted to tell her. "Now listen carefully to me, Kate. This . . . here and now . . . the two of us together . . . this is your first time."

The weekend that Sol flew up to Boston, Dottie went to her first political meeting. She was vaguely frightened to attend, since her first two months at NYU had been largely an intimidating experience for her. Everywhere she looked, thin, confident girls roamed the urban campus looking as if they were all former cheerleaders and prom queens. Dressed in matching cashmere sweater and skirt outfits with the circle pin that had become de rigueur along with the string of pearls, they made her feel like a klutz. Despite her loss of weight over the past summer, when she looked in the mirror she still saw chubby, frightened Dottie.

Early on, she vowed that she would change that someday, that she would be a person with whom to reckon. Someday, she thought, someday I will banish this feeling forever from my life. Someday I will never again be frightened in a room full of strangers. Then they will all look at me and wonder how they had the incredible luck to meet the remarkable Dottie Langford. I'll show them, I'll climb to the top of every Jewish and Gentile heap I set my mind to. And when I get there, I'll look down and wave indulgently at all of them. Mark my words. Someday I'll do it. Someday.

But for the moment Dottie's most pressing problem was finding a niche in the intimidating and clique-ridden layers of college life. She knew that she could not join the cashmere set; it was totally beyond her to make such an overture. And the various clubs set up for students to join smacked of too much rigidity and organized intellectualism. Yet she knew that if she were a part of a group, some of the bumpier roads of college life would be smoothed for her.

Thus, when the rally in support of the Hungarian students was announced, Dottie decided to go. She had been following the progress of the protesting students in Budapest for several weeks. For the first time in her life she identified with heroes—people her own age who had the courage to die for a conviction.

It was during that time when Dottie began to look around her with a new and more critical perspective. The students who spoke up, the ones who challenged accepted notions and livened the classes, were not usually the boys dressed in tight slacks with a buckle in the back and a button-down Brooks shirt, nor the girls with the circle pins impaled on their Peter Pan collars. They were the ones dressed in more radical uniforms: dungarees and sneakers, old sweat shirts and turtlenecks.

These students, ruffling the fringes of bohemia,

were the ones who hung out in Washington Square singing Pete Seeger union songs to the accompaniment of a usually skilled guitar player. And they were the ones who carried a copy of *On The Road* in a conspicuous place and sipped espresso at the Café Reggio.

Dottie knew she was a fake of sorts. She wasn't really a beatnik, despite her parents' negative pronouncements. (She saved two of her good dresses and a matching outfit to wear on her visits home.) But eventually she joined the group by the gesture of dressing like them. And her first real act of commitment was taking part in the protest rally. Despite the fact that the students who perched on the extreme left end of the political fence were embarrassed by a movement that opposed the communist regime, for many in her generation this revolution had become their Spanish Civil War. So, much as Dottie was intimidated by it, she felt compelled to attend.

The atmosphere of the room was electric, even vaguely sexual in the way in which strangers touched, bonded together in what had become a futile common cause. They wept bitter and unashamed tears as they listened on a portable radio to the final message of an unknown Hungarian teletypist: "SOS The Russians are too near. SOS Good-bye friends. Good-bye friends. God save our souls."

At the end of the message there was a stunned silence. Silent tears streaked Dottie's face. Then she turned without thinking to the boy standing next to her, seeking refuge in the arms that he put around her so naturally.

When it was over, finally, they walked together to the Reggio for coffee, rehashing the events of the past few weeks as if they were old friends. They talked into the evening and Dottie was surprised at how simple the meeting had been, how uncomplicated and natural.

His name was Marty Feldbaum and Dottie had, at last, fallen in love.

Dear Dottie:

School hasn't improved much. I keep wishing I were somewhere else, away from Harvard Yard and status symbols.

Somehow, I feel that a city isn't the place I should be. Watching seasons change in the midst of concrete seems vaguely obscene to me. I should be somewhere else, but I don't know where.

Classes are difficult, but my grades are good. I figure that as long as I'm here, I may as well do the best I can. But I wish I could figure out what it is I should *really* be doing.

Daddy says all this really doesn't matter. That what counts is the fact that I'm going to get a college degree. Mother just nods her head, as usual. And, also as usual, I disagree with them. I know Daddy means well, or at least appears to. But I cannot shake that abiding feeling that he basically disapproves of me. I feel that I have failed, that I am, and always have been, some kind of vague disappointment to him, that I am some kind of mysterious mistake that was entered without his knowledge on the orderly ledger of his life.

On to other things. Kate was here last weekend with Sol, as I'm sure you probably already know. She was supposed to stay here, but she never made it. Those two people are so in love it makes me ache. (Not to mention jealous . . .)

But I do worry about Kate. She's really in a dilemma about what her parents will think. The last thing she said to me, in tears actually, was "what am I going to do?" And I really wished I could tell her. But I fear she's too locked in to family feelings. I'm afraid for her and afraid for Sol. Neither of them deserves what I suspect will happen, i.e., that Kate's parents will win, and she will give up Sol. Maybe something can get resolved over Christmas.

And speaking of Christmas, I can't wait to see you. I've really missed the Troika and think we should call a meeting to order *tout de suite* upon our return.

In the meantime, I drift and work hard. But I don't feel the adrenaline, the challenge. I keep thinking there's something I should be doing, but I don't know what. Got any ideas? Besides Kate's perennial solution of a man, that is. I don't like living this way. But I can't come up with an acceptable alternative at the moment. Maybe by Christmas.

Love to you, Ashley

The greatest single problem that Ashley had during that school year was living without Alexander. His absence left her off-center, without a direct focus for her sexual and emotional energies.

"With my future so obscured, my present seems to hold nothing except emotional chaos," she had written to Alexander in a moment of controlled panic. She had awakened in the middle of the night, awakened from a recurring dream that always disturbed her. It was a single vision, one out of another age, another time, as if her subconscious mind had taken a photograph of Ashley as she was in the eighteenth century. It wasn't that the vision was fearful. It was lonely.

Wearing a long white gown, she lay on a large bed. The room was stark, made of gray rough-hewn stones. Leaning on one elbow so that she could see out the open window, she watched the back of a man as he rode away on a horse. That was all. But she knew, beyond reason, that this man was important to her. And she knew, beyond hope, that she would never see him again. It was this last part that disturbed her so, that left her feeling totally abandoned. And she wondered even then if her destiny would, indeed, be chaos. Or even worse, if it would simply be lonely.

As much as she refused to admit it, Marty Feldbaum rescued Dottie from anonymity. He was the easygoing kind of man who knew a lot of people, who could fit in anywhere. And when Dottie was with him, she felt safe, the kind of safety she valued most. She was no longer on the outside looking in. Dottie was now part of the crowd, primarily because she was a part of Marty.

For someone with as strong a will as Dottie possessed, this would seem to conflict with her long-term goals. But, like so many people who become achievers later in their life, hidden behind her ambition was a frightened, insecure child longing to be protected from the assaults of unthinking actions and tactless remarks.

Consequently, more than love, more than admiration, it was gratitude that bound Dottie to Marty. That, and the deeply ingrained sense that without a man she would be nothing. With little effort on Marty's part, all his opinions, thoughts, ideas became hers. Even her need to be someone had been buried listlessly at the bottom of her mental hope chest. It was Marty's need to get his doctorate in philosophy that became her ambition, his need to become a teacher that became her goal.

Thus, it was a simple step from that to decide that they should get married.

"Do you really think so?" asked Dottie, thrilled at the exotic prospect of putting her husband through school, of being his helpmate. School had been boring for her, a truth that she did not want to admit to Marty. Working had to be more exciting than the American Constitution, she decided.

"Of course," Marty had answered. "I have a grant that would help us out a lot. We could make it."

"And I could work," offered Dottie.

"And go to school, too?"

"No. I'll skip college for now. Once you're settled teaching, then I'll get my degree. I don't mind waiting. I really don't."

"If it's what you want, Dottie." Then he leaned over and kissed her.

"Of course it's what I want, or I wouldn't say it," she replied, immersed in her own self-deception.

They went to bed together for the first time that night. Having little more experience than Dottie, Marty led her carefully through the act.

When it came down to the actual event, Dottie was only marginally responsive. Marty's delighted enthusiasm couldn't make up for her lack of enjoyment. It never really occurred to her that something was missing. It was as if sex with Marty took on the guise of a restless passion, one destined to wilt before it ever reached full bloom. The result was that Dottie considered sex something that men enjoy more than women. Not that it was bad. It was just something that she would not actively seek. How could she, when it simply wasn't that interesting, she thought.

Throughout the spring, Kate was careful to tell her parents about the various dates she had at college. They were delighted with her going to the Dartmouth Winter Carnival and the Sigma Chi spring prom at MIT. She had stopped talking about Sol altogether. Consequently, Dr. and Mrs. Henderson had relaxed their vigilance, merely assuming that whatever infatuation their daughter had with Sol had become obscured with time. It was simply no longer an issue.

But it was for Kate. Despite her willingness to keep Sol a secret, she was tormented by fear of her parents' disapproval. She deeply wanted to be the good girl they assumed she was. It was the basis for functioning in her family, a responsibility she did not take lightly.

Consequently, when they suggested a trip to visit her aunt in San Francisco that summer, Kate accepted without complaint.

The first thing Dottie announced when the Troika met in early June was that she was getting married.

"To Marty?" asked Kate.

"Who else?"

"You've got to be kidding," said Ashley. "Why do you want to do that?"

"If I have to face another summer in the Catskills with my mother scouting the surrounding territory for every available single male, I might die," joked Dottie. None of the three was willing to suggest that there might be more truth to her flip comment than she was willing to admit.

"What do your parents think?" Kate asked, always the dutiful daughter.

"Nothing, yet. They don't know."

"Oh, come on, Dottie," coaxed Ashley. "You can't do that to them. You're the first person in your family to go to college. They're counting on you."

"Yes, I can do it," said Dottie a mite too smugly. "Because that's where we're going right now."

"Where?" asked Kate.

"To my wedding. Marty's picking us up in ten minutes. It's all planned. We're going to City Hall."

Understanding the essence of what had driven Dottie to this, Ashley pleaded with her to reconsider. "Don't do it, Dottie. Please . . ."

"And don't do *that*," countered Dottie. "My mind's made up."

"How are you going to live?"

"Marty has a grant for graduate school next year and I'll work, too."

"But—"

"No buts," said Dottie firmly. "We've made up our minds."

Since there was nothing else to be done, Ashley and Kate accompanied the couple downtown to witness a ceremony framed in the institutional green of City Hall.

The words were brief and the feeling was business-like, as Dottie and Marty were hurried through the ceremony to make way for the next waiting couple.

As a fait accompli, they then all traveled to Dottie's apartment on the Upper West Side to break the news to her parents.

"*Vey ist mir* . . ." was all Mrs. Langford could summon as a response to the news.

And she repeated the line on the following day when she went to see the apartment where Dottie and Marty would be living on Horatio Street in Greenwich Village.

It was a third-floor walk-up in a tenement building near the river. Had it not been for Dottie's unflagging enthusiasm, Mrs. Langford would have dragged her daughter right out of the place she could only describe later to her husband as squalid. It was obvious that a colony of roaches had made their home there long before Dottie arrived. And the sink and bathtub—the latter located in the kitchen—were encrusted with years of scum that the previous tenants had neglected to clean.

"All it takes is a little work, Mother," Dottie explained doggedly. "It's all we could afford. And, besides, once it's cleaned, I'll get some bright curtains and a pretty bedspread. It will be fine."

"And speaking of that, just where *is* the bed?" Mrs. Langford asked in an amateurish attempt at sarcasm.

"There," pointed Dottie to a mattress on the floor.

"In my opinion, it's going to take a lot more than curtains to make this place livable."

But Dottie, in her usual determined fashion, made it livable within two weeks. When she invited Kate and Ashley down for lunch at the end of June, they both wished that they could make sincere exclamations over the state of Dottie's home, tell her how clever she was in the way she fixed it up with so little money. Instead, they told her how much flair it had; when what they really meant was that it was gaudy.

The luncheon itself was intended to be a going-away party for Kate, who was leaving for San Francisco the next day.

"What's the matter?" asked Ashley.

"I'm scared of flying," said Kate with a smile.

"No, really. Tell us," Ashley coaxed.

"Sol. I'm going to miss him."

"From what I've gathered, he's going to miss you, too," added Dottie. Then she plunged in. "Is it still so bad with your parents?"

"Yes," answered Kate. "Although talking about it with you makes me feel lousy."

"Look," said Dottie plainly. "I know a lot of Jewish families who would disown their children if they married a Gentile. As a matter of fact, I think that's the only thing that allowed my parents to accept Marty. He was a nice Jewish boy and they could, at least, be relieved about that. The point I'm trying to make is that I understand what your parents are feeling."

"But on the other hand . . ." said Kate, urging her.

"But on the other hand," continued Dottie, "it is my brother who's involved. And I worry for him. Much as I've tried to stay out of it, I worry for him. He doesn't deserve being hurt. He's too good."

"I know," answered Kate softly. "That's one of the reasons I'm going to San Francisco. To give it a chance to cool off. Maybe then . . ." her voice drifted into a bewildered void, not understanding what would happen next.

"It would seem to me," offered Ashley in a rare moment of naiveté, "that if the two of you are really in love, then your parents would accept it."

"I know mine would," said Dottie.

"Mine wouldn't. Ever!" said Kate bitterly.

The day ended on that note of anxiety and uncertainty. Dottie added to it, since it was quite apparent to her friends that she was only playing grown-up, with little responsibility beyond the confines of her new home. It was a relief for Dottie, this abandonment of ambition. A deliverance. The trouble was, worried Ashley, that once Dottie tired of playing house, she would not know what else to do. Her job had been done, efficiently and methodically. Dottie had exercised the option on her nesting instinct, and when it ran out, she would have no place to turn except Marty. Sweet, kind Marty.

For the second time that year Ashley approached her father about the possibility of not returning to college in the fall. The problem was, of course, that she could not present him with any viable alternative for her future.

"What would you do instead?" John Van Every asked his daughter with a slight challenge in his voice.

"I don't know. I just think it's a waste of time for me—not to mention your money."

"Let me be the judge of that," he said, taking a sip of his sherry.

In an effort to beef up her argument, Ashley brought up a forbidden subject. Without warning, it just slipped out of her. "Well, it seems to me that your mother did pretty well without a college education."

Her father's reaction was instant, yet controlled. Speaking through clenched teeth he said, "My God, how I rue the day that she came to visit you."

"I'm glad she did," said Ashley stubbornly, suddenly flooded with the memory of that day when she was nine years old.

She had just returned home from school when the doorbell rang. Answering it, Ashley was confronted with a woman who introduced herself as Marguerite Martinez, an old friend of her father's. She asked if she could come in. Although she had been taught never to talk with strangers, Ashley let her enter as if they had been lifelong friends. It seemed natural, she explained later to her enraged father.

Ashley told the woman then that her parents were not at home, but that she would be welcome to stay and see them when they did return.

"Call me Nana," said the woman. "That's what most children call me," she added, smiling.

They sat in the library, the woman and the young child, talking for an hour. Nana asked many questions about Ashley's father, all of which she answered as honestly as she could. And she asked about Ashley; if she had grandparents, if she traveled, what she did, what she loved, how she felt about her world.

Finally, Nana said she thought it best if she left without seeing Ashley's father. Disappointed and on the verge of tears, Ashley begged her to stay. It was important, she felt instinctively. For all their lives.

But the woman left. Not before Ashley clung to her, hugging this intimate stranger in an outburst of emotion she had rarely felt.

Holding her close, Nana stroked her long black hair. She told her how pleased she was that Ashley was such a beautiful girl. "Inside, as well as outside," she had added, to clarify her feelings to the child.

"Will you come again for a visit?" asked Ashley just before she closed the door on this woman.

"Perhaps someday," she had answered. "I would like that very much."

When John Van Every arrived home, Ashley waited

until he had mixed his cocktail and settled in his leather club chair before she asked innocently, "Who's Marguerite Martinez?"

Her father froze, his drink midway between the table and his mouth, fluttering suddenly with the sound of ice against crystal. That sound, seeming louder and more intrusive than it was, had become an integral part of the memory Ashley held of that day.

"How do you know that name?" he asked, his whole body making an obvious effort to regain control.

Ashley cringed at the memory. She sensed something was terribly wrong without knowing what. "She came for a visit today. Who is she?"

"A famous photographer," John Van Every offered tersely.

"I know," said Ashley. "She explained to me that she took pictures for a living. I think that's a wonderful thing to do." Then she paused. "But she didn't tell me she was famous."

"I see," said her father, very noncommittally.

"Who is she?" persisted Ashley.

"A photographer. I told you already," he snapped.

"I know that. But who *is* she?"

John Van Every settled in his chair. Ashley knew from looking at him that he was considering something serious. She had learned to read his body language long ago, to sense his moods, in her repeated efforts to please him. She knew even then that she should have dropped the subject. But it seemed too important to do that. The woman, herself, had seemed too important. And so Ashley waited—waited for some explanation from her father that would put the afternoon in an understandable perspective.

Finally, he spoke. "I've often wondered whether I would ever have to offer this explanation to you, Ashley. Of course, I've hoped I wouldn't. Some things in life are better left unexplained."

Ashley stood before him, ingesting every word,

waiting for the flash that would clarify the situation.

She waited patiently for her father to continue. "A long time ago when you asked me about my parents—your grandparents—I told you that they were both dead. In a way, that was true. They were dead to me. And I thought that was enough. My father is really dead. Just like I said. But my mother . . . my mother is Marguerite Martinez, that woman you met today."

Stunned, Ashley just stood there. She hadn't the slightest idea of what to say. Finally, she uttered, "Your mother?"

"Yes."

"But why?"

"Frankly, that's between me and my mother, Ashley. Suffice it to say that we don't get along."

"No! That can't be," cried Ashley. "She's a nice woman! I liked her!"

"Be that as it may," John Van Every said in a voice coated with false calm, "we don't see eye to eye on some major issues. And, because of that, we don't see each other."

"Ever?"

"Ever," he said conclusively.

"But Daddy—"

"No buts, Ashley." That was his final word and she knew it. "And I would appreciate your not bringing this up in the future. As far as I'm concerned, the subject is closed."

"Period?" she asked shyly.

"Period."

For a long time afterward Ashley looked for her grandmother when she walked to and from school. She looked for her in restaurants and theaters. But there was never a Nana waiting for her. She even looked in the phone book, hoping to find her address. But there was no trace, as if their meeting had only been a dream.

And now, ten years later, Ashley brought up the

subject again. She had guessed about Nana not going to college, and discovered that her remark was on target.

"I believe I asked you, a long time ago, never to bring her up again, Ashley." His voice was chilly with feigned indifference.

"I'm almost twenty years old, Daddy. I'm an adult now. Why won't you tell me about her?"

"Because it won't do any of us any good."

"But I *need* to know," said Ashley, the pleading in her voice taking on a significance in its own right. "I've never forgotten her, Daddy. And I keep thinking that maybe she would understand what's going on inside me."

"I can assure you, Ashley, that her capacity to understand is minimal."

"Why can't you let me be the judge of that?"

"Because I need—"

John Van Every's voice turned to the torrent of ice that Ashley rarely experienced, but recognized immediately. She knew then that the conversation was useless. "As far as Marguerite Martinez is concerned, Ashley, you need know nothing. Nothing. Do you understand?"

"Yes, Father, I understand."

"And do you also understand that you shall return to Radcliffe in the fall?"

"I'll do it," she answered gathering her courage. "For one more year. And if I don't find anything in it after that, I'll leave."

"Are you telling me or asking me," he said in an impassive voice.

"I guess . . . I guess I'm telling you, Daddy. Because one more year is all I could stand." She was holding her ground against him, despite the fact that her mother had just walked into the room—a woman for whom direct confrontation was tantamount to the declaration of war.

"What is it?" asked Martha Van Every.

John turned to his wife. "Ashley and I have come to the agreement that she will stay in college for one more year. If, at the end of that time, she still wants to quit, it will be acceptable to us." He looked directly at his wife, but Ashley knew his words were for her alone. "If she does choose to quit, however . . ." He paused significantly for his daughter's benefit. "Then she will be on her own. She can expect no further help from us."

"If you'll excuse me for interjecting a realistic note into the situation," her mother commented, not fully understanding the dynamics of the previous conversation, "Ashley won't need any help from us. She comes into her trust at the age of twenty. My mother wanted it that way."

And that was how Ashley discovered that she had a trust fund. Her first thought was not about the money, however. It was an instant reaction, one directed against the kind of family that expends its energy keeping secrets in order to protect, instead of revealing truths in order to grow. She considered it just one more way in which she was a misfit amidst those closest to her. And she wondered if she would feel the same kind of alienation in the company of a grandmother whom she had met only once. She really hadn't the slightest idea. But she made up her mind to find out.

All the way home from San Francisco on the plane, Kate thought about Sol. She had not seen him for six weeks. Her preoccupation with him during that time had lost its obsessive quality. Time and distance had done the job that parental interference could not. That did not mean, however, that she had lost interest in Sol. Her love for him had simply moved into a more realistic perspective.

The one area from which she did receive some support during her vacation in California was from her brother, William, It had been almost eight years since she had spent any significant time with him. He had moved away to college in California when Kate was still young. Then, having entered Stanford medical school, most of his energy had been directed toward his profession.

But while Kate was in San Francisco, he went out of his way to see her, almost as if he were getting to know her for the first time. And the fact was, this had been the first time they had really communicated on an adult level.

Although William favored Kate in his coloring, with his sandy blond hair and blue eyes, there was a distinct difference in their appearances. A strength of character emanated from his face. His features, aristocratic and sculpted, had a power about them, as if time and wisdom had left an indelible mark. There was nothing soft about him, for he had fought hard to work his way out from under the influence of his parents, and he had no intention of ever returning to that state of enforced dependence.

When Kate finally understood that she had a friend in her brother, she told him about Sol. They were having a farewell dinner the night before she returned to New York, and it was a relief to talk to someone who had a shared experience of the obstacles she was up against, who understood the formidable strength of her parents' influence.

"I don't envy you," he commented when she told him. "It's a battle I hope I never have to fight."

"Why?"

"Because, even now, I'm not totally confident I would win. You've got a lifetime to fight. A lifetime of social and emotional and psychological brainwashing."

"I know," Kate answered quietly. "What do you think I should do?"

"Well, what I think you shouldn't do is run away and get married. That won't fix anything."

"I've considered it."

"And the result would be mayhem. It would be better if you could bring them around to your way of thinking."

"And how do I do that?" she asked plaintively, fiddling with her napkin. "How do I make them see that Sol is a worthy person in his own right?"

"From what you've told me, he's good at what he does. Give them a little time to discover that for themselves. And give yourself some time. How about coming out here for college, instead of staying so close to home?"

"I think I'd be lost. I don't think I have what it takes. Besides, all I've ever wanted to do is be a wife and a mother."

"That's what you've been taught to want, Kate. What about the time when you wanted to be an archaeologist?" Clearly, Will was not going to allow her to deceive herself.

"That was a long time ago."

"Before mother and father told you that women didn't become archaeologists. I know. I was there."

"Well, it was just a fantasy . . . a childish fantasy." Kate's voice drifted in the remembrance of it.

"Only a childish fantasy because you allowed it to be, Kate. As soon as they made it clear that a future like that was unacceptable, you stopped trying. I remember. Until that time, you were always reading science books and pretending your dolls were Eskimos."

"And right after that I stopped playing with my dolls altogether."

"You killed your own dream."

"I suppose so," said Kate, uncomfortable with the turn the conversation had taken.

"That should tell you something, Katie."

"What do you mean?"

"Well . . . have you been happy with that decision?"

"To tell you the truth, I haven't thought about it in years."

"Conveniently packed away?" he asked. She could not help but hear the soft sarcasm in his voice.

"I suppose."

"Listen to me, Katie." William leaned across the dinner table and touched her face. She could feel the conviction in his voice. "I want to tell you that there is nothing worse in this life than being haunted by what I call lingering regrets. They're caused by weakness and indecision and lack of strength. God knows, we have enough of them without asking for more. These are the big ones, the ones that won't go away. I am convinced that the loss of Sol will come under the L.R. heading." Will smiled at his phrasing. "You will regret his loss far more than you will ever regret defying our parents. And it's a regret that will follow you for a long, long time."

"I know what you're saying, Will," Kate answered. "I just don't know how to go about changing it."

"Neither do I," Will said, leaning over and kissing her. "But I suggest that you start finding out."

On the ride home from the airport Kate thought about Will, how grateful she was for his support and understanding. She had left San Francisco two weeks ahead of schedule, because she could not bear the indecision of her life any longer. But the closer she drew to home, the more anxious she became. It was as if her course were fixed by the lifetime she had lived, and to chart a new path would require more strength than she had.

All the resolve she carried home with her on the plane seemed to melt in the face of her parents. And she was left with barely enough strength to tell them, the first evening of her arrival, that she was going to the Village to Dottie's for dinner.

The walk to Teddy's was a short one. Kate had not told Sol that she was returning early, for she did not have enough confidence in her own will to guarantee that she would see him.

While she was walking, she considered once again how deeply concerned she was about Sol's happiness. She wondered if it would be possible for him ever to be content, if he were forced to battle her parents every time they had to see one another. She understood that the Langfords would be less than happy if they were to marry. But she also knew that she would, ultimately, be accepted into their family.

A secondary concern also flashed into her consciousness: Sol had no real profession. Would it be possible for him to make an adequate living? The prospect of living poor frightened her, for she knew that she could expect nothing from her parents if she married Sol. The thought also shamed her, since she wanted to think she was beyond such petty considerations. But the fact was, Kate was brought up without wanting. And she did not know if she could now do without. She suspected, sadly, that it could be too late to embark on such an uncertain and strained future.

The men standing at the bar turned to Kate as soon as she opened the door. Her looks alone invoked enough interest for her to have had ten dates that night.

She couldn't find Sol immediately. The bartender, recognizing her, smiled and pointed to the far end of the room. Sol was there, sitting in a booth, deep in conversation with a young woman.

Jealousy and fear clutched at her insides as she watched him. The woman was obviously interested in him, and Sol was doing nothing at all to discourage it. That had been their agreement, of course—that they were both free to see other people. They had never reached the point of mutual exclusiveness. She wished then that they had.

Kate walked over to the table where Sol was sitting. He looked up as her shadow crossed over his face.

"Kate!" His being opened up to her.

"Surprise," she said, smiling.

"It certainly is." He hesitated for a moment. "Oh, I'd like you to meet Sarah Gelman, a friend of mine." He turned to the woman next to him. "This is Kate Henderson."

Amenities exchanged, Kate didn't know what to do. She stood awkwardly by the table.

"Here," gestured Sol. "Sit down. What are you drinking?"

"Cognac, I think," answered Kate.

"And I think it's time for me to go," said Sarah Gelman. She smiled as she said it, but Kate sensed the tension of her words.

"Please don't," said Kate politely. "I didn't mean to intrude."

"You didn't, really," said Sarah smiling. "I really do have to be off."

"Nice to meet you, then."

"Yes. Good to meet you," said Sarah as she slid from behind the booth and stood up. Turning to Sol, she leaned over and kissed him on the cheek. "Thanks for the drink, Sol. And the conversation. I enjoyed it." Then she walked through the restaurant and out the door.

"I'll be right back," said Sol. "Don't go away."

He approached the bar and asked the bartender for a cognac. As he waited, he looked out the window and waved to Sarah. She smiled, then got into a taxi that had pulled alongside her.

"To surprises," said Sol as he tipped his glass to Kate. Sitting beside her, he touched her face with the back of his hand.

Kate smiled and took a sip of her cognac. It felt good, the strong fiery liquid rolling over her tongue.

They talked for a long time. As usual, Sol kept a keen eye trained on the restaurant. This back booth provided a good vantage point from which to survey it. And he would frequently look up during their conversation and nod at a patron or signal silently to the bartender. It had taken Kate a while to become accustomed to this, because she always felt that Sol wasn't really listening to her. But she finally realized that he could do both without intruding on her words or his. And so it was an accepted part of their ritual.

Finally screwing up the courage to ask the question she wanted to pose the minute she saw Sol, Kate asked, "Have you been seeing Sarah much?"

"Sometimes," he said, noncommittally.

"Do you like her?"

"We're friends, if that's what you're asking."

"More than friends?"

"Sometimes, Kate."

"Is she Jewish?"

"Yes."

"The kind of girl that your parents would approve of?"

"Yes. But so are you, Kate. You know that they've always liked you."

"But I'm not Jewish," she responded stubbornly.

"That is a fact," he said smiling. "You're Kate. And I love you."

Kate blurted out her next words before she changed her mind. "I don't think we ought to see each other for a while." She realized she must have been planning this all along. She did not know it, because she could not confront her own lack of strength.

An astonished sadness clouded Sol's eyes. Then he asked, "Did you meet someone in San Francisco?"

"No."

"Tell me the truth, Katie. That's the only thing I can deal with."

"I did tell you the truth, Sol."

"Then why?" he asked, making no effort to mask the pain that had invaded his voice.

"Because we should both try to find someone who will fit . . . who will be accepted by our families."

Sol took a deep breath and then looked directly at Kate. "We've been over this too many times for me to go into it again. You know that I believe in love, Katie. No . . . I don't think it will conquer all. But I do think it gives a kind of special strength to the people involved. At the moment, I can't see any way I can convince you that we could make it. That's something you have to learn for yourself." He paused, not quite knowing how to say it. "I not only believe in love, Katie. I believe in my love for you. As I hope you do. So, if you think we ought to stay apart for a while, I'll go along with it. Not because I want to. I just don't see any alternative. If we ever get together for anything permanent, it has to be of your own free will. Not because I pushed you into something."

"I know," she said in a tiny voice, fiddling with her napkin, as she twisted the paper corners into tight cones.

"Before we separate, Kate, I have to know something."

"Yes?"

"Do you still love me?"

Resigned to an immediate future of wandering, Kate answered him simply. "Yes, I still love you."

"Then remember that," he said. "And remember that I think of you and trust you."

"I will."

"And Kate?" She looked at him, her eyes filling with tears. She knew that there could be no cowardice of heart in this man, that he possessed a kind of anachronistic nobility that would not allow him to be anything except what he was. She was the coward. And she did not like herself for it. "Come back to me when you're ready. I'll be waiting."

"Oh, Sol," she cried, ready to dissolve.

"No . . . don't do that—to yourself, or me. I don't think I could bear it just now, love." His voice turned gruff as he stood up. "Here. Come outside with me now so I can get you a taxi. This good-bye is taking too long."

John Van Every was out of town on the sultry August day that Alexander Lain called Ashley. Caught completely off guard, Ashley was breathless when she heard his voice. They had written many letters since they had parted. But transatlantic telephone calls were most infrequent.

"How is Paris?" asked Ashley, pulling herself together with a superficial question.

"I don't know, since at the moment I'm in New York." She could hear the smile in his voice.

"It's about time," she said, her imagination fluttering in ten different directions. "For how long?" she asked.

"That's the problem," replied Alexander, suddenly serious. "Only until tomorrow. I got a last-minute request to deliver some papers. I could have used someone else in the office, but I rather liked the idea of playing courier. I hope you don't mind . . ."

"Mind?" she said, her voice alive in the old way. "Just tell me where you are and I'll fly over."

"I'm staying at the St. Regis and I should be there in an hour. Can you meet me then?"

"You bet your ass."

"We'll have dinner later."

Moving directly to the point, Ashley asked, "How do you feel about my spending the night?" Since they had met, Ashley always had to get home in order to avoid a conflict with her parents. This time, however, with so few hours to share, she was unwilling to make that concession.

Alexander answered her with, "How do I feel? Superb."

"It's settled then," she said. "I'll meet you in the bar of the St. Regis in an hour."

"Right."

Since the fight she had over Nana, Ashley and her parents had called a sort of truce. It had been a peaceful, if not bland, summer because of it. In a way Ashley was grateful. She had learned years before that it was important to reserve her strength for the big battles. She didn't believe in expending her energy in wasteful ways. But now she had a battle before her that was worth the fight. And she could think of no other way to accomplish a victory except by using the truth.

Mrs. Van Every was sitting in the study when Ashley approached her, carrying her overnight bag.

"May I interrupt for a minute, Mother?" she asked in a tense but polite voice.

"Of course." Mrs. Van Every smiled, looking up from her book. "What is it?" she asked, noting the bag.

"I'm going to be spending the night out."

"Oh . . . with Kate?"

"No," she answered directly. "With a man."

"I see . . ." She swallowed, her mouth suddenly dry. "To be frank, I really don't know what to say."

"Then let me talk for a minute," Ashley responded gently. "I'll try to explain."

"All right."

"A year ago—last summer—I had an affair. To be perfectly straight with you, it was with a man in Daddy's office."

"Oh, my goodness. I'm glad your father's not present to hear that."

Ashley smiled. "So am I."

Mrs. Van Every nodded. "Go on . . ."

"Well, the essence is that I fell in love. But then he had to leave. He's in the Paris office now."

"You know," said Mrs. Van Every in a reminiscent voice, as if she were seeing something for the first time. "I wondered why you seemed so peaked last summer. I worried about you, you know. I understood that something was wrong. And now that it's out in the open, I'm glad you've told me."

"It's easier without Daddy here."

"Of course," Mrs. Van Every said pensively. "It's true. And I'm sorry it is. He wouldn't be pleased at all."

"He's not pleased, no matter what I do," Ashley responded. "He never has been. No matter what I do, it's wrong."

"That's not so, Ashley!"

"Yes, it is," she said, her voice low and pained. "You just don't want to believe it."

"Since we're being so honest with each other, I suppose I would have to admit you're right." She looked at her daughter, her eyes filled with tears. "But don't ask me why. Because I can't give you an answer."

"Can't or won't?"

"Can't. I honestly don't know why. I used to try to talk to him about it. But I gave up a long time ago."

"I guess I should give up," Ashley responded. "But I can't. I need him."

Taking her daughter in her arms, she whispered, "So do I. But I feel as if I have failed you because of my need for him. He's all I have besides you, Ashley. All I have. Forgive me for it."

Stepping away so that she could see her mother's face, Ashley asked, "Are you going to tell him?"

"I see no need to," she responded, a bare smile playing about her lips. "It would cause too much of a scene. And I've never been very good at that. I was never able to stand up to him . . ." Her voice drifted, as if she were lost in her own ineffectiveness.

"You're stronger than you think, Mother."

"I wish that were true, Ashley." Pain was etched deeply into the lines of her face. "But I accepted this deficiency in my character a long time ago. And I see no need to deceive myself about it at this late date."

"I love you, Mom."

"I love you, too, Ashley. I love you dearly."

"Shall we skip dessert?" Alexander asked with a smile.

"I'll go along with that."

"Be my guest?" he inquired with a sweeping gesture of his arm toward the bed.

"Absolutely," Ashley replied.

They had met as planned in the bar of the St. Regis. But they had not even finished their first drink before Ashley suggested they go up to his room.

"I can't stand not being able to touch you," she had said.

"We'll order dinner in the room," he replied as a kind of erotic afterthought.

And so, after lobster and champagne, neither of them appreciating it as much as it deserved, Alexander suggested that they continue their communication in bed.

"Let's take our time," whispered Alexander when he saw Ashley beginning to undress. "It's been too long. I've wanted this too much to hurry now," he said, his voice husky with desire. "Let me undress you . . . very slowly."

His arms reached around her as they began to kiss, nibbling, exploring, consuming. Ashley raised her arms as he lifted the T-shirt over her head. She was not wearing a bra. Her firm full breasts welcomed him, the nipples already erect. He leaned over and kissed them as she clutched his head, her face raised in the total enjoyment of his touch.

Slipping the skirt off her hips, she stood before him in only a pair of black bikini panties.

"My god you're magnificent," he managed to say. "Even more beautiful than my dreams."

Then she reached down and unbuckled his belt, slipping his slacks down. He removed his shirt as he stepped aside, leaving his clothes in a heap on the floor. Then, unable to bear the tension, Ashley removed her pants and they pressed their bodies together, naked and free, their hands wandering endlessly over each other's body.

There was not any place they did not kiss, their bodies tangled and alive, moving all over the bed. Ashley gestured to him, eager.

"Not yet," he gasped.

"Yes," she said. She could not bear the emptiness of herself for one more moment. She needed his filling, his fullness, as if her life depended on it. "Please now."

When he entered her, throbbing and alive, she knew then she had, for a little while, come home. Alexander was with her, in her, and they called to each other out of a longing and love that belonged outside time.

All night long she lay in his arms, his love washing over her in waves of desire and contentment. And when dawn came, she wept in his arms, wondering how she would bear the coming days without him.

It was not in the arms of Marty that Dottie discovered herself that summer. From the beginning she had fooled herself into believing that her marriage would be the avenue on which she would discover who she really was. And it was a deceit that would, ultimately, result in sadness.

In order to earn the extra money that they needed, Dottie had joined the services of a temporary employment agency. Since she had no idea of what it was she might like to do, she worked for an insurance company, an advertising agency, and a Seventh Avenue clothing manufacturer before she was sent to the Jacot Agency to clean up some clerical work for the president.

Expecting a man, she was surprised to discover that the president was a woman. She only learned later that this was one of the most important literary agencies in the city of New York.

Having no knowledge of the book world, from the beginning Dottie was fascinated by the authors, manuscripts, machinations, and triumphs that the business entailed.

It was a fast world, one in which an agent had to be smart and knowledgeable, talented and determined. Otherwise there would be no market for the books that he or she handled. But most of all, it was a world that combined challenge with literature, and a place where a woman could rise to the top without prejudice.

When she told Marty about it the same day she had first met Madelaine Jacot, he was far from captivated by the sound of it.

"I'm happy you like the job, Dottie," he told her. "But I'm even happier that isn't a world where you will have to stay."

"What do you mean?" she asked innocently.

"Oh, you know," he replied inoffensively. "I've told you already that I'm sorry you have to work right now. But I want you to know that in one more year—two years at the most—it won't be necessary for you to work. Thank goodness you won't have to be a wage earner once I'm settled in teaching."

"But I like it," Dottie objected. "I just wish that I would be offered a permanent position there."

"Obviously, it would be a compliment . . . no doubt about it. But it would also be a comment about my abilities to make a living." He spoke so casually that Dottie understood he did not really even consider this an issue. "And, besides, you're going back to school as soon as I get my degree."

She spoke softly. "I think I'd rather work, Marty."

"What?" he asked, suddenly alert to the implications of the conversation. "Think how you'd feel being a professor's wife without a degree."

"I'd feel fine if I were working . . ." she offered.

"Well, I doubt there would be many high-powered interesting jobs for a woman in some small college town in the Midwest." He paused for emphasis. "And that *is* where I'll probably have to start out, Dottie. You know that. We've talked about it for so long that I feel like I'm boring you with the repetition."

"I know we have, Marty." She made her voice as softly convincing as possible. "But I had never really worked before and I didn't know how much I'd like it."

Marty threw his hands up. "I'm glad you like it, Dottie. Truly I am. But you'll get used to academic life. I promise you. And, besides, children will take up enough of your time so you won't have a chance to be bored."

He leaned over and kissed her then, ending the discussion.

At the end of August Dottie was offered a full-time job at the Jacot Agency. By that time she had come to understand that she had made a huge mistake.

Despite the fact that the two worlds were connected by the written word, the gulf between literary lunches and the sheltered groves of academe was enormous. Dottie was certain of only one thing: She loved Marty very much, but she knew she could never live in the shadows of his world. If she did, she would smother him, make him pay for his life with a price of doubt and misery. She did not want that for him, nor did she want it for herself. The problem was, of course, how to solve the dilemma.

* * *

It was early in September when Dottie invited Ashley and Kate to her apartment for dinner. Marty had gone to visit his parents in upstate New York for the celebration of their twenty-fifth anniversary, and Dottie was grateful to have the apartment to herself. She also wanted to talk to her friends without Marty's presence hovering in the background.

Ashley brought champagne and Kate brought shrimp. Dottie's contribution was spaghetti stuck in globs that were pasted together with a flour-laden clam sauce.

"Maybe someday when you get married," joked Ashley, "you'll learn how to cook."

"Judging from this," contributed Kate, "I wouldn't count on it."

"Let's just say the bulk of my talent lies in other areas," said Dottie, by way of moving into the subject she had been waiting to discuss throughout the evening. The specters of Alexander and Sol had intruded, but now she sensed the time was right and she plowed into the conversation. "I've been offered a full-time job at the agency."

"Terrific," said Kate.

"Doing what?" asked Ashley.

"As a secretary in a literary agency. And I intend to take it."

"So?"

"Marty doesn't want me to work," she said in a combination of dejection and defiance. Then she explained her dilemma to her friends. They listened carefully but could offer no solution. Finally Dottie verbalized the thought that she realized she had been harboring since she went to work for Jacot. "I want out."

"Of what?" Kate asked.

"Of my marriage."

Clearly shocked, Ashley said, "But you haven't even been married for three months."

Dottie nodded, mute in her misery.

"And Marty's . . . nice, Dottie. He's a nice man."

"I know." Her reply was tinged with shame. "He is a nice man. And a good man. I'm aware of all that. But this summer . . . working and all . . . this summer has given me a taste of . . . what it will be like. All wrapped up in an insular inbred community. I think I would die if I actually had to live it."

"Can't you work something out?" asked Kate. "Surely there's a solution." Then, as an afterthought, she said a bit uncertainly, "You do love him, don't you?"

"Yes I do," Dottie answered. "And do you know what will happen to this man that I love if I were to stay with him?" In the accidental discovery of her innate strength, Dottie spoke with a confidence that was new to her, despite the painful ramifications of her discussion. "If I stay with him, just as sure as I'm sitting here, I'll suck him dry. I'll use him up and there won't be anything left of him. It's no use saying that I should have known that before I married him. The fact is, I didn't. So there's no point in rehashing the issue. I can only tell you that he does not deserve what would happen." Her voice suddenly turned to a plea. "And I don't, either."

Ashley and Kate were at a loss to offer any solution to what was obviously a situation that could produce little result except pain.

Finally Ashley made the inevitable suggestion. "Then you'll have to file for divorce."

"It's not as simple as that," said Dottie evenly.

"Why not?" asked Ashley. "Do you need a lawyer? Daddy knows lots of them through his business. I'll get you a name."

"Thanks. I would appreciate that." Then she paused, searching for the guts to continue. "But there's more to it than that. And this is where you come in, Kate. I need you to get the name of a doctor for me."

"Why?" she asked naively.

"I'm pregnant."

## CHAPTER 3

Very simply, Kate was terrified. In her entire life, she had never had to ask her father such a defiant question. Not only would he be angered by her request, but he would interpret it as a direct insult against those ethical members of his profession who still believed in standards.

Standards. A word she had grown to hate and respect. "Hendersons have standards," her mother would tell her when she was not behaving in a manner that was expected. "Hendersons don't do that, Katherine. Standards. Remember standards." And she did remember them. The problem was, often they were impossible to live up to.

Here she was again, once more defying the Henderson standard. And she felt wretched.

"I thought you knew better than to ask me something like that, Katherine." The disdain and disapproval in her father's voice were blatant.

"But I told you, Daddy. It's for a friend. She needs help. She really does."

"Are you certain it's not for you?" he asked, thinking of her recent trip to San Francisco and wondering if she had met a man there and become pregnant.

"I promise, Daddy," she persisted. "It's not for me."

"Ashley? Is it Ashley?" he demanded harshly. "I always thought she might get herself into something like that."

"No, Dad. It's not Ashley." Kate was beginning to lose confidence that she would be able to assault this bastion of professional ethics. He was wearing her down.

"Well, whoever it is, she should have asked for help before she got herself pregnant. It's a little late now."

"It was an accident, Dad. Can't you understand that? Can't you understand that these things do happen?"

"I hardly think it's necessary for me to remind you of my medical specialty, Katherine." He paused for effect, then condescended to continue the distasteful conversation. "So I do understand. And I also understand that the law says that if you get yourself pregnant, you are to give birth to the baby. Not abort it."

"Oh, for God's sake." Kate surprised herself at the force of her reaction against his godlike intractability. "You're a gynecologist. You must see this all the time. What do you tell a woman when she's pregnant and doesn't want to have the baby?"

"It's really very simple, Kate. I tell the woman that she can put it up for adoption if she wishes. But that, in my experience, she will learn to love the baby if she decides to keep it."

Kate understood that arguing about the issue was out of the question. Pulling out her last card, she pleaded. "Dad? Just this once? I'm begging. I really am. Can't you help? Just this time, as a favor to me?"

"All right, Kate. I'll give you the name of an . . . abortionist. Just this once." The stony anger in his voice frightened her. He would give her this and then mark it down as payment due—and she knew in how many ways he would collect his debt.

* * *

It was dusk when they reached the street in New Jersey. Ashley was driving and it was difficult to read the house numbers. Kate had promised her father she would not go. Dottie, sitting next to Ashley, said nothing. She just waited.

At the end of a winding dirt road, set back from the neighboring homes, they found it: a modest, ill-kept frame house.

When they reached the door, a man answered. The first thing they noticed was the rank smell of alcohol that permeated the air that surrounded him, as if he carried it with him always, a permanent fixture of his addiction.

But he smiled, showing his tobacco-stained teeth, and said, "Come in," with just enough grace to prevent their swift exit. Holding Ashley's hand, Dottie was led into the house like a frightened child visiting the doctor for a tetanus shot.

They stood in the living room a moment.

"Do you have the money?" he asked. "I said cash, remember."

Ashley reached into her pocket and withdrew an envelope. Handing it to him, she said in her most businesslike voice, "Three hundred and fifty dollars. In cash."

He reached out his hand to take it, and she was relieved to see that it did not tremble. He walked over to a desk, opened a drawer, and placed the envelope inside without bothering to count the money. It was as if he knew that no one would dare shortchange him—that their journey had been difficult and it would not be worth the price of rejection they would pay, were they to deceive him.

"Come," he said, as he motioned with his arm and walked out of the room. They followed him into the kitchen, which seemed to be reasonably clean. The table, covered with a white sheet, stood close to the sink. The window shades were drawn and a gooseneck lamp was sitting on a stool at one end of the table.

"Climb up here and lie down," he directed. "Your head at that end." He pointed away from himself.

Dottie did as she was told.

"No, no. Take off your underwear first." He was annoyed, as if he were dealing with a half-wit.

Dottie slipped off her girdle and stockings, then her underpants.

"Now," he said. "I have no help, so I cannot give you an anesthetic. Do you understand?"

Dottie nodded.

"It will hurt . . . but you must not scream. You must not make noises. Under any circumstances."

Ashley looked at Dottie. Her eyes were dilated with fear.

"I'll stay with you," Ashley said in the most comforting voice she could manage. "I'll hold your hand."

Dottie squeezed her eyes shut tight to hold back the tears.

"Only stay if you are certain you will not faint," the doctor said to Ashley. "I cannot have that."

Then he spoke to Dottie. "Put your feet up here." He pulled two ladder-back chairs to the end of the table. Wrapped around the top rung of each chair was a towel. "This is for padding," he said as, splaying her legs, he tied her ankles to the chairs with strips of gauze. "You must not move your legs. Do you understand?" Dottie nodded. "If you move them, I could injure you." His tone was so matter-of-fact that it charged the air with a low-key intensity.

"Scoot down farther to me," he said, adjusting the light. To his right, at about Dottie's hip level, was a tray of forbidding-looking instruments that lay, gleaming, on a white cloth.

"I will begin now," he said.

Reaching over, he took the speculum from the tray and placed it against Dottie's vagina. She winced from the coldness of the steel, its indifference to the temperature of her body. Inserting it, he opened the instrument, stretching her so that he could see inside. Reaching again to the tray as Dottie watched, he took a long curved instrument in his hand. Ashley leaned over, trying to shield Dottie's view as he did this, kissed her on the forehead, and then stroked her gently with her hand.

"You will feel this," the doctor instructed indifferently. "I am going to sound the uterus. Check its depth and angle." Dottie winced with the insertion of the tube into her cervix. But she did not utter a sound. She squeezed Ashley's hand, more in fear than pain, as she felt the movement of the doctor, smelled his fetid breath wafting toward her.

"I must dilate you up now. This will hurt. It will hurt a lot." He spoke as if he were totally indifferent to the pain she would feel. "You must not make a sound."

"Ahhh," cried Dottie. She was not surprised at the pain. It was surprise at the kind of pain she felt: stabbing and sharp, piercing such an incredibly vulnerable part of her body.

"Hush!" commanded the doctor. Then he was silent.

Pulling the dilator out, he placed it back on the tray, only to take a larger version of the same instrument into his hand. Once again he inserted it. This time Dottie was ready and did not utter a sound. "Good." He nodded, never looking up from between her legs. "Now you know and will make no more noises."

Sweat formed in pitiless beads on Dottie's forehead. Not wanting her to lie there that way, Ashley leaned over and wiped her brow with the sleeve of her blouse. "I'm with you," she whispered. "I won't leave you."

Dottie said thank you with her eyes. She could feel her legs beginning to cramp, wished she could take them down, flex her calves and ankles to relieve them of the pain.

The doctor took a third dilator off the tray, even wider. Reaching over for a sponge, he wiped the pink smear off onto the gauze.

Dottie could feel something long and stringy pull gently through her vagina. As he wiped the dialator, it disappeared.

"Now," he said, seemingly satisfied with the results. Dottie thought it was over and squeezed her eyes shut again. This time in relief.

"Now we can begin," the doctor said. "This is what you came here for." Both Dottie and Ashley were appalled at the implication of his words. It hung over them like a foul-smelling ghost come to haunt them, torment them.

The doctor reached over to the tray once again, taking the gleaming steel curette in his hand. When he first inserted it, the clang of metal against the speculum disturbed the silence. A tolling bell, Dottie thought.

The doctor gently pushed the curette in. Dottie started to cry out. Without looking up, he instructed Ashley. "Put your hand over her mouth if she is going to make noise. She must not scream. Do you understand?"

With that statement, he had relegated Dottie to the status of nonperson, one who was incapable of understanding the simplest instruction. Dottie was a body—no more, no less—to be dealt with in the most expedient fashion possible.

Grabbing what looked like a diaper, he placed it roughly under Dottie's buttocks. Ashley could see grotesque lumps of stringy, mucous red blood plop out onto the cloth as the doctor gently moved his hand. Dottie could not see it. But she could feel it, this loss of herself into the hands of a stranger; could feel it, warm, fibrous, thick. An anonymous muck emphasizing the spectral pain that shot mercilessly through her body, leaving her mute in its wake.

"Not yet," muttered the doctor as he explored the four quadrants of her violated uterus. "Not yet." He began to feel the familiar sandpaper scraping as his curette grazed the walls of the womb, indicating that the material had been removed. Like an old-fashioned washboard, it was bumpy, filled with ridges, yet gritty and rough. It was only a feeling, one with which he was well acquainted. But it always seemed as if the sound of the scraping was audible over the muted moans that usually filled the room at this moment.

"One more time," he said quietly. "I will check one more time. Then it will be over." He moved his hand carefully, holding the curette, scraping, grating against the walls of the now-clean uterus. Then he removed the instrument, once again bumping it against the speculum, sounding its toll, bringing with it the final remains of the bloody mess, fibrous and scarlet, making no attempt to hide the globs of blood from Dottie as he wiped it carefully with the crimson sponge.

"There," he said, as he removed the speculum. "It's done."

Dottie began to shake. The pain in her legs, almost as intense as that in her belly, racked her ankles, calves, and thighs as he untied her. Involuntary trembling blended with her dizziness, causing her to believe that she had lost all control, lost herself in the intensity of the experience. Although there were no more instruments to be prodded and inserted indifferently into her body, the cramping continued, a leitmotiv to her fear and relief. Ashley leaned over and wiped Dottie's face, ever so gently, ever so caring, as the doctor turned his back on them.

"You will continue to feel cramping for a half hour or so," he said as he began to clean up the instrument tray. He spoke as if he were lecturing to a class. "You will bleed for several days. Perhaps pass some clots. Then it will be over."

Ashley helped Dottie sit up. She grabbed a Kotex that was sitting in a box on one of the chairs and gave it to Dottie. Then she held her as she put it between her legs, securing it with her underpants.

As they were leaving, the doctor stopped them at his door. With sad, watery eyes, kinder than before, he looked at Dottie and said, "If in a few days you do not stop bleeding, if you begin to feel more pain or run a fever, that will probably indicate an infection. Do not come to me. I will not know you. I will never have seen you before." He paused, then added. "I'm sorry you got yourself into such a mess. I'm sorry."

Dottie huddled in a limp heap on the front seat of the car. She did not cry. Occasionally, without looking, without taking her eyes off the road, Ashley would reach over and touch her, caress her head. All during the ride home she kept thinking that the pain she had just experienced would be nothing compared to what she would feel when she told Marty she wanted a divorce. This pain would fade in the anguish of the more difficult task that lay before her.

Ashley thought that when she got home, she would be sick.

Marty had just begun his last year of graduate classes and was filled with enthusiasm for the months that lay ahead. His life was laid out for him, simple and uncomplicated. He had a wife whom he loved, who was supportive and nourished him, and he had work in which he was totally involved. What more could a man ask?

"There is a chance," he said to Dottie with a smile, "that I may have a job offer coming from a small college in Ohio. I just heard about it today. It looks pretty good."

They were sitting together after dinner, just two weeks after Dottie had her abortion.

"Oh?" Dottie asked politely, in order to cover her pity for him. "That's wonderful."

"Actually, for a small school, they have a pretty good reputation in philosophy. It would be a great place to start." Dottie winced inwardly at the naive enthusiasm in his voice. "You'll like it, Dot. I've heard that it's a very pretty campus. Intimate. Small-town atmosphere and all that."

Dottie knew then that she could not delay telling Marty any longer. She could not allow him to continue his dreaming that they would be together the next year. It was unfair.

Much as she wanted to avoid this conversation, she knew that the time had come, that she had to tell him before she lost courage.

It took her a few minutes to find the opening word, as if the next half hour were weighted with a loathsome pain that would return to torment her at unexpected moments. Much as she loved Marty, she knew that she could not allow him to nurture his illusion of a shared future with her. It constituted a kind of dishonesty for which she had no tolerance.

"Marty?" she spoke softly. "I have to talk to you about something."

"What is it, love?" he asked solicitously, not even remotely suspecting the blow that was to come.

"I won't be with you."

"What do you mean?"

"I . . ." Dottie hesitated then, choking on the words. "I won't be with you next year."

Suddenly alert to the tone of her voice, the stiff reluctance of her body, he asked, "What in God's name are you talking about, Dottie? Of course you'll be with me. We'll be together, Dot."

"I can't go with you, Marty." There was shame in every syllable she uttered, and pain in every word.

"Are you sick?"

"No. I'm not sick, Marty. Just sick in my heart because I know that we made a mistake."

"A mistake?" he asked, refusing to comprehend what she was saying. "A mistake about my job?"

"No," Dottie answered, forced into the position of spelling everything out when what she wanted was to get this scene over with. "The mistake is our marriage, Marty. We should never have gotten married."

"Don't be silly," he countered, relief in his voice. He was convinced she was talking nonsense. "We love each other, Dottie. Of course we should have gotten married. Don't say such things."

"I have to, Marty. I have no choice."

Dottie knew then that she would have to lay it all out for him, that he would never accept her words if she did not speak with unforgivable plainness. She could not remember ever having had a more painful conversation in her entire life.

"I don't want to be a part of the life you've planned, Marty. It's not for me, living in some small town and being a professor's wife. I want more. I *need* more."

"But you said it was enough, Dot," he protested in the manner of a betrayed child.

"And at the time I thought I was telling the truth. I really did. I couldn't know that I would find myself in work. Just as you've found yourself in yours, Marty. It's not so different. I need to work."

"Work?" he asked, dazed.

"That's what I want, Marty. A career."

"As a secretary?" he asked, suddenly contemptuous as a defense against the feelings that were flooding through him.

"In the beginning I have to be a secretary. I can't start at the top. You know that. But it's worth it to me."

"But what about a family, Dot? Don't you want children?" He was clearly incredulous.

This was it: the subject she wanted to avoid at all

costs. And yet, in his instinct to defeat her, Marty had brought it up.

"No . . ." she answered, tears in her eyes. "I don't want children." Not now, anyway, she thought to herself. Not under these circumstances. "What I want, Marty, isn't children. I want a divorce."

"You can't be serious, Dottie! You simply cannot mean that." Marty enunciated every word distinctly, as if his saying it would make it so.

Dottie looked at him, her heart breaking for the pain she was causing, and knew that there was nothing she could do.

"I do mean it, Marty. This just isn't going to work. And the sooner we face that fact, the better."

Marty started to shake his head in protest, moving it from side to side as he spoke. Except for the change in direction, he reminded Dottie then of one of those trick birds that keep dipping their mechanical heads into a glass of water just as long as it is set before them.

"No." That was the only word he could utter. His head continued this sidewise motion as if it were independent of his body. Tears welled up in his eyes, tears of dread and sorrow, as he asked in a very low and frightened voice, "Is it another man?"

"Oh, my God no!" Dottie cried, much louder than she intended. And it struck her as odd that he probably would have preferred that to her wanting to leave him for a job. "It has nothing to do with another man, Marty. It's inside me. There's something that needs more. More than your kind of life can give me. I can't explain it, only—"

"Whatever it is, Dottie, I'll help you get it." He spoke with a ravaged bravado that they both recognized as a piece of a hopeless collage pasted onto the insecure background of his own doubt.

Pity shot through Dottie then. But it was combined with a quiet contempt for his naked need of her, a contempt she vowed she would not allow to show. She did not have to work hard toward this end, for she was so caught up in his pain that the thought passed only briefly into her consciousness.

"I'm sorry," she said at last, not knowing what else to say. "I'm sorry, Marty."

Putting his hands over his face, Marty began to cry. Deep, wrenching sobs drained the last of his dignity from him, a situation that Dottie had hoped to avoid. She took no pleasure in his defeat, for it only placed a greater burden of guilt on her.

"I love you!" Marty managed to utter at last. "I need you!"

"I love you, too, Marty," she whispered. "I never stopped loving you. Unfortunately, that has nothing to do with it." She took his head in her arms and pulled him to her bosom, cuddling him, rocking him, as she would the child she would never have.

When he was finally able to speak, Marty looked at her. His eyes reflected her betrayal. "I don't believe you. If you loved me, you wouldn't do this."

"You're wrong, Marty. I do love you. But I still have to do this." She did not know what else to say without driving the stake of her determination deeper into the last of his wounded pride. She did not want to devastate him, although she knew she had done just that. She simply wanted out, and she wished more than anything that she could be the one to pay the price, to feel the full weight of the pain. "Things are rarely as they seem. You know that, Marty. You deserve something better. I can't give you what you want. What you need."

"You're right," he said, catching his breath. "Things are never the way they seem."

Dear Dottie:

I was delighted to hear about your new job and that your parents have finally gotten over your divorce. I don't think they ever understood that it was, in truth, an act of kindness on your part. Please don't misunderstand. What I mean is that you were too strong for Marty, or at least the wrong kind of strong. And it seems to me that, for both your sakes, you did the right thing.

I assume, although you didn't mention it, that your parents are less than pleased at your decision to go to work instead of return to school. Certainly I have received a lot of flak about my lack of degree-attaining ambition. Especially Daddy. It still amuses me when I think of his threat to leave me on my own, when I discover that I am to have a pleasant income beginning in June. I do wish, though, that we were more compatible. It has never ceased being painful to me, this feeling like a misfit in my own family.

How do you like living alone? It occurs to me that maybe next fall we could get an apartment together, something nicer than a Horatio Street walk-up. I think for the moment that I am going to stay in New York and try to find a job. God knows doing what. Maybe that way I will discover what it is that I should be doing. Somehow I feel that it's there for me, just out of sight, just out of reach. I am convinced of its existence, but its elusiveness continues to haunt me, make me deeply and absurdly sad. It's very much as I feel about Alexander: I know he's there, but he's too far away to touch.

And speaking of . . . I am contemplating a trip to Europe this coming summer before I settle into the ranks of the wage-earning masses. Want to come along? Do you think you could get the time off? The way things look now, Kate is going, too. It would be great. The ultimate Troika reunion.

Are you game? Maybe, if you get a week or two vacation, you could meet us in London or Paris.

Much love to you.
Write soon.
Love,
Ashley

It was not a series of disastrous dates that caused Kate to call Solomon in November. It was, in fact, precisely the opposite.

Since arriving back at school in the middle of September, Kate had encountered a string of boys who would have made her schoolmates squeal with delight. They were usually wealthy and intelligent, predominantly attractive and Gentile. But none, not even on a limited basis, could engender in her the fullness of feeling and the confidence of being that Sol managed to create by the silent touch of his hand on her face.

On a Friday night in November, having spent a pleasant evening in the local bar with a date who offered too little excitement and too many whiskey sours, Kate returned to her dorm and called Sol at Teddy's.

The first thing he said when he was summoned to the phone was, "It's very noisy in here, Katie. But yours is the only voice I wanted to hear."

It was a short distance from that sentence to his arrival the next afternoon on her campus.

Having fallen in love for the second time with the same man, Kate spent every moment she could manage with Sol. It was difficult over Christmas vacation to keep him a secret. The tension and anguished guilt created by deceiving her parents undermined her confidence in her decision. The by-product, of course, was the tainting of her relationship with Sol.

"Sol isn't the answer, Kate," Ashley said to her just before New Year's.

"What do you mean?" she asked. "I keep thinking he is, Ashley."

"You're the answer, Kate. Can't you see that? It's time to reconcile what you believe with what you've been taught."

"I believe in Sol."

"Then for God's sake do something about it! Can't you see that if you're fortunate enough to know what it is you want, then you're obligated to pursue it?"

"I don't know if I can."

"What else is there, Katie?"

She thought a long time before she answered. Finally, she whispered, "Family."

Despite that response, she continued to see Sol. The most blatant deception came over her Easter vacation. Rather than go home and spend a holiday of lies, she told her parents she wanted to go to Bermuda. And, of course, they sent her the money for the trip. That was where so many nice young men and women spent their vacations; surely Kate would meet a lot of acceptable young people there. Instead, she met Sol.

By summer the strain of her double life turned sour. And Kate welcomed the prospect of a European vacation, despite the fact that it would be without Sol.

Both Dottie and Sol came to the ship for a bon voyage party before Ashley and Kate sailed on the *Rotterdam* for Le Havre. Of course, the Hendersons and Van Everys were there, and the room was filled with champagne and flowers.

It was a festive occasion. But there was a strain hovering, somber and palpable, in the tiny stateroom. Two days before Ashley sailed *The New York Times* carried a small article about a show that Marguerite Martinez was preparing in London.

It was unfortunate, on that Sunday morning, that

John Van Every looked over her shoulder just as Ashley was reading about it.

Too late Ashley put down the paper, reaching for the book section as if nothing had happened.

"Will you be in London then?" John Van Every asked in a low, controlled voice.

Her heart beating double time, Ashley answered, "When?"

"No games, Ashley. You know very good and well to what I refer."

"Yes," she answered.

"Then I forbid you to see her."

Ashley thought for a long, abysmal moment. "I don't know if I can go along with your wishes, Daddy. It's asking so much . . ."

John Van Every's face hardened. His lips compressed into a thin, hard line, and the blue of his eyes turned to ice. Even Ashley, accustomed to his obduracy on this subject, shrank from his gaze, for she could see nothing except contempt in his attitude toward her. There was no yielding in him.

"What I ask for is loyalty. To me and your mother, Ashley. To the *Van Everys*."

Knowing that she had nothing to lose, Ashley responded with a question. "But *why*?" she begged, her voice washed with pain, her face indicating the depth to which her world had suddenly been ravaged. "You've got to tell me why!"

"You're wrong, Ashley," he said, using the tone of voice he reserved for a child who was not quite capable of comprehending a truth. There was an edge of condescension in his stance. "As long as you remain under this roof, I don't have to tell you anything, except what I choose to reveal to you. The only thing I have to tell you is that you are not to see that woman. I forbid it."

Reaching toward him in a gesture of conciliation, Ashley tried to touch his face. But her father stepped backward, as if he would suffer some unspeakable contamination if he were touched by her. This, more than anything John Van Every could say, cut painfully into the heart of her. Standing before her father, mute with misery and dread, Ashley waited for his concluding words as if she were a prisoner awaiting sentence for a crime she did not commit.

"I feel it is my duty to warn you," he said coldly, "that if you see Marguerite Martinez in London, I am not certain yet what I shall do. I can only tell you that the consequences shall be long-lasting and irreversible."

With that, John Van Every turned his back on his daughter and walked out of the room.

On board the *Rotterdam* Mrs. Van Every did her best to smooth over the tension created by the confrontation. She tried to reassure Ashley that it was not as desperate a situation as it appeared. And then, in a rare moment, she confessed that she had argued the previous night with her husband. Ashley understood how much courage this had required of her mother, and she was humbled by it.

"I told him that it was immoral for him to behave this way with his own daughter," Mrs. Van Every said. "I told him that, Ashley. And I do believe that, given a little time, he will come around to my way of thinking."

"Thank you, Mother," Ashley said, as she hugged her. "I hope you're right. I truly hope you're right."

At the bon voyage party Mrs. Henderson greeted Sol politely. And after a moment of hesitation Dr. Henderson did the same. Thinking that his affair with their daughter was over, they could afford to be gracious.

It was not until she noticed Sol giving Kate a present that Mrs. Henderson recognized the situation for what it was. All Kate's unexplained absences, her vagueness, suddenly fell into place. The smile on

Kate's face as she hooked the tiny gold bracelet on her wrist confirmed her tumbling suspicions. All this time her daughter had been seeing that ignorant giant of a man.

Being, of course, a well-bred woman, Mary Henderson did not make a scene. But she did not ever remember a time when controlling her rage had been so difficult. The only mitigating factor was that Kate was sailing for Europe. Perhaps she'll meet a man there, she thought. Even though she would live far away, a European is preferable to a Jew.

With promises that she would meet Kate and Ashley for a Troika reunion in London, Dottie returned to her Madison Avenue office.

It had taken her about one week on the job to understand that this could be the avenue that would lead to her goal. Being a literary agent was one of the few areas in which a woman could rise to the top. She watched her boss, Madelaine Jacot, with a combination of awe and admiration. She had risen through the ranks a few years earlier and guarded her position jealously; yet she was strangely willing to offer Dottie advice and counsel when she asked.

Madelaine was a woman who had never been attractive. But there was an air about her, a confidence and self-assurance that carried with it its own kind of beauty. Her straight brown hair was always pulled tight to the nape of her neck in a bun. Her dark eyes, outlined with dark pencil, flashed with a challenge offered, or an obstacle overcome. It was obvious that she enjoyed the heat of battle, and that this penchant had earned her a reputation of being a formidable opponent in negotiations. She was tall, almost raw in appearance. But she artfully disguised this fact by dressing in superbly tailored clothes. In all, Madelaine Jacot was a woman to be reckoned with, both in her personal life—which was questionable, but rarely confirmed—and in her business associations.

Dottie liked Madelaine instantly when she first met her. It was not so much liking, really; it was admiration. Instinctively she recognized a kindred spirit who had drunk greedily from the cup of success. And Dottie wanted to share it if she could.

As was her custom—with the approval of Madelaine, of course—Dottie read most of the manuscripts that the agency was handling. Although she was only a secretary (whose typing skills were questionable and whose shorthand skills were nonexistent) she understood the importance of being up-to-date on the authors the agency handled. It had to do with being prepared if opportunity knocked, although she was not at all certain what guise that would take. She only knew that it was essential to be ready when the time came.

This necessitated, of course, taking home manuscripts and reading them at night. There was never enough time during the day to attend to such details.

The very day that the *Rotterdam* sailed with Ashley and Kate, Dottie picked up a manuscript that had been rejected by almost every major publisher in America. It was one that Madelaine had mentioned she would probably be returning to the author, the final and most demeaning rejection in a writer's quest for publication.

Reading that night, Dottie was awed by the power of the novelist, by his insight into character, his strength and originality of language. He had composed an intricate tapestry detailing the vagaries of the human soul. It was complicated and erudite, violent and earthy. Dottie felt as if she had been picked up by a wild and baroque locomotive and taken for a profound journey.

She understood the problems with the manuscript,

of course. It was long and unwieldy, almost nine hundred typed pages. And it was not an easy book to read. It demanded the active and literate participation of the reader. In an era where the simplistic thriller and established author reigned supreme, this latter was a quality that did not carry with it a high quotient of desirability from the publisher's point of view.

The following morning Dottie checked the files on *Spartan's End.* Every letter carried with it lofty praise. Yet every letter said no. Not one publisher was willing to take a chance on a book that was expensive to produce and difficult to sell.

During a lull in the afternoon, Dottie mentioned to Madelaine Jacot that she had read *Spartan's End.*

"Oh?" commented Madelaine, her face expressionless. "What did you think?"

"I think it's brilliant."

"I agree. It's a pity I can't sell it. But I've already spent a fortune on mail and messengers—not to mention my own time—and not one publisher has responded with even a conditional no. Every one has turned it down flat."

"I know," said Dottie. "I checked the file."

"While we're on the subject, you may as well return the manuscript to Jack today. I just can't do any more with it." She paused for a moment, as if she were, herself, remembering the power of the book. "It's funny. I've never even met him. I don't know what kind of person he is. But I sure as hell feel sorry for him. He told me on the phone that he had spent four years writing this book. Not such a long time for an author, I suppose. But a hell of a slice out of one man's life."

Dottie looked at the manuscript. Typed on the front page, she read: *Spartan's End,* a novel by Jack Barclay.

The idea must have been floating in the ambitious regions of her imagination since she had finished the book in the early morning. But she did not recognize it until that very moment. "May I handle it?" she asked directly.

"What do you mean?" responded Madelaine, her voice taking on a barely detectable hardness.

"May I handle the book?" she repeated as innocently as possible. She did not want to appear threatening, a lioness waiting to spring. So she softened the image, dressed it up in the guise of literary concern. Although her concern was, indeed, sincere, her motive was not. "What I mean is, I think this is really a brilliant novel and it deserves to be published somewhere by somebody. It deserves to be preserved between hard covers. I just thought I might be able to keep on trying. You know, with smaller houses. Or even new ones."

Madelaine looked at her, assessed the situation. Then with a concealed air of contempt she said, "One of the first things you learn as an agent is what property is appropriate for which house. You've been here almost a year now, Dottie. I would think you'd have learned that by now."

Dottie was hesitant. "I think I know what you mean."

Madelaine cut her off, as if she had a hidden need to demonstrate her superiority. "The only way this book will sell is through a house that has enough financial backing to withstand the loss. Surely you know that, Dottie. They usually balance something like *Spartan's End* against a popular seller. They like the prestige, and eventually chalk off the investment as a flop d'estime, if you will." A wry smile crossed her face.

Persistent in the face of what was a subtle putdown, Dottie said, "I'd like to try anyway. It would take it off your hands. I promise I won't even bother you with it. And I'll use book rates for mailing; no messengers. I'll even pay for the expenses," she added as an attractive afterthought.

"Well, the book is a deserving one. So if you really think that much of it . . . then it's yours, Dottie. Give it a try. God knows, I agree that it ought to be published. I sell enough crap to be painfully aware of that fact."

Inside Dottie soared, flew on the winds of premonition and supreme confidence in her own judgment. Outwardly, she smiled with humble gratitude at her boss and said, "Thank you. Thank you so much. I really appreciate this."

Just to make certain of the conditions, Madelaine added, "You *are* still a secretary, of course."

"Of course," agreed Dottie. But not for long, she thought. Not for long. Luck and time. That's what I need. Time to learn, and luck to hold hands with the chutzpah that I didn't know I had until today.

Dottie prepared the manuscript for mailing to another publisher that very afternoon. And she also wrote an encouraging and positive letter to Jack Barclay on stationery with the prestigious Jacot letterhead. In it she informed him that she would henceforth be handling his novel.

That evening Dottie had dinner with Marty. After their initial separation, filled with recriminations on his part and guilty apologies on hers, they had somehow managed to form a bridge over their differences and become friends.

They met at the Grand Ticino in the Village, a small family-run restaurant where they could get a complete meal with wine for three dollars. Neither of them had much money, since their previously pooled resources had been barely enough to survive on. So Marty had moved back into university housing while Dottie had kept their apartment.

It was a strange relationship, one in which both treaded softly around the sensitivities and vulnerabilities of the other. Hanging over this was the fact that

Marty would be leaving for Ohio at the end of the summer, and they felt a mutual need to complete what they had begun almost two years before.

They had the binding element of being reasonably adult when they shared their first sexual experience, an initiation that carried along with it loyalty to a mutual trust. Although Marty had moved on to other girls—not without anxiety, he had confessed to Dottie—she had remained celibate since they parted. She never confessed to Marty that her vague disappointment in their sexual relationship had quenched her thirst for it. She was not against sex. She merely had no desire to seek it, as if it were an acquired taste like Scotch or buttermilk.

Soon after they had given the waiter their orders for dinner, Marty mentioned casually to Dottie that the university had leased one of those new Xerox machines for the professors' use.

"It's going to make carbon copies obsolete someday," he said.

Not really interested, she said, "What do you mean?"

"It can make as many copies of a page as you wish. Instantly. All you have to do is push a button."

Suddenly alert to what he was saying, Dottie asked, "Do you mean to tell me that it makes copies instantly? Good copies?"

"That's right." He nodded.

Dottie considered then how slow the process of publishing was. An author only had two carbons that were passably readable. And most publishers would only accept the original manuscript for consideration anyway. Carbons were not only difficult to read; they were a dead giveaway to the editor that the manuscript was being shown to someone else at the same time. And editors did not like that.

"What are you thinking about?" Marty asked. "You have an absolutely goofy smile on your face."

Dottie then explained to him about the problems of submitting a manuscript. "The greatest drawback is the time it takes. If each publisher keeps the manuscript six weeks—and that's getting a fast response—you can only reach about eight people a year."

"If you're thinking what I think you are, Dottie my love, the answer is no."

"But it can't be," she said. "With ten copies, I could cover the publishing industry in no time at all."

"It's unethical, Dottie."

"How do you know? It's never been done. At least, not that I know of."

"I don't know about *your* ethics. But it is unethical for me."

"What in the hell do you mean?" There was fire in her voice.

"I mean that it has been made quite clear to the teaching staff that this machine is not to be used for anything other than university purposes."

"They don't have to know, Marty. Don't you see?"

She told him then about Jack Barclay, about how brilliant his book was and how much he deserved to be published. It was for the sake of art, she argued, fully aware of Marty's soft spot.

"Do you have keys to this room where the miracle machine is housed?" she asked.

"Yes, we all do."

"We'll go in the middle of the night. I'll help you, Marty. I promise. We won't get caught. And if we do, I'll take the blame."

"You're wrong," he said stubbornly. "I'll take the blame. I'm the one with the key."

Dottie steamed over him like so much rubble in her path. "Look, it can't take you more than five minutes to teach me which buttons to push. Then you can leave. I promise I would never tell them how I got in."

"Jesus, Dottie," he said uncertainly. "I don't know. If the manuscript is nine hundred pages, that's one hell of a lot of paper you're going to be using. They would notice it was missing."

Capable of seizing the moment, and desperate enough to use his love for her to her advantage, Dottie's mind raced past his in a flash of inspiration. "I'll call Xerox, Marty. I'll buy my own paper and bring it along. I won't use one sheet that belongs to the university."

"Well . . ." he said, drawing out the word, searching for more objections for Dottie to obliterate.

Dottie leaned across the table and took his hand. "How can you refuse, Marty? It's art. For the sake of art."

His fear thoroughly ravaged by her ambition, he finally collapsed. "All right, Dot. I'll do it. For you. And for art," he added as a soothing afterthought to his conscience.

Dottie picked up her wineglass in a toast. "Here's to larceny in literature," she said, extraordinarily pleased with herself.

Les Deux Magots was only a few blocks from the hotel on the Left Bank where Ashley and Kate were staying. As they walked to the restaurant, famous for being Hemingway's Paris hangout, Ashley could barely contain the searing delight she felt at the knowledge that Alexander would be there waiting for her. It had been almost a year since she had last seen him, and time had not lessened the impact he had on her. Now she was to have two weeks with him, moving them into new territory in their relationship.

He was standing outside under the canopy, and as soon as he saw them approaching, he walked down the street to meet them.

"You're beautiful," he said as he greeted her.

His blue eyes looked straight into the heart of her and immediately found the answer to his silent question.

Yes, she said with her eyes. Yes. Then she smiled, her warmth spreading over him like a familiar blanket, soft and comforting.

Remembering Kate, Ashley made the introductions. Until then they had not noticed an attractive Frenchman standing slightly to one side.

"And I would like both of you to meet my friend, Edouard Jonas," said Alexander.

"*Enchanté.*" He inclined his head slightly and smiled at them.

The introductions completed, the two couples entered the restaurant and were shown to a table by the window.

They exchanged routine small talk about their plans for traveling through Europe, while Ashley and Kate each sipped their first glass of Pernod, feeling marginally wicked and definitely grown-up.

Having spent a wonderful dinner, over coffee—the French *café noir* both Ashley and Kate would grow to love—Edouard suggested that they go to a club he knew in Montparnasse.

It was the perfect ending to their first night in Paris. One of the numerous clubs built in cellars under the city of Paris, it was dark and smoky, with haphazard rooms connected to one another with no apparent design in mind other than to enchant visitors from the new world.

It was a crowded, popular place, but Edouard knew the owner and was thus able to secure for them a table hidden in a niche in the main room.

The club was Greek and they drank ouzo and listened to the compelling rhythms of the balalaika as they tried to make themselves heard over the din of the crowd.

Ashley and Alexander were the first ones to join the dancers. As Kate watched, she felt increasingly like a voyeur. Alexander knew the dance, but Ashley did not. Following him in a rhythm deeply sensual and primitive in its message, she faced him, arms languidly outstretched, moving slowly back and forth to the pulse of the music. They were alone, wrapped in the privacy of their own mating ritual, oblivious to anyone else in the room.

Without a word Edouard took Kate by the hand and led her onto the dance floor.

"I don't know how to do this," she said, feeling slightly awkward. She thought he was an attractive man, which confused her all the more.

"Just follow me," he instructed with a smile.

Kate did as he directed, allowing the music to flow over her body, becoming part of its rhythm. For the first time in her life, she gave herself up to it. A long way from the fox-trot lessons I used to have in cotillion, she thought. There she had been taught how to do the box step, how to accept an invitation to dance with gracious deportment, how to keep her white gloves spotless and execute a commendable curtsy to the chaperon. But she had never, until that moment, felt the music.

At three in the morning, happily exhausted, they decided to call it a night. Feeling somewhat awkward, Ashley asked Kate privately if she would object to spending the night alone. She explained that she wanted to go home with Alexander, and Kate nodded that it would be all right, that she understood. And she suddenly wished that Sol was with her so that she, too, could sleep in the arms of a man she loved.

Late the next morning the two couples met again for brunch. It was Sunday and all of Paris was talking about the Algerians. That summer the revolutionaries had moved their bid for freedom to Paris. The police had begun their abrupt and sometimes brutal raids on the Algerian quarters of Paris. The morning newspapers were filled with accounts of the latest raid, and Alexander expressed a decidedly antiestablishment view in his support of the rebels.

"They deserve their freedom," he said passionately. "They have been treated with disgusting contempt by the French."

"Ah, my friend," replied Edouard in his best English. "They are a filthy people. They deserve what they have received."

"If you treat a man like a dog for a long enough time, he will begin to act like one. But that cannot possibly justify the treatment itself."

"They will be put down in short order," Edouard said confidently. "They have neither the brains nor the means to sustain a true revolution."

Alexander, in his desire not to spoil a pleasant day nor a good friendship, put up his hand. "I would suggest that we place this topic on our very limited list of things not to discuss. I don't believe in politics coming between friends. Especially when it is quite apparent that neither of us will budge from his position."

Edouard nodded and tipped his glass to his friend. "Perhaps I am too French to see beyond the bounds of my nationality. But I, too, agree with you. The morning is too fine to spoil."

Throughout this conversation Kate and Ashley were fascinated. The mere idea of revolution titillated their imaginations, for they had never experienced anything so exotic, so . . . foreign.

It was fortunate that Kate liked Edouard. It had already been planned for Ashley and Alexander to spend a week by themselves. And it made it easier for Kate if she had an escort to take her places. She was actually rather pleased at being alone in Paris. Having spent almost twenty-one years in the privileged shelter of the wealthy, she wanted to try being on her own. This decision had not been made without anxiety, of course, because it did take a certain amount of courage. But she managed quite well, visiting museums and parks and cafés with increasing ease; sometimes going out for dinner with Edouard. And so the days slipped by, each one bringing with it new experiences and confidence. But not one day passed without her thinking of Sol.

Having been offered the use of a country home in Normandy, Alexander took Ashley there the very day she separated from Kate.

For one week they lingered in the essence of their own loving, cherishing every moment they spent together.

"Will you come to London in August?" asked Ashley. They were sitting by the side of a small lake, watching the sunset turn the water cerise, then deep purple.

"I can probably only manage a long weekend. But I'll fly over then. Just let me know."

"I'm missing you already, even though we do have another week together in Paris," Ashley said, kissing his hand absentmindedly.

"I'll miss you."

"I wish you were coming with us."

"Knowing you, my absence won't prevent your having a good time touring Europe, my love. You have learned so beautifully how to live each moment that I envy you."

"Too bad I can't apply that to my future plans," she said.

"I do wish you'd stop worrying so much about that. It's certainly not a very unusual situation, not to know what you want to do. It will come."

She looked at him, questioning. "How can you be so sure about that?"

"Because you have the courage to pursue a dream. You just don't know what it is yet. You're beautiful in everything you do. And you're strong. This career problem is just the last piece to fit in your personal puzzle, that's all. You're generous to everyone except yourself. Give yourself a chance before you declare the battle lost. Okay?"

"Okay." She kissed him again. "When did you say you were going to be in New York?"

"Next April. I'll probably be there six weeks, and I fully expect to find you immersed in some career by the time I arrive."

"How about both of us getting immersed in some marriage plans?"

"That's a thought, too."

"How about now, instead," she said with a mischievous gleam in her eye. "And I'll pursue my career madly under the blessing of a Paris sky."

"Ashley, Ashley," he muttered, shaking his head. "It's not that I don't love you. You know that. And if you were older, I would jump at the chance. But I will not be responsible for clipping your wings when you're just learning to fly. You deserve more." He paused. "We'll have our time. Someday we'll have it."

"I hope so," Ashley responded, a dark cloud passing over her confidence. "I'm just so accustomed to doing things now, to taking advantage of the moment, that the idea of waiting frightens me."

"Don't let it. Don't let anything spoil us. Just love me as much as I love you."

"That's an easy request," she said, leaning on his shoulder.

Near the end of August, two days before Dottie flew to London, she took Marty to lunch at "21." The purpose of the celebration was twofold: She wanted to thank him for his covert cooperation in the successful Xerox copying of ten copies of *Spartan's End,* and she wanted to bid him a proper farewell, since he would be leaving for his first teaching post in Ohio the following week.

She was an inveterate eavesdropper. Marty used to tease Dottie that sometimes he felt the people sitting at the adjoining table should pay for her lunch, since her participation with them had been somewhat excessive. That day was no different.

Just as Marty was prepared to regale her with the details of his latest paper, she rolled her eyes toward the next table. He immediately picked up her signal and stopped talking as Dottie fiddled with her eggs Florentine, looking down at her plate.

"Saxon Press is the one," said the older gentleman. "Nigel Stephenson told me about it just last week. Of course, it's confidential, but he did say that he was looking for the big one. The prestige book. Said he's tired of publishing books for the lowest common denominator and wants to upgrade the image of the house."

"Didn't you have anything to offer?"

"Of course. But he said he wanted first rights. That he didn't want to follow in America's footsteps, publishing something that's already come out here."

Dottie thought of how all summer she had waited for the rejected manuscripts of *Spartan's End* to filter back to her. Again the book was invariably praised in the process of being turned down.

"So what's he after?" asked the second man.

"Something that would change his image. Money he's got. Prestige he hasn't. Said he'd pay up to twenty thousand pounds for the right property."

Soon afterward the men rose from their table as Dottie silently thanked them. Then she looked at Marty, whose patience was wearing thin.

"How many pounds to the dollar?"

"What?" he asked, lost in his own thoughts.

"How many English pounds to the American dollar?" she repeated.

"About three, I think."

"Not bad. Sixty thousand dollars."

"What in God's name are you talking about?"

Dottie explained the conversation she had just overheard, adding that Saxon Press was a publishing house in London, where she would just happen to be in two days.

"Ah, so," said Marty with a big smile. "Good show, Dot."

When they left the restaurant, a wisp of sadness passed through Dottie's heart, as if she had come to the end of an important phase in her life. She understood that, in Marty's leaving, she was not only saying good-bye to him. She was bidding a final farewell to a chance to live an ordinary life, to settle down with a husband and children.

She knew that she did not want this. And yet there was a secret part of her that found it difficult to let go of something that had been such an integral part of her upbringing.

Not knowing what to say, Dottie hugged him. "I love you, Marty. Good luck."

"Good luck to you," he offered, the pain of her rejection still alive in the recesses of his eyes. "I hope you find what you're looking for."

"I do, too," she said, her eyes brimming with tears. "I do, too."

Dottie landed at Heathrow at five in the morning. Before leaving, she had checked with Madelaine once again about her authority to handle *Spartan's End.* Madelaine had replied that if she could sell the book, she damn well deserved to negotiate the terms.

Ashley and Kate were having coffee when Dottie arrived at the hotel in Chelsea. They spent several hours catching up on what had happened over the summer, then went to the Queen's Elm, a local Chelsea pub, to celebrate the first European reunion of the Troika.

That afternoon, buoyed by a sufficient amount of wine, Dottie made her call to Nigel Stephenson. When the secretary answered, Dottie identified herself as representing the Jacot Agency in New York, and she was put through immediately to the publisher of Saxon Press.

"Yes?" he said in a clipped Oxonian accent.

"My name is Dorothy Langford, Mr. Stephenson, and I'm with Jacot in New York. I'm only in London for a few days, and I wondered if it might be possible for you to be my guest for lunch."

"Possibly," he replied noncommittally, his voice drifting into the empty space of the phone.

Dottie realized she would have to hook him, or he would be "busy" for the remainder of her stay. "A salesman is the one with the instinct for the moment," her father used to tell her. "Remember, Dottie, a salesman has a product that is beneficial, but not indispensable. Your job is to sell the benefit. There's a difference between negotiating and selling. Not everybody knows that. Only if the product is indispensable can you negotiate. Otherwise, you just sell." Dottie knew that neither she nor the book was indispensable. But if she could represent them as having a touch of that quality, she might have a chance. She also knew that she would have to make her pitch right there on the phone, or her prey would be lost to the dozens of other manuscripts that crossed his desk daily.

"Mr. Stephenson," she began with a deep intake of breath. "I have something that I think could be of great value to you. Perhaps it sounds brash of me—and please forgive me if it does—but I do think it would benefit you if we were to have lunch."

"Oh?"

"I have the big book, Mr. Stephenson. The one you're looking for."

There was a pause, too long for Dottie. Yet she allowed it to continue. The ball was in his court.

"Would tomorrow be acceptable for lunch?" he inquired.

"That would be delightful. Is the Connaught convenient?" She had chosen the most elegant hotel in London.

"Quite."

"At one o'clock?"

"Very good."

"Thank you, Mr. Stephenson. I'm looking forward to meeting you."

Dottie had done her homework on Nigel Stephenson. She knew that he was upper class, Oxford educated, the son of a publisher, married to the same woman for twenty-seven years; he was the father of two grown children, one of whom worked for Saxon, and was a man who observed all the proprieties and to whom image was important. Her hope was that, being American, she could get away with a forthrightness that would be unacceptable in an Englishman or Englishwoman. She also knew that there was a distinct possibility that he would check up on her before their luncheon date, that he would discover that she was, indeed, only a secretary empowered to handle one single property. Gambling on the fact that the reputation of the Jacot Agency would carry her, she still opted for American brash, hoping that an end run to the goal would be successful where a conventional play might not.

Dottie wore her most expensive dress, with her hair pulled back to the nape of her neck, and secured by a subdued silk scarf. Her makeup was applied judiciously, creating a conservative and reliable appearance. It was a look calculated to counterbalance her words, words she planned carefully.

After the initial amenities had been exchanged, she wasted no time in getting down to business. She faced the elegant gray-haired man, dressed in a three-piece pinstripe suit and school tie, and smiled disarmingly. Reaching to the floor beside her chair, she picked up two manuscript boxes and set them on the table.

"As you may or may not know, Mr. Stephenson, I

am just a secretary with Jacot. With one exception. I handle this novel. And the reason is, the novel is difficult to sell. In fact, to be perfectly honest, almost every decent publisher in America has turned it down."

"Oh?"

"They've turned it down because they're afraid. Afraid to take a chance on a quality first novel. And afraid to spend the money its production would require." She paused for a moment, to give him a chance to absorb her words, as well as to try to assess their effect. The placid look on his face indicated nothing. "As you can see, it's very long. It's also exciting and brilliant and remarkably well written. And I'm convinced that the man—or the house—that publishes this novel could build a reputation on this book alone. It's that kind of novel. It has that kind of power."

She paused, then waited for him. Refusing to give in to the instinct to fill the conversational void with chatter, she just smiled. Finally, he said, "What makes you think that Saxon is the house for, for . . ."

"*Spartan's End*," she said, supplying the title. "It's my understanding that you're looking for a property to enhance your reputation."

This time he raised his eyebrows in an indication of mild surprise. "And how, may I be so bold to ask, did you ascertain that fact?"

"Don't worry. It's not general knowledge, if that's what you're asking. Just chalk it up to my budding career as a literary agent."

"Indeed," he said, nodding.

Dottie's stomach lurched as she took a casual bite of her shrimp. This is it, she thought, now or never. She looked straight into his eyes, swallowed, and said, "You might as well take it along with you, Mr. Stephenson. Because you're going to end up buying it, anyway." She almost vomited with the chutzpah of her last statement, hoping she had not overplayed her hand, that she had caught him at the very moment he was off balance.

"Well, now," he said with an arch smile, "if that is, indeed, the case, we'd best finish lunch so I can get started reading it this afternoon." He looked at her, picking up his glass of wine. "I hope you'll permit me to say, Miss Langford . . . Miss Dottie Langford . . . that I admire your courage."

"My balls, you mean."

His English sensibilities were shocked, but there was a glint of respect in his eyes.

"Guess what?" said Ashley the following morning. "My grandmother's in town." Until then Ashley had not shared Nana with her friends. It was too painfully private until she had fully come to terms with it. "Here's the announcement of her show right here in the London *Times*," she said with quiet pride.

"Your grandmother?" asked Kate. "I thought she died."

"It's the other one," Ashley replied.

"I thought she was dead, too."

"Only to my father. He and my grandmother are . . . estranged."

"Why?"

"I don't know," Ashley answered. "But I think I'm going to have to find out."

"Well, it shouldn't be so difficult," Dottie said.

"There's only one catch. Daddy has forbidden me to see her."

"Ouch," Dottie said without humor. "That's a tough one. Have you ever met her?"

"Only once. When I was nine years old."

"I don't envy you this," said Kate.

"There's a little article in the paper about her," said Ashley thoughtfully. "It says that she's staying with Mr. and Mrs. Chester Wallensky, the owners of the gallery, in their houseboat at Whistler's Reach, wherever that is."

Dottie immediately reached for her map of London. It took just a few moments to locate it. "Here. It's here in Chelsea. Not so far from here. Near Battersea Bridge . . . and World's End," she added wryly.

"You all right, Ashley?" asked Kate.

"Yes . . . I'm just afraid, that's all. Afraid of the consequences."

"You should excuse me for butting in, Ashley," said Dottie with a particular hard ring to her voice. "But both sets of my grandparents died in concentration camps, and all my life I've wished I just had one. Just one whose lap I could crawl up on and talk to, and listen to stories about how life used to be when they were young. And so I can't quite understand how you could avoid seeing her."

"I can't either."

"What did you say she's doing here?" Kate asked.

"She's having a show. Photography. From what I can gather, she's pretty famous. A recluse of sorts." She paused, thinking, then expressed her worst fantasy. "She never came back after that time when I was little. Maybe she doesn't want to see me."

"There's only one way to find out," said Dottie, always practical.

Ashley stood. "So let's take a walk to Whistler's Reach," she said with somber determination.

Just as they were leaving the hotel room, the telephone rang. Ashley returned to answer it.

"Hello?"

"Miss Langford, please," stated an efficient female voice.

"One moment, please." Ashley motioned to Dottie. "It's for you."

"Yes?"

"Miss Langford?"

"Speaking."

"Nigel Stephenson here."

Dottie clenched the receiver, then said. "Yes, Mr. Stephenson. How are you?"

"Very well, thank you," he replied. "I just wanted to tell you that you were correct. Saxon is going to publish *Spartan's End.*"

"Oh . . ."

"Are you there?" he inquired politely, with a hint of amusement in his voice.

"Oh, yes. Yes, I'm here, Mr. Stephenson. I'm just a little overwhelmed, that's all. I didn't expect you to read it so quickly."

"Everything you said about the book is true. It *is* brilliant and I do want to publish it."

"That's wonderful . . . marvelous. I'm glad you believe in it."

"I'm a very busy man, Miss Langford. Let's get to the point. I'll pay three thousand pounds, advance against royalties, with the normal percentages."

Appalled, remembering the twenty-thousand pound figure she had heard in New York, Dottie objected. "But, Mr. Stephenson . . ."

His voice turned hard. "Three thousand pounds, Miss Langford."

I'm in no position to negotiate; I have no strength from which to deal, she thought. Like Daddy said, sometimes you can only sell. And, by God, against all the odds I've done that.

"All right," she said, maneuvering for some symbolic victory. "But you have to pay it all up front."

He conceded on an essentially meaningless point. Either way, he would pay her. It was just a matter of how. "All right, Miss Langford. All up front."

"Good."

"Shall I have the contract drawn up and sent to your New York office?"

"That would be fine, Mr. Stephenson. Just fine."

"Good enough. You'll be hearing from me soon."

"Mr. Stephenson?" Dottie hesitated. "Thank you."

"For what, Miss Langford? I should say you've done rather well for a twenty-one-year-old girl who's only been in the business for a year."

He did check up on me, she thought. "Thank you, Mr. Stephenson."

"Thank *you,* Miss Langford. It's been a pleasure."

"Good-bye."

Dottie hung up the phone softly, not quite able to believe the conversation that had just taken place. "I did it," she whispered. "I did it."

"Is something wrong?" asked Ashley.

"I did it," Dottie repeated, louder this time. Then, throwing up her hands, she yelled, "I did it! I sold a book! I sold the unsalable book!"

Ashley and Kate immediately smothered Dottie in hugs and kisses, words of astonishment and congratulations blending happily in the joyous atmosphere.

Dottie knew, finally, that her faith in herself had been justified. And she also knew that she would hold on to this feeling for the rest of her life.

As they walked to Whistler's Reach, Kate was preoccupied with the letter she had received from her mother the day before. She did not have the slightest indication that it was coming, and was thus shocked when she read it out loud to Ashley and Dottie.

> My dear Katherine:
>
> Soon you'll be returning home, a prospect which delights us all. I do hope that you have had a wonderful vacation abroad, and that you will always look back on this as a very special summer.
>
> But before you return I feel obligated to discuss with you a rather unpleasant subject.

Namely, that of Sol. Your fascination with him at the bon voyage party—not to mention the rather extravagant gift he gave you—did not escape my notice. Imagine how disappointed I was when I saw that, and was suddenly struck with the knowledge that you must have been seeing him all along. You must also be able to imagine the disappointment in you that your father and I experienced. More than just heartsick, we were angry. Because we have always felt that we could trust you to do the right thing. It was part of the standard by which you have been raised.

Your father and I have discussed the subject thoroughly and have decided to offer you one more chance, the rules of which are simply this: When you return to New York, you must give up Solomon Langford once and for all. We will allow you to see him one time for that purpose only. Then we forbid you to see him again. There is simply no other option.

We do hope you have a fine time in London and return home in good and positive spirits. Your father and I send our love.

Mother

"That's some letter," Dottie commented. "Welcome home." Dottie was hurt for Kate, worried for Sol.

"Yes, that's some letter," Kate rejoined bitterly.

As she walked, Kate could not help but compare her situation to Ashley's. They had both been forbidden to do something by their parents. Ashley had chosen to defy it, feeling it was more important to seek out love than to feed hate. To her, the inherent morality of her situation was clear.

Kate wished that William were there to talk to. Somehow, she felt that her brother would be able to help her see beyond her immediate sense of panic.

Neither of her friends was able to do anything except commiserate with her, for both Ashley and Dottie understood that Kate's defiance of her parents would have to be a solo endeavor. They could not help weigh the price nor share the consequences. That belonged to Kate alone.

Kate looked at Ashley and envied her. She's not going to toady to the Watermelon Baby, Kate thought. I hope, when the time comes, that I don't either.

Ashley was the first in line as the Troika walked across the plank to the houseboat. Single file, they approached the front door. She looked around and smiled tentatively at Kate and Dottie.

"I'm afraid," she whispered.

"Go for it," Kate returned. "Don't stop now."

After hesitating briefly, Ashley knocked on the door. They waited only a moment before a short, dumpy woman opened the door. Her face, framed in unruly white hair, looked at the three young women inquiringly.

"Yes?" she asked, her eyes kind, even with their question.

"Hello . . . ah . . . are you Mrs. Wallensky?" Ashley asked in a tentative voice.

"Yes, I am."

"Ah . . . my name is Ashley Van Every." She was so frightened that her grandmother would reject her that she could barely utter her own name.

"Yes," Mrs. Wallensky prompted.

A deep, clear voice called from the interior of the houseboat. "Ashley? Ashley Van Every? *My* Ashley?"

Looking behind her, Mrs. Wallensky stepped aside as a tall, elegant woman approached the door. She was dressed in gray raw silk slacks and a smocked flowered blouse in muted tones of dusty rose, gray, and blue. "Colors," she would tell Ashley later. "I love them. Perhaps because I spend my life working in black and white." But then, standing in the doorway, the impression was not so much of color, as of total and powerful presence. Ashley could only look at her grandmother for a long moment, flooded with memories of those hands stroking her head, holding her close.

Then she said gently, shyly, "Nana?"

"At last, my Ashley," Nana cried, her voice husky with emotion. "My Ashley," she repeated as she took her into arms that were warm and loving and serenely familiar.

Ashley felt as if she had come home. Finally.

## CHAPTER 4

Marguerite Van Every Martinez brought the three girls into her life with as much skill and ease as she excluded others. When they entered the houseboat, they were, in part, entering another phase of their lives. For despite their avowals of friendship, of past and future loyalties, the inevitability that their lives would take diverse directions would have insured the Troika's drifting apart into an unknown future. Not in enmity, nor even indifference. It simply would have happened. But Nana bound them together and gave the Troika a second life.

Out of love for a granddaughter whom she barely knew, Nana gathered the three into a corner of her life that she reserved for private needs. Rarely was one admitted to this sanctuary because necessity dictated entrance there. Nana Martinez was a woman who dictated necessity.

Marta Wallensky, a friend of Nana's for thirty years, understood immediately the importance of the occasion and bustled around producing an early luncheon for them. Business could wait, she thought, as she cut the crusts off the cucumber sandwiches that she prepared to accompany the sherry she had already offered the group.

Ashley stood and raised her glass in a formal toast to her grandmother. "To Nana," she said, her voice choked. "And to this day. Because I found her."

"And to my granddaughter," she returned. "Because I've waited so long." Tears glistened her eyes, making them bluer than they were, brighter than they had been in years.

Ashley sat next to her grandmother, content in her presence, yet filled with questions. Finally, she looked to her and asked, "Why?" Nothing else, just that one simple word.

"My dear dear Ashley," she said, reaching over and brushing an imaginary hair from the side of her face. "There are so many things I have to tell you. And"—she paused—"so many more that I cannot. For the moment, let me say that I have been deliberately excluded from your life. But you should understand that—even though we only met once—I never, for one instant, stopped loving you. I simply understood that one day we would come together. And when that time came, there would be no secret on earth that could prevent us from touching, from forming the closeness that I have known could exist between us. A closeness, I might add, that I have missed terribly."

Ashley nodded, content for the moment to accept this judgment. She looked at her grandmother and marveled at her beauty. They looked nothing alike. Nana was fair-skinned like her father. Although her hair was almost gray, it was apparent that it had once been light. Her face was oval, with defined but not wide cheekbones like Ashley's. But they did have the same mouth: wide and full and warm. What made Nana Martinez beautiful was not just physical. It was her entire aura, one wrought of pain and dignity, carrying with it an essence of nobility that emanated from her like a beacon on a dark, homeless night.

Despite this, she was not contained. Energy flowed from her in the form of extravagant gestures and mobile expressions, at once strong yet sensual. She was a woman who had wrestled with her ghosts and brought them under control. But she was wise enough to understand that any victory—over fear or passion or another human being—was temporary at best. And that the gifts life offered could be bestowed forever, or taken away without warning by a fate too capricious ever to trust. Therefore, she consumed moments as they were offered, earthy in her understanding and humble in her gratitude.

"That's a beautiful bracelet, Nana," commented Ashley after their lunch. It was, indeed, a work of deep and lasting art. Wrought of silver and brass, it was inlaid skillfully with five large natural turquoises in a thick band around her wrist. Although it was quite heavy, there was a delicate quality to it, a result of expert workmanship and a fine eye for design.

"Thank you." Nana beamed at her, her skin wrinkling in tiny lines around her eyes, the result of years of laughter and squinting into a white sun. "An old dear friend made it for me," she said as she slipped it off her wrist. "And I would very much like for you to have it. This is very special to me." She handed it to Ashley.

Slipping it on her wrist, Ashley held her arm up to the light. "It looks as if it were made for me," she said quietly.

Perhaps it was, thought Nana. More than you'll ever know.

"And now . . . I hate to interrupt our lovely day," announced Nana, "but Marta and I have work to do. My opening is tonight and we're overdue at the gallery." She looked at the girls and smiled. "Of course you'll come. Seven o'clock. On Old Church Street near the Chelsea Arts Club."

"Where does she live?" asked Kate as they were walking home.

"Near Santa Fe," answered Ashley. "As far as I know, she's lived there all her life. That's where Daddy was born. And I only know that because I saw it on his passport."

"Jesus!" said Dottie, awed. "I'll be damned if I can figure that one out. I don't know why anybody wouldn't want to claim her for a relative. She's extraordinary."

"I just don't know," Ashley said sadly, running her fingers over the rough texture of the bracelet.

The gallery was filled when the Troika arrived. But Nana Martinez, photographer, would have been noticed immediately in any crowd. Hers was a presence that dominated.

She wore a long loose-fitting gown of natural handwoven linen. It had a V neck and long sleeves, gathered in cuffs at the wrists. A plain gold band encircled her left ring finger, and on her right hand she wore a silver ring crafted of jet and coral. Around her neck, falling in a sweeping delicate curve, she wore an extraordinary necklace of ten strands of turquoise beads, honed like hishi into tendrils fine as the wire of a paperclip, yet fluid, graceful.

Nana was surrounded by admirers, but as soon as she saw her new children enter, she left the crowd and walked immediately over to them.

"I abhor these occasions," she said by way of greeting, rolling her eyes in a gesture at once funny and serious. "But it comes with the territory, as Marta insists on reminding me. And so I venture out of hiding once in a while to enter the world of commerce, hoping it will be sufficient once again to keep me fed and clothed."

She hugged each of them, then took them over to the bar where she procured three glasses of champagne for her very special guests.

"Let me tend to this nonsense," she told them, waving her hand in the general direction of the crowd. "We'll find time later to talk. In the meantime, take a look at the show. But please don't ask me about the photographs. I can't stand it when somebody asks me what a picture *means*. For me, it simply *is*."

Hung skillfully around the room were sixty black-and-white photographs. Each contained a vision so unique, made a statement of such clarity, that they were at once awesome and intimate in their impact.

Although Nana had traveled around the world, photographing the exotic as well as the mundane, the title of the show was "New Mexico." It spoke of her love of the land, her affinity with its light and shadow, and her identity with its inhabitants and their surroundings.

There was a close-up of a columbine, a flower common to New Mexico, that was startlingly fecund and female in its sensual curves and enclosures. Rock formations, desert sands, adobe walls, and weathered crosses took on new meaning; scrub oak and cactus became unique. And faces, young and old, were touching in their intimacy, universal in their message. It was as if Marguerite Martinez had scooped up a common world with the lens of a camera and ennobled it with her vision.

When the girls met Chester Wallensky, the topic of Dottie's success with the Saxon Press came up in the conversation.

"Do you mean Nigel Stephenson?" he asked with interest.

"That's the one," Dottie answered.

"Tough customer, that man." Chester shook his head slowly. "It's a wonder you're still wearing your clothes, since he does manage to take anything that isn't nailed to the floor. I dealt with him once on an art book. Took me to the cleaners, he did. Legally, of course. He just outmaneuvered me, that's all."

"I think he outmaneuvered me, too," said Dottie sheepishly, explaining about the three-thousand-pound sale, when she had heard the twenty-thousand-pound figure in New York.

"I think you did quite well, my dear. After all, you were quick to pick up on a fragment of conversation and turn it into success. I'll bet the old man is still wondering how you found out what kind of book he wanted. Just too proud to ask. Pleasures me to think about it," he chuckled.

"I never thought of that," Dottie said.

"I rather imagine one of the reasons he took the book in the first place was that he knew it had been turned down so many places. He wanted to enhance his reputation. If he can make a success out of this—and I suspect he'll try damn hard . . . publicity and all that—then it will make him look even better. He was the one who took the chance where the others withdrew. Very crafty, that man."

"It doesn't make me look that bad either," Dottie said with a smile.

"Absolutely, my dear. You'll be the agent who persisted. No doubt it will help your reputation. And the best part is you were perfectly honest with him. The minute I think somebody is trying to pull the wool over my eyes, I turn mean." Chester put his hand on her shoulder. "You did a good job, Dottie. Forget the money for now. It will come."

They all stayed quite late at the party. Ashley was

delighted, especially awed and proud that she came from such blood. And Nana flowed with love for her granddaughter, treasuring the rare gift of a child that the gods had chosen to bestow on her when she was sixty years old.

The Troika spent a happy two weeks in London. Often accompanied by Nana, they attended receptions and art shows, went to the theater and museums.

At different moments each of the girls spent time alone with Nana. And she was able to touch them each in unique and binding ways.

Kate, especially, appreciated Nana's presence. Although she had managed to tuck her fears about Sol into a private corner that did not intrude on her fun in London, she did tell Nana about him.

"I spent most of my life wanting to get married and have children," Kate said. "And now that I've met a man, my parents are confusing the very ambition they instilled in me."

It was quite apparent that Kate's dream had melded into her destiny. And she had finally made friends with it, out of love and out of need.

"Is that all you ever wanted?" Nana inquired.

"Almost. Once, for a while when I was little, I wanted to become a famous archaeologist. But I put that aside."

"Why?"

"Because my parents told me that girls didn't become archaeologists."

"Are you that easily dissuaded?" Nana asked.

Kate lowered her eyes, wishing that she could offer a different answer. Finally, she said, "I suppose I am."

"It may well be that you were meant to be a wife and a mother and nothing else, Kate," Nana said gently. "But I do think you should consider the possibility of not giving up your dreams so easily. It cheapens the worth of everything. Life's like that, you know.

You can't explode a dream and expect not to be harmed by the blast."

And so Kate returned home with Dottie, full of resolve to walk in her own path, rather than the one her parents would choose for her.

Ashley stayed on in London for another week. She wanted more time with her grandmother. And she wanted Nana to meet Alexander. Somehow, she felt the need for both of them to touch, as if she could keep them more alive in her memory if each had known the other.

Although she did not admit it to herself then, Ashley also stayed on so that she would not have to see her father. She dreaded the confrontation with him that would inevitably take place. And she hoped that her association with Nana and Alexander would give her additional courage when she would need it most.

When Dottie returned to New York, she was met by a very pleased Madelaine. Taking Dottie out to lunch at one of the restaurants reserved for important occasions and tax-deductible expense accounts, Madelaine congratulated her.

"I can hardly believe it myself," said Dottie.

"Of course, the price was rather . . . modest, shall we say."

"Not for a book that had been turned down everywhere." Dottie felt the necessity to defend her position, even though they both recognized that the sale was a coup.

"I called Jack," said Madelaine. "But he told me you had already cabled him from London."

"I thought he'd want to know immediately. He's been waiting a long time for this."

"By the way," said Madelaine. "I'm having a few friends over this weekend. Would you be able to come?"

"I'd love to."

Dottie understood all too well that this luncheon and invitation to the party were to stand in lieu of a commission or bonus on the sale. Otherwise, it would have been mentioned immediately. But she smiled, swallowing her irritation, making the decision right then and there never to let it show. She had an apprenticeship to serve, knowledge to glean. And she was in the perfect place to get it. Patience, she thought. It's the key. And when I'm ready, no one will stop me. No one. I'll do my work and learn everything I can about this business. Daddy always told me that the ability to wait for the right moment can mean the difference between success and failure. And, by God, when that moment arrives, nobody will stop me.

Ashley's last night in London was spent in the company of Alexander and Nana. Alexander had arrived on Thursday for a long weekend, and their time together passed as if the three of them had retreated to their own private country.

The Wallenskys had gone to the south of France and left them in charge of the houseboat. Anchored in the Thames, a home of uncommon beauty had been created out of a converted barge. Within its walls Ashley, Alexander, and Nana came together in their own season, sharing a fragment of time that blossomed from the heart of their common love. It was an idyll grounded in honesty, a sanctuary purified by truths explored and moments remembered. It was as if they had always known one another, and in the wonder of this discovery they sought new ways to grab hold of it before it was too late.

"Nana?" asked Ashley on their last evening together. "Why didn't you come to see me again, after that time in New York?"

There was no attempt at evasion in Nana's answer, although they both understood that the essence of their stories would have to wait to be told until John

Van Every could be made to understand how very important the revelation was. "That day when I came to visit you," Nana said, "I had every intention of waiting until your father came home. I had hoped we could meet after all that time and put our past behind us. But when you told me, innocently, of course, that your grandmother was dead, I understood the depth of John's desire to keep me out of his life. And I knew that seeing him—or you—would not change his mind. I'm sorry it happened, because I know it must have hurt. But now," she smiled gently, "these past two weeks have made it all worthwhile." Nana looked into her granddaughter's familiar eyes and smiled.

"I wish you had waited," said Ashley. "I would have *made* him understand."

"Is he that intractable?" asked Alexander.

"Indeed he is," replied Nana with a hard edge of remorse coloring her memory. "As a matter of fact, I'm quite concerned about what Ashley is going to tell him when she returns."

"I'll tell him the truth."

"And if that doesn't work?" asked Nana.

"It has to work," replied Ashley with an anguished determination. "We need to be a family again."

"I'm afraid for you." Nana spoke quietly. "I cannot help but feel guilty that I have placed you in a terrible position of having to choose between me and your parents." Nana leaned forward and touched Ashley's face, punctuating her words with love. "And if that time comes, Ashley, you must choose them. I'll not be responsible for severing another parent and child. It's a curse. It has been a relentless source of pain for me all my life, and I will not have you live it, too."

"I'll fix it, Nana. I promise."

Nana said softly, "He sends me money, you know."

"Money? Daddy sends you money?" Ashley was shocked.

"Indeed he does. Twice a year a certified check arrives for me in the mail. And I've never," said Nana with a stubborn pride, "I've never spent a penny of it on myself. Thank God I never needed to."

"What have you done with it?"

"Invested it."

"How?" Ashley asked.

"In another future. I wish I could tell you about it. But I can't . . . not now."

Exhilarated, they stayed up late that night. They talked about Ashley's lack of career plans, which bothered her more than it did Nana or Alexander. Both of them expressed similar confidence that she would discover what it was she wanted when the time was right.

They discussed Alexander's trip to New York the following April and made tentative plans—hinged, of course, on John Van Every's ability to forgive—for a family reunion in Santa Fe.

Before she went to bed, Nana expressed one more time her anxiety about the tenuous position in which Ashley had been placed.

Ashley hugged her. "Don't worry, Nana. I promise I'll make it work. I love you all too much for it to fail." She looked at Alexander, overflowing with love for him. "I promise you this: We'll all dance together at our wedding."

Madelaine Jacot lived in a six-room penthouse on upper Fifth Avenue. From her apartment Central Park lay before her like a child's imaginary garden, surrounded by twinkling lights at night, creating a city dweller's ideal.

Inside everything was clean, contemporary, in perfect taste. Leather-covered Breuer chairs outlined a chrome-and-glass dining table; pale gray plush carpeting, expanses of it, set off the monochromatic scheme. Glass étagères and a coffee table made of an antique etched-glass window set into an impeccably designed pecan frame shone with reflected light. Two sofas of muted blue flanked either side of the fireplace, with a Rya rug, the only splash of color, in deep blue and purple, placed between them. It was a home where good taste—purchased from an expensive decorator—was blatant, and fingerprints were anathema. It was precise, expensive, and uncluttered, a perfect reflection of its owner.

When Dottie arrived, wearing a simple black dress with a strand of opera-length pearls knotted around her neck, she was slightly nervous and unsure of what to expect. Just as she had learned to dress very simply because she knew that she had little talent for fashion, she also understood the necessity of being in control of potentially awkward social situations. Since she had only a vague idea of what to expect, her sense of control was minimal. Besides, her confrontation with a room full of strangers was her nemesis. More than any other human encounter, this was the one that frightened her most of all. This party was, after all, a command performance staged by a pro, and Dottie was only a bit player.

A bar, tucked artfully into a recessed corner of the living room, was set up for the guests, and a uniformed maid passed hors d'oeuvres unobtrusively among them. It was fashionable then to call about fifty people a "few friends." As Dottie looked around, she recognized faces from all the major areas in contemporary literature, from publishing to writing. Telling herself to stand up straight and look like she knew what she was doing, Dottie took a glass of wine from the tray a waiter offered and slowly sipped it as she surveyed the scene.

Madelaine was everywhere, talking, touching, laughing. This was her element, and fluttering in the middle of it, she was an expert—a strangely plumaged bird who behaved artfully in her natural habitat. Dottie watched, making mental notes, thinking she had best learn how to do it, despite her fear of crowds. Entertaining was part of the game and she was out to win at any cost.

At one point during the evening Madelaine took Dottie by the hand and led her over to an author who had just begun to flirt with fame. He was a Jacot client, a writer capable of anticipating the future in novels that were set in the present. The result of this literary shadowboxing was the creation of a world that was grounded in contemporary reality, yet which took on the timeless quality that all first-rate works of art maintain.

"This is Dorothy Langford, my secretary, Patrick. I thought you'd like to meet her. She's the one I told you about who sold Jack Barclay's book." Madelaine's introduction was casual, yet Dottie was pleased to hear that she had been talking about her sale of *Spartan's End.*

Shaking hands with Patrick McAuliffe, Dottie smiled, remembering his funny bawdy book that had just gone into its seventh printing.

As Madelaine floated away to join more strangers by her hostess efforts, Patrick asked with a quiet smile, "Is your appearance in this august company by choice or demand?"

"I wouldn't miss it for the world." Dottie delivered the line deadpan.

"I used to be grateful for parties like this. I was definitely poor enough to appreciate the free drink and food."

"And now?" asked Dottie, drawn by his magnetism.

"Now I'm neither as poor as I used to be nor rich as I want to be. But I am certainly enjoying the transition."

They talked for most of the evening. Dottie found herself increasingly attracted to him. He was funny and bawdy and blunt. Like his books. She also sensed an acute intuition behind his more brash facade, a quality that made him particularly appealing.

The room began to thin out around eleven, as the guests prepared to move on to other parties or other beds. Feeling suddenly awkward, Dottie started to make her excuses to Madelaine about leaving, hoping, of course, that Patrick would ask to take her home.

"Oh, don't go, Dottie. Stay and have a cup of coffee. It's early yet." She touched Dottie's shoulder, making her feel as if she were a child compelled to do the bidding of a stern and dictatorial parent.

"Of course," Dottie said, nodding, with a polite smile.

With a quizzical look on his face, Patrick bowed his head to her in a silent gesture of good-bye, then left. It made Dottie uncomfortable, for a reason she could not quite touch.

"So . . ." said Madelaine as she settled with their coffee, sitting next to Dottie on the sofa. "Did you enjoy yourself?"

"Of course," she responded. "I like Patrick. He's charming. He has the look of a winner."

"You're very sharp," said Madelaine as she reached out and touched Dottie on the shoulder. "Very."

Then Dottie understood. Although she had never been approached by Madelaine, all the little gestures of their common past fell into place. The innuendo and the rumor. And the smiles. She thinks I'm a lesbian, Dottie thought. She's simply assuming it. I guess this is the literary version of the casting couch. It just never occurred to me. Enter the reading room and follow the script, she said to herself. Trouble is, I don't know my lines. Once more with feeling . . .

Here goes, she thought, as Madelaine leaned over and kissed her on the lips. Could be worse. Besides, if this is what I have to do to get some clients of my own, I always said I'd do anything.

Feeling Madelaine's hand on her breast, which was

neither enticing nor repelling, Dottie closed her eyes and gave herself up to the experience.

When she left Madelaine's apartment the next morning, Dottie was confused. She realized that swimming around in her subconscious was the hope that she would like the feel of Madelaine's body next to hers. At least she would feel sexual. As it was, what bothered Dottie was that she found her experience with Madelaine no more interesting than her times with Marty. It gave rise to the tormented suspicion that she was neuter, that she was an outcast in a sexual purgatory, condemned to a longing from which there could be no deliverance.

She could not help but smile at the irony of meeting Patrick the very night Madelaine made her move. For a moment when she had been talking to him, Dottie felt that her attraction to him was more than just intellectual. And she had hoped she might have a chance to explore it. Instead, the experience had pushed her farther into a nether world that she did not want to inhabit.

She wished then that Nana were there for her. She did not quite understand why, except that she was convinced on a gut level that this wise woman would somehow understand what was happening to her, that she would be able to make sense out of the tangled skeins of her feelings and perhaps pull a few threads free so that they could be examined. She needed help, she thought. Because she knew only one thing: She did not want to live her life as a neuter. The thought of it was painful. What was unbearable was that she had not the slightest idea if there was any hope, any deliverance.

After Dottie had traveled downtown to her apartment to change clothes and shower, she thought of Madelaine. She knew that when she walked into the office on Monday, her boss would greet her with a cordial smile. She sincerely hoped that was all.

* * *

Kate lay, numb and exhausted, on her bed. The faint shadows of the early morning light played with delicate insistence on her bedroom wall. She had not yet slept, and she felt weary in every part of her body.

When she returned from London, Kate had been greeted enthusiastically by her parents. It was not until the following day that her mother brought up the subject of Sol. All the way home on the plane, Kate had steeled herself for this moment, determined to fight for her right to live her own life, even to make her own mistakes. But faced with her mother's smiling and quiet resolve to save her daughter from a disastrous marriage, Kate felt her vows crumbling, and with it, her self-esteem.

Shortly after her conversation with her mother, Kate had called Will. She needed the comfort of his family ties, of his immediate understanding. As soon as he answered the phone, Kate felt a rush of tears flood her eyes.

"Katie? What is it?" he asked.

"The same old thing, Will."

"You and Sol?"

"You guessed it."

Kate then proceeded to tell him about the letter she received while she was in London, and about her parents' ultimatum.

"Damn the ultimatum, Kate! If you want Sol, fight for him. Mother and Father aren't gods, you know. They're human just like you and me. It's about time you recognized that and stood up for yourself. Stop being so frightened of their rejection."

She was crying openly now. "I couldn't bear it if they disowned me, Will. I really couldn't," she sobbed.

"That's the weapon they're using against you, Kate. Your own fear."

"It's a powerful weapon, Will."

"Look, Kate, I know what I'm saying. As long as

you're afraid, they'll abuse you. You have to get hold of yourself. Believe me, if I could do anything, I would. But this one's on you, Kate. There's nothing I could do."

Kate paused for a moment, then asked, "Can't you talk to them for me, Will? Maybe it would help. Please?"

He sighed audibly. "All right, Kate. I'll talk to them. But I know in advance that it won't do any good. Yours is the only action that can make a difference."

"I'll try. I really will. I just need your support."

"You've never been without that, Kate. Never."

The following afternoon Kate and her mother had a quiet chat over a glass of sherry at cocktail time. Kate was already pouring her second glass when Mrs. Henderson brought up the subject.

"Will called this afternoon," she said to Kate in a suspiciously casual voice. "He mentioned something about you and Sol. And I told him that his attitude was naive, Kate. It was foolish of you to bring your brother in on this. He has no business interfering."

At that moment Kate wanted literally to scream invectives at her mother, to rip her self-assurance to shreds. She thought if she had to stay in her sight one more minute, she would die of it. Then she thought of what it would feel like to be banished from her sight forever. Only then did her emotions succumb to her mother's will.

Once again she considered the possibility that her parents were right in their judgments. Up until now they had been right in almost everything. Perhaps she oughtn't to step out of her class, reject her background. She had not been raised for that. She was a good girl.

For an entire week Kate wrestled with her pain before she called Sol. And as soon as she saw him, the first words she heard were not his, but her mother's: "How can you want to spend the rest of your life with that giant of a man? A man whose religion is alien to you, who has no career possibilities beyond working in a bar? Is that the life you want to lead?"

But when Sol touched her, his hand on her face with his fingers curving gently to the back of her head, she was frightened that she would never again know the feeling of being completely loved with the purity with which Sol loved her. And she wondered if she could live without it.

This one thing she knew: It was easier to end her relationship with Sol than to suffer the pain of her parents' rejection. She was simply not made for defiance. She was not strong enough.

Kate had arranged to meet Sol at his apartment, because she did not want any interruptions.

Sitting next to her, Sol looked directly into Kate's eyes.

"Is it over?" he asked softly.

Tears streamed down her face in her longing to be able to deny it. Finally, she said, "Yes."

"Then there's nothing I can say. There's nothing I *will* say to make you change your mind." He spoke with a control born of his innate pride. "I had hoped, of course, that you would choose me. Despite the fact that I know I'm not what your parents would want for their only daughter."

Kate reached out to touch him, but he shrugged off her hand. "Don't do that," he said. "I don't want to feel the touch of you right now. I couldn't stand it."

Crying openly now, Kate sat next to him, feeling more helpless and more desolate than she had in her entire life. Finally, she said, "I love you, Sol."

And he looked at her, unwavering. "I know you love me, Kate. You just don't love me enough."

Lying in bed, watching the sun spread through her room, Kate was transfixed with shame at her own cowardice of heart.

* * *

The evening Ashley returned home from London, she sat with her parents in the library, having a cocktail before dinner. She was animated in her account of her travels, telling them which cities she liked best and which museums, cathedrals, monuments, mountains were the most spectacular.

Without warning, John Van Every interrupted her account. "And London, Ashley? Did you see your grandmother in London along with the changing of the guards and the crown jewels?"

His hostility was unmistakable. Ashley heard her mother's sudden intake of breath.

Looking straight at her father, Ashley's heart skipped a beat. Then she answered, "Yes," in as strong a voice as she could muster. Before he could say anything, she leaned toward him in a rush of words. "And, Daddy, please don't speak for a minute while I tell you about it." Her words tumbled over each other in her haste to get through her story. "It was good, Daddy. It really was. She was nothing like you said. Nana doesn't want to live like this. I don't either. We're a family, Daddy. And Nana says—"

John Van Every stood up, towering over Ashley as he interrupted. "I don't give a damn what Nana says, Ashley. It cannot possibly make any difference."

"But it's got to, Daddy. It's got to! She loves you. And so do I. Whatever it was that caused the two of you to fight is over for her. It was finished a long time ago. She wants to see you!" Reaching up to him, she continued. "Please listen to me, Daddy. It's the most important thing that's ever happened to me."

"That woman is forcing you to choose between us, Ashley. It's a despicable thing to do." His voice was stony, impassive.

"No! It's not true!" Ashley was crying openly now. "And if it were, I'd choose you. You're my father and I need you."

She tried to grab his hand. But he backed away

from her. John Van Every spoke as if he were tainted forever by a vendetta that was consuming him. "You seem to forget, Ashley, the most important thing: Before you left for Europe, I forbade you to see her. And so whatever happened between the two of you, however you feel about alliances, cannot possibly negate the fact that you defied me."

"It was for the sake of all of us." Ashley sobbed. "For all of us. I want us to be together."

Mrs. Van Every leaned over her daughter, taking her in her arms. Looking up at her husband, she spoke, disregarding the savage emotion that was spilling from him. "Don't do it, John. Please don't do this to us! She's our daughter!"

Flailing wildly, he screamed. "Stay out of this!" And then he slapped her hard across the face.

Stunned, she put her hand to her face as Ashley cried, "No!"

He never even heard her. His voice was without emotion when he spoke. "You defied me, Ashley. I told you then that the outcome would be harsh. And it is, for all of us. Look what you have done to your mother. I must ask you to move out of this house. Your behavior in London was treacherous. And I no longer want you here to be reminded of it."

Without looking at her again, John Van Every walked out of the room.

Taking Ashley in her arms, Mrs. Van Every rocked her as if she were a small child, cooing soothing noises through the veil of her own fear. "He'll get over it, Ashley. We'll work on it together. He'll get over it. He's a stubborn man. Full of pride. Give him a little time. That's all. Just a little time, darling. Please. We'll make it all right."

Ashley could not stop sobbing. "How can he do this?" she wailed. "He walked away from his mother and now he's walking away from me. And he hit you! I don't understand. I don't even know why."

"We'll fix it, darling. Please don't cry now. I love you, Ashley. I'll always love you."

"I don't even know why," Ashley wailed.

When Dottie took Ashley to see the apartment she had found, Ashley was delighted. She had been living with Dottie on Horatio Street since her father had banished her from the house. And the tiny apartment in a dirty building had added to the depression she was suffering.

A two-bedroom apartment on Twelfth Street, just east of Fifth Avenue, the new location was perfect for them—convenient to the buses and subways, and to the secondhand bookstores that created a world of their own on Fourth Avenue.

What made the pain of Ashley's separation bearable was the comfort of her mother. Although John Van Every also forbade his wife to see Ashley, she continued to do so, offering her daughter comfort at every possible moment. Thus, Ashley was not completely cut off from parental loving.

"He'll come around, Ashley," her mother had counseled. "Just don't expect too much too soon."

Ashley had tried to talk to her father. She had even written him a letter. But it had been returned unopened.

"I won't give up, Mother."

"And you shouldn't. I know how much it means to you." She hesitated for a moment before asking the question. "Have you spoken to her . . . to Nana . . . since you returned?"

"Yes. She said she was afraid this might happen. You know, she told me that in London, but I just couldn't believe her. It seemed impossible."

"I know," said Martha. "Before we married, I tried to get him to mend the rift between him and his mother. But it was impossible. I just never dreamed that he would do it to his own child."

Ashley hesitated a moment before asking, "Do you know what caused it all?"

"Only that it has something to do with the man who was your father's father. No more than that."

"Daddy wouldn't forgive you if he knew you were seeing me," Ashley said softly.

Mrs. Van Every smiled. "Then let's hope he doesn't find out, dear. I wouldn't be very good at standing up to him. But I do want you to know that I love you and I always will. And even your father's anger can't prevent that."

It was that love and assurance that allowed Ashley to pick up the pieces of her life and start over again. She was even looking forward to moving into the apartment with Dottie. Somehow it meant that things were going to work out for her.

She was also relieved that she was not returning to college. In her two years in Boston, Ashley had never felt that she was in the right place, doing the right thing. It was as if she were removed from the experience, as if her life were lived in mirror images, always slightly askew and vaguely confusing.

On moving day Sol rented a small truck so that he could help them haul their belongings to Twelfth Street. They didn't have much that was usable, and Ashley, especially, was looking forward to furnishing it. Her mother had removed some of Ashley's smaller possessions from her home and brought them to her, so at least she had a reference to her past when she looked at her books, or used the Spode dishes that her grandmother had left her.

When Sol arrived on Horatio Street that morning, Ashley's heart went out to him. Although he greeted them warmly, he moved with a kind of plodding insistence. A spark had gone out of his life, and he did not know how to rekindle it.

Though momentarily tempted, neither Dottie nor Ashley could really be angry at Kate. They were disappointed, of course, but they knew that they could not demand more than Kate was capable of giving. They also knew that Kate was suffering deeply. They were acutely aware that she was punishing herself, and that was worse than whatever her friends could say or do.

They worked all morning unloading the furniture and carrying it up to the top floor of the building. By mid-afternoon, they were finished. Ashley and Dottie functioned well together. Dottie did not care where any of the furniture was placed, so long as the apartment was reasonably comfortable. And Ashley was concerned about every detail, her need for visual pleasure dictating the placement of the smallest vase.

"Where do you want this, lady?" asked Sol as he carried the last article of furniture into the apartment.

"Over there, I think," said Ashley, pointing to a space by the large windows that overlooked Twelfth Street.

"That's it, then," said Sol. "I'll be right back."

When he returned, Sol was carrying an ice bucket, a bottle of champagne sticking rakishly from one side. In his other hand there were three champagne glasses.

"Oh, Solly," Dottie cried. "That's perfect. I never would have thought of such a thing."

Sol opened the bottle with finesse, filling all three glasses before the trio lifted them in a toast.

"To new lives," he said solemnly. "To success and happiness and sweet dreams."

Then the three of them settled onto the sofa.

The room looked surprisingly complete, considering the fact that they had just moved in. Ashley had insisted on putting the rug down immediately, which instantly offered a sense of completion. But best of all was the light that poured in from the wall of windows at the end of the room. After the dark dreariness of Horatio Street, it was as if they had walked into the sunlight after traveling for months in a tunnel.

"This is a great apartment," Sol said approvingly.

"And you're going to be our first guest for dinner," said Ashley, hugging him. "What's your favorite dish?" Then she added, "Not that I'm much of a cook. I hope you have a little tolerance for beginners."

"Absolutely," he said, putting his arms around her. He knew what Ashley had gone through with her father and understood her need for male affection and approval. "Except I didn't think you had mastered the boiling of an egg by now."

"I'm taking a special course in eggs and coffee," she said.

By dinner time they decided to go out and get pizza, since they had not yet stocked the refrigerator. Sitting at the table by the window, Dottie felt slightly high from the champagne. She was not drunk, only tipsy enough to loosen her tongue.

"My God," she commented with more vehemence than she anticipated. "Just look at all of us! It seems that we all decided to get ourselves into a mess at the same time. Kate's taken to her bed with shame, Ashley's been banished from her house, Sol is nursing a broken heart and . . ."

"And you?" asked Sol.

"And I'm trying to figure out whether or not I'm neuter," Dottie concluded in bewilderment. She had not intended to say such a thing, but once she had, the sentence sort of hung in the air without anyplace to go.

In a quiet, nonjudgmental voice, Sol prompted, "Tell me about it, Dot. What is it?"

Swallowing uncomfortably, she said, "I'll take it from the top." Her voice was brittle when she spoke. Then it turned soft as she began to explain her bewilderment about sex, how she could not understand what the big deal was, since it had never been anything except mildly exciting with Marty. "It bothered me so much that I decided to try something else," she said softly. "I went to bed with Madelaine Jacot." By this point she was able to explain without embarrassment, because she had a simple confidence that neither Sol nor Ashley would judge her negatively. "But it wasn't any better with a woman than with a man," she concluded lamely. "And now I don't know what I am."

Sol reached across the table and took her hand. "I want you to listen to me very carefully, Dot." He spoke in a low, controlled voice, behind which hid a phantom of anger. "You're my sister and I love you. And I think you know that I've never lied to you. And I'm not going to start now. Do you understand?"

Dottie nodded, feeling wretched inside.

"You are not neuter. Just because you've never experienced that kind of passion doesn't mean that you aren't capable of it. I know that. But you have to learn how to be less afraid. To let go. You always want to be in control, and that's not so good when it comes to sex. You have to learn how to trust yourself, Dot. You have to be open to love."

"And look what happened to you when you opened yourself to it," she returned, a brittle edge in her voice. "That scares me. I don't want to be hurt that way."

"And you know what?" Sol said, smiling. "I don't want to be hurt this way either. It's all a risk, Dottie. There's no guarantee that the Watermelon Baby won't get you. We've always known that, you and I. Since we were little and walked in the woods holding hands because we were so frightened. But I can only speak for myself now. And I can tell you this: Despite the fact that it didn't . . . couldn't . . . work out, the risk I took was worth it. Because I know how it feels to be loved."

Having graduated from junior college the previous June, Kate was at loose ends until she landed a job as a buyer trainee at Bloomingdale's the following November. She seemed satisfied with the job, with the edge of glamour that was more imaginary than real that surrounded it. It also filled a gaping hole in her listless life.

Ashley had gone to work for an advertising agency, but she was working simply to be working. Her trust fund from her grandmother was paying her a handsome monthly income, and she could have lived comfortably without lifting a finger. But she recognized the inherent trap of idleness, and even though she found the work only mildly interesting, she decided to live with it awhile in order to give it a chance.

She filled her spare time fixing up the apartment, scouring the secondhand stores on First and Second avenues for unique pieces of furniture.

In her efforts to keep busy, Ashley decided that the Troika should have a Christmas party. She had met a few people at work whom she liked and thought it would be a good idea for the three of them to expand their social horizons.

"Expand my social horizons?" asked Dottie wryly. "You gotta be kidding. Where did you pick up that phrase?"

Ashley laughed. "All right. Have it your way. We need to meet some new people."

"Right," agreed Dottie.

The day before the party, Jack Barclay walked into the Jacot Agency unannounced. Dottie looked up briefly from her desk as he entered, wondering if he were a messenger or a writer. Messenger, she decided, as she took in his clothes. No, writer, she thought, reversing her decision. A poor writer in search of an agent.

"Good afternoon," he greeted her. "My name is Jack Barclay and—"

"Oh!" Dottie punctuated her response by standing

up and putting out her hand. "I'm Dottie. And it's certainly a pleasure to meet you."

Walking directly around the desk, he approached Dottie and enveloped her in a bear hug. "My God! What I owe you!" he said, his words more an offering than a statement. "You are one sensational woman." It crossed Dottie's mind then that no one had ever before called her a woman, except as a conventional courtesy. She liked the sound of it, used in this new way.

Stepping back, Jack kept his hands on her shoulders and stared straight into her eyes. "Dorothy Langford, my guardian angel," he said, smiling broadly.

Dottie liked him, liked the feel of him. "Pleased to meet you," she said with mock formality.

He moved away from her then. There was a panther quality about him; he was a man in full command of his strength. He would have to be like this to write *Spartan's End,* thought Dottie. No Caspar Milquetoast here.

He was on the short side, just a little taller than Dottie. But his build was broad, stocky, carrying with it an inherent power that made him appear larger than he actually was. He had a full blond beard, the kind a man grows because he doesn't like to shave, not because he is hiding a weak jaw or long upper lip. His hair was shaggy, also blond, badly in need of a haircut. And his blue eyes flashed with the bold spirit of a man who knows the name of his dream.

"A friend of mine was driving to New York and I decided to come along for the ride," he explained as he looked her over with disconcerting directness. "But I thought you'd be older. Perhaps a little old lady who was prone to the ill effects of drafts and who took pity on a writer who was about to fail."

Recovering sufficiently, Dottie responded, "No. Just a little young lady who believed in your book."

"I predict great things for you, Dorothy Langford. Great things."

Trying to find a balance with which she could settle his vigor enough to carry on a normal conversation, Dottie asked him, "Would you like some coffee?"

"Sure would. It's colder than an Eskimo's ass out there. I'm used to the sunny climes of California."

Delighted with her company, Dottie walked over to the hot plate and put some water on to boil. "Madelaine's not here right now. She should be back after lunch. I hope you can stay."

"Forget her," he said. "I came to meet you."

Dottie felt the glow of his compliment spread over her, a new and even exciting sensation. "Thank you," she said quietly.

"My pleasure," he responded, rubbing his hands together. He was a man frequently in motion, not because he was nervous, but because there was a vital energy that lived just under the surface of his deeply tanned skin, compelling him to find outlets for it, short of a punching bag or a roll in the hay. "I want you to be my guest for lunch," he said. "Anywhere. I'll take you anywhere. But it has to be good. A woman like you deserves the best," he stated flatly, as he finally took off his overcoat to reveal a well-worn tan corduroy suit that draped haphazardly over his body without the slightest pretense to fitting.

A fashion plate he's not, Dottie thought, smiling to herself. But he's wearing a tie. That should get him into the restaurant, she decided. A restaurant where writers eat, so the maitre d' will know he's an eccentric artist instead of a slob.

"And that would be my pleasure."

She took him to Le Valois, where he ordered their lunch in surprisingly good French and ate as if he had last seen a meal in Venice Beach, where he lived.

Their rapport was immediate, continuing nonstop

throughout lunch. Dottie couldn't remember when she had been so enchanted by a man.

When they returned to the office, Madelaine was already there and had read Dottie's note that she had gone to lunch with Jack Barclay.

Madelaine immediately invited him into her office, closing her door after giving Dottie some instructions about a letter to be written. Feeling the deliberate snub, Dottie turned to her work, vowing once again not to get caught up in the kind of petty feelings that could only sap her energy.

Half an hour later Madelaine buzzed Dottie and asked her to step into her office. Smiling woodenly, she gestured for Dottie to sit down.

"Jack and I have been talking," Madelaine said evenly, by way of moving into a subject that did not please her. "I told him that I could surely get an American sale on *Spartan's End* once the English edition is published. Nigel told me that he's hot on the book and he intends to go all out on pushing it there. That could mean a lot."

"A hell of a lot," Jack agreed happily.

"However," Madelaine continued, drawing out the word. "This determined young man here claims that he won't have anybody handle his book except you."

Dottie smiled politely, a novice in a poker game she knew the basic rules for, but had never played. A wave of triumph and gratitude washed over her impassive face. "Thank you for the compliment," she said to Jack. "I'm flattered."

"I trust you, babe. That's all," he said matter-of-factly. "I believe in you."

Dottie understood then how she should operate with her future clients. It was a matter of making a writer believe in you. This, of course, grew out of a mirrored sentiment, the end result of which was loyalty. No, not just an end result, she thought. It's a mutually beneficial payoff.

"And so," said Madelaine, as she stood and gestured elegantly with a sweeping movement of her hand, "he's yours. American yours, as well as English yours."

"How much mine?" asked Dottie. It was a loaded question. She gambled instinctively that Jack's presence would increase the meaning of "yours" into something more than permission alone.

Knowing exactly what she meant, Madelaine rose to the occasion. "Fifty percent yours. You split the commission with the agency."

"Deal," said Dottie, moving to shake both their hands.

When they were alone once more in the outer office, Dottie took the opportunity to ask Jack to come to her party the following evening. With all the confidence she had gained in a short period of time, she was shy about talking to him.

She had deliberately not asked Madelaine to the party. Madelaine had never mentioned a word nor made a reference to the night they had spent together. In her effort to maintain some kind of working relationship, Dottie had remained polite and efficient in the office. The few times that Madelaine issued an invitation to her, Dottie was cordially unavailable.

The awkwardness decreased as Dottie plunged herself into her work. She devoted herself to it with a raw determination combined with an unwillingness to admit defeat. This was heightened, of course, by her pure, unbridled ambition. Nothing was going to stop Dottie Langford from climbing to the top.

Kate arrived early to help with the party. Christmas week had been a very busy time for her, but she showed no ill effects from the stress. The job itself was a structure around which a young woman of means could build a viable day. And so she persisted in dancing to the confining rhythms of her parents' tune, finally able to combine coasting and hope into a recognizable day. She could also use her employee's discount at the store to purchase clothes. For the party she had chosen a long, pale blue, pure silk shirtwaist dress. It not only emphasized the blue of her eyes and the frailty of her figure; it demonstrated amply that Kate was turning into a beautiful young woman.

The effect was heightened by her nervousness at the fact that Sol would be at the party. This would be the first time she had seen him since their parting at the end of summer. She did not know whether she was looking forward to the meeting or dreading it. But the anticipation of it added color to her cheeks and a sparkle to her eyes that was normally not present.

Martha Van Every had arrived at the apartment earlier that afternoon, her car laden with glasses, silver trays, and an enormous ham she had cooked that morning after her husband had left the house for a weekend business appointment. Since he had parted with Ashley, he worked even harder, filling his days with appointments, meetings, and manufactured excuses to keep himself busy.

Mrs. Van Every stayed only long enough to help the girls get organized with their first party, then left, wishing them all a happy Christmas.

Before the first guest arrived, Ashley smiled at her friends and said, "I have some surprises for us." After receiving the proper response, she gave them each a present that Nana had sent for Christmas.

For Dottie, Nana had chosen a hand-wrought silver Star of David, with her good wishes enclosed for a happy Hanukkah.

Kate's gift was a plain bracelet, of hand-hammered silver, at once delicate and strong.

When Ashley opened her present, she was awed. It was a necklace of tiny turquoise beads, similar to the one Nana had worn to the London opening.

Ashley, whose interest in clothes was practical and minimal, wore the same dress that had caused such parental unrest at her highschool prom.

Nana's necklace was stunning against her skin. The strands of turquoise were perfect with the V neck of the gown, moving with her as she moved, fluid with a life of their own as they brushed against the gentle mounds of her breasts. Ashley had finally grown into the strength of her face and had become a striking young woman. Her shining black hair, piled on top of her head in a simple twist, emphasized her long neck and the defined lines of her face.

There were quite a few guests in the house when Jack Barclay arrived. Immediately, the room took on a life that had not existed before. He was a man who could turn going down to the corner for a Coke into an adventure, Dottie thought, as he greeted her with a kiss on the cheek. Handing her a bottle of champagne with a bow tied around it, he whispered into her ear, "This is to be saved. For you and me to drink. So put it away."

She smiled, feeling awkward, bereft of poise. But she caught hold of her anxiety before it caught hold of her. Smiling, she said, "Come. Let me introduce you."

"Not before I tell you how lovely you look," he said.

And, indeed, she did look lovely. Dottie's face, which used to be full, had begun to be defined into that of a woman instead of a girl. She was not naturally pretty like Kate, nor striking like Ashley. She never would be, and she knew it. But she had begun—through the careful application of makeup and the perseverance of one who understands limits as well as possibilities—to develop a style of her own. The finishing touch, of which she was completely unaware, was the glow that success cast upon her. Just as pregnancy enhances some women and a new lover illuminates others, success had graced Dottie with an aura that not only enhanced her looks, it made her genuinely attractive for the first time in her life—even desirable, an attribute that Jack Barclay was far quicker to recognize than Dottie herself.

Two things happened at the party that would set it apart in the collective memory of the Troika.

The first was that around eleven thirty Sol walked into the room. For Kate, he was the Christmas present that she both desired and feared. For Sol, there was nobody else in the room, except Kate.

She immediately concerned herself with slicing ham, refilling drinks, and finding busy work to calm herself. When he finally walked over to her, she was alone in the kitchen.

"Merry Christmas, Katie," he said, his voice catching.

"Thank you. And . . . Happy Hanukkah." She had never even said that before, and she felt awkward, as if she were a small child who had learned to say the right thing without understanding what it meant.

"You're beautiful." He leaned over and kissed her on the cheek. Then his arms were around her and she was safe inside the shelter of him once more.

"I've missed you," she whispered. "I've missed you so much, Sol."

"I've missed you, too."

He started to move away, but she said quickly, "Please don't. Stay here."

They spent an hour talking. Kate well understood that Sol would never ask to see her, to be with her. These words, if they were to be spoken, must come from her.

"Sol?" she said, holding his hand. "I don't want to live without you. I really don't. Please. I want to see you again. We'll work it out."

"I have to be honest with you Kate." He spoke in a low, controlled voice, looking directly at her. "I don't think I will ever love anyone the way I love you. But I don't trust you, Katie. You've given me no reason to.

We've tried it twice and each time you've buckled in to the wishes of your parents."

"I won't this time, Sol. I promise you."

"How can you be sure?" he asked.

"Because when I stand here with your arms around me, I know that's what I want. Not a job. Not a pretty life. Just you, Sol."

There were tears in his eyes when he spoke. "I want you, too. Want you more than you can ever know. But, just at the moment, I don't think it will work."

"Please."

He took a deep breath. "I haven't told Dottie yet. But my parents have loaned me the money to open a restaurant of my own. The deal should be closed in a month or so." He paused, mouthing words that went against the message of his heart. "I want some time, Katie. Give it to me. Please."

She nodded.

"If I can create a success of my own, maybe then I would be more acceptable to your parents."

"I'll help you do it, Sol. Let me."

"No." His was the final word. "I'll do it on my own, Kate. Then it belongs to me. Besides," he said, "it will give you some time to think. I couldn't bear having you leave me again. And to be honest, I don't really have any confidence that it wouldn't happen again if your parents put up a big enough stink."

"It won't happen, Sol." But she was not certain. She did not feel totally confident, remembering the power her parents held over her, that she would be strong enough even then. She wanted to believe it. Just as Sol wanted to. But she had not learned to have faith in her own courage. Instead, she lied about it, hoping that would make it real.

"I'll be waiting for you, Sol."

"Time," he said. "A few months. Then we'll see."

* * *

The other thing that happened to make the party memorable was Jack Barclay and Dottie. She had spent the greater part of the evening playing hostess alongside Ashley. In truth, it was easier for her than mingling with the guests and talking to strangers.

Occasionally screwing up her courage, Dottie would make it a point to introduce herself to the people whom she had not met, friends of Kate's and Ashley's from work. Simple as it appeared to be, Dottie had a painful time talking to strangers. Her sense of inferiority manifested itself in her conviction that people would find her boring; that she would make a faux pas or forget a person's name. In addition, she had never cultivated the art of small talk, a superficial technique that simply did not blend with her more straightforward personality. Dottie did not understand that those people who were meeting her for the first time liked her for precisely that reason. Dottie's ability to ask direct questions and derive interesting answers was what made her good and memorable company.

It was obvious that Jack Barclay felt the same way about her. As if he were timing his absences, when he felt he had gone too long without talking to Dottie, he would slip up behind her during some conversation and wait patiently to be included. Dottie, immensely proud, introduced him as her client, one whose book had been sold to a very prestigious English publisher. Although it had been six months, Jack still delighted in being introduced as an almost-published author. His book was scheduled to come out in April.

"Is this your first?" asked a friend of Ashley's.

"The very first," he answered, grinning as if the child inside him had taken over. There was absolutely no attempt at a genteel and adult response to a question that carried with it so much joy.

"What have you done to make a living until now? Teach, like other authors?"

"God no!" he answered explosively. "Teaching can ruin a writer. This writer, anyway," he amended. "Takes too much mental energy to teach. I was a bartender in a joint down the beach from where I live. Still am, as a matter of fact. The advance on the book just allowed me not to work as often, that's all. I don't think publishers understand the meaning of a living wage."

"Don't worry," said Dottie. "Very soon you'll be a full-time writer."

"I don't know how I'll manage," he said, pride and anticipation resting easily on his shoulders. "I suspect I'd continue bartending anyway. Even if I had a best seller on my hands. Otherwise, I'd become a hermit. Going into my room to write and never coming out again."

It was a good party. All three women looked back on it with the feeling that they had done a first-rate job on their maiden voyage into the world of entertaining.

When the last guest departed, Jack was still there. Sol had taken Kate home and Ashley was in the kitchen washing dishes.

Jack walked over to the table that Dottie was clearing. "Come," he said. "Come have a drink with me."

She turned to him, her brown eyes flickering with green tints as the light of the candles reflected in them. "I can't, Jack. I really have to help clean up."

"No problem," he said looking around. "I've had to clean up my beach shack after parties that lasted three days nonstop. This job is a piece of cake."

"Oh?"

"Sure," he said, grabbing a load of glasses and carrying them into the kitchen. Working swiftly and efficiently, they finished the job in half an hour, laughing most of that time.

Sensing their need to be alone, Ashley surveyed the stacks of clean dishes and commented casually, "Lord,

I'm exhausted. Throwing parties is a tiring avocation. So if you don't mind, I'm going to turn in now."

Jack smiled at her, thinking what a beautiful older woman she would be someday. The kind he would like to write about. "I'm happy to have met you," he said. "I'm sure it won't be the last time."

"It was a pleasure meeting Dottie's first client," she said. "My friend here is very lucky."

Alone with Jack, Dottie walked back into the living room, nervous at the prospect of what to say or do. With Marty, it had been easy. They were both novices functioning on the theory of the blind leading the blind. But with Marty it had also been disappointing. And the memory of it made Dottie want to flee from the arms of Jack. It would be better not to know, she thought.

In a transparent effort to catch hold of herself, Dottie started talking. Even before she sat down on the sofa, she began. "I'm tired, too. Exhausted really. You know, that was my first real party. Could you tell?"

Jack looked at her, smiling, allowing her to run down.

"Did you have fun?" she continued. "I'm really glad you could come. At one point during the–"

Losing his patience, he leaned over. Without a word he took her chin in his hand and kissed her. He kissed a young woman who had once been married, but who had never experienced anything as powerful as this simple kiss.

"I . . ." she began again nervously.

"Hush," he said, kissing her again.

Pulling her closer to where he was sitting, he turned her around so that she was facing him, curled into his arms.

He kissed her face, her eyes, her lips. Shyly at first, then eagerly, she kissed him, nibbling his lips, running her tongue over them. Exploring, touching. He held her close, his hands kneading her back and shoulders.

"My God, Dottie. I love the way you feel," he whispered. "Soft and strong, all at the same time."

With one hand holding her near, the other moved gently over her body, caressing, inviting. She was breathless from him, feeling her mouth and throat turn dry as he continued to touch her. His hand reached the hem of her skirt and moved onto the smooth stocking underneath, moved up to the top of her leg where the stocking ended.

The touch of his hand on the bare, sensitive skin inside her thighs made her shiver. Gently he stroked her. Patiently. He was in no hurry, he said with his hands. Yet the urgency of his touch, the passion expressed, closed over them, soft as a cloud. Her hands wandered to his chest, then to his strong shoulders, which felt like bands of flexible steel as the muscles moved on his back.

"Come to bed with me, Dottie," he whispered. "Come to bed."

"I can't," she breathed. "Ashley . . ."

"She's fast asleep by now. Don't worry. She won't care anyway."

Dottie did not move, suddenly frightened by him. Frightened by his strength and frightened by the desire that he invoked in her.

"What is it?" he asked, leaning away from her so that he could see her face. "Tell me."

She just shook her head, totally unable to utter a word.

Jack took her face between his hands, holding it so that she could not look away. He spoke softly, yet with absolute confidence in his words. "Listen to me, Dottie. I don't know what is going on inside your head. I can't pretend to know. I don't know whether you're afraid or just not interested in what's been going on . . ."

"Oh, no, it's not that," she protested. "It's just that . . ."

"What?"

She closed her eyes, embarrassed. "You're right. I'm afraid."

"It's not your first time, is it?" he asked incredulously.

"No."

"Then, whatever it is, I promise you, Dottie, I'll do everything I can to make it all right."

She could only look at him.

"Now," he said. "Let's go to bed. And let's not talk about it anymore. Just be with me . . . stay with me . . . we have a lot of time."

They stood up shakily, untangling their bodies. Then he took her by the hand and led her into her bedroom.

"Let me see," he said, as he pulled the sweater over her head. "You're beautiful," he whispered, cupping his hands gently over her breasts. "You need to believe that." She held his head close to her, breathless from the surprise of wanting him so much.

He made love to her with the experience of a man who has known many women and understands how to please them. But it was not programmed or automatic. It was sensual and erotic and filled with secret pleasures. Yet still he did not enter her. He touched and kissed every part of her body. And he waited for her to want it as much as he did. Finally, she could stand it no longer, and she moved her body under his with a sigh of anticipation and relief.

He watched from above her, her head flung back, her mouth open and eyes closed. He watched as her lips moved in silent tribute to their loving. And he watched as she came, gasping, astonished and sated. And when he came, she held her arms around his strong back with a triumph and intensity that had been a stranger to her until that night.

"Never," she said to him afterward, her eyes filling

with grateful tears, "that never happened to me before."

He leaned over and kissed her eyes.

"Never?" he asked.

She simply nodded, confirming suspicions that he had harbored when he sensed her initial hesitation. He felt it in the tentative quality with which she touched him, as if she were trying out feelings for the first time like an awkward child on her first visit to a department store to shop for a new outfit.

"I think," he said with mock seriousness, "we can have a lot of good times trying to repeat the experience. Stick with me, kid."

She giggled then, curling into his arms.

When she awakened the following morning, there was a moment of surprise at the fact that she was lying next to a man. It's been a long time between drinks of water, she thought, smiling to herself. She started to move then, but his arms pulled tight around her and they made a long lazy kind of love.

Dottie was pleased to discover that Ashley's presence at breakfast was not awkward at all. Seated at the table by the window, indulging in champagne and strawberries that Jack had bought along with some sweet rolls at the corner deli, the three of them talked and laughed as if they were old and intimate friends. The crisp winter sun shone through the window where they sat, warming them happily.

After breakfast, in a gesture that totally lacked subtlety, Ashley said she had some errands to do and she would be back in the late afternoon.

They spent their privacy wisely. Dottie could not stop being astonished at how she wanted to touch him all the time. When they weren't making love, they would lie next to each other and talk, telling each other stories about their past and about their dreams. During all that time she did not stop touching him. The serenity she felt when she held his hand carried with it a peaceful completion she had never experienced. It was not until Dottie's father called in late afternoon with the news about Sol that the peace was shattered beyond recognition, beyond remembrance.

Ashley walked in the door of the apartment the moment the phone rang. She could hear Dottie pick up the receiver in the bedroom.

"Dottie?"

"Hi, Dad. What's the matter?"

"It's Sol."

"What about him?" she asked, already frightened.

"He's in the hospital, Dottie."

"Oh, God. Tell me."

"Well, he had some sort of seizure at the restaurant late last night. We didn't want to worry you about it, but now . . ." He stopped to gain control, still choking on his words when he continued. "They think he has a brain tumor."

"Oh . . . my . . . God . . ." said Dottie, drawing the words out in the process of sorting her pain.

"They're going to start running some tests in the morning. First thing."

"Where is he?"

"New York Hospital."

Dottie could feel Jack's hand on her shoulder, offering comfort for something he did not yet understand.

"I'm going straight up there," said Dottie, already grabbing for her clothes.

"Visiting hours are over, Dottie."

"I'm going up there, Dad. I'll call you when I get home."

Ashley stood in the doorway and waited for Dottie to say something. Instead, she simply rose from the bed and started looking for her shoes and stockings.

"What is it?" asked Ashley anxiously.

"Sol." Dottie's answer was brusque in her effort to

maintain some kind of control over her tears. "He's in the hospital."

"With what?"

"He had some kind of seizure. They think it might be a brain tumor."

"What can I do to help?" Jack asked, feeling helpless.

"Nothing. Thank you," she said without even looking at him. She had already left him.

"I'll go with you," said Ashley.

They all moved quickly. There was no time for a proper good-bye. Jack simply kissed Dottie on the cheek before he put her and Ashley in a taxi. That was all.

They were silent on the ride uptown. There was nothing to say, nothing to do except wait. Ashley reached out and took Dottie's hand to hold.

Dottie asked the floor nurse what room Solomon Langford was in.

"Four-eighteen," she replied. "But visiting hours are over."

"Not for me, they're not."

"I'm sorry, ma'am. But there are no visitors allowed now. That's the rule."

"Screw the rule," replied Dottie. "He's my brother and I'm going to see him." She turned, and with Ashley silent at her side, they marched down the hall, checking numbers until they found his room.

Wrapped in a hospital gown that was clearly too small for him, Sol looked at his sister when she strode into the room.

"Stormed the gates, I see," he said, offering her a foolish grin.

Dottie walked to the bed, leaned over, and flung her arms around her brother. "Oh, Solly, what happened? Are you all right?"

"Now . . ." he said comfortingly. "Do you think it's at all possible for a tiny little thing in my head to get to a man as big as I am?" He put his arms around her and enclosed her inside his love. "And, besides, with two beautiful women to visit me, how can things go wrong?" He looked over and laughed at Ashley, his eyes welcoming her. She walked to the other side of the bed and kissed him. He pulled her into the group, and they were silent for a moment. Then he patted them both gently, sitting them up on the bed beside him. He was so simple in his love, so pure in his intent of comforting his visitors, that Ashley and Dottie were touched even more deeply.

"Tell me," said Dottie.

"There's nothing to tell. I just got another headache and saw some wavy light. Next thing I know I'm lying on the floor beside the bar."

"Another headache?" asked Dottie. "How long has this been happening?"

"Oh, I don't know." He spoke lazily, as if it were nothing to worry about. "A long time, I guess."

"Why didn't you see a doctor, Solly. Why did you wait so long?"

"I didn't want to worry anybody. And you don't know this yet, but I'm going to open a restaurant of my own. And I didn't want to put myself in a bad light by being sick or something."

"Does it hurt a lot?" asked Dottie, a sob focused behind every word.

"Sometimes."

"I'm sorry."

Ashley sat next to him, holding his hand, trying to swallow the tears that insisted on reaching her throat with clawed fingers.

"Just think," Sol speculated. "Maybe that thing's been there for a long time. Maybe that's why I'm so dumb." Dottie winced at his words. "That's what the doctor said could sometimes happen." He smiled easily, then swallowed. "Dottie, would you do me a favor?"

"Of course," she said, barely able to get the words out.

"Would you call Kate for me? I'd like to see her."

Dottie buried her face in his huge, comforting chest near his heart. "Of course I'll call," she mumbled, overcome with pain and fear.

## CHAPTER 5

On the day after New Year's, after two weeks of testing, they operated on Solomon Langford.

Because she did not think that she had the right to intrude on the Langford family at the hospital, Kate waited all day in Dottie's apartment for news of Sol's condition.

During that time she paced endlessly up and down the length of the living room, unable to remain still, unable to concentrate on anything except Sol, her beloved Sol. She remembered the hours she had spent with him, the joyous, sensual times. And she berated herself for having parted with him, wondering if she might have been able to help him if she had been around.

"How is he?" she asked when Dottie returned home, weary and tear-stained, from the hospital.

"They don't know," Dottie answered in a monotone.

"What do you mean?" Kate asked, alarmed.

"They said it might be several days before they have a good idea about his recovery."

Kate took a deep breath, then asked, "How bad is it?"

"They're not sure, because they had to cut through so much brain tissue to get to it. The goddamn thing was the size of a lemon. It wasn't even a tumor. Just a cyst. But it was the size of a goddamn fucking lemon there in his brain." Kate could not tell if Dottie was going to scream or cry. "They don't know if he'll have some paralysis. Also . . . they don't know about his mind. If . . . if it will be . . . all there."

Five days later, after she met Kate uptown, Dottie went with her to see Sol. Kate had gone to the hospital every day during lunch, but they had not allowed any visitors outside the family until that day.

"Don't be shocked, Kate." Dottie tried to warn her. "He apparently has amnesia about the operation. The doctors said he would never remember the time directly before or after the operation. That's been cut out of him forever," she said bitterly

Kate saw him before Dottie did. He was at the end of the corridor staring out a window. Sitting in a wheelchair with a sort of tray across it to prevent him from falling out, he seemed to be talking to himself.

They approached him from the back. He did not turn around to see who it was. Dottie leaned over and kissed him gently. "Hi, Solly," she said. "How's it going?"

He turned his head slowly and looked up at them. Smiling uncertainly, he questioned them with his eyes. He looked first at Dottie, then Kate, a wisp of recognition passing briefly across his eyes before it returned to the mangled recesses of his mind where remembrance was lost or confused in the swollen tissue of his brain.

A huge scar reached from his right eyebrow, curved over the top of his shaved head, and moved on back to the base of his skull, tracked by black stitches looking like small tarantulas that had been placed there to hold his head together.

He resembled nothing so much as a giant mongoloid who had outgrown his high chair. His hands seemed to have a life of their own as they fluttered in hapless movements on the tray of the wheelchair. His head moved independently of his facial expressions.

Having grown up in the midst of a medical family, Kate had a fairly precise idea of what to expect. Consequently, she was not shocked at his physical condition. What crossed her mind, instead, was a kind of spectral rage at the unspeakable annihilation of the essence of Sol. That, and an ineffable sadness that he did not know who she was.

Trying to hide her private lament, she spoke softly to him. "I'm happy to see you, Sol."

"Got . . . to . . . get . . . package . . . wr-wr-wrapped," he said, his hands struggling with an imaginary box set before him. "Can't . . . tie."

"Here, let me help you," said Dottie, her voice that of an eternally patient mother. She leaned over and began to mime the motions of tying a package. "There." She stood up and smiled. "Is that better?"

"No," he said, smiling, nodding his head in a barren indication meaning yes. "Th-th . . . ank . . . sss."

"Sticky," he said, his brow furrowed as he pulled at a finger.

"What?"

Understanding what he meant, Kate leaned over. "I'll get it off," she said gently. "It's here, isn't it? I'll wipe the sticky stuff off with my handkerchief."

She wiped his hand and put her handkerchief back in her purse, as if that small act would allow her to stay in control of her sorrow.

Sol looked up to thank the nice lady for helping him. Bewilderment lingered in the dark of his eyes as he stared at her. Without understanding why, he reached out and touched her face, his fingers curving through her hair to the base of her skull. It was an impulse born of another time, as if his hand remembered what his brain could not.

Kate did not move. A sob escaped from her quivering lips, but she refused to forsake the touch she cherished most of all.

Slowly, he lowered his hand. He then seemed quite content to sit there in the presence of the two nice people who had come to deliver him from a world he did not understand. He only knew vaguely that he did not work so well. He had spent hours that day sitting in his wheelchair, trying to solve the riddle of his existence in such a strange place. The harder he tried, sitting there, the more his thoughts became muddled with the words. And what did come to the surface made no sense at all.

Finally, with great effort, he spoke. "Sol," he said, smiling with his accomplishment, just before Dottie and Kate left.

Dottie sobbed all the way home in the taxi. Kate was too stunned to do anything except hold on to her friend in a mute pain of such intensity that she thought it had become a rapidly growing presence, putrid and stinking, inside her gut.

Jack Barclay stayed in New York for another week before he returned to California. During that time he saw Dottie one evening. But she was preoccupied with Sol and her parents, and was distracted and removed in his company. It was clear to him that she would continue that way until Sol's recovery was assured. And so he returned to his beach shack. The last thing he said to her on the telephone before he left was, "We'll have our time, Dottie. I'll be waiting." She barely heard his words, although in the recesses of her mind she felt a sudden sense of loss.

On a bright Saturday morning Ashley went with Dottie to see Sol. In an effort to find relief from their merciless burden of grief and anxiety, Dottie's parents planned to take a break from hospital visits and drive to the country for the day. And so Ashley and Dottie planned to spend most of the day at the hospital keeping Sol company.

Physically, he had improved. Even mentally, they could see the difference. The doctors, who had been extraordinarily kind in taking the time to explain the situation to the Langfords, said that they still held out hope, that the trauma and swelling in the brain would have to subside completely before they could offer an accurate prognosis. To accommodate the swelling after the operation, they had been forced to remove a small portion of his skull. A plate, for protection, could be surgically implanted later. In the meantime only skin and the baby fuzz of new hair covered the opening.

When they first arrived a therapist was sitting in the room with Sol. On the table before him she had spread three cards, each with one picture on it.

"Good. Very good," she was saying as they walked in. "And what is this?" she asked, pointing to a picture of a spoon. "Come on, Sol. Tell me."

"Fffork . . ." he said, smiling.

"No," she said patiently, "it's a spoon. Say it now, spoon."

"Ssspoon," he repeated after her.

"And what do you do with it?"

He looked at the picture for a long time, his brow furrowed in intense concentration. "Eat?" he asked, looking at her.

"Good! Very very good, Sol!" exclaimed the therapist, smiling broadly as she touched his face. Then she turned to Dottie. "He seems to be coming along. It's slow, but it appears to be coming back to him, Miss Langford. It will take a long time, of course. A very long time. But I think it can be done."

Sol looked at Dottie then. His eyes brightened.

"Dddd . . . ot," he said. And Dottie ran over to

him, giving him a great hug around his immense body, blinking away tears in her eyes she was determined not to allow to escape.

Ashley and Dottie spent the day with him, keeping up an almost endless strand of chatter in their effort to maintain the connection that was strung so tenuously between them.

At one point Dottie mentioned their lake home, the trees and the woods. Once again a flash of recognition passed over him. "Wa . . . water . . . m . . . baby." Then a haunted expression spread slowly over his face.

"No, no," soothed Dottie, marveling at the random pattern of his returning memory. "There's no Watermelon Baby, Solly. That's just a game we used to play when we were children."

He relaxed then, sinking back into his chair.

"Sleep," he said quite clearly.

Ashley and Dottie tucked him into bed like a small child, fluffing the pillow and smoothing the sheets.

Just as they were about to leave, Kate entered. She had hurried to the hospital the moment she finished work.

"Oh," she said. "Is he sleeping?"

Kate had been visiting him every day. She would sit next to him and talk for hours about things they used to do. Sometimes he would recognize her, sometimes he would not. She could never get used to the vagaries of his behavior. Even on the days he did know her, Sol never touched Kate again after that first time. His touch, of course, was what she wanted most. As a substitute, she would sit next to him and hold his hand, convinced that would help him get well.

Dottie told Kate that they had just put Sol to bed. So she walked over to the bed and kissed him gently on his forehead. Touching him with a serene gesture on the side of his face, she whispered to him. "Sleep well, Sol. Have sweet dreams."

When the Troika left, they decided to go downtown and have a bite to eat in an Italian restaurant in the village. It had been a difficult day.

Sol slept only a short time. Startled by a noise in the corridor, he awakened suddenly and moved slowly out of bed. He walked to the door and figured out how to open it. As he moved quietly to the end of the hall, he was pleased at how easily his feet were working for him. At the window he looked down to the river, so peaceful and calm in the late afternoon. He had already learned that when he reached out to touch the tiny toy boats, his hand would hit the glass, preventing him from picking them up and playing with them. Pretty. They were pretty, moving so slowly in the water, chased by their own wakes. Like the toys he used to play with in the bathtub.

A nurse walked up silently behind him.

"Sol?" she said gently. "You shouldn't be here all alone. I thought you were sleeping."

He looked at her, trying to put the strange sounds together, to make sense of what she was saying.

"Come," said the nurse, taking him by the arm. "I'll take you back to your room."

"Come" he understood. Also "room." That was the place he did not like. It was so tiny. He could not move enough there. Sometimes it was hard to breathe in a place so small.

He looked at the stranger who had her arm on his. As he looked at her, somewhere deep inside understanding of what she wanted him to do dawned and he resisted.

"Yes!" he cried out, his head nodding "no" in an angry gesture of defiance. "Yes!" he repeated, shoving her away from him as easily as a person might flick a fly off his sleeve.

* * *

Ashley had to stop by the apartment to get some cash before they went out to dinner. The telephone was ringing as she walked in with Dottie and Kate.

"Hello?" Ashley said into the receiver.

"Is Miss Langford there? This is New York Hospital calling. An emergency."

She handed the phone to Dottie, fear creeping over her with a loathsome insistence.

"Yes?"

"Miss Langford?"

"Speaking."

"It's your brother, Miss Langford. He's walked out of the hospital."

"He what!"

"We have a very serious problem, Miss Langford."

"Go on," said Dottie, already moving into the midst of a nightmare.

"He walked out and we couldn't stop him."

"But why?"

"He's a large man, Miss Langford. Even in his weakened condition, he is very very strong. The problem arose when we tried to stop him. He became violent. And as you know, he not only has the drain implanted, but there's that small portion of his skull that was removed. We couldn't risk damaging that by fighting with him."

"You mean to tell me that you don't know where he is?"

Kate felt her heart beating double time as she listened.

"Please, Miss Langford. We're doing our best. And we know exactly where he is. But we need your help."

"How?"

"We have a doctor following him. Also a squad car. The police have been notified. But every time someone tries to get near him, he becomes agitated and violent. We can't touch him. He's outside wandering around, and we thought if you could come here, perhaps you could talk to him. Get through to him."

"I'll be right there."

"Wait. We'll have a police car pick you up in front of your building. They've been alerted. We've just been waiting until we could reach you or your parents."

"I'll be right downstairs."

When she hung up the phone, Dottie ran into the bedroom. Functioning in that remarkable state of calm that some people acquire in the eye of the storm, she grabbed a blanket off her bed, remembering that Sol had always hated to wear an overcoat and wanting to make sure he was warm.

"Come on," she said to Ashley and Kate. "I'll explain on the way."

Minutes later they were in a squad car racing to the hospital.

Flanked by her friends on either side, Dottie talked all the way uptown, chattering nonstop, as if she could keep Sol safe as long as she could find words to speak.

"You know, Mom and Dad are going to invest in a restaurant for Sol. He was so happy when he was manager of Teddy's. And he was good at it. He wanted to do it for himself and he wanted to do it for you, too, Katie. He told me so. I've always hoped he would find something like this. He's not dumb. But both of you know that already . . . It was just that book learning somehow defeated him. He had started to do lots of reading in the last year or so. It was almost as if he had to grow into it. But he was never really defeated. He just kept on plugging away. He kept trying till he got it, that's all. That's how he is . . . I could feel it today when we were there. He was frustrated because he kept trying and he didn't understand what had happened to himself. He kept looking at me. Like he wanted me to tell him why . . . Oh, God, I could scream just thinking about it. It makes so much sense. I know why he ran away. If he didn't remember the operation, then he couldn't figure out why he had to stay there. He always hated being penned up. A walk in the woods was what he loved most. He was free there . . . He's such a moral person. He always had a deep sense of right and wrong. And he was never afraid to face anything. If he believed in something, he just wouldn't let go. That's why he got himself out of the hospital. Because he didn't feel they had a right to keep him there. He just didn't understand . . . he couldn't . . . I remember when we were children, we would play this game: 'Yes means no and no means yes.' And that's how he is right now. He's a child. And we have to take care of him for a little while till he gets better. Because he doesn't understand yet. But even in a child there can be moral outrage. And that's what he's feeling right now. I know—"

"Miss Langford?" said the patrolman who was sitting in the front seat. "We're getting close now. We have to drive carefully. But you should be ready." Dottie could hear the static of the police radio blurting out disconnected messages. "Heading east on Sixty-first Street toward the river."

"As soon as we see him, Miss Langford, you can get out. Just try to talk to him. If you can get close enough to calm him, we have a doctor following him with a tranquilizer. But it has to be administered without a fight, as you know. Just see if you can get him to return to the hospital with you. That's the best thing to do if you can. If not, try to get him to stand still long enough for us to get him with the hypodermic."

Kate had the savage thought that Sol was being handled as if he were an animal escaped from the zoo. And, indeed, that was how he being treated: as a rare and exotic speciman to be captured, but not harmed.

As soon as they turned off First Avenue onto Sixty-first Street, they saw him. Towering over the other people on the street, walking in and out of traffic, he was barefoot, with the back of his hospital gown flapping open.

Ahead of him a policeman was clearing the way, moving people out of his path, telling irate drivers to stop their cars until Sol and his entourage passed. Dottie jumped out of the car, with Kate and Ashley following.

Running along the street, her blanket dragging on the ground as she ran to him, Dottie passed a doctor in his white hospital coat patiently following Sol's erratic course as he zigzagged his way down the street.

"Sol!" Dottie called to him. "Solly!"

He stopped slowly and turned to her. As she approached, he looked as if he would run from her in panic.

"Easy, Miss Langford," she could hear the doctor say in a low, cautious voice. "Approach him slowly."

Dottie stopped. So did Sol. "Sol?" she said, smiling. "It's me. Dottie."

He looked at her, standing still in the middle of the street.

Ashley and Kate stood next to the doctor, holding their breath, as if one exhalation would break the spell. They could hear the doctor saying, in a prayerful voice that reeked of pain and compassion for this gentle lost man, "Come on, Sol. Let her talk to you. Come on, Sol . . . you can do it."

Kate prayed then. Feeling helpless and terrified, she reached out to him with her love.

Dottie held out her hand. "Sol? I've come to help you."

He stood motionless, waiting. Dottie took a step forward. He did not move. She took another, slowly, testing him with every step.

"Here," she said soothingly. "I have a blanket for you. You must be cold." She held it out in front of her, as if she were bribing a confused child with a toy. Her heart wept as she looked down at his bleeding feet, cut from the trash on the streets, cut and unfeeling in the cold.

"Sol . . . here . . . here's the blanket." She was close enough to touch him, close enough to put her hand on his face. He looked down at her and smiled.

"Dot?" he said, very distinctly, as if he had been practicing the word. "Dot?"

"Yes, it's me, Sol. Here. I'll just put this blanket around you. It will keep you warm."

He stood still, arms hanging limply at his sides, obedient and compliant. Dottie stood on tiptoe and draped the blanket over his broad shoulders. As she did so, she whispered to him, "I love you, Sol. I love you. And I'll take care of you. So don't you worry now. Just stay with me and let me take care of you."

He pulled the blanket tighter around himself.

"Thhank . . . sss" he said to her, nodding his head no. "Thanks."

He stood still for a moment longer. Dottie put her arms around him, her head resting on his huge chest.

"I'll take care of you. Just come with me," she coaxed.

She felt his body stiffen with the suggestion.

"That's all right . . . it's all right, Sol. We'll just stay right here. We don't have to go anywhere. Don't you worry."

He relaxed again as she rocked him slowly back and forth, back and forth. Her arms were around him, her head pressed close. She felt the presence of someone else, but did not move. She just stayed with Sol, rocking, soothing, crooning to him, "I love you, Sol. I'll take care of you always. Stay here with me because I love you."

Behind him, the doctor moved closer, his lips uttering a silent plea, making his decision to push the needle right through the blanket into his buttock. There was no other way to administer the Thorazine; it had to be done quickly.

But Sol sensed his presence. Suddenly whirling, knocking Dottie to the ground, he turned and flung out his right arm over his face. He saw the needle then. Saw the white hospital coat. But it was the needle, the sharp sharp teeth of the Watermelon Baby. The Watermelon Baby come to get him. Lashing out, the hypodermic flying into the air, he started to run in a blind, confused panic.

"Wwat . . . r . . . mel . . . bab . . ." he cried out in his frenzy.

Somewhere inside he could hear Dottie calling to him. But he had to get away from the Watermelon Baby before it was too late.

He ran to the end of the block, his white gown a banner trailing behind him.

When he reached the end of the block, he saw it. The Fifty-ninth Street bridge, spanning the East River. The same one he had admired from his window and tried so hard to touch.

Running toward it, he could hear the footsteps behind him. Footsteps of terror. The kind of terror that could easily rip open the heart of a child. A red flashing light closed in on him, a shrieking noise. That would be the monster's scream. "Sol!" He could hear that voice, the one he loved, the one that made him feel so good. But the siren was louder, and he ran toward the bridge as if it were his last hope of escape.

There was no end to his strength. For he would do anything to get away.

Dottie ran closest behind him, the others following. There was no tiredness in her, only the need to touch Sol one more time. To tell him that it was all right, that it was only a game they used to play. There is no Watermelon Baby.

He ran up the exit ramp onto the bridge, the honking horns, the shouts echoing in his head. Whirling, turning, dervishes come to drive him mad. The cacophony, bouncing crazily off the walls of his limited understanding, closed in on him.

Running out onto the bridge, past the screaming motorists, past the cars, he looked down. And then he suddenly stopped. There, just below him, was a pretty boat in the river. It was bigger now and he wanted to touch it. He put out his hand. There was no glass to stop him this time, and he smiled, suddenly calmed by the sight. He did not hear Dottie calling to him. He did not hear her call his name, nor the words "I love you" floating on the air. They were Kate's words, Ashley's words. He did not hear anything at all. He just looked at the tugboat and loved it, wanted it.

Moving up beside him, Dottie was silent. She only came near enough to touch him one last time before he reached, laughing, too far over the edge, away from his terror to the pretty boat.

All their lives they would remember him: his body—frail in its enormity, vulnerable in its nobility—a black silhouette, arms outstretched toward a dream, captured in a shaft of dying sunlight. For one moment he was still, motionless in midair like a dancer hesitating at the apex of a magical, breathtaking leap, before falling to the water in a long sigh of freedom and relief.

# CHAPTER 6

My dear Dottie:

Ashley telephoned me immediately about the death of your brother, a man who was loved by so many people. My heart reaches out to you in your grief.

Enclosed is a small stone plaque from the Anasazi period in New Mexico, with a turquoise bird carved in the center. Ashley told me that the woods and trees and wildlife were a part of Solomon, which is why I have chosen this particular gift for you.

This is a very old and symbolic work of art, as valid in design today as when it was first made by an unknown craftsman. I send it to you because I feel that often, when confronted with such ravaging grief, we feel that the beauty has passed out of our lives. It is not so.

Sometimes we need to be reminded of the simple existence of beauty, of its endurance and even its necessity. Since man first fashioned crude drawings on the walls of caves, that need has been with us.

Sol's death seems now a cruel mockery of this. But his beauty does exist in you and the others who loved him.

Much as I would wish it to be different, I cannot offer you real solace. I know you felt that, in many ways, Sol was your child. And losing a child—no matter how—is probably the most grievous, unspeakable pain that one must ever bear.

But I do offer my love and sympathy to you. I want you to know that I am thinking of you, that in some infinitesimal way I bear a part of your pain in the hope that it will lighten your burden.

Please take care of yourself, my dear Dottie. And know that I am thinking of you. And that I love you.

Nana

Of all the people who grieved for Sol, Kate's was the grief that was most savaged by guilt. During the months after Sol died, she berated herself for not having had the courage to marry him.

"If I had married him, I might have been able to help him, to get him to a doctor before it was too late," she confessed to Ashley.

"Nonsense," Ashley replied. "Stop doing that to yourself. There's nothing for you to do now except remember him with love and move forward in your life."

By that time Kate's grief had dug into the heart of her, stripping her of any pretense of living. Like an automaton, she moved through her days, aware that she had reached a crossroad in her life and had made the sad choice of moving straight forward on the ordinary path her parents had chosen for her. And now, just as her brother Will had predicted he would, Sol had become one of those lingering regrets that would live within her for the remainder of her days.

There were times—too many of them—when Kate would dream of Sol's hand caressing her face. The sweetness of those moments brought with it a golden light that illuminated her hunger on dark and lonely nights. But when she realized that it was only a dream, she would wake up crying and mouthing a silent scream.

On those nights, unable to fall asleep again, she would creep through the house to the bar and pour herself a generous portion of cognac, then take it back to bed with her. Sitting alone in her room, scorched by the memory of Sol, by her betrayal of him, she would drink until the liquor made her woozy. Only then would she fall into a restless and furtive sleep, in which dreams of Sol had been drowned in amber serum.

In April Alexander came to New York. He had been very discreet about his relationship with Ashley, telling no one in his office about it for fear the news would somehow be leaked to John Van Every. He knew that he could be fired from his job for this transgression. In addition, he did not want to cause any more pain for Ashley in her relationship with her father.

By March, weary of her job at the advertising agency, Ashley had taken a job with an independent playwright. Despite her title of assistant, she was nothing more than a gofer for a turgid ego.

And so it was with a sense of helplessness and gratitude that she welcomed Alexander. He stayed in New York for six weeks, during which time Nana came for a visit.

Alexander and Ashley decided that they would be married the following spring. Ashley fervently hoped that by then the rift between herself and her father would be mended. The thought of a wedding without his blessing became increasingly painful, and Ashley vowed that she would move mountains to make the attempt to ease the rift in her family.

Dottie's brother had been buried in January. During the following year it then became necessary to bury her grief. Her method was no stranger than most. She plunged into her work with a vengeance, leaving little time for remembering and feeling.

She, too, awakened in the middle of the night with nightmares. But her vision was of Sol falling. Always in the dream she was reaching out to catch him. And always he was just beyond her touch, alone and plummeting to earth.

Because of an overload at the office, Dottie was given three new clients to handle—each a novice writer trying to break through the pragmatic barrier of publishing.

With utter calm, with deep determination, Dottie sold their books. She sold them because she believed in them, and she sold them because the sheer weight of her ambition compelled editors to believe in them, too. She also sold *Spartan's End* to an American publisher. But she did not see its author.

The memory of Jack Barclay had been blurred by the death of Sol. The pleasure and joy she had experienced in his presence had been overlaid with tragedy, thus robbing her of its full impact.

"We'll have our time," Jack had told her. But there was no longer a Dottie to take it, a Dottie who was receptive to loving. In her place was a robot, determined to subdue the pain of her own grief, determined to survive.

By the end of that year the collective progress of the Troika had come to a halt. Ashley was mired, by then, in a third job, and her career ambitions had become a joke to her friends. Nothing she did could satisfy her needs. No dialogue could break the noise inside her mind, alleviate the pain of her floundering. What she wanted was Alexander and satisfying work, in that order. What she got instead was confusion.

Knowing that she was an intelligent and capable woman, Ashley felt an acute pain from her lack of direction. Hers was the pain of not knowing who she was. There was even a vague shame at her inability to focus on something satisfying, on something fulfilling. Instead, she wandered, waiting for the day she would see Alexander again, waiting for his frequent letters, for his occasional phone calls.

Kate's talent for avoiding truths finally asserted itself. And she buried Sol in that special vault she carried deep in her consciousness where all her fragile conflicts and crystal dreams were carried.

She continued to work at Bloomingdale's, doing her job efficiently, but without imagination or flair. Drifting, she waited for her husband to show up on the screen on which she had projected the movement of her life. She walked smiling through her days—a smile frequently tainted by memories, and occasionally aided by alcohol.

The smile only turned real again the day she met Christopher Griffin. He was a resident in Obstetrics/Gynecology who worked under her father at the hospital. He was tall and attractive and had crinkles at the corners of his eyes when he laughed. And he delivered Kate from mourning and confusion as soon as she met him. He was everything her parents would want for her. She was, once again, a good little girl.

In January 1961, under the mantle of Kennedy's inaugural words, the Troika met once again. This time it was because they all wanted to celebrate the prospect of a better year.

Both Ashley and Kate talked of wedding plans. Kate's would be first, followed by Ashley's at the end of April.

Dottie's plans did not include marriage. But finally peering out over the edge of her abyss, she began to think once again of Jack Barclay. Not as a client. But as a man.

* * *

Kate's wedding was not everything that Mrs. Henderson wished for her daughter. But it was everything that Kate wanted.

It seemed that with the advent of Christopher in her life, Kate had slightly more courage to stand up to the demands of her mother, exerting more of her own will in her final effort to grow up.

The ceremony itself was perfect, despite the fact that it was not large enough to suit Mrs. Henderson's idea of a wedding.

Attended by Ashley and Dottie wearing pale pink silk, Kate wore a wedding dress she had found in a secondhand store on First Avenue. Her mother had been appalled when she brought it home. "A secondhand wedding dress for my only daughter!" she had exclaimed. A gown from Bergdorf was more what she had in mind.

But Kate wore what she wanted and the dress was exquisite. It had a high neck with a bodice made entirely of ecru lace. The sleeves were long and tight, with a satin sash that cinched her tiny waist, opening in the back into a long full train over the satin skirt. She looked as if she had just stepped out of an antique sepia photograph, the kind one sees when visiting maiden aunts, framed in maroon leather with cut velvet matting.

William flew in for the wedding, and Kate doted on his company before the ceremony.

They stayed up late talking the first night he arrived. It was William who, in a moment of honesty, verbalized speculations that Kate's other friends had harbored silently: that perhaps she was marrying Christopher on the rebound from Sol; also, that marrying a doctor garnered the greatest amount of parental approval.

Kate denied it vehemently, of course. But that was the night she became violently drunk. She had to attend her final bridal shower the following day with a vicious hangover.

When Kate returned from her honeymoon, she moved into domesticity with a vengeance. She told Dottie and Ashley that she had never been happier in her life—that she was now complete and could think of nothing nicer than that she would soon become pregnant.

Still determined to make amends with her father, Ashley was waiting for him at her parents' home one night when he returned from the office.

"What are you doing here?" he asked, as soon as he saw her.

"I'm going to be married in April, and I want you to give me away."

His mouth tightened in an effort to control his rage. "In case you hadn't noticed, I've done that already."

Determined not to cry, Ashley reached out to him. "Please, Daddy. I love you. I need your blessing."

"You forfeited that right a long time ago, Ashley. There's nothing more to be said."

Without waiting for her reply, without acknowledging the anguished cry that followed him, John Van Every walked out of his house until his daughter left it.

Ashley was stunned. Somehow, she had convinced herself that her marriage would make the difference, that her father would, at last, come around and make a move toward reconciliation. Instead, he had not even asked the name of the man she was to marry.

She experienced a new kind of abandonment then, as if she were a drowning victim going down for the third time.

"Be patient, Ashley," her mother had counseled. "It takes time. Perhaps when the wedding is closer . . ." Her voice drifted off inconclusively, as if she could not actually believe her own words.

"I'm trying," Ashley muttered through her tears. "And I'll keep on trying. But I wonder if it will ever do any good."

Martha Van Every held her daughter tightly, trying with all her heart to love Ashley enough for two parents instead of one. But she understood that her love alone could never be enough, that Ashley's craving for her father's acceptance negated that possibility. And it broke her heart to think that her husband might never reach out to his daughter again.

*La bombe plastique* is an explosive device used originally in World War II. Made of a TNT compound, it is a rubbery substance that feels similar to putty. It is stable, light, and pliable. It can be cut or stuck to a surface with relative ease. And it can be detonated by means of a fuse or any other number of electrical devices. Although it was used effectively during the war, it was the Algerian revolutionaries who perfected its use in guerrilla tactics.

For a long time the guerrillas had carried on the revolution in their own country. Finally, they brought it to France, where it culminated later in the infamous Blue Night in Paris.

From the beginning the terrorists appreciated the effectiveness of carrying the battle to the enemy's territory. The explosions burst upon the citizens of Paris with awesome effectiveness.

On a cold February night a man happened to be walking home on the sidewalk when another man started the engine of his car nearby. The driver, a long-sought target of the Algerians, had no idea that a *bombe plastique* had been attached to the car underneath his seat. It was detonated, of course, when he turned the key in the ignition.

In an explosion of this sort the chemical compound is suddenly heated to a high temperature and then shocked, turning it instantaneously into a hot gas which, under intense pressure, must escape. One hundred yards away the tremor can be felt, shaking the body in an unforgettably sickening way.

In that car the seat simply blew directly up into the driver's body, leaving little evidence that there had ever been a human being there in the first place.

As if in slow motion, the car left the ground and then returned. That was not enough release, however, for the pressure the gas created. Just as air will escape from the hole pricked in a balloon, the remaining force of this explosion escaped in the one route left for it—the open front window of the car on the curb side.

The man walking home that night happened to be passing that window the moment the bomb was detonated by the turn of a key. Like the lens of a camera, the window neatly focused the blast directly on him.

The first thing that happened to him was that the radiation of heat blistered all the exposed parts of his body; on that night, only his hands and his face were uncovered, for it was cold and he was wearing an overcoat. Immediately afterward his clothes were blown off by the shock waves of energy transmitted through the air. The shock waves also crushed him, blowing the flesh off his legs and torso along with the dirt from the gutter that flew with it. For a long moment his obscene blistered head was left standing on a barren spine before it collapsed, with incredible and hideous gentleness, to the ground.

In the late afternoon Ashley sat at the table reading a letter from Alexander that she had received that day. In it he described the tragedy of the escalating war and the sudden increasing fear of the citizens of Paris.

He continued with more personal words:

> I was deeply sorry to hear that your overtures toward your father have failed so miserably. I

know how much pain you must be feeling and wish I were there to help you.

In the light of that, I have started to look for another position. I cannot be associated with a firm in which he works. I'm too angry at his abandonment of you and have lost all my respect for him. Do you want to continue living in New York? I know there would be jobs there for me if I wanted them. I rather favor staying in Europe. Perhaps England for a change. How do you feel about that? Would you like to live in London? Let me know soon. I am not that set on any one place, since a home with you will be wonderful anywhere. And I want it to be a place that you will love as much as I do.

And speaking of love, Ashley. Even though we are separated, the love I feel for you has become an integral part of me, one which carries me through difficult nights and makes good days even better. I feel so complete in the knowledge that we will be married in five weeks, that even the missing of you is easier.

Take care, and be good to yourself. You deserve such fine things that sometimes I feel privileged that I am a part of your life.

I love you, Alexander

Ashley smiled to herself, then walked to the kitchen to pour herself a glass of wine before she read the paper.

The apartment was dark when Dottie arrived home that evening. She had worked late typing contracts, the job she hated most of all, and was relieved to be home.

She didn't see Ashley sitting by the window at first. Turning on the light, she fumbled with packages and cursed the cold rain that was falling outside.

When she did notice Ashley, there seemed to be no recognition of Dottie's existence on her part. She sat as if she had been turned to stone, staring at the rain that splattered on the windowpanes.

"What is it?" asked Dottie as she walked over to where Ashley was sitting.

But there was only silence in response. Silence, and the dull, broken expression on Ashley's face.

Frightened, Dottie shook her. "Ashley? Ashley!" she said harshly. "What's the matter?"

Ashley lifted her hand off an article in *The New York Times* that was spread open on the table. Dottie leaned over, squinting to read it.

> PARIS, AP, February 23—Late last evening Algerian revolutionaries once more brought their battle to Paris. André Louvan, long a leader of the counterrevolutionary forces, was killed in an explosion of a *bombe plastique* that had been set to go off when he turned on the ignition of his car.
>
> An employee of Charter Investments, Alexander B. Lain, was also killed in the blast. Formerly a resident of Philadelphia, he was apparently an innocent bystander.

## CHAPTER 7

Thus, just as the atmosphere in the apartment on Twelfth Street had begun to take on a new and optimistic light, it was once more plunged into darkness.

It was as if Ashley and Dottie had embarked on a journey through a long and somber night, from which they would both emerge forever changed.

During the next year Jack Barclay wrote Dottie one letter shortly after Alexander died. In it he told her that he was retiring to his cave in order to write his next book, and that she should not expect to hear from him while he was working. Consequently, she drove herself even farther into the mania of achievement, taking care to step around Madelaine's oblique advances, while at the same time plotting her own.

Ashley's recovery, however, was not so simple. The death of Alexander had left a raw and gaping hole in her life.

Martha Van Every spent hours with her, holding her hand, talking, trying as best she could to pull her daughter out of the shadows.

But it was Nana who finally offered her the hand that could give her a start. She had come to Ashley as soon as Dottie had called her about Alexander. And she had stayed for a week, sharing the sorrow. She tried to persuade Ashley to come to Santa Fe, but the answer was always the same. "I cannot come to your home as long as my father rejects me. It would be the last form of betrayal."

Ashley quit her job and spent her days in a morass of mourning, caring neither about herself nor her friends. Finally, in November, Nana could stand it no longer, and she made another visit to New York.

"It's time now, Ashley. Time for you to move on. You can't do this to yourself any longer."

"I can't seem to do anything else," she replied in a monotone.

Nana settled back in her chair. "You know, I actually admire you, Ashley. You have that rare quality of one who knows how to celebrate life. Even when you are confused, when you don't know what to do with yourself, you've taken the moment and squeezed all you could out of it. Because that's the way you are."

"Well, I'm certainly doing a lousy job of it now," Ashley commented dryly.

"No . . ." replied Nana. "That's where you're wrong. You've not been afraid to confront your own sadness. You've done it. I've watched you, heard it in your voice when I called." She paused for a moment, trying to find the words for what she wanted to express. "You've not been afraid to explore the abyss. Most people, when they are at the edge, will pull back in alarm. You had the courage to plunge in and feel it, to understand its tyranny and its malevolence. It's no longer an unspeakable stranger to you, Ashley. That's the important part. Because you'll never never be afraid of it again. You've been there already."

Ashley looked at her grandmother for a long time. Then, through sobs of relief and gratitude, she finally said, "You make me hungry for life, Nana. All of a sudden I feel greedy."

"It's about time," said Nana with a smile. "So if you won't come home with me, then we'll just have to find something right here for you to do. No more silly jobs to pass the time, to make you feel marginally occupied. If you don't know what to do with yourself, then at least have the sense to fill your time with something really useful."

Taking her grandmother's advice, Ashley found a job working in the pediatric ward of New York Hospital. The salary was minimal, but the compensating factor was Ashley's sense of doing something worthwhile.

Throughout the winter she worked at the hospital three days a week, putting her heart into everything she did.

Dottie worked harder than ever, selling manuscripts regularly, building a reputation for herself as a formidable agent. Even though her client list was limited, she was a success, and she reveled in the respect she was being accorded by more and more people with whom she came in contact. It was a treasured compensation for her lack of a social life.

By spring, just as Dottie had begun to form a tentative friendship with the loneliness in her life, a manuscript box arrived in the mail from Jack Barclay. Unfortunately, there was only a very brief covering note with it.

Dottie was fearful that he had become involved with someone else; she tormented herself with visions of him lying next to another woman, was afraid that he had fallen in love. Two years is a long time for anyone to wait, she thought. We each chose it, though. We each opted out.

"So call him," said Ashley one evening as she returned exhausted from work. Since her emergence from mourning and her job in the pediatric ward, she felt better. Although it was not work that involved her in the way she wished, every time she caused a sick child to smile, she received payment enough to keep her continuing.

"I think," said Dottie in a depressed reply, "if he had wanted to see me, he would have called, written. Or added a letter to the manuscript."

"There's only one way to find out," Ashley said as she picked up the phone and handed it to Dottie.

Two days later Jack Barclay re-entered Dottie's life with as much force as he had left it. He opened the door to Dottie's office without knocking and stuck his head inside.

"Long time no see," he said by way of greeting.

"Long time no kiss," replied Dottie as she ran into his arms.

"I hope I have chosen the precise day to arrive on which you don't have any engagements for lunch," he said.

"Give me five minutes and I'll be free," she said happily.

"Not yet, not yet." He closed the door to her office, pulled her back to him, and kissed her. Memories flooded back upon them, tumbling over the erotic side of her, caressing places that had been left untouched since she was last with him.

Ten minutes later they walked out of her office.

As they walked arm in arm up Fifth Avenue on the way to the Oak Room at the Plaza, Jack asked about Ashley.

"Fine, now," said Dottie. "But it was touch and go for a while."

"Oh?"

"Her fiancé was killed in Paris by one of the Algerian bombs."

"I'm sorry." He hesitated before asking. "And you? What about your grief? Tell me about it now. I want to know."

She related the story of Sol to him in dispassionate words to cover the sorrow she still harbored. "And my grief?" she said. "It's not gone, just buried. But it's nothing compared to what my parents have gone through. Sol's death destroyed them without killing them. They just sort of . . . grew old before my eyes. And there wasn't anything I could do. Nothing . . ." Dottie's voice just sort of drifted into the breeze.

"Well," said Jack as they seated themselves in a corner booth in the bar. "The sad subjects have been covered now. Not forgotten, mind you." He reached over and brushed his hand against Dottie's cheek. "And I think we should devote the remainder of the day to unmitigated joy. I'll do my humble best to make a significant contribution."

"So let's celebrate," said Dottie.

"Celebrate what?" he asked.

"The brilliance of *King's X*," she said.

His eyes sparkled with the reference to his new book. "I thought you'd never mention it. And I was afraid to ask. After all, you're the only one who's read it."

"I'm flattered."

*Spartan's End* had been quite successful in England and mildly successful in America. It had sold enough copies to put some hard cash in Jack's pocket, to earn him a growing reputation because of the good reviews, and to please the publishers. Dottie had no doubt that because of that, his second novel would be easier to sell.

When she told him, he leaned back in his chair, took a deep breath, and said, "That's the first time I've felt really relaxed in a year.

That evening, in a rush of touching, Jack and Dottie made love. With a fulfilling release of emotion, Dottie settled into the feel of him once again. All this, she thought, has been dammed too long inside. Never again. Please.

When Kate heard that Jack Barclay was in town, she decided to have a dinner party. In her determined efforts to be superwife, she spent two days preparing, thoroughly enjoying all the simple tasks of putting a first-rate meal together. She orchestrated her dinners, planning them carefully so that each new dish complemented the last.

She asked Ashley if there was anyone she would like to bring and received the expected answer: no. It was not a sad or self-pitying refusal. It was simply that since Alexander's death she had no desire for the company of a man. It was not a necessary part of her life, nor even a desirable one.

Certainly there had been doctors at the hospital who had been attracted to her unique kind of beauty. But she wasn't interested. She often thought that she would like to find a man who was a friend instead of a lover. But that was asking a great deal.

Instead, Ashley filled her days doing things she

wanted to do: She went to scores of movies, her favorite pastime; she attended concerts and museums and bought a horse she kept for early-morning rides in Central Park. She worked hard at the hospital, mourning the death of some of the children, or crying tears of relief when others died, because they were finally delivered from such tormented suffering. And she rejoiced at the recovery of others. She enjoyed dinners with friends and hours in the company of her mother. Her father continued in his exclusion of her. But by now that had become a more muted color in the spectrum of her life, a life that searched always for affirmation.

The evening of the party was festive. Kate was particularly delighted, because her brother, Will, was now living in New York while he did his residency in orthopedic surgery. She did not realize how very much she had missed him until he returned. She sought him out often for advice and she accepted most of his judgments without question, even though he persisted in warning her of the dangers of such a course.

"When will you ever learn to trust your own instincts, Katie?" he asked in an attempt to make her see how this attitude was a serious impediment in the progress of her own growth.

"When I grow up," she answered teasingly.

"Not funny, Kate. Not funny at all," Will answered. "If you insist on behaving like a child, you'll continue to be treated like one. And that's a condition that, sooner or later, you'll grow weary of. But by then it might be too late."

In spite of Will's judgments, Kate adored him without reservation, and she was delighted to invite him to the party as a companion for Ashley.

By the time the six of them had finished the marinated fish accompanied by a crisp Meursault, it was a congenial party. More than anyone, Jack Barclay infused a vitality into the group, making all of them feel wittier and more charming in his presence.

When dessert was served, Kate tapped on her wineglass like a master of ceremonies, pausing dramatically before she spoke. "I have an announcement." She smiled beatifically, looking at Chris. "Finally, ladies and gentlemen, I am pregnant."

She had been waiting for this moment. For a year after she married, she had filled her days with a domesticity directed toward a baby in the house. But she did not become pregnant and had grown increasingly despondent. This was her moment of triumph, and when she saw a shadow pass over Chris's face when he heard the announcement, she dismissed it. She would not allow anything to blur the joy of this moment.

After dinner the six of them moved to the living room for coffee. Kate had been an extraordinarily gracious hostess, running the entire evening with the velvet glove of good taste and pleasurable conversation.

She was very proud of her apartment. Since Chris was just starting in practice, there had not been a great deal of money to spend on extras. But she had picked up a few key pieces of furniture in secondhand stores and refinished them. The result was a room that was warm and inviting and comfortable, with just a hint of formality about it.

And now, she was thinking with pleasure, she would have a baby's room to fix up.

Ashley talked politics with William, mostly about the fact that there were now American soldiers in Vietnam, that the service might interrupt his medical training.

Jack entertained them all with stories of the growing hippie population on Venice Beach and the agonies of writing a novel when you're hungry.

After the party, when Kate was getting ready for

bed, she asked Chris what had happened to him when she announced she was pregnant.

He answered softly, perhaps to prevent the annoyance from creeping into his voice. "I just thought it was a private sort of thing, that's all. You should have told me first."

"I'm sorry," said Kate, genuinely contrite. "I really am. It's just that Ashley and Dottie know how much I've wanted to become pregnant and I thought they should join in the celebrating. And even though I did spring it on you, I didn't think you'd mind. You didn't get home from the hospital until five minutes before the company arrived. And . . . and I thought the surprise might be fun for you."

"I assume you went to your father's office with the traditional sample of urine," he commented.

"Yes."

"Well, I wish you had come to me, that's all."

"I'm sorry, Chris. I won't do it again. I promise." She spoke like a chastised child. Standing on her tiptoes, she kissed him on the cheek. "I love you."

"I love you, too."

Kate lay awake long into the night, wondering how she could have been so stupid as to botch such a happy announcement. She thought of being a mother and how much she hoped she would be a good one. I don't care if it's a boy or a girl, she thought. But, please, God, let it be healthy. That's all I ask.

Unable to sleep, she finally crept out of bed around three in the morning and walked into the living room. Pouring herself a large snifter of cognac, she sat alone on the sofa and sipped it, hoping it would put her to sleep. A vague anxiety, nameless and untouchable, hovered over her. She could not grasp it even though it had become a part of her life. There was no way she could deal with it because she did not know its name, could not discover its hiding place in the nebulous corners of her mind.

* * *

"Tell me again," said Jack as he nuzzled Dottie, kissing her on the belly.

"You're just like Lenny and the rabbits," Dottie said, her hands stroking his shoulders.

"So tell me about the rabbits, anyway," he said.

Dottie took a deep breath, smiling, then repeated her words one more time like a litany. "I am convinced—even though it may take the world a little time to catch up with it—that *King's X* is going to make your fortune and your reputation."

"So go sell it," he mumbled, kissing her breasts, becoming excited once again by this strange, strong woman.

"That's exactly what I intend to do, if I can stay out of bed with you long enough to find the time."

"Well, since I depart for western shores tomorrow, the next time I hear from you, I shall expect it to be a phone call regaling me with vast sums of money and promises of instant fame."

"Right. But for the moment I have other things on my mind, if you please." She slipped her hand beneath him, stroking him.

"I *hope* I please," he said, moving on top of her.

The next morning Jack came to Dottie's office to tell her good-bye. Every time Dottie saw him, she seemed better to herself than she remembered. Not just more attractive. But more interesting, more exciting.

Madelaine recognized it, too, as soon as she saw the two of them together.

"Well, now . . ." Inherent in her voice was the arched eyebrow of sudden insight. "Good to see you, Jack." She paused significantly. "How long has this been going on, pray tell?"

"What?" asked Dottie, displeased.

"Well, the two of you, of course," commented Madelaine in an obvious effort to be casual.

Madelaine was not casual enough, however, because she could not conceal fully the tiny note of jealousy that crept into her voice. She had always thought of Dottie as somehow being hers. For Madelaine, it was a small step from being a business protégée to being a sexual one. Even though they had been together only one time, she still regarded her secretary with a possessive air.

When Dottie had evinced no further interest in her, Madelaine had decided just to wait, to bide her time. Eventually, she kept telling herself, Dottie will come around. She was in no hurry, because there were others to be had for sexual encounters.

But now, with Jack Barclay, the complexion of the picture changed. And Madelaine did not like the tone it took on, nor the indirect rejection it implied. She did not like it one bit.

It never even occurred to Dottie. She simply assumed that Madelaine understood it was something that happened a long time ago. Besides, she had Jack.

Two weeks after Jack returned to California, in an effort to relieve her work load, Madelaine gave Dottie five more clients to handle. Despite her personal feelings, Madelaine knew that Dottie was a first-rate agent. Being a pragmatist in everything she did, Madelaine had no trouble at all making the decision.

It was at that time that Dottie decided she should be living uptown, that an agent's image should be matched by her living conditions. An apartment on Twelfth Street, furnished haphazardly and shared with a roommate—immediately leaving her open to all kinds of speculation, she was wise enough to recognize—was no longer adequate for her needs.

"Ashley?" said Dottie, on one of the few evenings when they were both home together. "I want to move uptown."

"Oh?"

"It's just that this place," she said, sweeping her hand around the room, "isn't suitable anymore."

Although both of them now had adequate money, it never occurred to Ashley to move. The apartment was comfortable and unpretentious, which was enough for her needs.

"I understand," said Ashley.

"I want to start looking for a place and I just wanted to let you know."

"Well, it may be time for a change for me, too. My accountant mentioned to me a month or so ago that I should figure out how to invest some of my money to get a better tax break. He said buying a house would be a good idea. Although I can hardly imagine myself doing it."

"Unfortunately, I'm not in a position to do that. I wish I were," Dottie commented, not without envy.

"In the long run you will be, my dear Dottie. Trust me. You will be. You'll make more money than you know what to do with. It's in the cards."

Ashley accepted Dottie's ambition as a norm, not as an aberration by which so many would condemn her in the future.

"I hope you're right," said Dottie.

"You have the eye of an artist," Nana said to Ashley as they stood in front of one of her photographs that they had hung in the gallery for her new show in New York. "You understand instinctively what it is that I'm doing."

Earlier that day the two of them had gone horseback riding in Central Park.

"It's too tame here," said Nana. "Sooner or later I'm going to get you to New Mexico. That's where you can really ride."

"I've ridden a lot in Connecticut," said Ashley.

Nana smiled. "It's not the same at all. I rode in my father's arms before I got a pony of my own when I was four years old. But I will never forget the first time I was given a real horse. I remember thinking then that I had never felt so free, that giving my horse its rein and galloping toward the mountains was the most wonderful sensation I had ever experienced. Besides that first moment when I lift my pictures out of the developing fluid—the anticipation and expectation—I like this the most. Riding."

"I'll get to New Mexico, Nana. I promise."

"It does seem to me, Ashley, that the time has to come when you give up on your father. Sooner or later, you'll have to recognize the fact that he won't change."

"Never!" said Ashley with a force that surprised even herself. "He's my father." Sorrow spread over her face like a dark cloud blotting out the light shining through a stained glass window. "Despite what he's done, I miss him so much."

"Ashley, my dear," Nana said with a gentle strength in her voice. "If it's that important to you, perhaps we should not see each other."

"Once again my answer is never. I want you both. And if it's the last thing I do, I'll make it happen."

"I often admire the uncompromising convictions of the young," Nana commented. "I just don't know how we all lived through it."

"I'll find a way."

That evening William Henderson picked up Ashley to take her to Nana's gallery opening. She had gone out with him several times since Kate's dinner party and enjoyed his company.

The first evening they spent together, she wished that she could fall in love with him. There was an innate goodness that shone from him. A grace. And she wanted to be a part of it. But, for the moment, he understood her need for friendship, and had asked no more of her than that she be good company for an evening.

But on the night of the gallery opening, they had champagne to drink, loosening their inhibitions. Especially Will's. He thought then how strikingly beautiful Ashley was. And wished he could enjoy her in bed. He understood instinctively, though, that it was only a wish.

On a more practical note, it was at the gallery opening that Ashley heard of a house for sale in Greenwich Village.

"It sounds perfectly suited for you," said Nana. "It's in the back of a town house on St. Luke's Place. Servants quarters or something. Over a hundred and fifty years old."

"I'll look at it this week," said Ashley.

When he took Ashley home, Will came in for a cup of coffee. Ashley was standing in the kitchen when Will turned her toward him and kissed her.

It was an undemanding kiss, but filled with longing. Ashley did not object. Nor did she enjoy it. When it was over, her head searing with memories of Alexander's kisses, she looked up at Will.

"I have to be honest with you, Will. It's not that I didn't like kissing you. But . . . but it's that I didn't feel anything." She stopped, then suddenly added, "Absolutely nothing," in a voice of savage despair. Abruptly, sobs burst out of her, sobs she did not know had been there. And she stood a long time enclosed in the benevolent arms of a man for whom she could feel nothing except friendship.

Kate's usual routine in any given day would be to get up early with Christopher and make him breakfast. After he left for the hospital, she accomplished whatever cleaning and chores had to be done, planned her menu for the day, and did some shopping. Sometimes she read, had lunch with a friend, or went to a movie. But she would always be home when

Chris arrived in the evening, looking fresh and pretty for him.

There were times, of course, when he would be held up at the hospital, delivering a baby or tending to an emergency. But Kate understood this, having grown up with it, and learned how to plan her meals so that they would be ready when he arrived home, no matter what the hour.

In July she was watching the evening news as it announced that Algeria had been declared independent following a general plebiscite in France. She thought of Ashley then, and reached over to pick up the phone and dial her number.

They chatted for a long time. They had not seen each other since Kate's party, and they had a lot of catching up to do. After making plans to meet Ashley for lunch the following week, Kate hung up the phone. It was at that moment she felt a tiny fluttering in her stomach, as if a butterfly were beating its wings gently against her.

So when Chris opened the door, she greeted him with a particular ebullience. "I felt it!" she said, hugging him. "I felt the baby move. Just a few minutes ago."

"Not the baby," Chris corrected. "Him. It's bound to be a boy. I know it."

"It's only bound to be healthy," Kate said, returning to her reality. "You ought to know better than to wish that. It's like a slap in the face of God."

"Well, at any rate," he said, smiling indulgently, "I'm glad you felt him."

"Well, doesn't it excite you?" asked Kate, her eyes still shining.

"Kate, my love," he explained while he mixed himself a drink. "You have to understand that I've been through this so many times that I just can't generate the excitement that you can. It's just not the same."

"You're right, it's not the same," replied Kate with determination. "This time it's ours."

Every once in a while an agent or an editor holds a manuscript in hand that he or she knows is a winner. It is almost as if the box containing the sheaf of papers carries with it a life of its own, as if its contents are palpable with success. Often it is a book that brings with it the enticing smell of money, a commercially viable commodity that will sweep the market with its impact.

Less frequently, and far more treasured, is the manuscript that carries with it the earmarks not only of commercial success, but of critical acclaim as well. A book that is well written, well conceived, and well executed. A book that does, indeed, exist in a life of its own, carrying with it a force and a passion that are present because it is a total original, because it is blessed with a special genius.

Such a book was *King's X*, and Dottie knew it from the moment she opened the box. She planned long and hard about its future, about the type of publisher that would be best for the book and the kind of publicity it should receive. For the first time in her career, she was in a solid, strong position to negotiate. Not just sell. And she did not intend to squander the opportunity.

It took a while for her to plot the game plan. But in a final burst of confidence, she submitted the manuscript to Adam Farling, editor in chief of Stafford House, the most powerful and prestigious publishing firm in America.

She did not know Mr. Farling personally, for Miss Dorothy Langford was much too low on the agent-laden totem pole for him to have bothered to make her acquaintance. As far as he was concerned, she was just part of the hoi polloi with whom he occasionally found himself at a large party.

Of course, he did know the Jacot Agency, and Dottie composed a note to accompany the messenger-delivered manuscript with the care that others might put into a prize-winning acceptance speech.

Fully aware that an agent's credibility is of the utmost importance, in her usual covering letters, Dottie might call a novel "promising," "very fine," or "beautifully crafted." It was her job to sell. But it was not her job to mislead. She counted on Adam Farling's respecting the name of Jacot enough so that he would also respect the words that she wrote. In her note to him Dottie stated simply that the enclosed, while being eminently commercial, was also clearly a work of genius, destined to become a classic.

Eight weeks later Adam Farling called and asked Dottie to lunch.

He was not the kind of editor who hung out at the momentarily popular restaurant. There are those places in New York that trade in chic, whose ambience is far more important than the quality of the food they serve, whose status is linked to the degree of fame the patrons flaunt. They come and they go, brief flashes in the tarnished pan of the perpetually insecure.

Instead, Adam Farling asked Dottie to have lunch with him at an obscure little Mafia hangout on Forty-fifth Street. This is not to say that Adam Farling was willing to forgo the large doses of stroking for his eternally thirsty ego that came with the territory of the fancier restaurants. To the contrary. The owner of this obscure little establishment—called Luigi only by his intimates and Adam Farling—fawned over his illustrious client as if he were a satisfactory substitute for the Messiah. That was because the editor in chief of Stafford House brought him the class and respectability that otherwise would have eluded him.

"It has the greatest pasta in New York," said Adam Farling when he invited Dottie to lunch. "Made by some old lady down on Thompson Street, and it's the envy of every restaurant in town."

Dottie arrived first at the restaurant. She was shown to the best table in the moderately sized room—right next to the recirculating lily pond that featured rubber frogs and plastic plants.

Having learned from previous experience that she could not drink more than a modest amount at lunch and still function properly for the remainder of the day, Dottie ordered a glass of white wine and a bottle of club soda. As was her custom, she would fill the glass with soda as she drank the wine, offering the illusion of joining her companion without really doing so.

Ten minutes later—most likely, minutes that had been calculated—Farling arrived. Dottie had never met him, but she had seen his picture numerous times in trade publications, as well as the daily papers. Leonine was the manner in which he was most often described. And indeed he was, thought Dottie, as she watched the maître d' bow reverently to him as he entered.

Having done her homework on him—considering him to be a friendly adversary—she learned that he was a man of considerable pretension, one who frequently glanced in passing store windows catching his reflection in a stance that could only be called preening. On the other hand, the image that he had carefully constructed over the years allowed him this egocentric flaw.

His full white hair, thick around his face and worn longer than the average man, accented his tan, obviously the kind of tan that was maintained year-round in various spas known for the quality of their seasonal sun. He wore an ascot instead of a tie, a touch that made Dottie want to giggle—a silliness enhanced by the fact that it was unusually gaudy, although "flamboyant" was the word that Adam, himself, would have chosen. His entire demeanor seemed to be pasted on in deliberately chosen patches.

That day he sported a beautifully tailored navy-blue blazer with gray flannel slacks. His shoes, soft and luxurious leather loafers, were obviously handmade. No golden initials of somebody else's name for him, thank you. He wore a heavy gold ring with a crest—presumably of his illustrious forebears—etched deeply into the surface, and gold and onyx cuff links decorated his hand-tailored shirt.

Clearly on the far side of sixty, he appeared to have a need to create an impressively youthful image while still maintaining the illusion that he, alone, possessed the wisdom that comes with age. A dandy in publisher's clothing, Dottie thought, as he approached her. With just a hint of ladies' man mixed in for good measure.

Dottie looked up and smiled when he reached the table.

"Miss Langford?" he said formally, extending his hand for her to take in a firm grasp.

"Mr. Farling," she returned with a demure nod. "It's a privilege to meet you, sir."

"I see you've already ordered a drink." He turned then to the owner. "My usual, please, Luigi," he said with the gracious stance of noblesse oblige and settled into his chair.

Dottie had deliberately worn her most beguiling dress on that day: soft, understated, and feminine. She had already decided not to tip her hand until he did. She was fully cognizant of the fact that this man had been eating little agents like her for breakfast since he first began in the business that was once known for its gentlemanly endeavors. And she did not intend to be just another little snack to sustain him in his old age.

They spent the time before their pasta was set before them with an appropriate flourish, engaged in literary small talk. He was waiting for her to bring up the subject of *King's X*. She didn't. She simply joined him in a congenial conversation, following wherever he led. He was, after all, the host for this occasion. Incapable of small talk in more ordinary circumstances, Dottie rose to the occasion on that day, lacing her wit with the perfect amount of charm, playing up to him with an ease that she actually began to enjoy.

Finally, having grown impatient with her, he broached the subject head-on. "I'll not beat around the bush, Miss Langford," he said, after beating around the bush for an hour. "I agree with you entirely about *King's X*, it *is* a work of genius."

"I'm so happy you think so," she said smiling humbly.

"And I do think you exercised good judgment in submitting it to Stafford House," he continued.

"I thought so myself," she responded, following his lead. "The book deserves the best." Careful, she thought. Don't lay it on too thick.

"As a matter of fact," he said casually, "I see no reason why we shouldn't publish it."

"Oh?" This time she moved instinctively into the stance of waiting for the opponent to fill the conversational gap. There was a long pause as he obviously expected more from her.

"There is, of course, the matter of the advance."

"Yes, of course," she agreed politely. Then she waited again.

He paused, furrowing his brow in an expression that created the desired effect of The Thoughtful Man—one who knows his mind and will exercise it carefully but confidently. "I'd say fifteen thousand would be a fair price."

Dottie looked at him, the shock of the low figure registering on her face. Finally, she responded. "I'd say, with all due respect, of course, that it would not be a fair price at all." She took a sip of her wine, reassessing the power of her opponent. "Not at all."

"Come, come, Miss Langford. Barclay's last book didn't do all that well. Adequate sales, that's all."

"It was that kind of book. Not as easy to read and exciting as this one."

"I don't think it's necessary, Miss Langford, to point out that it will cost somewhere in the neighborhood of thirty thousand dollars to print, bind, and distribute this book all over the country. And I am the one, after all, who assumes the risk."

"And I don't think it's necessary to point out what you and I both know, Mr. Farling, that there's virtually no risk in this property. It's a winner."

"Perhaps," he agreed conditionally. "But, again, it's still dependent on the throw of the dice."

"I agree that it's a crap game," said Dottie, deliberately following his metaphor to its mundane conclusion. "But this one is destined to win. It won't crap out."

Farling settled back into his chair, holding his head up slightly to conceal the folds of skin. "And what if I were to agree with you?" He paused, took a sip of his espresso that had been generously spiked with amaretto by Luigi just moments before. "If I agree with you," he repeated, "just what kind of advance are you talking about?"

Here goes, Dottie thought. The big roll of the dice. "Fifty thousand dollars."

"For a second novel, Miss Langford? Of a virtually unknown writer?" He smiled. "Preposterous."

"Not for *this* second novel. It's a bargain."

"Ah, the illusions of youth," he countered with a marginally smug look invading his hooded eyes.

Dottie turned tougher. "Young I may be, Mr. Farling, filled with illusions I am not. This novel is going to make a great deal of money. You know it, and I know it."

"I couldn't possibly consider giving you that kind of

money for an advance. Twenty-five, perhaps. But no more."

"It's worth a hell of a lot more money than that, Mr. Farling. A lot more."

What now, thought Dottie, confused. Where do we go from here? I've got the best publisher in the business offering me measly money. Do I move on to another publisher or lose money for Jack? And, she added with cold honesty, status for me?

"So where do we go from here, Miss Langford?" He asked, echoing her own thoughts. "Is your figure final?"

"Let's just say it's slightly negotiable," she responded, hoping he would come up with something that resembled the money she had set as the figure she could get for the book. She had also set her bottom limit at thirty thousand dollars. And there was no doubt that she could get it from almost any reputable publisher in town.

"Twenty-five, Miss Langford."

Dottie thought a moment, considering the man sitting across from her very carefully. She knew, beyond any doubt, that he was trading on his reputation. The book was good. There were others who would snap it up. Besides, she thought, Jack not only deserves the money, this is his freedom money, the stuff that will make him independent until the royalties start coming in. It's Jack's money, not mine, she thought. And I have to get it for him.

Dottie smiled graciously. "I'm sorry to have wasted your time, Mr. Farling. But that's not enough. I'll have to take it to someone else."

"All right, Miss Langford. As you wish." There was a light note in his voice. Not the gravity that having lost an important round should have engendered.

This immediately put her on alert. She thought their business was completed. But her instinct, still untried but remarkably accurate, put her on guard. Oh, God, she thought. Do I just sit here and smile while I wait for him to pull something out of his sleeve? Or do I leave?

Before she could make her move, Adam Farling reached with utmost grace and finesse up his monogrammed sleeve and extracted the hidden ace that had been planted there weeks before.

"It has come to my attention, Miss Langford, that you have been handling the first novel by a Sarah Jacobs without much success. As a matter of fact, if my information is correct, it has already been rejected by seven publishers."

Dottie swallowed her anxiety and nodded in affirmation.

"It's a good novel, Miss Jacobs's book," he continued like a man who was telling a story about his first sexual encounter—humbly arrogant. "And it's certainly worthy of publication, I would say. But it won't get published because it is not well-enough grounded in plain old American commerce. Wouldn't you agree?" He smiled.

"Not particularly," Dottie countered, trying to remain noncommittal, while thoroughly agreeing with him. He was correct, she thought. The only way Sarah's book will sell is by a fluke. Dottie had agreed to handle it because it was good, not because it was an easy sale. And she also understood that the author would turn out more popular books in the future, as she became more familiar with her craft. But she still did not know what it was that Adam Farling was leading to.

"Come, come, Miss Langford. Let's put our cards on the table."

"It appears to me, Mr. Farling, that you're in the process of doing just that. And the pack includes an extra ace." She tried to lighten the remark. "Or a joker that's suddenly been declared wild, at the very least."

"There's no need to feel that way," he said with an

indulgent smile. "It's not an extra card I have. Merely a solid, bona fide business proposition."

"And what might that be?"

Aiming directly at the target, he said bluntly, "I'll give you three thousand for the Jacobs book and twenty-five for *King's X.*"

I have just been had, thought Dottie with a kind of perverted admiration for such a skilled opponent. I've been had in spades, with a pretty ribbon tied around the entire neat package. He, too, recognizes Sarah's future potential to turn out a best seller. He wants in now, when he can get her cheap. And I never even submitted the novel to him.

Stalling for time, Dottie asked, "If I may be so bold as to ask, how did you get ahold of Sarah Jacobs's book?"

"Oh . . . a friend of a friend. You know how that goes. I did him a favor by reading it. Before you ever accepted her as a client."

"I see." And she did see. The name of this particular game that he played so well was simply this: sell one author down the river for the benefit of another. In essence, one writer subsidizes the other. In ignorance, of course. These kinds of things are always kept from the writer, she thought. And, in the deal, I gain permanent entrée to Adam Farling, one of the most powerful men in publishing. Good for everyone except Jack.

For several minutes Dottie just sat there, desperate to get a handle on a viable alternative to his offer.

"Come, come, Miss Langford," said Adam Farling, reading her mind. "I dare say that a young woman in your position can allot little room for conscience. This is business. You're in the big leagues now. And here we never play it for laughs." He paused, waiting for the effect. "Nor do we always play strictly by the rules. I would think you'd have learned that by now."

Vowing silently to herself never again to be caught

without an additional ace of her own, Dottie stood up and reached over to Adam Farling to shake his hand.

"Thank you very much for lunch, Mr. Farling." She spoke with all the dignity she could muster for one who had just been taught such a tough lesson. "I'll have to get back to you with my decision. Is day after tomorrow suitable?"

"Quite," said the spider to the fly. "I'll look forward to hearing from you."

## CHAPTER 8

St. Luke's Place is considered by many people to be the loveliest street in Greenwich Village. Speaking eloquently of another era, it is lined with ginkgo trees from end to end. Gas lights and wrought-iron fences decorate the houses, little changed from when they were first built in the early nineteenth century.

Ashley stopped at number 23, admiring the house that faced the street. To one side of the house was a tall, narrow wrought-iron gate with the number 23½ worked skillfully into its design.

She had called the owners early that morning and had been told to walk through the gate, that the house in the back would be open for her inspection.

She stood in the street for a long time, unsure of whether she wanted to go any farther. The purchase of a home for herself was a giant step in her progress toward total independence. But it meant commitment, one that she was not at all certain she wanted to make. She had lived so long in a subdued emotional chaos that she had become convinced that it was a permanent state of being. Despite the fact that it would be a relief to move beyond it, she had no confidence that she could make a smooth transition. Even for someone as adventurous as Ashley, trading the known in for the unknown created an increased anxiety level, one that seemed to loom larger as she stood before the gate.

Finally gathering her courage together, she opened the gate and walked down the narrow horse walk that ran alongside the house from the sidewalk to the back garden.

Even though she was aware of the existence of these smaller buildings that had been built behind houses throughout the city, Ashley was unprepared for the perfect charm of this particular one.

The house, originally quartering servants from a neighboring farm near the Minetta Stream, was situated at the back of the lush green courtyard. Covered with English ivy, the two-story brick home gave the distinct impression it was settled comfortably at the end of a long-forgotten country lane.

Inside the ceilings were beamed and the floors were constructed of wide planks of pine, uneven and filled with knot holes. At one end of the living room was a stone fireplace, large enough for cooking, with a smaller arched brick baking oven to one side, built deep into the stone. The windows looked out on the trees in the courtyard. The only other room on the first floor was the kitchen, which Ashley knew immediately would need major renovation.

At the top of the narrow staircase, there were two small bedrooms and a bathroom. Deciding that the dividing wall should be knocked out in order to make the upstairs into one large room with exposed brick walls, Ashley visualized exactly how it would look when the renovation was complete.

It was only then that she realized she had already

mentally purchased the house, she was treating it as if it were already hers.

She stayed in the house for over an hour, overcome with her sense of happiness at her feeling of being totally comfortable in her new surroundings. It was as if she could finally start to move forward in her life again, confident she would find the answers to all her questions if she would only try hard enough.

She could feel the weight of her past lighten as she sat there, as if an albatross had been magically removed from her shoulders. The house symbolized a new beginning for her, and she left it reluctantly, closing the door softly behind her.

Then she walked to the nearest phone to call her lawyer so that she could make this house officially hers.

Dottie sat quietly in her office. Several times she reached for the phone, each time withdrawing her hand in an act of unusual procrastination.

As soon as Dottie returned from lunch with Adam Farling, she had told Madelaine all the details of the deal she had been offered.

Not at all surprised, Madelaine discussed the ramifications with Dottie, helping her make up her mind in what was obviously a difficult decision.

And so now, having come to her conclusion, Dottie finally picked up the phone and made the call.

"Yes?" said Jack Barclay, as if he were involved in something so intense that the mere act of answering was a chore of the first magnitude.

"Jack? It's me. Dottie." Her voice was deliberately light, cheerful.

"Hey, babe, it's good to hear your voice."

"Do you remember what you said should happen the next time I spoke with you?"

He moved quickly. "You sold it?"

Dottie took a deep breath. "Not only did I sell it,"

she said, dramatically pacing herself, "I sold it to Adam Farling at Stafford House."

"How much?"

"Twenty-five thousand, Jack. With a guaranteed print order of fifty thousand copies." She had at least managed to wheedle that concession from Farling.

"Well—" responded Jack.

Dottie interrupted. "I know it's not as high as the figure we discussed, Jack. I just couldn't get it. But it *is* Stafford House. The very best."

Dottie could hear his intake of breath. "That's great, Dottie. Just great. It's not as much as I thought it might bring. But just thinking of all that money gives me a hard-on."

Dottie laughed, deluged with the relief that flowed over her. "Well, I wish I were there to do something about it."

"I wish you were, too."

"The way things look right now," said Ashley dryly, "I don't know why we're bothering to move to new homes."

"You have a point," responded Dottie.

It was October, at the height of the Cuban missile crisis, and Dottie hovered under the threat as if all the missiles were pointed directly at her own heart.

Ashley's attitude, despite her remark, was more pragmatic. "Live now, worry later," she had said to Dottie when it began. "I'll be damned if all this is going to make me stop in my tracks."

The first thing Dottie did when she found her new apartment was to call Kate. They had been out of touch over the summer, and Kate, especially, was glad for the break in her routine when she heard her friend's voice on the phone.

"I need your help," Dottie explained.

"What can I do for you?"

"Help me decorate my apartment."

And so, the first evening Dottie was free after she moved into the brownstone on East Seventy-fourth Street, Kate arrived to help.

Negotiating the stairs with a graceful agility not usually associated with a woman who is seven months pregnant, Kate rang the bell.

"Welcome to my new home," greeted Dottie, flinging open the door dramatically.

It had taken Dottie almost six months to locate the exact apartment she wanted, and the time spent had been worth it. It was situated on the parlor floor of an old town house, and the ceilings were almost eighteen feet high, with ornately carved woodwork all around, bearing the burden of years of coats of paint.

On the wall opposite the entrance was a black marble fireplace, and at the end of the room by the street were two large bow windows, framing a tree growing at the edge of the sidewalk.

At one point in time an unknown tenant had knocked out the wall joining the living room with the darker room behind it, creating an open space of almost forty feet. Behind that was the kitchen, the hallway beside it leading to the back of the house where a bedroom and tiny study overlooked a small garden.

"It's just marvelous," exclaimed Kate. "How much is the rent?"

Just as writers always talk money, seasoned New Yorkers discuss the price of apartments without any feeling that they are moving to the edge of poor manners.

"Two seventy-five," answered Dottie. "That's not the problem, though. I know it's a great apartment. And I can afford it. But what I don't know is what to do with it."

"Not much," said Kate.

"Easy for you to say. But, unfortunately, I'm not in the position to hire a decorator. And fixing up a place with taste is hardly my strength. That's where you come in."

"I'll do what I can," said Kate, obviously pleased with the compliment. She had, after all, finished doing the baby's room months before and was delighted with the prospect of something to fill her time. Kate was a person whose mind began to function at full speed at the sight of an empty room. She mentally arranged furniture with the same ease as Dottie unconsciously edited a manuscript when she read it.

By the early part of December, the apartment was finished. Kate, with her own brand of magic, had found somebody to strip the paint off the woodwork, leaving the original wood exposed. The floors were also stripped, stained to a rich dark brown, and varnished to a high gloss. Working carefully within the budget that they had set, she bought a beige sofa on sale, placing it in front of the fireplace with its back to the entrance of the room. Behind it, she put a long narrow hunt table, where magazines and books found a temporary home. It could be used as a buffet, Kate explained, if Dottie had a party.

On either side of the fireplace were two club chairs in rich burned orange, with the color picked up again in the hand-woven throw pillows tossed casually on the sofa.

The rest of the room was sparsely furnished, with a long refectory table and six simple chairs creating the dining area.

The overall impression was one of good taste combined with comfort and casual elegance, an effect that Dottie alone would never have been able to achieve. It was also a room in which she could entertain, secure in the knowledge that the image she projected was the correct one: a young and successful woman on the rise.

Neither Kate nor Dottie acknowledged the fact that the apartment was just a block away from Teddy's. It had taken them both time to become accustomed to passing it without tears springing to their eyes. The gaping hole that Sol's death had left in their lives had still not been completely filled. Kate, especially, wondered secretly if it ever would be.

At the end of November Kate went into labor. Chris was still at his office, but she did not call him. Nor did she call the obstetrician whom Chris had chosen for her. Instead, she sat on the sofa and timed the contractions. They had not yet begun to hurt in an unmanageable way, and she actually took pleasure in the sensation of the beginning of birth. It was a feeling of being fully alive, of participating alertly in an experience for which she was convinced she had been born.

Finally she called Chris, and she was in the delivery room by midnight, her legs straddled in the stirrups and arms strapped down to the sides of the table, a sensation that sent shivers of panic through her. She had already been given injections of Demerol and scopolamine and was quite woozy from the drugs. But she kept mumbling to her doctor, "It's not so bad. Really. Please don't put me under. Want to see. I have to see. Please."

As the baby was passing down the birth canal, the anesthesiologist placed a mask over her face, giving her unwanted whiffs of gas. Her hands struggled from the straps, trying to pull away the mask, but she was helpless.

When she awakened, lying in the recovery room, Chris was with her.

"It's a boy," he said.

"Healthy?"

"Yes."

Tears of gratitude and relief fell in large drops down her cheeks. She did not know until then how fearful she had been that it would be a girl. She was deeply afraid of Chris's disappointment and knew, finally, that she had done well.

They had already decided that a boy would be called Michael Henderson Griffin. She repeated the name softly, then fell back to sleep.

When the nurse first brought Michael to her, Kate was complete. He fitted into her arms so naturally, she thought.

Unbuttoning her bed jacket, she put him to her breast, swollen with milk.

Standing next to her, the nurse asked with surprise, "You're going to breast feed him?"

"Of course," Kate answered, as she moved her nipple over his perfect tiny lips until he opened his mouth and began to suck lustily in another of nature's instinctive miracles.

"It's . . . it's just that we weren't informed," said the nurse. "I have orders here for your injection of Dellademone to dry up the milk."

"Simply remove the orders, that's all," said Kate firmly. She looked down at Michael, nursing contentedly. She was pleased with herself, with the way her usually small breasts were swollen with milk, full and nurturing.

Ashley moved into her new house just before Christmas. It had taken longer than she thought to renovate it.

"But the result is worth it," she said to William, as he stood in the living room with her for the first time.

"Indeed it is," he agreed. Then his voice turned serious. "Ashley? I want to talk to you."

"All right," she said, sitting down on the sofa.

Since he had kissed her that one time, they had continued to see each other. But Will had never again touched her. Now Ashley sensed that he was no longer willing to put up with that.

"I don't know how to say it, Ashley, so I'll just get it out." Will swallowed. "I'm in love with you."

She reached over and took his hand. She had known this was coming. And she did not know what to say, how to refuse him without hurting him beyond the inevitable pain.

"I'm sorry. I really am, Will. I wish I could tell you that I was in love with you. But I'm not."

"This is a lousy way to celebrate your new house. But I don't feel I can go on this way. It's . . . not enough."

"I understand, Will. I really do."

"Do you understand that I can't see you anymore?"

She looked to him, her eyes filled with tears. "I'll miss you. I really will."

She sat alone in her new house after William had gone. Despite Nana's help, since Alexander's death she had moved imperceptibly away from the edge—that position she had always occupied so naturally—and unconsciously resolved to walk a safer path where pain was not so acute, nor grief so terrible.

She understood, of course, that her feelings for Alexander were bound up in a complicated scheme of passion and emotions that had nothing to do with her present reality. It was not so much that a person had died. It was as if a dream had been wrenched from her soul and crushed needlessly under the heel of a stranger's boot.

Since that hideous moment when she had first read of his death in the paper, Ashley had no trouble filling her days. It was the nights that defeated her.

Often she would wake up, sweat saturating her sheets, with visions too terrible to remember haunting her dreams. Always she would see Alexander at the moment of death, scarred instantaneously beyond recognition into an obscenity that had nothing to do with a human being. She did not know how very close these visions were to reality. But the knowledge she did have caused her to retreat into the safety of a loveless world.

During her visit to New York over Christmas, Nana had tried to talk about it.

"You can't understand, Nana," said Ashley sadly.

Her grandmother smiled with the indulgence of one who had lost her innocence long before Ashley, who had lost her dream to an accident, also. "I suspect I understand more than you give me credit for, Ashley. I know, for instance, that there is no safety, ever."

"There has to be, Nana. Otherwise, how would we live?"

"Most of us don't," she said simply, understanding that very few of the young can comprehend how capricious, how utterly illogical, are the visitations of fortune, good or bad.

"And Solly," said Ashley. "He didn't deserve that. Sol . . . of all people."

"Ashley, my dear, you can apply that to most things that happen in this world. Few of us are ever willing to try to shape events. Most of us are content to allow things to happen, like a shallow river washing over rocks simply because they are there."

"Well, I'm here. And yet I don't feel it."

"You will. I told you after Alexander died that you were a person who understood the value of living. You haven't forgotten it. It's just a temporary lapse. If you weren't in love with William, it wasn't because you were incapable of it."

"That's how I feel."

"It was because the two of you simply weren't suited. Give yourself some time."

"I'll try, Nana."

"You'll get there, dear. You've seen the worst already. Soon you'll begin to move forward."

And so Ashley continued living her days. She worked hard at the hospital and filled the remainder of her hours with determined efforts to come all the way back. But, in truth, she skimmed the easy treats off the surface of her life, like a child dipping its chubby finger into the icing of a cake. She hadn't the slightest idea that it would take an even greater personal tragedy to return her to her rightful place at the edge—the place where sunsets are richer and storms more fearsome, where one weeps at the flight of a red-tailed hawk and shakes an angry fist in the face of the stranger who wears the crushing boot. Or, better yet, laughs at him in the acceptance of the knowledge that there is nothing left to lose.

New Year's Day Madelaine Jacot held an open house in her Fifth Avenue apartment. It was lavish in its extravagance and deliberate in its intent: to cull new contacts and favors out of a pride of literary lions.

Dottie arrived early, having been informed that she was to play hostess to the lesser lights that would be gilding the scene, instructions from Madelaine that Dottie found particularly demeaning.

It had been a difficult morning, since New Year's would be forever associated with Sol in her mind. Dottie had recovered from his death, as much as anyone recovers from the death of someone they love. But there were times when the memory of him created such an aching void in her that it was difficult to function normally.

Standing alone looking out over the park, Dottie thought of him, of the times they would run hand in hand through the woods together. She was not aware, at that moment, that there was someone behind her. Finally, she turned around.

"If it isn't the ambitious Miss Langford," said Patrick McAuliffe. "It's been a long time."

"Too long," she said as she turned to him. "How are you?"

"More important, how are you?" he asked. "I heard you did quite well by Jack Barclay at Stafford House."

"Well enough, I suppose. Although I do wish it could have been a little better." She was racked by a guilty conscience over the trade-off deal she had made at Jack's expense.

"I understand they're going to treat it as a really big book," he said, imitating Ed Sullivan. "After mine, of course."

"Of course," she agreed, smiling.

"How is it that you haven't gone out on your own yet?" he asked. "I would think you'd have had enough of living in Madelaine's shadow."

"I may have been in the shadows, but I've certainly learned a lot in the process."

"Enough to form your own agency?" he persisted.

"Why do you ask?"

"Because I'm thinking of changing."

Dottie was shocked at this revelation, knowing that Madelaine had no inkling that one of her star writers was plotting an insurrection. Despite her surprise, it was certainly not beyond her ambition to recognize a propitious moment when she saw it. "Would you be willing to change to an unknown?" she asked carefully.

"Funny you should mention it," he responded with equal care. "I've been thinking of doing just that." He paused. "If the unknown were willing to roll up her sleeves and focus on my needs when necessary." Stopping, his eyes swept the room imperceptibly. "Instead of throwing parties to gain new clients when she doesn't have the time for the existing ones."

"I see," said Dottie, nodding her head. "Theoretically speaking, of course . . . if this mythical person were to go out on her own, how would she know that a writer—one of your stature, just as an example—

would go with her, instead of some more well-known agency?"

"Would a written agreement do?"

New Year's Day Ashley and Nana decided that they would attempt to assault the fortress of John Van Every one more time.

"I'm scared, Nana," Ashley whispered as she rang the doorbell of the home in which she had grown up.

"I'm scared, too, dear," Nana replied evenly, taking Ashley's hand in hers.

Martha Van Every opened the door.

"Mom?" Ashley asked in a weak voice. "Is Daddy home?"

"Yes. He's in the library. But—"

"Mom . . . this is Marguerite Martinez. And we've both come to see him."

"I'm afraid . . ."

"So are we, Mother. But let us come in anyway. Please?"

"All right," she agreed reluctantly.

Sitting in his leather club chair waiting for the New Year's Day football games, John Van Every was just reaching for his cup of coffee when they walked in.

"Daddy?"

Startled, he looked up at his daughter, his face contracting with an oblique displeasure. He had grown grayer and older since Ashley had last seen him, and she was saddened to see the changes in him that had taken place.

"Daddy?" Ashley repeated again. "It's New Year's. And we've come to see you because we don't want to spend another year without you. Both of us."

"Hello, John," Nana said almost in a whisper.

"Mother . . ." he said, acknowledging her presence with a nod of his head.

He stood up and walked over to where they were standing so awkwardly near the door of the library.

Nana spoke in a soft but determined voice. "We need you, John. We truly do. We want to be a family again."

He started to say something, but she held up her hand. "No . . . please. Let me finish. This should never have happened in the first place, John. None of it. Looking back on it, I cannot understand why everything couldn't have been worked out. Between all of us. But I want to tell you that the water has gone dry that's run under the bridge. I haven't betrayed your confidences. Ashley still doesn't understand how all this began. I've always felt that if she were ever to learn what happened between us, it should come from you."

"I thank you for that, Mother." Although his words were excessively formal, his voice belied the pain he felt. He could barely utter the words, and it was quite apparent he was struggling to quell his thunderous emotions.

"I lost my anger years ago, John. What happened then is a part of a past that I don't recognize anymore. What happened, and the consequences, has been worked out satisfactorily for everyone. For all of us," she said significantly. "You're my son, John. And please believe me when I tell you that I love you." Tears were streaming down Nana's cheeks by then, but she made no effort to wipe them away.

John Van Every's face contorted with an internal agony that Ashley had never seen. She was shocked at the power of it, at the raw and desolate torment of his expression. She wanted to reach out and touch him. But she was afraid. It was apparent that he wanted to speak, but words were beyond his power.

Nana continued through her tears, as Ashley watched in awe. "But the end result of all our stubbornness is that your own daughter is paying an abominable price for our mistakes. And I count on you now to recognize the injustice of this. It is not fair to put that burden on her shoulders. It is simply not fair."

Finally, Ashley spoke. "Daddy? Please . . . I need you." She reached out to him, but he recoiled as if she were a threat to his life.

His behavior was bizarre, as if his own malignant passion had eaten away slowly at his core. There was a savagery in his agony, one that had surpassed his ability to withstand its assault. He was a man trapped in the decaying slime of his own rotting hatred, and he no longer knew how to extricate himself. His pain was at once pitiful and loathsome. His voice cracked when he finally spoke. "I . . . I've gone so far down this road that . . . I don't know how to return." Tears pooled in his eyes, as if he wanted more than anything to reach out to his mother and his daughter. But it had been too long, and he did not know how.

"I'll help you, Daddy. We'll all help," Ashley pleaded.

"I . . . don't know," he mumbled, an edge of shame in his voice.

"Please, Daddy. I'm losing the people I love and I can't bear it any longer." Once more Ashley reached out to him. And once more he retreated from her, fearful and desolate, and terribly alone.

With great effort he spoke. "Time. Give me time . . . Ashley . . . Mother. I need that."

"All right, Daddy. I know how painful this is for you, so we'll leave now. But I'll be waiting for your call."

"How soon is dinner?" asked Chris, as he came into the apartment. "I'm starving."

"Not for a while yet," answered Kate. "I spent most of the afternoon trying to get Michael to stop crying long enough to do anything, and I just didn't have a chance to start dinner."

"Christ!" He spoke with an irritation that had begun

to invade his voice frequently of late. "Do let me know when the time comes that my needs will take precedence over Michael's. After all—"

"Chris, please. I'm so tired. Please don't do this. I haven't had a full night's sleep in three months, and I am exhausted beyond any feeling I ever thought I'd have. I took Michael to Dr. Leighton's for a check-up today and he says it's natural, all this crying. Just colic. That perhaps if I weren't so nervous, Michael would calm down. And I'm trying . . . I really am. But I just can't get used to it. He's so little and it looks like he's in pain." By the time she had finished talking, tears were spilling down her cheeks. She simply had no strength to control them, despite the fact that she knew Chris hated scenes like this.

Her weakness was increased by the fact that she was aware Chris had developed a kind of residual jealousy toward Michael, and she simply did not know how to meet both their needs.

"Here," said Chris, reaching out to the baby in her arms. "Give him to me. I'll take care of him while you fix dinner."

That afternoon, while rocking Michael in one arm and holding a book in the other, Kate had finished reading *The Feminine Mystique*. Despite the fact that she was the living symbol of Friedan's thesis, Kate found the book irrelevant. She was so certain she had what she wanted—even though this had been a difficult period for her—that she viewed the book as preposterous and extreme. It was, of course, impossible to allow the idea to enter her carefully structured life. Very simply, it was too threatening to take seriously.

By summer Ashley had spent hours thinking about her father. Every time she saw her mother, she would ask about him. And every time, she received a variation on the same answer.

"I know he's thinking about you, Ashley. But he

seems very confused right now. As if he doesn't know how to walk on a less lonely street. I know he would like to call you, dear," Mrs. Van Every would say with a note of concern and comfort in her voice. "And I think he will. But just not yet. He'll come around. Give him time. Please."

"Do you really think he will?" Ashley would ask.

"Yes. I really do," her mother would answer.

In June, when the *Fanny Hill* obscenity suit was in full swing, Dottie decided to open her own literary agency. It had not been an easy move. Even Dottie, having learned to perform very well when her back was against a wall, had major trepidations about informing Madelaine Jacot of her move.

"You what!" Madelaine hissed, when Dottie told her.

"I want to start my own agency."

"With what, my dear?" her voice was flagrant with contempt. "Twelve novice writers and a ream of paper?"

"With Jack Barclay and Patrick McAuliffe, primarily."

Madelaine's eyes bore a hole straight through her. "Did I hear you say Patrick McAuliffe?"

"That's right." Dottie shuddered inside.

"How dare you . . . how dare you do such a thing. Stealing one of my best clients!"

"I didn't do it, Madelaine. He did." Dottie searched frantically for some solid ground under her doubts.

"You ingrate!" she spat at Dottie. "I take you in, I teach you the business. And now this. You everlasting motherfucking ingrate! How dare you!"

Dottie spoke evenly. "I didn't steal him, Madelaine. He was the one who came to me."

"I'll never believe that, Dorothy Langford. Never."

"It's the truth."

"Just why should I believe you, pray tell. You're the one who sold your own lover down the river."

"At your advice," Dottie countered, regretting one more time what she had done.

"You'll pay for this." Madelaine hurled the words at her from an impossible distance, as if each one carried a separate explosive. She stopped for a moment before she left the room. "And don't you think you won't, Dottie. Because I'll see to it personally."

Chris had begun to stay out later and later after Michael was born. Although it nagged at her from time to time, Kate was often relieved that she did not have to deal with her husband's increasingly negative judgments of her, with his impatience at her inadequacies, his anger at her bewildered tears.

He was away at a medical meeting when Michael became ill. Kate called the pediatrician, who labeled it a virus and gave her the standard instructions about how to treat it. Despite the light diet and aspirin, Kate was up most of the night with him.

At first, it was just vomiting. When that was under control, the diarrhea began. Being a doctor's daughter, she did not react as mothers unfamiliar with illness might, calling the pediatrician in the middle of the night, overcome by panic. She dealt with it in the only way she could: by being there and caring.

She held him for hours, rocking him gently. When he began to cry, she knew that the cramps had begun and that shortly he would have another bout of diarrhea. Holding him on her lap with a towel under him, she would massage his belly, sing to him, and even recite poetry in her efforts to distract him from his pain.

She understood, then, a parent's need to protect a child from all pain, to save him from both physical and emotional threats. She knew that there was nothing she would not do for this child, and that for the remainder of her life she would never waver from that feeling. Then, she would have gladly borne his anguish, wished she could.

By morning he showed no improvement, and Kate took him to the doctor. Knowing Kate's medical background, Dr. Leighton could not quite conceal his displeasure that she, too, when pushed to the wall, behaved just as neurotically as any other frantic mother.

"As you can see, Kate, he's active. If he were really ill, he wouldn't be crawling around like this." He looked at Michael pulling himself up, holding on to his mother's chair. "But I'll give you some Donagel, anyway, just in case the diarrhea continues."

Kate nodded, feeling silly, and thanked him for his time. Then she walked Michael home slowly in his carriage, grateful it was a warm, sunny day.

By six o'clock in the evening Michael was asleep. Kate intended to stay up to check him periodically. But worn out from the lack of sleep and tension from the night before, she fell into a deep and exhausted sleep.

Around midnight she awakened suddenly. Uncertain whether or not it was a baby's cry that she heard, she went into Michael's room. He was awake, just lying there. But he was perfectly silent. He did not even look over to her as he usually did when she walked into the room. He did not move. He lay there, inert, in a pale-brown, watery puddle.

She picked him up in her arms, then took him to the changing table and cleaned him. Still holding him, cooing and making comforting nonsense sounds, she stripped the sheet off the crib and dumped it into the bathtub. Then she called Dr. Leighton.

In a voice trembling with fear, she described what had happened. He advised her to stop behaving in such a nervous manner, that such behavior would only agitate Michael further. He also told her to increase the doses of Donagel, and that she could call him in the morning if there was no improvement.

As soon as Kate hung up, she called William.

"Yes?" he answered sleepily. She was grateful he wasn't at the hospital that night.

"Will? It's me. Kate. And I'm scared."

Quickly alert, he asked. "What is it?"

"Michael. He's sick. I know he is, even though Dr. Leighton says it's just a virus. He's sick, Will, and I don't know what to do."

Understanding that his sister was not given to panic over minor medical problems, he said, "I'll be there as soon as I can." And then he hung up.

Before William arrived, Kate had had time to examine Michael. Picking him up, the first thing she noticed was that he felt lighter. She was unconsciously attuned to his weight, and feeling him now, she thought that this fact was probably why she had called Will, even though she had not recognized it at the time.

Then she took off the light blanket that covered him and stood him on the changing table. His little belly stuck out in a peculiar way. It was distended and hard. His buttocks seemed to have shrunk, and his legs were spindly instead of the chubby ones they had been only the day before. But what seized her with abject terror was the look of his eyes. In the period of just a few hours they seemed to have sunk back into his head, glazed and dull, resting in dark orbs. It occurred to her then that if she had met this child on the street, she would not have recognized him as her own baby.

She was shaking by the time William rang the doorbell.

He took one look at Michael and said, simply, "You're right, Kate. He's sick."

As he spoke, he gently pinched a portion of Michael's skin between his thumb and forefinger, then let go. Rather than spring back into place, the little mound of skin returned very slowly to its former position, as if the elasticity had been drawn from him, leaving him with the flaccid skin of an old, old man.

"How sick?" Kate asked, her eyes wide with fear.

"Very. We need to get him to the hospital."

The day after Dottie told Madelaine about her move, she called Jack on the phone.

"How do you feel like flying to New York and helping me celebrate?" she asked.

"Celebrate what?"

"I'm ready to open the agency."

"Mazel tov, as they say in your language. So where's the champagne?"

"I'm thinking of having a party in two or three weeks. Can you come?"

"Wouldn't miss it. I want to see the look on Madelaine's face."

"That, I'm afraid, you *will* have to miss. I don't think she'd be in the mood for a party."

"Angry, huh?"

"Very."

"Well, we'll have a celebration anyway. Shall I plan on staying at your place?"

"Where else?" she said happily, grateful for the presence of this extraordinary man in her life.

Ashley was playing with Michael Griffin, her godson, when someone walked up behind her. It was Michael's third day in the hospital, and Ashley had told Kate to go home and take a nap. Kate resisted, but Ashley convinced her that no one could tolerate the strain under which she had been without a break. Ashley promised to stay with him until Kate returned.

"Thank you for looking after my nephew," said William picking up Michael's chart, which was hanging on the end of the crib. Scanning it briefly, he said, "He's improving. A few more days and he'll be fine."

Ashley looked up, a fuzzy puppet on her hand. "I just got him to laugh," she said proudly. "The first time since he's been here."

"God knows he needs it," said Will. "I didn't know if he was going to make it. Dehydration's dangerous in such a little fellow." Will leaned over and stroked his cheek. "He lost one sixth of his body weight in two days."

"I know some women who would sell their souls for that to happen," said Ashley, smiling. Then her voice turned soft. "It's good to see you, Will."

"How are you?" he asked, feeling awkward.

"Fair to middling, as my grandmother says. I suppose that means getting by."

"I'm glad."

"And you?" she asked.

"The same. I still think of you."

"Well, I should hope," Ashley said, hoping to inject just the right degree of lightness into her voice.

But William didn't buy it. "You know what I mean, Ashley."

"Yes . . . I know what you mean. And I'm sorry. I'm still the same in that way."

"Sorry to hear it," he said, leaning over and kissing her on the forehead. "Ashley?"

She looked at him expectantly.

"I want you to call me if you ever change your mind." She attempted a weak smile. "And even if you don't change your mind, I'm still your friend."

"Thank you, Will." She was infinitely touched by him and wished she had not closed the doors on that part of herself so tightly. He is a good man, she thought.

Michael Griffin was in the hospital for five days. As soon as William had called him, Chris took a plane home. When he walked into the pediatrics ward, he saw Kate lying in the stainless-steel crib with Michael asleep in her arms. She looked up as he entered, and then began to cry softly.

Understanding that Michael's needs were being taken care of—though belatedly—Chris knelt by the side of the crib and took Kate in his arms.

"Katie . . . Katie . . . I'm sorry I wasn't at home to help you. And . . . I'm sorry I've been so rough on you. Are you all right?"

Fighting a losing battle to keep her tears under control, all she could muster was a weak nod. Until that point she had maintained all her strength and directed it toward Michael. At last, with Chris there, she could allow a little weakness.

When she could finally speak, she said, "I had a fight with Dr. Leighton." She had dreaded telling Chris this, for fear he would become angry at her for confronting one of his colleagues at the hospital.

"He told me," Chris said. "Under the circumstances, I couldn't conjure up much sympathy for him."

Kate nodded, again remembering the scene she had thrown in front of the nurses' station.

"I'm sorry, Kate," Dr. Leighton had said. "I really didn't think it was this serious."

"Sorry?" she asked Dr. Leighton incredulously. "You're *sorry*? Is that all?" The Kate who dreaded confrontations with a fear that flirted with the pathological spoke to him in a low scream. "You should be one hell of a lot more than just sorry. I simply cannot believe this has happened. You treated me like some flighty neurotic mother who didn't possess decent enough judgment even to be believed. And now you tell me it's a milk allergy. From the milk I put in my coffee, no less. But I'm not even sure you were aware that I was nursing him . . ."

"Go ahead," said Dr. Leighton calmly in the standard voice he used to soothe distraught mothers. "Say anything you want. It's good for you. I'll understand."

Appalled at the condescension in his voice, Kate lost all control. "You just presumed I was exaggerating! Just presumed it! How dare you do that? Michael could have been treated at home if you had just done me the simple honor of believing what I told you. But no . . . you thought you knew better than his own mother. You just presumed it. But here he is now, stuck full of needles and suffering needlessly. All because of you. You goddamn sonofabitch."

"Calm down, Kate. He's going to be all right."

"You're goddamn right he's going to be all right. No thanks to you, I might add. I'll have my brother send you the bill. In the meantime, he's going to be all right because I've gotten another doctor for Michael. So you can just go fuck yourself!" With that, she turned and walked down the hall of the hospital back into Michael's room.

"I heard from two different sources that you weren't very gentle with Dr. Leighton," said Chris.

"No. Not at all."

"I'm glad, Katie. You did the right thing."

"I did?" she asked with infinite relief that she was receiving support from her husband.

Three weeks after Kate and Chris brought Michael home from the hospital, they went to Dottie's party. It was catered and expensive. Kate noted with pride that the room worked well for entertaining.

Dottie, of course, was playing hostess. And doing a superb job of it, Ashley thought with pleasure. She wondered how much of it had to do with the fact that Jack was with her. Ashley envied Dottie then: envied the fact that she could love someone, be a part of a man's life. Even if it was mostly long distance, she thought, it was still worth having. She had done it, herself, with Alexander. She would have given anything for him to be standing next to her at that very moment.

"Who is that magnificent woman?" Patrick McAuliffe asked Dottie.

Even though she was with Jack, Dottie felt a surprising twinge of jealousy nag at the back of her unconsciousness.

"Her? That's my friend Ashley Van Every," answered Dottie. "Do you want me to introduce you?"

"No. I'll take care of it," he said as he started to make his way across the room. "Thanks a lot, Dot."

He approached her from behind. "Ashley Van Every?" he said in a familiar voice.

Expecting to see someone she knew, Ashley turned to look into the laughing eyes of a stranger.

"Yes?" she said quizzically.

"I'm leaving for Dublin tomorrow. But when I return, we'll get together."

"Oh?" she asked, her intrigue outweighing her slight scorn at his approach. "How long will you be in Ireland?"

"About a year, I think. May I get you a drink?"

"I never accept drinks from strangers," she said.

"But I'm not," he said. "A stranger, I mean. My name is Patrick McAuliffe and I think I've always known you."

"Indeed," she said, feeling the pull of his attraction. Finally, she thought. And he's going away already. What the hell. I probably won't care by the end of the evening anyway.

"Indeed," he answered.

From Dottie's point of view it was a successful party also. Even Adam Farling stopped by, in what was obviously a public vote of confidence for this unknown agent. Nobody in the literary part of the room missed it.

When she thanked him for coming, Adam leaned over and kissed her on the cheek. "I owed you one," he said with a conspiratorial smile. "Now we can start even."

Soon after Patrick brought Ashley a glass of wine, they were separated by the vagaries of cocktail party conversation and the greetings of old friends. Ashley was amazed at the distress she felt when he was not with her. And it became acute when he did not return to her at the first opportunity.

She began to wonder if she had imagined their initial encounter, if he had intended nothing more than to be polite.

Before midnight, he came to her again. "I have to go now," he said. "My plane leaves very early and I have a long way to go before my packing is finished."

"Oh," she said, the disappointment there for him to read.

"I'll see you when I come back." He spoke directly, without artifice. "Until then," he said, taking her hand and holding it. She moved totally into the feel of him, memorizing his touch. Leaning toward her, he whispered, "I'll miss you." Then he brushed his lips against hers in a kiss so gossamer-light she could not be certain afterward that it had actually happened.

"Strange how you can miss something you never had," Ashley said later to Kate.

"Not so strange at all," Kate responded.

While Dottie worked fiendishly to establish her business, Kate spent the summer playing wife and mother. With more and more frequency Kate felt her life closing in on her. There was a claustrophobic quality to her existence. And yet, when she would ask herself what the cause of this debilitating malaise could be, she could not come up with an answer.

At first, she looked within herself for a clue, but she found nothing except emptiness. When she examined her relationship with Chris, she could see many things that might be changed on a superficial level. She knew that her sex drive had diminished considerably since Michael's birth. But she also understood that it had to do with exhaustion, with too many chores that required major expenditures of energy, yet did not pay her back with any sense of satisfaction.

She had a futile sense that—no matter what she did—there would never be an end to it, a time when she could look back and say to herself that this was a job well done. Cleaning, child care, cooking, entertaining—all these things were done, only to be repeated soon afterward. There was never a time in her life when anything was finished. Like Sisyphus, she merely struggled through her days, neither looking forward to the beginning nor the end.

In most things she did there was a sense of quiet despair, of a sluggishness of movement, as if she wandered through her days walking in water up to her neck. There was no hope for relief nor time to seek it. There was only a present filled with a listless bewilderment. And she stood by helplessly and watched as her horizons narrowed and her life took on the inexorable color of anxiety and dread.

Although they went away for the month of August to a beach house on Long Island Sound, the change of scene was not enough to pull her out of what she could only describe as a vague discontent.

"What is it?" asked Chris as they sat on their porch overlooking the water, drinking a cocktail before dinner.

"I don't know," Kate answered honestly. "I wish I did."

"Jesus!" said Chris with a vehemence that surprised them both. "You sound like every other woman of child-bearing age that comes into my office. They don't know, they say. Something's just wrong. More, they say. They want more. But they don't know of what. And, for the life of me, I can't figure it out."

"You mean I'm not the only one?" Kate asked naively, yet with a sense of relief.

"Hardly," he replied. "It's as if they bring the same

taped message with them. It's an epidemic. And what boggles my mind is that these women have everything. My practice is hardly filled with deprived females. And yet they act as if they've been forced to go on welfare. Sleeping pills. Or tranquilizers. That's what they want. Anything to get them through another day or night. And when I ask them what the problem is, they don't know. They just say they're unhappy."

Kate got up to fix herself another drink, obliquely threatened by the conversation, but unwilling to let go.

When she returned, she said, very simply, "I'm one of those women, too. And I don't know what's wrong."

"For God's sake, Kate," exclaimed Chris, throwing his hands up in the air in a gesture of total exasperation. "You have a healthy child, you have a maid once a week and a sitter once a week. You live in a nice apartment and you have a husband who makes a good living. I'm beginning to agree with Freud: What is it that women want?" He spoke with such contempt that Kate thought later she would have preferred it if he had slapped her. The effect would have been shorter-lived. As it was, she carried his disdain with her as if it had been stuck to her guilt with sticky anxiety and a quiet sense of dread.

"Mother?" asked Ashley as she reached for the sugar bowl. They had just spent a pleasant day shopping together for some fall clothes and were having a cup of tea before Martha Van Every returned home. "Does Daddy know that we see each other?"

"He may suspect. But I don't care, just as long as he has no proof."

"What do you think he'd do?"

"Get angrier than I'd like to think about."

It had been several months since Ashley had asked about her father. She knew that it was a subject of unbearable sadness to her mother and did not like to cause her the pain that the question evoked. Instead, she had waited patiently for his call that never came.

"Do you really think he'll call me?" asked Ashley.

Mrs. Van Every looked straight at Ashley, not wanting to avoid her eyes. "I think he wants to call you, dear. But I am also beginning to suspect that he doesn't know how. He did mention Thanksgiving the other day. That it would be nice to have an old-fashioned family dinner. I know it's a long way off. But I think he'll come around by then. He's just not . . . been himself lately."

"What do you mean?"

"I don't really know," she answered speculatively. "He's more agitated, more restless, than he's ever been . . ."

Ashley's response was more animated. "Oh, wouldn't it be lovely to have Thanksgiving together. I'd like that so much. Do you think I could call him and tell him that?"

Her mother thought a moment. "No. Wait a little while. Let's see if he won't make the first move now. I think that's what has to happen."

Kate started going to the park on sunny days, taking Michael in his carriage. Even when the weather was not very good, she would bundle him up and take him out for an hour. The camaraderie that was formed—mothers on one bench, maids on another—would become a part of the texture of her life. The women talked, at first hesitantly. But in difficult times, they created a sort of unspoken support system.

"I think," said Kate to a friend named Anita one day, "that if I have to look at that child for another five minutes I just might flush him down the toilet."

"So what else is new?" asked Anita.

Michael was very mobile by now, crawling over the playground with amazing ability to find the thing on the ground that should not go in his mouth, but inevitably would.

As Kate watched him, she said, "I think if I have to take one more cigarette butt out of his mouth or kiss one more boo-boo, I just might do it."

"Tell you what," said Anita. "Give him to me. I'll take him home with us for lunch. You go to the movies or something. Or just go home and take a nap. Come pick him up around four. Okay?"

"Anita?" Kate said, tears forming in her eyes. Her hands were shaking. "I don't know what it is. I don't understand it. But thank you."

"I don't know what it is either. But you're welcome."

"You, too?"

"Me, too." Anita nodded.

It was just such a day as that in November when Kate was talking to Anita about Thanksgiving dinner. She was particularly glad she had called and invited Ashley, since she had no plans.

It was in the middle of exchanging stuffing recipes and watching their children that they first heard it.

"Kennedy's been shot." The words came from a dream. They couldn't be real.

"What?" asked a woman standing a few feet away.

"What was that?" asked Kate as she held out her arms for Michael, so happily secure in the knowledge that his mother would catch him.

"Kennedy's been shot. He's dead."

Kate flashed back to the first time she had really developed a liking for Kennedy. It was when he went to Germany in June and had made the "*Ich bin ein Berliner*" speech. In contrast to the rest of her family—including Chris—whose conservative views made political hash out of the entire Kennedy clan, Kate adored him. When she heard he was dead, she had nothing to say. Finally, moving out of the initial shock, she looked around her.

Some women were crying openly. Others just sat there with stunned expressions pouring over their faces. She even heard one woman say, "He deserved it, the creep." Kate knew she would never speak to that woman again.

The ordinariness of the day took on new meaning as snatches of radio reports began to filter through the air. It was a flash in the face of time, that day, burning an indelible image forever onto the surface of Kate's life.

She sat closer to Anita in their mutual effort to protect themselves from the outrage that had just assaulted their collective senses. Silent tears streamed down Kate's face, as she hugged Michael closer to her.

Those silent tears were still very much in evidence when spring came. Only the reason for them had changed. Kate was pregnant again and frightened that she would not be able to cope with two small children.

Sometimes the tears were brought on by something real. At other times it was the most insignificant incident that caused her to cry. But she felt herself inexorably losing what little control she had left over her life—the life that she had waited all her years to begin living.

Kate didn't really drink more frequently. It was just that when she did drink, she consumed more. This was not aided at all by Chris's growing disdain for her floundering attempts to discover what nameless tormentors were assaulting her senses.

"What do you want from me?" he asked in an irritated tone of voice one evening in April. "I hear it all day long. I don't know what to do with those women. And, God knows, I don't know what to do with you."

"I know what you can do with me," Kate answered in a despondent voice. "You can help me."

"Help with what?"

"I don't know."

"I have the strangest feeling, Kate, that we've had this conversation before. The whole family seems to be suffering from this strange malady of yours." He paused significantly. "Not to mention our sex life."

"I know," she said, cringing with guilt about her lack of interest in sex. "I don't know what's the matter. I just don't feel . . . any desire. I'm neuter."

"Well, if that's the case, I'm sure I can find someone who isn't."

Even for an obstetrician, who is frequently on call at night and other odd hours, Chris had been gone from home an unusual number of times lately. He had a perfect excuse, of course. But Kate had sensed a change in him. And his last remark washed over her, not as a threat, but as a confession of a fait accompli.

Chris went to bed early, pleading exhaustion. Kate drank several cognacs as she thought of him in the arms of another woman. Her head spun with forbidding images and unspoken threats.

Got to stop thinking about it, she thought. And I've got to stop drinking so much of this, too. Or I'll pickle myself and stay young forever. She giggled at the thought. But I don't feel pickled. I feel like I've been vacuum-packed and placed on the wrong shelf of life. I love Chris. I love Michael. But there are times when I'm so bored that a nap is the high point of my day. And now a new baby. Whom I already love. So why do I feel like I'm going mad? Because I've been spoiled and it's all too much for me? Right. I have been spoiled. Given everything. Except dear, dear Solly. I had to fight for him. So I didn't get him. Too much a coward to do it.

She could feel, at that very moment, Sol's hand touching her face and the infinite comfort that simple gesture brought with it.

But that's all over now, she thought, and I'm living the good life. I got exactly what I wanted . . . or thought I wanted. I simply eliminated the options that caused problems. Like archaeology. And now, while I live the good life, the world will pass me by. Somewhere along the way I dropped out. Or dropped in. Don't really know which. I dropped out because I was afraid to finish the race. What race? What's the prize? But I chose it and I'm whining now. Whining. Hate whiners. So does Chris. That's the way the cookie crumbles. So pick up the pieces and move on. Get on with it. What pieces? Of me? Of my marriage? Of the other woman? God. Sounds like a soap opera. A very drunk soap opera, I might add. So tell the audience. Which will it be? The whiner or the other woman. The latter, of course. I'd choose her, too. Got to find something to do. Something to keep me sane. Something—

The telephone rang. Midnight calls were not unusual in her home, and so Kate waited for Chris to answer it. Shortly after it stopped ringing, Chris walked out into the living room.

"It's for you, Kate," he said, looking very serious.

"Who is it?" she asked, trying not to slur her words as she sobered to the unusual situation.

"Marguerite Martinez. Long distance. She says it's urgent."

Kate walked down the hall to the bedroom, trying to pull herself together, the adrenaline rushing through her veins to mix with the alcohol.

"Hello, Nana?" she said, her hand shaking slightly as she held the receiver to her ear.

"Kate, my dear. I'm so sorry to bother you. But it's Ashley. She needs you."

# CHAPTER 9

Kate picked Dottie up in a taxi. It was well past one in the morning when they arrived at Ashley's house on St. Luke's Place. Knocking gently on the door, they waited in silence for her to answer.

"Oh," Ashley said, smiling automatically when she saw her friends. "You're here." There was absolutely no expression on Ashley's face when she spoke. It was as if the life had been sucked from her, leaving a beautiful but placid robot in her place. "Come in," she invited them, as she turned and walked into the living room, taking her place on the corner of the sofa and curling into a ball. Her arms clutching her knees, she did not utter another word. Her eyes were dry, her body was perfectly still.

Not knowing what to say, Kate sat down and put her arms around Ashley. Only then did she make a true and honest noise. She cried out. Not to her friends. But to an unknown fate that moved in a fickle dance around the fires of her own life, unpredictable in the direction of its obscene pointing finger, unreliable in its mercy. Her voice, a muted wail that echoed off the jagged edges of the night, filled the room with its sorrow, never once forming a sound that was truly a word, yet conveying in its message the universal language of all those who mourn.

The only words Ashley could finally utter were: "He called me this afternoon, he finally called me." It only moved her further into the depths of her own sorrow, for her father had invited her to dinner the following night. Then he took his wife for a drive, and both of Ashley's parents were killed in a bizarre automobile accident on the West Side Highway.

Nana had told Kate on the phone that he had also called her. But that he sounded disoriented and confused, as if vengeance had finally eaten into the heart of him.

Then Martha Van Every had talked to Nana, relating to her the fact that her husband was "not himself," her New England understatement for blatantly unstable behavior. He was insisting upon taking her up to the Cloisters for a drive.

That was all Nana knew. But she was afraid that perhaps it was not an accident at all, a suspicion she never related to Ashley. She was wise enough to understand that hatred had carried her son to desolate and malevolent countries where death had become a blessing, because the alternative of living within these tormented boundaries was too unspeakable to bear.

The following afternoon Nana arrived. She was now the only relative left to Ashley besides a dried-up uncle, her mother's brother, who was a second-rate investment banker. "The will of God works in strange ways," were the words of comfort he offered Ashley when he arrived at her parents' home to help with the funeral arrangements.

"Yes, Uncle Jackson," Ashley responded dutifully as she kissed him automatically on the cheek. She felt absolutely no kinship with this man whose idea of a gift, every birthday and Christmas, was a twenty-five dollar savings bond to be tucked away for some unknown future. Joy was an alien concept to him.

Dottie canceled all her appointments for the next few days and Kate arranged for her mother to look after Michael. Thus, together, the three of them helped Ashley through the numbness of her mourning.

A few days after the funeral Ashley asked Nana why she did not appear as upset as she was.

"I grieve for the sorrow you feel, Ashley. But I buried your father a long time ago. I can't do it twice in one lifetime."

"Tell me about it, Nana."

"This isn't the time. Not now. I do want you to know, though, that I never, for one moment, stopped loving him."

"I always assumed that, Nana."

Nana smiled and kissed Ashley on the forehead. "Why don't you plan to come to New Mexico this summer. You can spend the next two months clearing things up here. And then you can come out to me in June. It's beautiful then."

"I'd like that."

On the flight to Albuquerque Ashley experienced a great sense of relief to be leaving New York. For the first time, the noise, the hassle, the dirt had begun to annoy her. Perhaps, she thought, it was because her senses, scraped raw from grief, were more vulnerable.

Because of her need to escape her immediate past, Ashley quit her job at the hospital. She did not know what her future would bring. But she was certain that it would not include a job in New York. She wanted to experience a new freedom: one which, despite money and mobility, she had never before known.

On the flight west she was fascinated to watch the flat plains below her—a patchwork civilized by man—stretch to meet the untamed mountains. They looked like rich brown velvet quilts draped in sensuous mounds between twisting silver braids of meandering streams.

The first thing that struck Ashley when she got off the plane was the quality of light that surrounded her. It was white and clear. But the feeling was pure gold, a muted bronze tint reflecting the colors of earth and sun. It bathed Nana's smiling face in a kind of gentle austere beauty that she had never before seen.

After a drive of over an hour this feeling was further confirmed when she saw the house where Nana lived, the house in which her father was born. It was a two-hundred-year-old adobe located at the far end of a wild canyon that had been homesteaded by Nana's father, Hans Van Every, in 1883. A Dutch immigrant, he had come to America seeking a newer and more spacious freedom. And he found it in this strange and enchanted land.

Originally just one large room, the house had been added to over the years, as needs dictated. Ashley had never seen anything like it. The living room was her favorite, welcoming and warm to a stranger come home. The ceiling was constructed of huge timbers, *vigas*, stripped of their bark. Between each *viga* were smaller branches, *latigas*, arranged in a herringbone pattern. The walls, of earth-colored adobe, were covered with baskets and blankets and books. The classic corner fireplace cast the perfect combination of flickering light, warmth, and the fragrant aroma of piñon wood.

Scattered on the floor, made of terra-cotta bricks, were Navaho rugs of muted earth colors of natural dyes. Woven with intricate skill and design, many of them resembled the Oriental rugs with which Ashley had grown up.

The furniture was a strong combination of Spanish and Mexican, all old, worn over the years to a rich deep patina. It was a pleasantly cluttered room made for living and loving. And Ashley was astonished at its beauty, and the immediate comfort she derived from it.

From her own room Ashley had a commanding view of the land that her great-grandfather had homesteaded. There was a spring near the house, rare in this frequently parched land, fed from the snows of the mountains beyond. The house, strategically set on a high point, was surrounded by a lush garden. Farther away jagged red and yellow hills changed to the gentler green of the Sangre de Cristo Mountains.

"It's magical, Nana," said Ashley in an almost reverent tone. "For some reason, judging from your photographs, I expected your house to be modern. Clean lines and all that."

Nana laughed. "I suppose the color and the clutter is a direct reaction to all that."

"Why don't you use color in your work?"

Nana thought for a minute. "I think it's because I have always felt it a challenge to take a photograph of light on the side of a hill and convey to the viewer that it is clearly golden, when, in obvious fact, it is gray-white. It's like Modigliani. Some of his women are beautiful. Extraordinarily beautiful. You know they are, despite the fact that their features are indistinct . . . or often not even all there. You can create with absence as well as presence. It's purely a matter of how you choose to say it. And I have always preferred the subtlety, the minute gradations of tone, that only black and white can express."

"Well, you certainly compensate for it here," said Ashley with pleasure and satisfaction.

After eating a dinner of lamb chops, *chiles rellenos*, and *sopaipillas* that Nana prepared easily, they settled themselves in the living room with their coffee.

"Now, Nana, tell me," said Ashley. "It's time." Taking a sip of her strong black coffee, she continued her statement. "Tell me about everything. Tell me about Daddy and what happened. I want to know it all."

In a rare and gentle accounting, Nana told Ashley how she had fallen in love with Juan Martinez when she was seventeen years old. "Which is, as you have probably suspected, why you look the way you do. He was half Mexican and half Indian. And, I might add," she said with a smile warming her memory, "he was very beautiful, indeed."

Nana went on to explain how, in those days of 1917, a Spaniard might have been marginally acceptable. But to marry a man who was Mexican was anathema.

Nana's father, of course, objected bitterly to her union with a man of such lowly origins. Despite his pleas against the marriage, Nana's will was a strong one. She married the man, this Juan Martinez, paying a high price for her early-twentieth-century indiscretion. As one Santa Fe matron had said when she heard about the wedding: "Marrying a Mexican just isn't done."

Juan moved into the house at the end of the canyon with Nana and her father. Nana's mother had been long dead of diphtheria, and her father would often exclaim how fortunate she was to have been spared this humiliation that their only daughter had brought upon the family. But slowly, grudgingly, he came to respect this man that Nana married. Even came to like him.

Not too long after his final and loving acceptance into the Van Every family, Juan Martinez was killed by a horse gone mad after eating locoweed.

"But not before I became pregnant," said Nana with satisfaction. "At least I was carrying his child. Your father. And I named him Juan."

"Juan? That was Daddy's name?"

"Yes. Juan Martinez."

Nana explained how Juan had grown up, plagued by his Mexican blood. He was a social outcast. "It never bothered me," said Nana. "I knew that came with the territory of marrying Juan. But your father, Ashley . . . your father couldn't bear it. Even as a child, it made him bitter. The irony was, of course, that the genetic dice had rolled in his favor. He looked Dutch. So rather than move beyond the social handicap, it still makes me sad to tell you, he ran from it. And when he was fourteen years old, he asked to be sent east to boarding school. It was a mistake for me to do it, the way I see it now. But then I thought I was doing the right thing. By that time I had gained a certain reputation in photography, and between the money from that and the income my father left me, I was able to do it." Nana stopped for a minute, making no effort to hide the tears in her eyes. "I can't help but think that if he had ever known his father, he could have found a way not to be ashamed. You must understand, my dear, that the Mexicans in those days—even now, to a certain extent—were regarded rather like the blacks in the old South." Shaking her head, she said sadly, "It wasn't the treachery that bothered me, really. It was his abject lack of pride."

"And I never knew," said Ashley.

"Of course you didn't. That was his way. He thought he could divide his life, and that his past would bear no significance for his future. So, when he moved east, he changed his name to that of his grandfather's, and anglicized the Juan to John. The transition was complete."

"Except for me," said Ashley. "It must have been difficult for him to look at me." Pain spread over her face in the realization that her very countenance was a constant source of ugly remembrance to her father.

"Indeed, it must have been difficult for him. But worse for you, Ashley. And there is nothing I can say to soften that hurt."

"Didn't he ever come to terms with it?" asked Ashley.

"Once I thought he might. He came home for the summer before he went to college. And he fell in love—in an astounding kind of irony, I might add—with a lovely Navaho girl. But he left her," said Nana, shaking her head. "He left her in shame, I expect. And he went to college and never came home again."

"But that wasn't enough reason never to see you again," objected Ashley.

"There are some things that I am still not at liberty to explain, Ashley. Because of promises I made a long time ago. Please believe me when I tell you that there was reason enough. At least, I thought so at the time." Nana looked straight at her granddaughter. "Believe me, Ashley. It was your father's decision. And nothing I could say or do could make him change his mind."

Seeing Ashley then, her exotic eyes absorbing all that was being thrust at her, Nana felt the unconcealed pride of her own blood. This person, alone, had made all her anguish bearable. She knew that Ashley would never turn her back on her heritage, and was grateful that she carried the compelling, dark good looks of her beloved Juan. She understood instinctively the necessity of never cowering to the judgments of little minds, a trait that she had developed over the years with a private and painful personal courage.

After Juan died, Nana never remarried; never even considered it. She had lovers, of course. She was much too alive to deny herself that. Shortly after her son started going to grammar school she became a photographer's assistant in Santa Fe. Although she did not need the money while her father was alive, Nana understood the necessity—even in those days—of having something of her own.

She began her career by taking pictures of visiting actors, lecturers, and entertainers who would come through Santa Fe on tour. That was how she learned her craft. The change from craft to art came gradually, as her vision and her imagination moved on to new subjects. And she slowly built a reputation for the extraordinary photographs that she took, ranking in the field with Stieglitz and Adams.

"Didn't you ever try to mend the break between the

two of you?" Ashley asked wistfully, as if her question could change the course of their personal history.

"When I heard you had been born, I wrote your father and asked if we couldn't put the past away. But his answer was to start sending me those checks. Twice a year they arrived. Like clockwork. But he never came with them."

"I wish he had," said Ashley in a faraway voice.

"So do I, my dear. I wish it with all my heart."

Ashley's voice choked with tears she had carried with her from the moment she learned of her parents' death. "I wish he had," she confessed, "because I cannot stand the pain I've been left to live with, Nana. I can't stand it anymore." She moved to the comfort of her grandmother's arms before she continued. "Burying them was bad enough. But to be left with this guilt, Nana. It's tearing me apart. I can't stop myself from thinking that if I had only gone straight to Daddy when he called me, I might have been able to . . . touch him. He might not have gone for a drive . . . I should have tried harder."

"I tell you the truth, Ashley," said Nana as she stroked Ashley's hair back from her face, "when I say that there is nothing either one of us could have done."

"But I came so close," Ashley wailed.

"In a way, my dear, you never did stop touching him. And I think he knew that. Or his agony would not have been so complete." Nana was not at all certain that she was telling the truth, but she spoke her words with conviction.

"How long will it take for me to stop feeling this way?" Ashley's voice was that of a lost child's, forlorn and hopelessly bewildered.

"I can't answer that."

"I'm so afraid, Nana. I'm so afraid that I never will."

* * *

Kate juggled the telephone receiver in her hand as she balanced Michael in the classic mother's stance: one arm around him as she held him on her hip, which was thrust out to form a small seat for his chubby legs to wrap around.

"Hello?"

"Kate? It's Dottie. How are you?"

"Fat . . ." she said, looking at her swollen belly.

"Are you so fat that you couldn't enjoy a decadent lunch with me Friday?" asked Dottie.

"Never."

"How about Laurent?"

"Sounds good, but too expensive."

"Don't worry. This one's on me."

"Just as well. I don't think I could justify spending that kind of money to Chris. What's the occasion?"

"My private celebration. The first anniversary of my own agency."

"That's a good enough reason to put on a couple of pounds. Congratulations."

"Gotta go. Long distance on the other line. One o'clock, okay?"

"Fine. See you then."

In the year since Dottie had been on her own, she had become something of a phenomenon in the business. Jack Barclay's book, *King's X,* had hit the best-seller list from the moment it was published to rave reviews. Not only was Dottie grateful for herself—because her commission alone insured that she could stay in business without the stress of underfinancing that plagues so many new agencies—but she was grateful for Jack. There was also the expiation of the secret guilt she harbored in the back of her mind, where her conscience made an occasional stab at her when she let down her guard. She had sold him short for the sake of another writer, but he was going to make far more in royalties than the money she'd shorted him on.

It also allowed Jack the freedom to come to New

York whenever he wished. He enjoyed flying in on the spur of the moment, seeing a play or having a sumptuous dinner with Adam Farling. He liked the frills that fame brought with it. As a matter of fact, he seemed to enjoy them too much, which bothered Dottie.

"What is this piece of nonsense I read about you in *The Times*?" she asked him one evening at dinner.

"You mean a writer's vision versus his private reality?" he said with an impish smile on his face.

Dottie nodded, rolling her eyes heavenward.

"What's the matter? You didn't like it? You're not jealous, are you, about me being called one of the most desirable additions to a dinner party in the constantly changing world of bachelor roulette?"

"Of course I'm jealous," she answered with a tease in her voice, yet revealing a more serious concern underneath. "I'm also your agent and want to know what you're working on these days."

"Ah, Dottie," he said with mock severity, "you may be my agent. But you're not my mother. And don't you forget it." He paused one beat. "I disapprove of incest."

Dottie put her hand on his. "Are you working, Jack?" This time she was serious.

"You know better than anyone, Dottie my love, that I never need to work again. I have written a classic for our times. And that's a quote. A mad vision of war. An even madder vision of peace."

"You didn't answer my question, Jack. What are you working on?"

"Getting drunk," he answered. But the joke fell flat.

"It would appear to me that it's not the mad vision of peace you're working on. But a private madness that has to do with the fact that you're not a man who can remain idle indefinitely. When writers do that, they run the risk of their talent beginning to fester."

Jack's face turned serious, then transformed into the

expression of a man in pain. "I know. And I don't know what to do. I'm scared, Dot. I keep writing and nothing happens. I just put the pages away and forget them. They're no good, Dottie. No good at all."

"Why are you scared?" she asked, clearly worried by the amount of liquor that he had consumed that evening.

"Writer's block? Too much fame? Riches? Wrong. None of the above."

Dottie waited. She knew he was teetering on the edge of being drunk. She also knew that he was on the verge of naming his demon, something that did not come easily to Jack Barclay. He was a man who made things happen, who created and shaped events to his liking. He was not a man who looked into his own motivations, because he was fearful of what he might discover.

"What I'm really afraid of, Dot," he said, lowering his voice, "is that I'm thirty-five years old and the best is over. I've done what I set out to do. And it's downhill from here on out."

"Why?"

Jack took a deep breath and exhaled slowly. This gesture, for him, was something akin to crying. "Because everything I write from now on, every goddamn word I put on the page, will be compared to *King's X*. I know. I've seen it happen to other writers. They go slowly crazy from it. Because they simply can't create another masterpiece. Being compared to other writers is bad enough. Being compared to yourself is downright destructive. It's insidious. It spawns monsters. And I don't know how to avoid it."

"You're better than that, Jack. It's just another kind of risk. And, God knows, you've never been afraid of that."

"How the hell would you know, Dottie!" His vehemence frightened her. "How the hell would you know? You're going to be twenty-seven years old and—"

"And I'm already a smashing success, too," she finished for him. "So I just might understand a little of what you're talking about. I don't mean to compare my talent with yours, mind you. I know the difference. But I still just might be able to understand what you're talking about."

"And speaking of your success, my hotshot agent," said Jack, slurring his words. He was clearly drunk now. "I heard a quote the other day, attributed to one Madelaine Jacot. This person said that you would make it to the top of the heap because there was not anyone you wouldn't step on, or sell out, to get there." He paused, looking at her with puzzled eyes. "What did they mean by that, do you suppose?"

Dottie wanted to retch, she was so frightened. Oh God, she thought, what if he finds out? I love him so much. I couldn't bear it if he found out what I did to him.

She reached over and took a sip of her wine, mentally calling on her voice to behave. "I suppose it means," she said with a slight smile, "that they are jealous."

"Well, good luck to them," replied Jack. "Good luck." He raised his glass to her, then leaned over and whispered conspiratorily, "Hey. Let's go back to your place. I happen to have something new. Even better than that Mexican stuff we've been smoking. It's starting to come in from Vietnam."

"All right," said Dottie, immensely relieved he did not pursue the other subject. "What is it?"

"The spoils of war," he said with a note of triumph tinged with bitterness in his voice.

When Kate met Dottie for lunch two days later, she brought with her a letter that had just arrived from Ashley.

Dear Dottie and Kate:

Lots of news. I'll save most of it till we see each other again. But, herewith, the highlights:

The mystery of my past is finally unraveled. My grandfather—Nana's husband—was half Mexican and half Indian. For the first time in my life, I look in the mirror and understand what I see. I also understand why I never received the approval from my father that I always wanted so much. This was the blood he hated. I cannot tell you how desolate this makes me feel. The knowledge, of course, helps. But the pain that comes with it is something I haven't yet learned to accept.

The irony, of course, is that I wonder if it ever occurred to him how much pleasure this single fact of personal history would have brought to me. Not only has it explained something that has puzzled me for my entire life; it has rooted me in a place. I feel as if I have always been waiting to come home here. The land, the people, the feel. I have experienced this incredible sense of relief since I arrived.

This does not negate my feeling for New York. Rather enhances it, I think. I suppose it would make some people schizy, having two homes, two allegiances. I thoroughly enjoy it.

Obviously, Nana has been an extraordinary guide through all this. Very patient. She tells me stories of her past, of my past. Giving me a perspective. And yet . . .

I remember, Kate, when Sol died and you told me how guilty you were feeling. I told you then that you had to get on with the business of living. I know now it isn't that simple. When Alexander died, there was no guilt attached to it. Just unbearable anguish. And I didn't get on with the business of living for a long time. But this time there is a part of me that lives in a kind of tepid emotional limbo. Thank God it's only a part of me. But I fear it's enough to do permanent damage.

Nevertheless, good things are happening, too. And there is enough of me left to enjoy it. A week ago a trailer pulled up the canyon and unloaded an incredibly beautiful Arabian stallion. Black, with two white socks and a star. And fast. All my life I have ridden on Central Park trails and cultivated country lanes. And now this. Nana has had to teach me how to ride western saddle. No posting. No fancy stuff. It demands that you become more a part of the horse, a part of his movements, rather than cultivating a comfortable counterpoint to them. Of course, this kind of riding is entirely different. Each to its own place, I suppose.

Nana has an Appaloosa. Sometimes the two of us are up before sunrise (can you believe it?) and out riding across the desert. I constantly marvel at the strength and purpose she has. We ride for miles and miles.

Often I go alone. Just me, the horse, and the wind. Nothing to stop me. And the mountain trails are magnificent. Nana says that before the summer is over, she'll take me to a special place she knows. Where she used to go with my grandfather. How's that for exotic? She never went back after he was killed. But she wants to show it to me. That touches me in unimaginable ways.

I plan to stay here through the summer and return to New York after the heat that leaves all you peons wilted has disappeared from the city. Return for Indian summer. Appropriate. After that, my plans are open. I don't know what I'll be doing. And for the first time I don't really care.

Nana sends her love and says that whenever I

can arrange it, there's room for all of us here for a grand reunion. Wouldn't that be great? Think about it.

I send my special love to you both. I do miss you.

Love, Ashley

P.S. I named my horse Troika. A.

Dottie folded the letter and placed it back into the envelope. "Ashley sounds better," she said, the relief apparent in her voice.

"Certainly an improvement over a few months ago," agreed Kate. "I was really worried about her."

"Me, too. She sank so far down that I didn't know if she could crawl out again."

"I've always trusted Ashley to be able to do that," said Kate with confidence.

"And speaking of Ashley," said Dottie, picking up her glass of wine. "I think we should be toasting to absent friends."

"While we're toasting," Kate said, "I want to ask you something special."

"And what might that be?"

"Chris and I want you to be godmother for this child here," said Kate, patting her belly.

Tears welled in Dottie's eyes. "It's probably the closest I'll ever come to being a parent," she said, the recollection of her abortion swimming in the murky pain of her memory. "It would be my privilege, Kate. You know it would."

Kate did not mention how hard she had to fight for this. Chris did not consider a Jewess an appropriate godmother for his child. But in one of her rare moments of assertiveness Kate had won. And seeing Dottie now, she knew that the fight had been worth it.

They spent a very pleasant lunch talking about the past and what was happening in the literary world.

They did not talk about what was happening to Kate. Dottie noticed that, by the time the meal was over, Kate was drunk.

In August Nana took Ashley on a pack trip to the hidden valley she had known so many years before with Juan. Protected by the Pecos Wilderness, Nana knew without asking that it would still be the same. Those fortunate people who would discover it could not help but leave it in the same condition in which they found it.

They reached their destination in the late afternoon of the second day. Leading their packhorse behind them, Nana and Ashley made their way along a rocky narrow path into the last clearing at the end of the canyon. Sheer stone walls rose steeply in a natural cathedral on either side of them. Just when it appeared that the trail would come to an end and it would be impossible even to turn around, a clearing opened up to reveal a waterfall cascading over the sides of a huge boulder, hollowing a deep basin out of the stone below.

The pool was clear and cold, harboring trout in the purity of its waters for their supper and music for their sleep. Surrounded by the lush growth that naturally graces such a location, the tiny valley was, indeed, an earthly paradise. It was the last refuge of a soul that had suffered too much, dazzling in its beauty, profound in its comfort.

Choosing a soft grassy area on which to make their campsite by the side of the waterfall, they unsaddled the horses and tied the animals to the low branches of a Douglas fir. The vanilla smell of its sap drifted into the perfect cleanness of the air.

"It's like Elysium," said Ashley as she hugged her grandmother. "I can't imagine a more beautiful place than this."

"Juan and I used to come here together when it became too difficult to be at home. Before papa learned to love him. I never returned after he died. Never wanted to until now. But I thought you should know it. Know how to get here. We all need a place for escape. Even if it sometimes comes to us just in our dreams. For years I have imagined this canyon. And now that I see it again, it is one of the few places in my entire life that has not disappointed me when I returned. It is still just as noble and splendid as when I first saw it." There was a dream in her voice. And a love.

Using her years of experience, Nana set up the tent quickly. Ashley helped when she could, her skills limited to three terms at summer camp when she was a child.

That accomplished, Nana said, "Now I shall set about catching our dinner." She took her fishing pole out of its case. She was a woman who knew where the trout lurked just as expertly as she knew the qualities of light that would create a great photograph. When she was young, she would lie on her belly on the bank of a stream with Juan. He taught her then how to catch a fish with her hands, waiting patiently until the trout swam by, then dipping quickly into the water and scooping the fish out onto the grassy bank with one movement of her arms. But now even she was forced to acknowledge certain limiting companions with which age traveled, and standing upright with a fishing rod was preferable to a body grown older.

Nana walked quietly downstream, keeping her body out of sight of the stream and the suspicious eyes of fish until she found the perfect covering from which to cast her fly onto the water. A woman of infinite compassion, she had no compunction at all about fishing for food. Killing for sustenance was always acceptable. Killing for sport was an abomination.

After she caught the fish, Nana would fry up some bacon she had brought with them, using the fat to cook the fish, which would be rolled in cornmeal, before simmering in the cast-iron skillet over the open fire. She saw some watercress growing in the stream and made a mental note to pick some after she had caught her fish.

Ashley, who was new to this kind of camping, unloaded the packhorse in preparation for dinner. She had just dumped an armful of equipment on the ground when she saw it. Fifteen feet away, crouched on the top of a boulder, was a mountain lion. Its huge teeth bared, a low grumbling curled through the air. Ashley could feel the hair on her arms stand up, as her heart beat with the uncertain rhythm of one whose life is in imminent danger.

At that same moment the horses began to jerk on their reins, making nervous, frightened noises.

"What is it?" called Nana, just returning with a full creel for dinner. She was totally unaware of what was happening. But she knew that the noises of the horses signaled danger.

Without taking her eyes from the lion, Ashley reached to the packhorse next to her, feeling along its flank for the rifle case that was strapped to it. She felt the snap, undid it, and lifted out the rifle. All that she knew about guns had been learned that very summer from Nana with some casual target practice. Oddly, as Nana had strapped the rifle onto the horse before their journey, Ashley asked why she was taking it.

"Because you never know when you might need it," she had answered in a simple statement of fact.

Having processed the smell of danger, the horses were pulling at their reins, which bound them prisoner to the tree. Whinnying and moving restlessly, they shook the highest branches above them.

"Come see if you can calm the horses, Nana." Ashley never took her eyes away from the cat, from the teeth that menaced her deepest self. "It's a lioness. Right over there." She spoke automatically, with the voice of one who functions superbly in a crisis, only to collapse in a helpless heap afterward.

By the time Nana reached the horses, Ashley was holding the rifle at the ready.

"It might go away," cautioned Nana in a whisper.

The rifle raised to her shoulder, Ashley sighted down the long barrel, aiming at the wild creature whom fate had designated her enemy.

For a moment Ashley thought there would be a reprieve, as the cat shifted her weight to her back haunches. Then the muscles tensed on the powerful hind legs.

"Get ready, Ashley," Nana said as she held tight to the reins of the horses. She no longer made any effort to lower her voice. It was too late.

"God forgive me," whispered Ashley. "Or help me."

Nana screamed, "Shoot!" as the lioness leaped toward Ashley and the packhorse in one magnificent leap. The crack of the rifle accompanied the jump, tearing a rent in the silence of the hidden valley.

Around them animals scurried to safety and birds in the surrounding trees fled at the noise. The horses reared, held from bolting by the branches of the trees and Nana's strong arms.

As if in slow motion Ashley saw the cat suspended in midair, moving inexorably toward her. Her scream pierced the animal just as surely as the bullet, and it fell wounded to the ground in a sickening thud. Still, the cat tried to raise its body, its teeth bared as it wailed in long, shrill howls.

Ashley stood watching it, stunned and sickened by what she had done, immobilized by the travesty she had just committed. Nana ran around the horse to her.

"Kill it, Ashley." Her voice was a command. There was no leeway toward mercy.

Still, Ashley stood and watched the struggling cat, watched it try to raise itself on its legs and attack her. But she did not move.

"Kill it," said Nana one more time. "You must. There is no choice. Even if it can't hurt you, you must do it."

When there was still no response from Ashley, without hesitating, Nana reached over and took the rifle from Ashley's hands.

Raising it to her shoulder, she shot the cat directly between the eyes. Blood spurted from the head of the lioness as it exploded from the impact of the bullet. In one long last scream of anguish and injustice, the animal died.

Then Ashley began to cry, great spectral sobs torn from the heart of her innate morality. "So beautiful," she mumbled incoherently. "So beautiful it should not have died. So beautiful."

Nana took Ashley in her arms. "You had no choice, my dear. No choice at all. You had to do it. When death is inevitable, you must not ever allow a creature to remain half alive. It is indecent to linger in pain when there is no hope."

Ashley nodded.

"We must bury it, Ashley. Now. Before every scavenger in the area comes."

The two women worked into the night with their one short-handled shovel, digging a hole large enough for the animal. Then they dragged it in and covered it with earth, packing it down hard around the already stiff body.

When they finished, Nana cooked the fish for them.

"I really don't feel like eating, Nana," Ashley had protested when she lit the fire.

"Nonsense," said Nana. "No more self-pity." She turned to Ashley, her face hard with the determination of one who has suddenly wearied of tears. "I've heard enough of that. And I want you to listen to me."

Ashley nodded, wide-eyed, having never heard her grandmother speak like that before.

"We do what we have to do, Ashley. That it is sometimes difficult does not negate the task. Now I grant you that you have been forced to grieve for too many people in your life. It isn't fair. I agree. But that is, frankly, beside the point. I won't have you moving into another funk over this. I—will—not—have—it. Do you hear?" She turned to Ashley, the light from the fire flickering across the strong planes of her face. "Enough. That lioness that you shot was just like your father. They were both wounded beyond help. Your father's stubborn determination to hang on to a vendetta that was no longer valid killed him. It ate away his insides just as surely as the bullet from that rifle exploded in the guts of that animal. Even if they had survived, neither could have lived with grace. They were beyond that. And to grieve, to feel guilty, about a matter that was out of your hands is life-negating and loathsome. And it will kill you, too, if you do not stop it. It is an insult to everything you stand for, Ashley Van Every."

"But . . . ?" Ashley protested.

Nana leaned over and took Ashley's tear-drenched face in her hands. "Stop it. No more excuses. I've been there, too, Ashley. And I can tell you that the only chance you have in this life is to seize the moment and appreciate the wonder that it offers. There's no secret, Ashley, to surviving with grace. You knew how to do that once. When we first spent time together. You weren't timid then. You were eighteen years old and you were one magnificent young woman. You were vital. And you could be astonished at the surprises that life offered. It's time to do that again. I will not have you slowly extinguishing the flame that burns in you. There's something more out there, and by God, you had better set about finding it. Right now. The only tyranny of the spirit is the one we create for ourselves. And if you allow that to happen, your life will be tawdry and anemic and you will be reduced to drawing your sustenance from second-rate pleasures."

She stopped and leaned over to kiss Ashley's comprehending face.

"Do you understand what I am saying?" asked Nana.

Ashley nodded.

"Good," Nana said. "Now eat your supper. It's getting cold."

Ashley lay awake long into the night. She thought of the lioness, and the fact that it must have been protecting its cub. And she thought about her father. And of her mother, who protected her as best she could with her limited strength.

In the morning Ashley set out to look for the cub.

"Where are you going?" Nana asked, as she organized her camera equipment.

"To see if I can find the lion cub," she answered.

"What makes you so certain that it exists?"

Ashley stopped. "I don't know," she said finally. "I just assumed."

"I see," Nana commented, loading film in the camera.

Obsessed with a need she did not yet understand, Ashley combed the area around the camp. Moving methodically in circles farther and farther away from the center, she searched as if her life depended on it. As the day progressed, she became increasingly anxious and desperate, imagining that the helpless and unprotected cub was waiting for her to rescue it from its harsh fate.

In the late afternoon, half a mile upstream, she looked up and saw a shallow cave situated up a steep and rocky incline. Exhausted, she began the climb, finding precarious footholds for her assent.

Her heart was beating with anticipation when she reached the cave. But when she looked inside, it was empty. There was nothing except dried twigs and leaves resting on the rocky floor of the cave.

Sitting down, she began to weep with an intensity

born of her own recently abandoned self. Relentless sobs racked her body as she cried for all that was lost that would never come again. It was an ending and a beginning for her, a final bow to the acceptance of fate, while at the same time refusing to give in to its demands.

She knew then that she would regret the killing of that lioness until the day she died. She had violated something sacred, and it left her with an everlasting sorrow. But she also knew, with a clarity that was new to her, that it had been necessary, that there had been no choice.

She understood, then, what Nana had tried to tell her. The cub—if it even existed—had presumably escaped and would survive. Just as Ashley would survive. Thus, during the course of one day in her own Garden of Eden, Ashley moved back to her rightful place on the edge, there to join her grandmother. Both women were keepers of unique visions. It was as if they contained a singular passion that had a life of its own—one that had skipped a generation, and come finally to rest in the newly cleansed soul of Ashley.

Neither considered this unusual. It was simply a fact of their lives—their peculiar destiny—to see and hear things differently. Wild and strange, sometimes terrible, it was awesome in its need and lilting in its intensity. They occupied a space open to few. Two spirits bound by a passion for living and a fullness of heart, they neither questioned its power nor examined its existence ever again. It simply *was*.

Just as she had promised, Ashley returned to New York in the fall. But not before she had received one final and lasting gift from Nana.

It happened on the pack trip: Nana began to teach her photography. She had naturally brought along her camera; she hardly could have been convinced to come without it.

Spending hours with the four-by-five camera, waiting for the perfect light to photograph one flower, Nana scorned the modern technique with which a photographer would take scores of pictures of his subject, counting on the odds to produce one or two good ones. Nana would take one or two, and expect both of them to be good.

As Ashley watched her, she began for the first time to appreciate the act of creating. More than that, she wanted to be a part of the process. She, too, wanted to capture a moment of time with her own private vision.

Thus, Ashley returned to New York for Indian summer. Armed with a new purpose and an imposing dream, it was a happy reunion. The late October days glowed with the warmth of a benevolent sun and the leaves fell gently onto the ground in the garden in front of her home.

In November Kate delivered her second child, named William after her brother. Just after Thanksgiving Dottie attended the baptism ceremony with all the pride of a new mother.

Understanding the renewed loneliness that Ashley would inevitably experience at Christmas, Nana flew to New York for the holidays, missing her traditional Christmas in New Mexico and the company of her few and cherished friends. But they could wait, Nana thought, when she saw Ashley at the airport.

She had grown even more beautiful since Nana last saw her. In fact, Ashley was dazzling in the sonorous glow that grew from within her.

Nana was overwhelmed by the love she felt for this young woman who had entered her life so late. And she was immensely grateful for her very existence.

Patrick McAuliffe walked into Dottie's office in early December and handed her a manuscript.

"Here it is," he said, placing it squarely in the middle of her desk with a gesture of pride tinged with misgivings. He, too, had to contend with the problem of competing in the public mind with his last book.

"And I thank you," said Dottie, getting up and walking around her desk to give him a kiss of congratulation and welcome. Once again she felt his attractiveness—that same magnetism she had acknowledged the first time she ever met him at Madelaine's party.

"Tell me about it," she said, settling him with a cup of coffee in the easy chair across from her desk.

"What's to tell?" he said with a studied casualness. "The title is *Vector* and it's about the different kinds of living and the different kinds of dying that we choose for ourselves."

"A real upper," Dottie commented dryly.

"No . . . actually it is. A life-affirming book, I mean. There's even a happy-ending love story."

"Between a longshoreman and a ballerina?"

"Between two people, that's all."

Dottie looked at him and smiled. It had been several months since she had seen Jack, and she was suddenly hungry for the touch of a man. This man. He's really quite beautiful, she thought, as she looked at his dark fiery eyes and curly black hair. Quite.

"How about a writer and an agent?" she asked impetuously, regretting almost immediately the vulnerable position in which her statement placed her.

Patrick leaned toward her, resting his hand on her desk. "Is that a general or specific statement?" he asked in the blunt manner of one who never appreciated the value of playing games.

Dottie sat quietly for a moment, assessing the situation with all the inexperience of a person who is savvy in business and naive in personal relations. "Specific, I suppose."

Patrick nodded his head slowly. "Dottie, Dottie . . ." he said with an edge of regret. "I thought about it once. But Madelaine made it quite clear to me then that you preferred the company of your own sex."

"What?" Dottie asked, confused.

"Well, your preferences are hardly a secret."

"My preferences?"

"You're a lesbian, aren't you?"

"She told you that?"

"Well, considering the source . . ." he said, drifting to an unverbalized conclusion.

"Look, Patrick, let me make it clear that I don't care what anyone's sexual preferences are. Each to his own. But mine are, and always have been, heterosexual."

"Really?" he asked, genuinely surprised. "That's going to be news to a lot of people in this town."

"You want I should prove it?" she asked, trying to make her question light.

Patrick spoke carefully, obviously uncomfortable at the invitation. "It's too late, Dottie," he said gently. "Just too late."

Dottie drew a deep breath, stung by the rebuke. Worse than that, she felt humiliated, reduced by a few words to the Dottie of old—the one who had to struggle against debilitating insecurities that threatened to defeat her with every step she took.

This was magnified by her concern that Madelaine had spread this rumor as a form of revenge, not as a final step in retribution, but a beginning one. She was plagued by the possibility that when she was with Jack, he would discover the deal that she had made with Adam Farling. She did not think he would tolerate such a revelation without punishing her. And she did not think she could bear that.

A sense of dread descended over her, as if a cloak had been dropped over her shoulders without warning. And yet she knew that she could not allow this to defeat her, for she had fought too hard and come too far to make even a perfunctory bow to its existence.

Stunned as she was, she looked at Patrick and smiled.

"I'm sorry, Dot," he offered. "I really am."

"Forget it," replied Dottie. "It's water under the bridge. Besides," she said, coming to a decision, "just to show you that there are no hard feelings, I'm going to do you a favor."

"Like what?"

"Like tell you that my friend Ashley's back in town."

Dottie envied the way his body turned alert, his eyes lit up at the sound of Ashley's name. And she envied her friend the treat that she had in store.

Two days after Christmas Ashley had a party. Just a few friends over to meet her grandmother. She and Nana had spent the time before Christmas decorating a tree and hanging garlands of pine over the mantel. The house was lovely and warm, and the fire was burning brightly when the guests arrived.

Dottie only told Ashley that she was bringing a friend. So much had happened to Ashley since she had met Patrick that Dottie was certain she had forgotten all about him.

Despite her own attraction toward him, Dottie was not the kind of person to begrudge his feeling for Ashley. She was even looking forward to seeing Ashley's surprise at meeting Patrick again.

She wished, however, that Jack could have been with her then. His presence would have filled the aching emptiness that was lurking somewhere in the vicinity of her heart.

Patrick wore gray slacks with a navy blazer over a maroon turtleneck for the party. Ashley thought he was the most beautiful man she had ever seen when he walked in the door with Dottie. He was not conventionally handsome by any stretch of the imagination. His features were too sharp for that. He had a lean face with piercing black eyes and hair to match. His nose looked like that of a boxer's, except it was a shade too chiseled for that. His mouth was large but firm, and his seemingly pointed chin broadened to blend with a wide square jaw. He was a man who believed in laughter, a man who believed in life. There was nothing tentative about him, as if he had accepted entirely the limitations of his destiny and the brazen expanse of his dreams.

"Happy New Year," he said to Ashley when he took her hand.

"I thought it was still Christmas," she replied.

"For them, it is," he said with a smile. "For us it's the New Year."

The first night Patrick McAuliffe spent with Ashley, after they had taken a very happy Nana to the airport, was everything he imagined from the moment he saw Ashley a year and a half before. Neither of them had felt any need to communicate with each other during the time Patrick had been in Ireland and Ashley in New Mexico. But it seemed that the period of waiting had simply been a time of preparation for one of the glittering gifts that life, in its rogue ways, can suddenly bestow.

They came together, not as two halves making a whole, but as two entirely complete individuals who would, from time to time, create an even greater entity. Because of that, Patrick knew, there would be conflict. They were both too strong to avoid it. But there would also be love and passion which neither had ever experienced.

They made love that first night like explorers in a new and exotic land. Much as she longed for him to be inside her, to fill her, Patrick would not allow Ashley to hurry. He kissed every part of her, lifting her at each step to a new plane of being. She could not get enough of it. After so long a time without love Ashley was greedy for his kisses, ravenous for his touch. She feasted on the banquet of his loving as if this were the end of a particularly overwhelming famine.

Intoxicated with his presence, she stroked and tasted every part of him, refusing to allow one morsel to escape without her notice.

Tentative and gentle at first, then passionate and wild, she cried out to him, calling his name, calling him to her. Borne on the wings of transporting passion, she flew to new heights where she existed only with Patrick in a strange and wonderful land. There they hovered briefly in an ineffable peak of passion that burst over them in incandescent showers of sated desire.

Ashley knew that she had come home once again.

His arms wrapped around Ashley, Patrick had fallen asleep floating on the erotic pillow that they had created together. But he was awakened abruptly around five in the morning by a night terror of an intensity he had not experienced since he was a child. It was a nightmare of dread so unspeakable and obscure that he was barely able to give it a name.

The room was dark and he felt like a child again, waking up in the middle of the night. He knew instinctively that each generation of children harbored its own terrors, remarkably like those of its ancestors. The dark. The rush of nothingness reaching out to threaten you as you walk past a black forbidding doorway at night; the hands ready to grab from the huge universe under the bed; the formless figures ready to leap should the protective magic of the covers slip off while you sleep.

"From goblins and ghosties and four-legged beasties and things that go bump in the night, God save us all." A primitive prayer that still applied to modern man, he thought. He understood well man's ageless need for light, for fire to fight off the demons of the dark—how the bonfire became instinctively ritualized in the lights of Christmas, in order to ward off the evil spirits that lurked in the dark of the long winter nights.

It had been years since he had awakened so frightened. Since he was a child in Texas.

He had grown up there, in the flat, arid land of the panhandle. His mother—a woman whose talent for life had been slowly snuffed out by too many years of living without money, too many hours of scrimping to realize life's simplest necessity—passed on to her son her passion for books. In truth, it was a deflected passion, for it had been born out of her overwhelming desire to escape what was happening to her: a growing old before her time; a paring down of dreams to the manageable size of mediocrity; an inexorable shrinking of the spirit to conform to the confines of a dusty Texas town. She was left with a husband who she knew was a loser, but whom she loved in a lifeless, habitual kind of way. And she was left with a son whose passion for words won him a scholarship to the local junior college.

Before he graduated, in an act not uncommon in a small town, Patrick married his childhood sweetheart. He was married for three years before their conflicting goals wormed separate ways to the surfaces of their lives. It had to do with the fact that Patrick had to write; he couldn't not write. His wife felt that this was, very simply, a childish aberration. And so, in an act of wisdom born out of ignorance, they divorced.

Patrick moved to New York and his ex-wife stayed behind, destined soon to marry a man whose dreams were as limited as hers. Patrick thought of her occasionally, hoping she was happy. But, finally, she came to rest in the suburbs of his heart—that lonely place that harbored those relationships carelessly relegated to the status of indistinct memory.

And now, he thought, as he looked at Ashley beside him, wherever I had to travel to get right here, the journey was worth the price.

When she awakened that first morning with him, they made love again, moving together to a land where security had no home—where risk and splendor coexisted in tenuous balance, each carrying with it the ultimate power to smother or to bless.

In the late spring, William Henderson completed his residency in orthopedic surgery and entered the army. A doctor, he was commissioned as a captain and sent to Fort Sam Houston for eight weeks of toned-down combat training. Before he left for Vietnam, Kate had a family farewell dinner for him.

Burying her anxiety for her brother in the detailed preparations for the party, Kate spent three days preparing all his favorite foods. The house shone and so did Kate. Her glow was due, in part, to the two glasses of wine she had consumed before her guests arrived.

"Are you scared?" she asked him after dinner.

"Not yet," he replied. "I don't think the war is big enough to really worry. And, frankly, I don't think it's important enough to warrant all the fuss. Those May Day antiwar protesters boggle my mind. After all, there are only twenty-seven thousand troops in the entire war. How bad can it be?"

Like most of the people with whom he associated, William could not possibly conceive of the fact that by the following November, the troop count would have increased to 170,000 and over one thousand American soldiers would have died.

Concerned for his sister, Will asked Kate how she was. "I get the feeling things could be a lot better in the Griffin household."

"Oh, it's not really so bad," she said smiling. "I'm taking a pottery course at the Y. I like it."

"You can do more than that, Katie."

"Well, with the children and all, I have a lot of limitations."

"That's not what I meant." He spoke gently but firmly to her.

"I know," she answered, lowering her eyes. "I just don't know how to begin. I don't even know where the starting line is, for that matter."

"The starting line is now."

"For what?"

"For anything that makes you feel better about yourself." He paused. "And that makes you stop drinking so much. I don't like it, Katie. It's destructive."

"Well, I hardly get up in the morning and snort a jigger of gin," she said, swirling the cognac in her glass in shy defense.

"I didn't mean that," said Will, trying to touch her consciousness without leaving an ugly mark. "You're too fine to let this happen, Katie."

She turned defensive. "I have two little children, Will. What do you want of me? To go out and get a job?"

"If that's what it takes," he said calmly.

"You sound like Betty Friedan," she said. "It's not that simple. And, besides . . . Chris doesn't want me to work."

"That's not the point, Katie. What do *you* want?"

She thought for a minute, trying to find the words to explain her confusion. "I used to think I had what I want. But I don't know anymore. Something's missing. And I don't know what it is."

"You," he answered.

"Who's that?" she asked with artificial brightness, as she got out of her chair to pour herself another drink.

Finally, she had to bid Will good-bye. She buried herself in his arms. "Be safe," she repeated over and over. "Please be safe."

The last words she spoke to her brother before he left were "I love you."

But in the morning, feeling miserable and hungover, she could not remember telling him good-bye.

Their conversation, too, had slipped into the vague regions of her memory where she could not really touch it. Because of the alcohol she had consumed, it was as if their farewell had never taken place. He was going off to war, and she did not even say good-bye.

## CHAPTER 10

In the middle of June Patrick and Ashley flew to New Mexico to spend the remainder of the summer with Nana. Having grown up in Texas, Patrick had a general idea of what to expect: adobe, dust, Mexicans, Anglos. But he was not prepared for the beauty that accompanied it. The color of the light blending with the drama of the land; the feeling of huge expanses enclosing him in an intimate embrace; the sense of history combined with the rawness of frontier America.

As they drove from the airport in Albuquerque to Nana's home north of Santa Fe, the sun was setting in a dazzling display, outlining the mesas with fire, turning distant storm clouds crimson with the waning light.

"Just a little welcoming show for your benefit," Nana said as she drove. Like most things she did, her abilities at the wheel of a car were solid and competent, with just a bit of flare to keep herself in practice.

It was dark by the time they reached her house. But Nana had left lights on and a fire ready to be lit when they arrived. The warm days carried with them the refreshing gift of cool nights, happily inviting the need for a fire.

After a simple dinner, accompanied by champagne, they went to bed early.

At breakfast—a magnificent meal of fried bread sandwiches of eggs, jalapeño peppers, bacon, and cheese—Nana commented to Ashley that she still looked tired.

"I kept hearing you wandering around in the middle of the night, and I was worried," said Ashley.

"I slept like a baby," said Patrick. "I don't know how you could be restless when there's air like this to breathe and this view to greet you the moment you open your eyes."

Nana looked at her granddaughter, then reached across the table to touch her hand. "Please excuse me for inserting a little disquiet into your day. But I think you have just encountered an old friend." She paused. "I wasn't up once last night."

"What do you mean?" She paused. "Who was it then?"

"Well," said Nana, obviously hesitant, "for want of a better word, I call him my ghost."

"Pardon me?" said Patrick, completely unwilling to believe that this modern enlightened woman could say such a thing.

"Are you serious?" asked Ashley, leaning toward her grandmother.

"Well, that's what I call it. Somebody else might say spirit or apparition. Or even just ESP of some kind. But it's been here ever since I can remember. And so I don't feel compelled anymore to analyze it. It's simply a part of my life."

"You sound so casual about it, Nana," said Patrick. "That's hardly the kind of thing you drop into someone's lap at the breakfast table."

"I thoroughly agree with you. I rarely ever talk about it. Because I know how people will react."

Nana paused, nodded her head. "And rightfully so. Who am I to say? It's just that he's been such a part of my life, that I really don't find anything unusual about it anymore. I never would have mentioned it, if you hadn't talked about the noises in the night."

"He?" asked Ashley. "Why he?"

"I really don't know. Just a feeling, I guess."

"Have you ever actually seen him?" asked Patrick.

Nana hesitated. "Well, as long as we're involved in the subject, I may as well tell you all of it. Yes. I have seen him. But only at special times. Usually it's just a feeling without actually seeing anything, a few noises like you heard, Ashley. A visitation without substantiation."

"Doesn't it frighten you?" asked Patrick.

"Oh, goodness, no." Nana laughed. "We've been friends all my life."

"Who is it, then?"

"I haven't the foggiest notion. I can only tell you that when my father homesteaded this land, there was a one-room adobe hut on it. Part of the kitchen. Where we are now."

"You mean it came with the house?" asked Ashley, both awed and amused. "Like your local resident ghost?"

"Maybe. I don't know. The area has always had its ghosts. In mines, houses, canyons. Around here, for a lot of people, it's an accepted part of life."

"Tell me about seeing him," Ashley said.

"That's the unusual part," said Nana. "To my knowledge, the only time he can be seen is when someone dies. Otherwise, as I mentioned, it's just noises. The first time I saw him was the night my mother died. I was eight years old. It hovered over my bed all night long. And in the morning she was dead. Of diphtheria, as I told you," she commented, directing it at Ashley. "And two nights later, my brother, Thomas, died. And he visited me again. I could see him quite clearly."

Her voice carried with it the memory. "He was just a shape, really. Amorphous. Filmy. Maybe just a feeling, a feeling transmitted from one mind to another that was powerful enough to take on form . . . I don't know."

"And when was the next time," asked Patrick, compelled to ask the question, even though he was not so certain he liked what he was hearing.

"The night Juan died. And then, with Papa, it happened again. He was in the hospital, but when I woke up and saw the ghost, I knew he was dead."

"That simple?"

"That simple," confirmed Nana. "I've always believed it was a presence come to comfort me. Never once have I felt frightened by it."

"Wish I could say the same for me," commented Ashley. "I'm not so sure about it."

"Remember . . . I was introduced as a child, when belief is simpler, unquestioning. As an adult, I'm not sure I'd like it either. But then it was like a visit from an old friend."

"That'll be the day," commented Patrick.

"A compassionate old friend," said Nana, as if she had not heard his words. "I do believe that there are things in this world that can't be explained by rational, intellectual processes. They just *are*."

"Didn't it ever occur to you, Ashley, how it was I came to call you the night your parents were killed? He visited me that night. I thought at first it might have been you. That's why I called. But it turned out to be your father, who was born here."

The summer was spent in an idyll for Ashley and Patrick. It was as if they had been granted one more chance at childhood. The sun shone bright and clear upon the surface of their lives together—illuminating instead of burning, blessing instead of scorching.

Ashley worked hard on her photographs under the

wise tutelage of Nana, learning new techniques in developing as well as photographing.

Often in the early mornings Ashley and Patrick would ride their horses to the top of the mountain or run them across the desert, laughing at the gift they had been given, reveling in its kindness, in its innocence.

"We're very lucky," Patrick commented one day as they were sitting on their horses watching the sun fall slowly behind the mountains.

"We are," agreed Ashley. "It's as if we've both—no the three of us," she amended, "have been suspended in a kind of time outside time. The other life is there. But it doesn't intrude on us now. They're related but not connected."

They continued to live in this retreat of the soul as if it were a permanent segment of their lives, forgetting that something like that could never last.

Nana knew better, of course. Long ago she had come to understand that any retreat, no matter how achingly lovely or deeply necessary, comes to an end—that the secret place where existence is sweeter is a dream that cloys if it is not mixed with the more common ingredients of everyday life. She knew its limits as well as its beauty. And she accepted it fully for what it was: a gift that graces those chosen with a sense of wonder at its existence, and a sense of ineffable bereavement at its loss.

The dream ended for Ashley and Patrick on the day that the first prepublication review of *Vector* arrived for Patrick in the mail.

Ashley had admired the book greatly when she read it in manuscript form. But she had reservations because it was not a book that was easily accessible to readers; it was threatening, a fact that did not bode well. It was the story of a man who was as daring in his living as he was in his dreams. It explored new regions of sensuality and unique forms of prose, both aspects that carried with them the power to turn off an adoring public. She kept these reservations to herself, however, hoping she would be proven wrong.

Unfortunately, the review confirmed her opinion. It went even further in rejecting the book. "Not only is Mr. McAuliffe's writing pretentious," the review read in part, "it is a flagrant effort to match his last novel in excitement and innovation. And it is an effort that fails miserably."

Patrick had been considering making a visit to his parents on the way back to New York at the end of the summer. This review now was the impetus for his departure, for he did not want to be with Ashley when he was experiencing such a public failure.

Neither of them yet felt bound to the other, being wary of a commitment that implied such permanence. The residual effects of Patrick's unhappy first marriage still haunted him at odd moments. And the specter of Alexander continued to invade Ashley's dreams. They were thus caught in a trap of their own making. Patrick knew that he could not ask Ashley to marry him when he was in the throes of failure. And she felt it would appear to be an act of pity if she were to reach out to him then.

This was further complicated by the fact that they had been together almost continually since Christmas, and they had both begun to experience the delicate suffocation that such constant companionship carries with it.

And so when Patrick announced he would be returning to New York via Texas, Ashley felt obligated to go along with him on his decision. It was a decision that slipped a wedge into the core of their idyll, moving it slightly off-center for the first time.

When she bid Patrick good-bye at the airport, Ashley felt as if a toad had jumped suddenly onto the glittering and elaborate banquet table from which she had been feasting. She only hoped that this feeling was a temporary retrenching instead of a permanent loss.

She did feel, however, that their time together was not yet over. In her heart she was convinced that what ran between them was strong enough to sustain them over a long period of time. They had delved too deeply into each other's souls for these feelings to be casually negated.

The first week in September Dottie and Kate came to Santa Fe for a vacation. It had not been an easy task to accomplish.

Kate, of course, had a more difficult time arranging the trip. The problem was not what to do with the children, for her mother had volunteered to take care of them while she was gone. The real problem was Chris.

"Your place is here, Kate," he had said to her. "Not running off to New Mexico on some tangent."

"It's not a tangent, Chris. You take trips. Why shouldn't I?"

"Mine are business trips."

"But I have no business, beyond my family and friends. Can't you see that?"

As if it was cued in a script of their life, Chris became angry. It was his way of controlling Kate when she stepped out of line. She had not understood this until that moment. But it flashed to Kate then that she feared his anger even more than his disapproval. He used anger like a whip, and she did not know how to cope with its blows. Instead, she retreated.

Every time he raised his voice to her, she instantly regressed to a little girl, fearing the wrath of her father. Despite the fact that she was almost twenty-seven years old, she was still a child in the confrontations with her husband—a child who feared the anger more than the spanking, who feared being abandoned more than she feared her own self-betrayal. Because she was a good girl. And it occurred to her then that if she were ever to get out from under the imprisoning blanket of this coercive threat, she would have to learn how to stand up to him.

"All I'm asking for is five days in New Mexico, not a year in Paris. That's all, Chris."

"You're not asking, Kate. You're demanding."

"Is that what you want? For me to ask nicely? For me to ask permission? There are times when we barely see each other for five days in a row anyway. Because of your work . . . or whatever," she added significantly. "It's not a big deal unless you make it one, Chris. Otherwise, it's just a small vacation. That I'm going to take." This was the first time she had ever approached him quite so defiantly. And her heart beat a strange new rhythm as she waited for his response.

"So take it," he said bitterly. "Go ahead and take it. Whatever I say obviously does not make any difference. Take it!"

And she did.

The night of their arrival they celebrated their reunion with champagne.

"I can't believe this place," said Kate. "It's a dry paradise."

"I've lived here all my life," said Nana, "and never grown weary of it. I've traveled all over the world, and I cannot remember one time that I wasn't anxious to come home." She paused for a moment, thinking. "Ah, yes, there was one time. A few years back I met a wonderful man in Vienna. I didn't want to leave him. At least for a while," she said with a smile.

Dottie and Kate looked at her as if they were conjuring up images of two prehistoric creatures coupling on the front lawn. By this time Ashley had become accustomed to Nana's sensuality, to her refusal to call it quits just because she had reached a certain age. So she just smiled at her friends.

Nana, of course, took all this in. "Don't worry, dears. I shan't embarrass you with a lover during your visit."

"I wish you would," said Ashley, laughing.

"So do I," replied Nana. "But for the moment the well is dry."

"Alas and alack," said Dottie.

"My sentiments exactly," concurred Nana with a mischievous smile. "My last lover was with me for about a year. We had a glorious time."

"What happened?" asked Ashley.

"I'm not totally certain. We're still very good friends, of course. But I think it was simply a matter of using up a passion. We were greedy and burned it all up."

"How sad," said Kate quietly.

"Not at all. It was quite wonderful. We had a grand time."

As the days progressed, both Dottie and Kate could see the changes that had taken place in Ashley. There was an ease about her, as if she had traveled forever to reach this spot. And once here, she blended with the sun and the stars and the light, becoming one with her environment, becoming whole.

Often now Ashley would carry a camera with her when they hiked in the desert. She was serving an apprenticeship with a master of the art and was growing progressively more proficient.

"I love it," she said one day as Dottie and Kate sat with her, waiting for the perfect light and the perfect shadow to appear on a tiny adobe church that seemed to spring out of the earth in simple and pure testament to the work of God. "It's the capturing of a moment that draws me, the conviction that it's possible to discover the essence of something and record it on film. It's as if I'm a part of it then, able to touch the particular and the universal at the same time. I've never felt so complete in my entire life."

Freedom and life emanated from Ashley. It was both pagan and refined, as if she alone had discovered a new country in which the polarities of her existence blended to create a different air to breathe, a rarer and more fragrant light in which to live.

Kate found herself wishing that she could share some of Ashley's light. But it was elusive, always just out of her grasp.

Despite the fact that Kate was excited to be with her friends in New Mexico, she seemed to be slightly off-center, as if she were perpetually losing her balance. She was listless, as if there were no motivation strong enough to pull her back toward a more balanced existence. She drank too much, one night waving her hand in a casual gesture and knocking her brandy glass off the table beside her. She was embarrassed, even humiliated, as Nana took her to bed and tucked her in like a helpless child.

The day before she left Nana took Kate for a walk. She wanted to try, for Kate's sake, to shine some kind of discerning light on the core of her obvious discontent and sadness.

"It is possible, Kate, to change what you don't like. You don't have to remain in this morass, you know."

"I don't have the strength to change, Nana." This was not said in self-pity. It was simply an unadorned statement of fact.

"Everybody does, if they would just use it," said Nana quietly. "When my husband died, I thought life was over for me. But I finally pulled myself together and got a job when . . . my son began school. I made a career out of a second-rate job. I'm not tooting my own horn here, Kate. I'm just trying to explain that we all have the power to change our lives."

"Do you really believe that, Nana?" Kate asked with an edge of hope peeking through her own unsureness.

"I really do."

Kate saw something glittering on the ground and leaned over to pick it up.

"Look!" she said, holding it up to the sun, "It's exquisite." It was a perfectly formed point, intricately flaked of black obsidian. Violet light shone through the glassy fluted edges, emphasizing the precision with which the unknown craftsman had worked two hundred years ago.

"Do you know how long it takes to make one of these?" Nana asked, holding the point in her hand.

"A couple of hours?" Kate asked, venturing a guess.

"About ten or fifteen minutes," said Nana. "That's why it's possible to find so many of them. It was easier to make new arrowheads than to retrieve the spent ones."

Nana handed it back to her.

Remembering her manners, Kate said, "Oh, no. It's yours. I found it on your land."

"Don't be silly, Kate. It's not mine, just because I own the land. It really belongs to its creator. And now to history. Keep it as a remembrance. I like to see your eyes light up when you look at it."

"I used to read a lot about archaeology."

"Don't you anymore?"

"Once I told Chris that I thought it would be fun to go on a dig, and he pointed out how long I would have to be away from the family. And that if I wanted to do something, I should choose something I could do at home."

"And?"

"I guess it kind of took the wind out of my sails. I lost interest after that."

"That, my dear Kate," said Nana with a hard edge to her voice, "is a classic case of copping out. You'll never do anything until you learn to trust your own opinions. The way I see it, you spend one hell of a lot of time finding reasons why you can't do something.

You flounder, you wallow, and . . . you drink. All in an effort to avoid choice."

"My choice is clear: to take care of my family."

"That's *one* choice, Kate. And, obviously, a necessary one. But there are others. Like finding something to do. Not in the way of a dilettante, but something to involve you for the rest of your life." She paused, then added, "Children do grow up, you know."

"But I don't know what I want to do."

"Nonsense. Consider, instead, the fact that you just haven't found it yet." She pointed to Kate's pocket where she had placed the point she found. "Like that. It's a brand-new discovery. But you loved it immediately. You've read about arrowheads since you were a child. But actually finding one placed this so-called common object in a new perspective. Suddenly it's more beautiful than you imagined. Your face lit up. You were a child again."

"It's like treasure hunting."

"Only because you impart that quality to it, Kate."

"I see," she said slowly.

"What you don't see," replied Nana, "is the fact that if you don't start to pull yourself out of this self-imposed mire, if you don't stop blaming your husband or your parents for your own fear of making a choice, a commitment, then you'll simply continue like this. And when you're my age, your memories will be filled with regret beyond bearing, your life will be bitter and filled with rue. And then it will be too late."

"I'm afraid it already is, Nana."

When Kate returned to New York, she showed the point she had found to Chris. His reaction was cool, and she put it away in her jewelry case, to look at on days she longed for something else.

A week after she returned a package arrived from Nana. Inside the wrapping was a book entitled *Archaeology of New Mexico*. The flyleaf was inscribed,

"To Kate, who can create her own treasures. With love, Nana."

When Patrick picked up *The New York Times* that November morning, he had already heard about the review of his book that was printed inside. It was only slightly less damaging than the prepublication review, and he winced at the power the review had over his own life. Conjuring up mental defenses for the negative point of view, he chastised himself for caring what one individual had to say about his work. But he did care. And the essence of the caring had nothing to do with the fact that the book would make little money. He had enough of an income from the first novel to survive if he was careful with his expenses. It had to do with the fact of his ego, his pride. It also made him doubt his ability to judge the written word, especially his own.

This was not made any easier by the fact that all the people he knew in New York would read this review. The prepublication one, damaging as it was, was only seen by those involved in the industry. This new one made his humiliation completely public.

Thus, when the phone rang, he was in no mood to talk, to listen to ego-assuaging words from well-meaning friends. The fact that it turned out to be Ashley calling from New Mexico did not make it any easier.

"Hello," she said, her voice soft with love for him.

"Hello."

"What's wrong, Patrick? I hear it in your voice."

"*The New York Times* published a lousy review of *Vector* this morning."

"Ugh. I'm sorry."

"Not as much as I am," he said dryly. "At least I can look forward to your coming back soon."

"That's what I'm calling about, Patrick. But maybe it should wait for a few days . . ."

"Go ahead. Pile it on," he said, his voice a mixture of irritation and amusement. "I seem to be the local garbage dump today."

"Well . . . Nana asked me if I would stay here through Christmas. She said it's really the loveliest holiday and I just don't think I can refuse her. Of course, she said it would be wonderful if you could come here, too."

"How gracious of her." His voice dripped with sarcasm.

"Don't . . . please don't Patrick. Nana didn't know it would cause any trouble. Please don't blame her." She paused, waiting for his reply.

"All right . . . all right, Ashley. I don't blame her. It's just that the timing was bad, that's all."

"I know. Tell you what. Why don't I call back tomorrow and we can talk about it?"

"I'm a grinch right now. It's a good idea." Although it was an apology in a manner of speaking, Ashley could still sense his annoyance.

"Okay. I'll call you then." She waited for a reply, but there was none. "Patrick?" she asked. "I miss you. I really do."

"I miss you."

"I love you, too."

"I love you, Ashley." And he hung up.

As soon as he had severed the connection, he regretted it. But not enough to call back. Feeling suddenly like a little boy who had been abandoned in his moment of need, he stormed around the house for the remainder of the day, alternately resenting and missing Ashley.

Around four the phone rang. It was Dottie.

"Just your agent calling to commiserate," she said gently. "It's a good book, Patrick."

"Thanks." He was almost sullen; having brooded for several hours over his miseries, he had moved easily into the mode of self-pity. He understood how unattractive his stance was, but seemed helpless to control it.

"Look," said Dottie. "Why don't you meet me in my office in about a half an hour and I'll buy you a drink."

"A sterling idea," he responded. "One that I thought of around two hours ago. And I don't mind continuing it."

"All right. I'll wait for you."

He was more cheerful by the time he arrived at Dottie's.

Buoyed by the drinks he had consumed before he left home, he decided to cultivate the talent of not caring what the critics said. He had heard that some famous writers didn't read any reviews, good or bad. And he recognized the wisdom of that decision. Still, underneath, the negative responses gnawed at him. And it was compounded by the fact of Ashley's phone call. To hell with them all, he decided, as he walked into the office.

Dottie greeted him warmly and sympathetically. Then told him she had just one or two things to clear up before she could leave.

"In that case," he said, "I shall make a quick visit to the bathroom."

He was in the middle of it, when the lights went out.

"Hey!" he called to Dottie. "Stop it with the lights, will you? I can't see a thing."

"Neither can I," she replied, her voice too far away for her to have been fiddling with the switch.

"Well, I hate to think of the mess in here when the lights go back on. I couldn't see the target."

He could hear Dottie giggling.

He walked out of the bathroom and felt his way across the room. "What happened?" he asked.

"I just looked out the window and all the lights on the block are out."

"Terrific. Let us hope that *The New York Times* is experiencing the same difficulty," he said with malicious glee. "Do you have a radio?"

"There's no electricity."

"A portable, I mean."

"No."

He opened the window and stuck his head out. "Jesus. It looks like every light in New York City has gone out."

"But I do have some candles," she said, feeling her way to the cabinet at the side of the room.

Standing at the window, they watched the high rise across the street. Slowly, magically, soft glows began to show up in selected windows, casting an eerie gentle light, a surrealistic portrait of an emergency.

"Let's go outside and see what's happening," he said.

They lit one candle and took turns holding it as they made their way out of the building, giving out with an occasional ouch when the hot wax would drip on their hands.

Outside on the street it was as if they had unexpectedly wandered into Mardi Gras. Cars moved slowly on the avenue, their headlights cutting bright swaths through the darkness. At the corner a teen-ager directed traffic with a flashlight. For a mystical reason known only to New Yorkers in crisis, no horns were honking, no angry shouts of frustrated drivers called out in the air. Patience and good humor prevailed. Everyone was talking and laughing, as if a holiday had suddenly been declared.

"This is terrific," said Patrick. "Come on, let's make our way to the local watering hole. I need another drink."

He led her uptown for a block and a half to a bar. When they entered, the atmosphere was joyous. Couples pressed their bodies together in corners, taking advantage of the dark. Candles flickered on some of the tables, offering just enough light for the waiters to see.

"Another ten minutes and this place will be jammed," said Patrick. "Come on. Let's grab that table."

They ordered a bottle of wine to start, then two steaks charcoaled on the gas grill and salad from the fast-defrosting refrigerator.

"Sounds like good emergency rations to me," said Dottie. "I don't know why I should be having so much fun in the middle of a crisis, but I feel high."

"So do I. It's a veritable festival." He picked up his glass in a toast. "To lights in the darkness," he said. And then he added, "And to God's formation of a special purgatory for critics. Where they are forever condemned to reading lousy books and writing with dull pencils."

"This is potentially the most adulterous night in history," said Patrick as he was walking Dottie home. It was quite apparent that all restraints had been removed by what Con Ed later claimed was an act of God. They had heard in the restaurant that the blackout would last for some time, and so they walked home slowly, enjoying the happy greetings of strangers and the eerie sensation of a city without light.

When they reached Dottie's house on Seventy-fourth Street, she turned to Patrick and asked, "Do you want a drink for your long journey home?"

"Always," he said, bowing.

Inside she instructed him. "I'll round up some candles and then we can build a fire. Okay?"

"Okay," he answered. "Where's the brandy?"

"On the table behind the couch," she answered. "In the round decanter."

They settled in with just the glow of three candles and a fire to light their night.

"Dottie?"

"Hmm?"

"Thanks a lot for calling today. You're terrific."

"Think nothing of it," she said.

He leaned over to kiss her. First on the cheek in the kiss of a friend, then on the mouth in the kiss of a lover. Their restraints had been removed, too.

"What the hell," she said, putting her glass down on the table.

"My sentiments exactly," he said, his hand moving to her breast.

Despite the illicit quality to their lovemaking, they were in no hurry. It was as if they had to allow time for their passions to assert themselves, for guilt to be buried in the locked parts of their consciences along with thoughts of Ashley and Jack.

Dottie never fooled herself into believing that Jack had no other women when she was not around. But Patrick had been faithful to Ashley, as she was to him, so his was the guilt that took the most effort to suppress.

They didn't bother to move to the bedroom. On the floor before the fire they caressed and explored each other's bodies. Naked, she eased on top of him. He held her waist, then moved his hand down, making her come first. Then he, in a gasp of pleasure, called out to her.

They lay together a long time afterward, afraid to talk about what had just happened. They both knew that they had betrayed Ashley. And as sobriety returned, the impact of what they had done rested heavily on their shoulders.

"She didn't deserve that," Patrick said finally.

"I know," Dottie whispered.

"There's no excuse. None at all."

"Except weakness and need."

"That's not an excuse, Dot. It's an explanation. And a pretty pitiful one at that."

"You're right. There's no excuse."

* * *

management, were waiting for her in her bungalow. There was also a message from Luke Kranz when she arrived: that he would meet her in the Polo Lounge before lunch.

Arriving at the appointed hour, she was shown to a tiny table in a surprisingly shabby bar. Kranz was waiting for her. She was relieved to see that she did not have to play the silly game of less-secure egos: that punctuality was considered a courtesy, rather than a method by which one demonstrated power.

He stood to greet her. "Miss Langford? I'm Luke Kranz. A pleasure to meet you."

"My pleasure, Mr. Kranz."

"Call me Luke."

"All right," she said, smiling as she looked at him. She was surprised that he was so tiny. No, spindly, she thought, as she peered down onto what she was certain was a toupee. His clothing was California natty; for the occasion he had worn what looked like a British officer's uniform with epaulets and a belted jacket.

In this surprising package was a man who played with talent like puppets on an endless string of special favors and ingratiating deeds. He had the power to put together parcels of talent for millions of dollars without doing more than making a couple of phone calls. Dottie could not figure out what a man of his stature would want with her.

After they had ordered drinks, Kranz moved right to the point. He was certainly not a man who indulged in those endless rounds of shadowboxing that Dottie called the Hollywood Shuffle.

"Despite the fact of your youth, Miss Langford . . ." he began.

"Please call me Dottie," she said politely.

"Despite the fact," he continued, "I would like very much to do business with you."

Dottie leaned forward in her chair. "Excuse me for

asking, but I can't imagine what kind of business you could possibly want to do with me," she said with perfect honesty.

"In good time, Dottie. In good time." He leaned back in his chair and took another appraising look at her. "As you know, I've been working alone for years. But I'm not getting any younger." He smiled. "Although I wish I were." His timing was exquisite, Dottie thought. "It used to be that I could pick up a phone and make a deal. That still happens, of course. But the industry is changing. And it's becoming more and more difficult to do that. The talent is spread out all over the world. Television is competing with movies. And actors are asking for preposterous sums of money." He stopped and took a sip of his drink. "Not that I'm against it. I always get my cut."

Dottie nodded, but said nothing.

"My weakest link has always been the publishing industry. Being in Hollywood puts me at a disadvantage in that area. On the other hand, it has its rewards. Big ones. But now I find myself in the position of needing an associate in New York. That's why I've asked you to meet with me."

"Me?" asked Dottie, stunned. "Please forgive my shock, but there are agents in New York with far more power than I have, who have the benefit of years behind them. Who have a long list of famous clients." She had decided from the beginning to play this encounter perfectly straight. He was out of her league.

"Precisely. And it is a matter of record that I know ninety-five percent of those agents and their clients already. So them I know. The young ones I don't. And I don't like being on the outside. Never did."

"Oh."

"Your reputation precedes you, Dottie. It is my understanding that you are the agent in New York with the best track record for discovering *new* talent. For nurturing it. Even for marketing it. Making stars out of satellites is a gift that I highly respect. I do not treat it lightly, as I suspect that others do. Foolishly, of course. Because your aptitude for this belongs to the future. My strength lies in the present and, regretfully, in the past."

"I'm flattered, Luke."

"Don't be. I'm doing business. Not seducing you."

"Nevertheless, in my opinion, your presence alone covers any generation."

"Most people share your opinion. But I am wise enough to know better. I know that the movie business is going to turn around in a couple of years. And when the train takes off, I want to be one of the passengers who gets VIP treatment."

After all this Dottie could think of nothing to say except, "You mean I came all the way out here to have a deal proposed to me that you knew I would accept?"

"I always prefer doing serious business in person."

"Well, I must say, it's been my pleasure."

"I take it, then, you find favor with my proposal?"

"I find favor with it, Luke. A lot of favor," she said, smiling. "It would be my pleasure to be associated with you."

"You'll find I'm an easy person to work with, Dottie. As long as the game stays honest, I'm a cinch."

Just as he was reaching over to shake her hand, a familiar figure appeared in Dottie's peripheral vision. Obscured by the dim light, sitting at a table with three other women, was Madelaine Jacot. Dottie shuddered, hoping that her former boss had not spotted her with Luke Kranz.

After Patrick left for Ireland, Ashley threw herself into her photography with a renewed passion. Although she missed Patrick, for the first time in her life her work carried her through her loneliness. She did a series of pictures about the remaining Jewish families who had refused to move from the Lower East Side as its ethnic makeup changed. And for her debut she was able to get the entire picture story published in a photography magazine.

She carried the issue proudly as she flew to meet Nana in June.

Although her visits to New Mexico had by then become routine, each time she stepped on the plane, she invariably experienced that special sense of anticipation that was born of a combination of love and her need for something new. Cheap thrills did not belong in her life. Deep experience did. Always, in the mountains, she found it.

The first morning after she arrived, Ashley hugged Nana and said, "Let's go for a ride. Take a lunch and spend the day in the meadow. We'll go see if the wood lily is blooming."

"I'm afraid horses and I don't get along so well these days," replied Nana ruefully. "Every time I go for a long ride, I pay the price of a sore back. I'm afraid, Ashley," she said, brushing an imaginary wisp of hair from her granddaughter's face, "that old age crept up on me while I wasn't looking."

"Nonsense, Nana. You're not old."

"Old enough to have arthritis," she replied. "I'm sorry. I really am."

"Come down to the stable with me anyway, while I saddle Troika. I'll just go out for a couple of hours. I've missed the mountains."

"You go for as long as you want," said Nana, her hands on her hips in a gesture of strength.

After she returned from the stable, Nana took some more aspirin. She had been running a low-grade fever on and off for several weeks, and she discovered that the aspirin kept it under control. She abhorred taking medicine of any kind. But this kept her active and, she rationalized, was used by most people who had bouts of arthritis.

Ashley rode up the mountain trail past the old log

cabin that had been abandoned years before. It stood by a stream, alone and isolated, the perfect refuge for a person who wanted to take a vacation from civilization. Dismounting, Ashley tied the reins of the horse to a branch and walked over to the door. As she pushed it open carefully, it creaked on its hinges, as if the effort were too much for such a neglected house.

But the inside was not neglected at all. Sometime in the past year—or had it been longer since she looked inside, she speculated—it had been cleaned up. Not that there were any amenities added; it simply showed signs of occupation. On the far side of the small room was a bed that had been built directly into the wall. On it a mattress stood on its side, deliberately placed so that air could circulate around it. A crude but serviceable table with two chairs sat next to the window near the door, and the glass had been replaced in all the windows. There was a wood stove for cooking to the left, and a simply built stone fireplace on the right wall adjacent to the door. The floor of pine planks had been swept clean, and in a corner a metal box, unlocked, contained a supply of simple canned goods, some bags of flour and salt, and two cast-iron cooking pots. The box was a deterrent to pack rats, but they had left indications of their presence anyway.

The first thing Ashley asked Nana, when she returned from her ride, was, "Who's been living in the cabin up the mountain?"

"Oh. You noticed," said Nana. "I have a friend who comes there occasionally to get away from it all."

"Is that part of your land?"

"Yes," she smiled. "It's part of my land."

"Who's the friend?" asked Ashley.

"Oh, someone you've never met. Just an old friend."

Ashley sensed that she did not want to discuss it any further; it would be an invasion of a privacy that she had long respected. So she let it drop, understanding how thoughtless it would be to pursue the subject.

Instead, they sat out on the terrace and ate a simple dinner of salad, fresh bread, and cold beer. The sun, coming late in its spring warmth that year, shone on them with its special clean light against a background of a deepening blue sky. Ashley thought then that she would always think of her grandmother this way: happy and peaceful, sitting in the sun.

Kate was mingling with her own species in her natural habitat when she met him. Looking at swimming trunks in the men's department of Bloomingdale's, she was preoccupied with which color Chris would like best, when she reached for a pair of deep blue ones on the counter. Simultaneously, a man's hand did the same thing, meeting hers in the area of the elasticized waistband.

"Oh," she said. "I'm sorry."

"No please," he said. "My mistake."

By the time their mutual apologies had turned to laughter, they had each purchased a pair of the trunks. Then he asked her to have a cup of coffee with him.

"Oh, I'm sorry. I can't." She was flustered and even a bit frightened by his direct approach. He spoke as if there were nothing that he ever doubted.

"Of course you can," he said, smiling.

"No. I really have to go. I have to pick up my children at school."

"I'm sorry," he said. "I would have enjoyed talking to a beautiful woman today." Then he paused. "And you are the most beautiful woman I've seen in a long time."

"Oh . . . thank you," she mumbled, as she turned to leave.

He put out his hand and touched her arm. He said to her, "By the way, my name is Benjamin Hoffer."

Two days later he called her at home.

"How did you get my name?" she asked immediately.

"Off your charge card. I have eagle eyes."

"Oh."

"Are your children off at school?"

"Yes. They left an hour ago."

"Then why don't you have lunch with me today?" he asked.

"Because I'm a married woman," she answered.

"That's not a good enough reason."

"I think it is."

"Just consider it a brief interlude," he coaxed.

She remembered how attractive he was. He was tall and dark with soft brown eyes that belied the force of his personality.

"No . . . I don't think so."

"Look," he said, recognizing her wavering conviction. "I'll be in Le Mistral at twelve thirty today. Sitting at a table for two. And I'll wait for you." He paused. "Do you understand me, Kate?"

"Yes. I understand. But I won't be there," she replied, at once drawn and repelled by his sureness. "My apologies in advance."

"I'll be waiting," he said and then hung up.

Waiting for what? she thought as she put the receiver back in its cradle.

Kate spent the morning frantically doing chores and odd jobs around the house, trying to keep busy. But all she could think of was Benjamin Hoffer. She wondered what would happen if she were to have an affair. She knew by now that Chris had been playing around for years. Why not me? she thought. At least it's better than being another convenient and tasteful accoutrement around the house. Antiques, charming wife, charming children, summer home, Oriental rugs, gourmet meals. I've turned into part of a package deal for a successful Park Avenue doctor.

At noon she made the sudden decision to find out.

Scurrying to get dressed, she hailed a cab at twelve twenty and gave the driver terse instructions, her heart beating so hard it almost pounded its way out of her chest.

"Le Mistral, please."

In July Jack Barclay surprised Dottie with an unexpected visit. He simply rang the doorbell of her apartment one evening.

When she saw him, Dottie flung her arms around him. "Oh God, I've missed you."

He put his arms around her in an automatic gesture of greeting. But there was no warmth in it.

"Come in," she invited, slightly puzzled. "This deserves a drink. What can I get you?"

"Nothing, thank you," he said quite formally.

She turned to him and looked straight in his eyes. Alarmed, she asked, "What is it?"

He sat down on the sofa in front of the fireplace. She took a seat in the chair next to him.

"Tell me," she said, trying to play it light. "You've met another woman and you're going to run off and get married."

His face was hard. There was no mirth in it.

"I've come to ask you something, Dottie. I won't beat around the bush because neither of us has ever been any good at games."

"Go ahead," she nodded.

"I saw Madelaine in California the other day. She was there on business and told me she heard that you are now associated with Luke Kranz."

"But I told you about that already," replied Dottie. "I spent the weekend with you after I met him."

"I know. But Madelaine also told me something else."

Dottie wanted to vomit and she sat before him stonily waiting for the blow.

"She told me," he continued, "that you sold me

down the river when you made the deal for *King's X*. She told me you took less money so you could sell Sarah Jacobs's book, too. That you and Adam Farling made the deal."

He stopped, allowing the ugliness of his statement to linger in the air.

The bitch, thought Dottie. She was jealous of the deal I made with Kranz and she's tried to ruin it. And Jack will never believe that Madelaine had anything to do with the decision.

Jack's face was brittle, immobilized by his anger. "Is it true?" he asked. "Tell me. I want to hear it from you."

Dottie looked up at him. It was too late for excuses, too late for reaching out to rectify an incident that had happened a long time ago.

"Yes," she said, her voice a maimed imitation of its usual self. "It's true, Jack."

"That's all I wanted to know." He stood up.

"But . . ."

"I don't care what kind of excuses you have, Dottie. I don't care what you have to say. I don't care that the sales made up for any of the money I might have lost. I don't care about any of that. It's irrelevant. Nothing matters other than the fact that it actually happened. You screwed me, and I have nothing . . . absolutely nothing more to say to you."

He turned and walked out the door, closing it softly.

One morning in early August Ashley went out for a ride. The wildflowers covered the meadows. Iris, bluebell, primrose, and columbine blanketed the mountains with a blaze of color. Penstemon contrasted their deep reds with the purple of aster and the yellow of buttercup.

Ashley rode to the special place that Nana had shown her, the place where the wood lily grew. The location was their secret. Rose-colored and rare, the flowers were almost extinct from the careless picking and transplanting of campers. And they protected the location of these wood lilies as if it were Nana's own personal cache of gold.

As she rode through the aspen and pine, a deer and her fawn bolted ahead of Ashley, running in incredible leaps over the logs with dazzling grace.

Ashley reined the horse to a halt, wishing she had seen the deer before she had frightened them. This is what it was like two hundred years ago, she thought. Pure. Untouched. She was grateful she was privileged to be a part of it now, for she had never known such simple peace as that which she experienced in these mountains.

On the way home she chose the trail that took her past the cabin. She thought about stopping to see if it had been used since her last visit. But she felt a sudden and unaccountable compulsion to hurry home. With a gentle nudge of her heels against Troika's flanks, she increased his pace down the mountain. She knew she could not go too fast, for the steep trails were too precarious for that. She also knew Troika could find his way, and she allowed the horse to negotiate the turns and twists of the trail.

Finally reaching the slope that led to the last stretch of level road, she pushed Troika into a gallop; leaning forward in the saddle, she rode with the wind, her hair flowing like a banner behind her.

As soon as she opened the door to the house, she saw Nana. She lay on the floor, helpless and unmoving.

Nana's eyes moved in her direction. "Ashley, my love. I'm so glad you're here."

Ashley ran to her. Kneeling down she touched her face and felt the dry hot presence of a very high fever. She leaned over to scoop Nana up in her arms.

"No!" she cried out. "Don't move me! It's my back."

# CHAPTER 11

"Why didn't you wear the dress I bought you?" Ben Hoffer asked Kate. His lips compressed in silent disapproval.

Kate looked at him, blanching at his attitude, yet feeling the embarrassed necessity to defend herself. Since she had begun to see Ben, slowly he had tried to take over her life. At first it was just little things: how she expressed herself, what kind of meals she ordered in a restaurant, how she wore her hair. And at first Kate liked it. She could relegate the entire running of her life to someone else. The arrangement made everything comfortable, because choices and decisions were no longer necessary. She moved from being automaton-wife to doll-lover, with little thought about the self-negation the behavior implied.

That evening, when Chris was out of town, she had planned to go to the theater with Ben. She had intended to wear the new dress he had bought for her. But when she tried it on, the dress just didn't seem right. And so she changed into something that made her feel more comfortable.

"I guess I just wasn't in the mood for it," she replied, in answer to his demanding question.

"It was purchased just for this occasion," he said. "This is the first time we've gone to the theater, and I wanted you to look perfect."

"What's perfect?" she asked, a slow anger beginning to burn inside.

"What's perfect is the dress I bought for you," he answered. "I certainly didn't buy it to hang in your closet and for you to wear with your husband."

Feeling suddenly contrite, she asked, "Do you want me to go home and change?"

"It's a little late for that now," he answered, his body stiff with the inherent rebuff of her act.

"I . . . I'm sorry, Ben. I guess I just wasn't thinking."

"Please remember it for next time," he said with a forced smile. "Come. We'll be late if we don't hurry."

"Ben?" she said, reaching to him. "I'm sorry."

"It's all right," he returned, kissing her on the cheek like the contrite little girl she was. "We'll have a good time anyway."

The hospital room was pale green. There was a crucifix hanging over the bed, and a Degas print on the opposite wall.

When Nana opened her eyes, she turned her head to Ashley.

Wincing in pain even at such a simple movement, Nana attempted a smile. "Looks like I've joined the millions of other Americans with back pain," she said.

"Looks like that," answered Ashley, trying to prevent the tears from overflowing.

"Don't worry, Ashley. I'm a tough old buzzard. You know that. Just a short stay here and I'll . . ." she drifted off, leaving her sentence incomplete.

"Does she do that often?" asked Paul Coston, her old friend as well as her doctor.

"Do what?" asked Ashley.

"Stop in the middle of a sentence."

Ashley's brow furrowed in an effort to get a grip on the thought. "Sometimes. But I've always known what she was saying, so it never bothered me."

"Does she get disoriented? Does she always know what time it is? The date?"

disease and it's gone too far. Tell me now," she demanded.

Clearly at that moment Paul Coston's pain almost equaled his patient's. But for her sake he did not look away, did not avoid the inevitable question. "Most likely irreversible brain damage. Then eventual death."

Nana closed her eyes. "Son of a bitch!" she whispered.

> Dear Jack:
>
> I've waited this long to write, because I was hoping you might call me. Even though we've always lived long distance, I miss the presence of you in my life. And I want to offer my apologies to you.
>
> I understand why it is not possible for me to be your agent anymore. But I have been hoping that we might at least be friends. I've always believed in you, as a writer as well as my friend. You do mean so much to me. Would you call?
>
> Yours, Dottie

Just as she had done with all the other letters she had written to Jack, Dottie crumpled it up and threw it in the wastebasket. She could never seem to find the right words to say to him. Somehow, everything she said sounded foolish.

She wished she could just dismiss him from her life. But it was, unfortunately, not that simple. She existed on the verge of obsession, dreaming of him at night, remembering times they had laughed together, made love all day long. He was an addiction that she could not shake.

Fired by her still-unwavering ambition, she continued to climb up the satisfying ladder of success. Not even Jack's absence could prevent that, nor Madelaine's presence, which had become malignant in her thoughts.

Deciding, finally, that a letter was simply not appropriate in this case, she smoked two joints one night before picking up the phone and dialing his number.

A rush of adrenaline spread through her stomach when she heard his voice.

"Hello?"

"Jack?" she said in a timid voice. "It's me. Dottie."

Before she could continue, the line was dead.

As so often happens when people enter a hospital, the psychological, emotional, and physical assaults on their bodies combine to create a sick person where only a few weeks before there was a healthy one. Sadly, despite the strength of her will, Marguerite Martinez was no exception. Her condition deteriorated rapidly once she was hospitalized. The tests, a combination of loathsome attacks on her body, left her weak, the anxiety left her frightened. And the pain, venomous and unrelenting, was her final cross to bear.

"No more morphine, Ashley. Tell them that. The longer I go without it, the longer I remain human."

"Please, Nana," Ashley begged. "Please have some so you can sleep."

"I can sleep all I want at night. They can give me the drugs then. Besides, before long, I'll be having all the sleep I'll ever want."

Sitting quietly beside Nana, Ashley tried to push her own pain to one side, compartmentalizing it for another time. Her sense of helplessness as she took care of Nana was overwhelming. She knew now that her grandmother was going to die, and she felt a sense of unutterable loss creeping into her life. There would be no one after Nana died, no connection to family except her Uncle Jackson. And that was no comfort at all.

Compounding this personal loss, Ashley suffered immensely from Nana's pain. It was as if her spine, too, had been ravished by disease, screaming its agony into her nerve endings, torturing her body as well as her soul.

Opening her eyes, Nana reached out and touched Ashley's hand.

"You shouldn't be sad, my dear. It's too late for that now," she said simply. "There are more important things we must discuss."

Nana seemed to recognize the times when she was lucid and sought to take advantage of them. More and more frequently she would slip into the past, confusing it with the present. Often she would talk about Juan as if he had just stepped out of the room for a moment. Ashley would sit next to her and nod, carrying on the fantasy.

But that day her head was clear. And she felt the compulsion to tell Ashley the last secrets she harbored before it was too late.

"There are some things I must tell you, Ashley. I made a promise once that I wouldn't do this. But I think he will forgive me."

"What is it?"

"Things I must tell you before you assume they are the ravings of a woman gone mad."

"I always know when you're telling me the truth, Nana." Ashley smiled. Days ago she had abandoned tears in favor of a tenuous control that would help her grandmother, not weaken her.

"Well, my dear, I tell you the truth now. And that truth is that you have a brother."

Stunned, Ashley gasped, "A *brother*?"

She could not believe what she was hearing. All her life she had hated being an only child, had wished she had a brother or sister with whom to share her feelings. But it had only been a wish. And now, confronted with the reality, she did not know what to think.

Her head spun with the knowledge, and a hundred conflicting emotions coursed through her. This is wonderful; will I like him; will he like me; will he be a part of my family; will he accept me. And then she focused on the final question: Who is he?

"Tell me, Nana," she managed to ask.

"Do you remember once that I told you your father came home one time before he entered college? That he fell in love with a Navaho girl?"

"Yes . . ."

"She is the mother of your brother. Or half brother."

"Where is he now?" Ashley asked.

"He lives on the Santo Domingo Reservation," she answered. "Near his mother."

"Why didn't Daddy tell me? Or you?" There was that strange quality of delayed pain in Ashley's voice, the kind one experiences when learning something so long after the fact.

"That's the reason we fought, Ashley." Nana knew that Ashley's system had experienced an overload, and she sought ways to tell her that would not be too painful. But the fact was, there was little she could say to ease the hurt. "The reason I'm telling you this is because I don't want you to think you are going to be left all alone, that there is another relative besides that dreadful Jackson."

"What happened, Nana?"

"John had gone back east when Marcelina—that was his girl—came to me and told me she was pregnant. When I called him, your father totally denied responsibility. He refused to come home. He absolutely refused to do *anything* about it." She paused a moment, thinking. "Looking back on it, I suspect that after he had denied one child, it made it a little easier for him to do it again with you. Either way, it was a dreadful act on his part. And we fought bitterly. So bitterly that we didn't see each other again until that New Year's Day we went to him together." She drifted momentarily. "Although I had forgiven him long before that."

"Is that what you did with the money, Nana?"

She smiled. "Yes. When your father's checks started coming, I gave every cent to Marcelina and Joseph. It seemed . . . right. That money sent Joseph to the university. That was my investment. And a fine one it turned out to be. He's an extraordinary young man. He's very talented, very special. He's the person who's been living in the cabin, as a matter of fact." Nana started to drift then.

"What is his name?"

"Joseph Rosetta," she whispered. "His mother's name is Marcelina. A beautiful woman . . ." Nana's voice began to weaken. "After this is over . . . you must go to them."

"There's time for all that, Nana. Right now, you just get some rest. You need it."

"I am a little tired," Nana admitted reluctantly.

"Sleep now, Nana. I'll stay with you." Ashley pulled the covers over her, gently tucking her in. "Sleep now."

"Oh . . ." said Nana, as she drifted off. "Tell me about the flowers. Is the wood lily in bloom?"

"Yes, it's in bloom, Nana. And I promise never to reveal its secret location."

"Hello, Sarah." Dottie stood to welcome Sarah Jacobs, who had called that morning for an appointment.

By then Sarah had published her second book to favorable reviews, and it was quite apparent to both Dottie and Adam Farling that she would eventually become a very successful writer. Her evolution was slow but sure, and it was inevitable that she would be a steady money-earner for both publisher and agent.

"Can I get you some coffee?" Dottie asked.

"No thanks. I can't stay long, Dottie. I just wanted to talk to you about something."

"Your next book?"

"Well, sort of."

"I'm waiting," said Dottie with a warm smile. Not only was she pleased with Sarah as a writer; she liked her personally.

"Tell me. Come on," Dottie coaxed, aware of how shy Sarah was.

"It's just that . . . I heard something the other day. About you and me."

"Who told you?"

"Madelaine Jacot. At a party."

"The bitch strikes again," said Dottie enraged, fully aware of what was coming.

"Did you do it?" Sarah asked. "Did you sell my first book because of Jack Barclay?"

"Yes. It's true. But, God knows it was to your benefit, Sarah. I don't think the book would have been published without that deal."

Hesitating, Sarah spoke falteringly. "I don't like it, Dottie. It's not right. I understand that you were trying to help me. But it's made me lose my trust in you."

Dottie reached out, her face suffused with pain. "Please Sarah, don't. It's in the past."

"I know. I understand that, Dottie. But I just don't trust you anymore. I could be next."

"I promise you it won't happen, Sarah."

"That's not enough. I'm sorry." Her face was genuinely sad. "It's just not enough."

Struggling with the rancid bitterness that had decimated her resolve, Dottie spoke the only words that she could think of. "I'm sorry, too."

After Sarah left, Dottie leaned down on her desk,

her head spinning with confusion and doubt. The chickens are coming home to roost, she thought bitterly. All my planning, all my hopes are beginning to dissolve before my eyes.

She knew it was not the end, of course. She had enough clients to protect her position. But this loss, coupled with Jack, symbolized something far greater than mere success. It was an ending, a blatant rejection of her ambition, of her dreams. It was a battle in which integrity and ambition fought a bitter fight. And, in a surprise ending, integrity had won.

Dottie wept then, wept for what she had been and what she had become. She wished things were different. But it was too late. She could feel the grip of her career slip imperceptibly downward, as if she were sliding inexorably down a long pole toward a very tawdry destiny.

When Nana was in the hospital, all her friends came to visit. Sometimes she would recognize them, other times she would not. Jacob Flesher came every day, sitting patiently next to Nana's bed, holding her hand, wiping her brow with a cool, damp cloth.

"Take a break, Ashley," he would say gently. "I'll stay with her until you return."

And so Ashley would wander the streets of Santa Fe, going into the shops, asking without interest the price of a bracelet or a handbag. She would nod politely, then walk on, always aware of what was happening to her grandmother, tormented by her condition, racked with grief.

When she returned to the hospital, she met Paul Coston in the hall.

"I know it's against regulations, Paul, but I want to start spending the nights here. Can you arrange it?"

"Of course."

"How long?" she asked, far beyond speaking delicately, dancing around the issue of Nana.

"I really can't tell. It is entirely possible that it could be some time yet, Ashley. She's a remarkably strong woman."

A sob invaded her voice. "It's so undignified. So ugly for her, Paul."

He answered softly. "I know."

"The awful part is," Ashley continued, "that sometimes she's very lucid. She knows what's happening to her. And she looks at me with such rage that it frightens me. Sometimes she just howls and I can't stand it for her."

Paul Coston reached over and touched Ashley's face. "She's even resisting the morphine. I've never seen anything like it. Powerful. An extraordinary will. She always was like that. Nobody else could have waited so long before it defeated her. They couldn't have borne the pain."

"I know."

Several nights after she had begun to stay at the hospital with Nana, Ashley fell into a deep and exhausted sleep. She had functioned so long on nervous energy that her body finally demanded a reprieve.

That afternoon Nana had awakened, partially lucid. It was then she told Ashley that there was no grace left for her. It was a statement, neither self-pitying nor defiant. Simply a comment on the condition of her being, a comment that emphasized the helplessness that Ashley felt so deeply.

Ashley was asleep when Nana stirred. She was not even aware of the fact that Nana had opened her eyes. Nor was she aware of the fact that she had pulled the intravenous tubes from her arm, the blood dripping slowly down her hand.

So determined was this magnificent lioness of a woman, she was capable of pushing her physical agony into a corner of her mind where the anguished rage of her soul abated long enough for her to make the moves to maneuver her body out of the high hospital bed. Slipping carefully over the edge, balancing herself on the bed, she steadied her body so that she could stand as upright as possible. Will alone pushed the pain beyond its own limits, and she took one step, then another. Blindly, instinctively, she opened the door.

The hallway was dim, clothed in the dulled hush of a hospital at night; the light from the nurses' station shined like a lost beacon from around the corner.

Holding on to the wall, Nana moved her stooped body slowly and silently along the corridor, feeling her way with her hands, leaving a scarlet trail behind her like the bloodied breadcrumbs of a hopelessly lost Gretel.

Inch by inch she moved, impelled by an instinct not just for survival, but for one last gesture to the living, an epitaph to life.

Her hand groped a metal handle on the wall. And she stopped. In a moment of recognition Nana paused. As if in salute to every dying person to whom some final and awesome attention must be paid, she pulled the handle.

Ashley jumped, startled instantly awake by the sound of the fire alarm. For one moment she did not know where she was. Then she registered the meaning of the sound and jumped from her cot, moving quickly to Nana's bed.

But there was no Nana. There was only the limp intravenous tube dripping its impotent contents onto the floor beside the bed.

Over the deafening noise of the alarm, she could hear people rushing down the hall, seeking the source of the fire. Thinking of Nana, she ran outside and looked down the corridor. There, in a heap on the floor, was her grandmother, still breathing, with a gentle smile on her face.

Ashley ran to her, almost colliding with an intern who had also seen her body.

"My God!" he exclaimed. "She's the one who pulled the alarm."

"Nana?" asked Ashley, stunned.

"Who else? Look." He pointed to the red handle of the alarm, just above them on the wall. "It's been activated. And she's the one who did it." He nodded his head in wonder and in oblique admiration. "But God only knows how she managed. Or why," he added as an afterthought.

Ashley looked at the almost beatific smile on Nana's face. "I understand why she did it. I understand perfectly."

Kate stood at the door to Ben Hoffer's apartment. She raised her hand to ring the bell, then hesitated. Puzzled, she thought a moment about what had caused her to stop. She was stunned to realize that she was dreading the meeting, that she did not want to see this man who had been her devoted lover.

Surprised at her own feelings, she tried to examine them. Very slowly, as if the message were being teletyped into her brain, she realized that when she was with Ben, she felt diminished, as if his control over her made her less of a person.

God knows, she thought wryly, I can't afford to lose any more of myself, or I'll turn into a living, breathing nothing. I can't allow it to happen.

Armed with this thought, she resolutely rang the bell.

Opening the door immediately, Ben greeted her with a kiss. Then he said, "I'm glad you could make it, Kate. But I hate to tell you that something has come up and I have to leave for an appointment uptown in an hour." He patted her gently, then added, "But I have a surprise for you, anyway."

Kate smiled at him and walked inside.

"Come," he said, leading her into the living room.

On the coffee table was a bouquet of roses and a small jewelry box.

Leaning over to smell the roses, she said simply, "They're beautiful."

He nodded, then replied, "Open the box now."

She stood up and laughed. "Wait just a minute. Give me a chance to catch my breath. I've only just gotten here."

"Kate," he said, shaking his head, his lips compressing ever so slightly. "When I go to the trouble to buy you a gift, the least, the very least, you can do is to open it when I ask you to."

Nodding, she picked up the box, but not without some effort. Opening it, she looked at the small earrings inside, just dots of gold attached to a post.

"Oh . . . they're lovely," she said. "Thank you."

"Put them on. Let me see how they look. I never did like those gold hoops you always wear. These are much more suitable for you."

Even Kate had her limits. And this was it. In a voice dripping with sarcasm, she replied, "Oh, if that's the case, then by all means I'll put them on immediately. I wouldn't want to disappoint you, Ben."

Ben greeted her words with a tight smile and then an exasperated exhaling of breath. "There's really no need to talk like that, Kate. Really there isn't . . ."

She stood before him, looking straight at him. "It's over, Ben." She was surprised at her own words.

"What are you talking about?" he asked, his body stiffening.

"It's over, that's all. I can't come over and play with you anymore."

"Don't be ridiculous, Kate. Did you have a bad morning getting the children off to school? What happened? It's best to recognize it, so you don't take your anger out on me like this."

"My anger is directed very deliberately at you."

"For God's sake, why?"

Understanding that his ignorance was genuine, Kate was suddenly sorry for him. "I'm not really angry, Ben. I'm just trying to tell you that it's over. But you won't listen."

"Of course, I'm listening to you, Kate. I just don't understand what you're saying. It's impossible."

"No," she said evenly. "It's not impossible, Ben. The fact is, it's over."

"All right, all right. We'll talk about it later. Just give me a moment, will you? I hate to interrupt this, but I have to change my shirt before I go to the meeting. Wait, and I'll get ready. Sit down. I'll only be a minute." He left the room.

Refusing to do his bidding, she remained standing. When he returned, he was just slipping his shirt on. Standing directly before her, without a word, he buttoned it up. He did it slowly, exposing his chest to her, his flat stomach, showing her what she would be missing.

Even in sex he made his demands. He always had. But she had loved it, she thought, remembering the last time they had gone to bed together.

He had undressed her slowly and then gently pulled her onto the bed. Lying there, wondering what he would do next, she reached for him.

"No," he directed. "Not yet."

His hands roaming over her body, he moved one down between her legs. Teasing her knowledgeably, he began the rhythm that he knew she loved. She came almost immediately, holding on to his back. He waited only a few moments before he started again. Whispering to her, he said over and over, "Again, Kate, again." Giving up to the pleasure, she closed her eyes and once more allowed it to happen, this time experiencing an orgasm of complete and satisfying intensity. Stopping to look at her, he smiled and kissed her, his tongue probing her mouth. But he did not take his hand away.

Wanting him inside her, she wriggled momentarily free of his hand.

"Oh, no." He smiled. "One more time."

"No," she gasped. "Can't. Already enough."

"One more time," he repeated, as he moved his hand back between her legs. When he touched her, the hypersensitivity caused her to blanch. But he refused to stop.

"No."

"Just close your eyes, Kate. Allow me to give you this pleasure. I want to."

She closed her eyes, but it didn't happen. Too much had already happened and she knew it was impossible.

She wriggled, but his finger kept moving.

"Can't," she said.

"Yes you can," he replied, his voice very low. "Of course you can. You will, Kate."

She tried, feeling the bare beginning of an orgasm. But it was useless, and she nodded her head back and forth on the pillow.

"No!" she said.

His voice louder, more demanding than he intended, he said, "I—want—you—to—come—goddamnit!"

Still the doll-lover, she obeyed his command. But there was no satisfaction in it.

And now, standing before him as he unbuckled his belt and unbuttoned his pants in order to tuck in his shirttail, he allowed her to see even more of what she would be missing.

Refusing to glance down, she said one more time, "It's over, Ben."

He nodded his head no, understanding how much she had always desired the sex with him.

Turning to leave, she said, "I'm sorry. I really am . . . you've been good to me. Generous."

He reached over and picked up the box with the earrings. "Here. Take these with you."

"I can't."

"But I bought them for you. You have to take them."

All she could say was, "I'm sorry, Ben."

He stared at her, as if he could not believe she were actually leaving him. His lips compressed into a hard line as she closed the door softly after her.

The evening after Nana set the fire alarm, the nurse came into her room to add more morphine into the intravenous tube that dripped mercifully into Nana. Noticing a small leak where the rubber tubing was spliced together midway between the bottle and her arm, the nurse adjusted the tubing.

Ashley watched, and then murmured, "Thank you," as the nurse left the room.

Ashley sat next to Nana, waiting for the drug to take effect. Nana's eyes fluttered, and she opened them briefly. Smiling wanly at her, she whispered, "I love you, Ashley. You gave me a new life."

"I love you, too, Nana," she replied, leaning over to kiss her on her sunken cheeks.

As if it were happening at that very moment, once again Ashley saw the mountain lion lying wounded on the ground before her, a magnificent animal brought low by an obscene hand of fate. "Kill it," Nana had said. But Ashley couldn't. Not then. But she could still hear Nana's voice, strong and clear and convinced: "You have no choice. When death is inevitable, you must not ever allow a creature to remain half alive. It is indecent to linger in pain when there is no hope." Those words, both an epitaph for the dead and a homage to the living, sang out in the room. It was as if Nana were speaking to her, telling her what to do. Only she wouldn't ever tell me to do it, thought Ashley, because she wouldn't want to burden me with it.

She looked at Nana lying there on the bed, wasted and alien and in pain. There was no grace left.

Without any deliberation, Ashley stood up and moved to the other side of the bed where the intravenous bottle hung, impotent and mocking. Taking the rubber tubing in her hands, she pulled it apart where the splice was. Holding the portion that led directly into Nana's vein, she tipped it downward, draining the contents into a water glass that stood on the night table next to the bed.

God have mercy on her soul, Ashley prayed. God have mercy on mine. She stood a moment with her eyes closed, then bent over the exposed and empty tube. God have mercy.

Taking a deep breath, she blew hard into the tube, pushing the last of the liquid into Nana's vein through the catheter taped securely to her arm. Giving it two more hard and long blows that would cause an air embolism in her lungs, she turned and reattached the tubes quickly.

Lying down next to her, Ashley took her grandmother in her arms. "I love you, Nana. I love you." Kissing her, not letting go, she continued, cooing the soothing words as if Nana were an infant. "I love you. Good night, Nana. Sleep well. Sleep now," she whispered. Refusing to close her eyes and allow Nana to die without bearing witness, Ashley assumed full responsibility for her act in the only way she knew. "I love you, Nana. Sleep now. Sleep." Ashley held on and waited. Waited for what seemed a compressed eternity. Waited not for her grandmother's death, but for her deliverance instead. Her deliverance from the indecency and lack of grace that she so abhorred.

Ashley's face was next to Nana's when she felt her jerk.

"I love you," whispered Ashley.

"Juan?" That was the last word, hoarse and soft and astonished, that Marguerite Van Every Martinez ever spoke.

# CHAPTER 12

Ashley arrived home at four in the morning. She had stayed with Nana for over an hour in a long and private farewell. Before summoning the night nurse, she wiped up the traces of the intravenous fluid that had dripped on the floor, rinsed out the glass on the night table, and kissed Nana one last time.

Paul Coston had come immediately to the hospital, observing the formal rituals of death. For one brief moment he looked inquiringly at Ashley, as if a silent question had died on his lips. Then he wrote on the death certificate: "Death from heart failure due to complications of tuberculous meningitis."

He suspects, Ashley thought. But then she dismissed the fear that accompanied the suspicion with the sure knowledge that he, too, loved Nana, and wished an end to her suffering.

The only question Paul Coston asked Ashley was if she would like to spend the remainder of the night at his home in Santa Fe, rather than make the long drive back to the house that now belonged to Ashley.

Wanting to be among familiar surroundings, she refused, even though she knew that it would only accentuate the emptiness, the bereavement she felt.

As soon as Ashley entered the house, she was startled by the comfort it offered instead. The very atmosphere seemed to erase the anguished edges of guilt that might have grown sharper as she considered the momentous act she had just committed—an act of love bound by the muted ribbons of risk and mercy.

Dazed, Ashley undressed methodically and slipped, weary and alone, into bed. Only then did she sense it. The presence. She knew that she was exhausted and confused enough to hallucinate. Perhaps that's what it was, just a trick the mind plays when it has been pushed to the far and lonely side of its limits, an illusion that accompanies the sanctity of mourning.

Reality or mirage, fact or fancy, she saw it. Saw him. For a few vivid and unforgettable moments he hovered near her, as a father would bend over an infant. It was not frightening or intimidating. It was simply an essence of being come to console, to relieve. An apparition of deliverance. Very slowly it faded, until it vanished with the morning light. But the feeling it left behind was one of infinite comfort.

Two nights later, after she told Dottie and Kate that she had killed Nana, Ashley derived a similar comfort from the presence of her friends. It was one that she had experienced before when her parents had died. And she was deeply grateful for their touches, as well as their conversation.

The night before, Ashley called Patrick in Ireland. The overseas connection did not allow him to hear the sorrowful inflection of her voice when he first heard her, and he launched into his enthusiasm for how well his book was coming along.

"It took me about a month, Ashley. But every day I write, I feel stronger. And I'm convinced it's good."

"I'm glad."

"Ashley?" he finally asked. "Is something wrong?"

"Nana's dead," she replied.

Weeping openly, he tried to talk through his tears. "I'm sorry . . . she was . . . one . . . magnificent woman." Regaining control, he said, "It will take me a couple of days to pack and get ready. But I'll get there as soon as I can, love."

"No," she replied, understanding how much it meant to him that his writing was moving so beautifully. "Finish your book first. I really mean it, Patrick. I want you to."

He hesitated. They had never played games, saying one thing when they meant another. But he did want to make certain that she was not merely giving lip service to the gesture.

"Are you sure, Ashley? You know I'll come to you."

"I'm sure, Patrick. I promise. We both have things we must do."

"Are you alone?" he asked.

"No. Dottie and Kate are coming, and . . . oh, I wrote you about my half brother. And I want to meet him. There are a lot of things to take care of. And if I do need you, I promise that I'll let you know, Patrick."

"Promise?"

"Yes."

"I love you very much, Ashley."

"I love you. We'll be together soon. And then we'll celebrate the completion of your book."

When they finally finished talking, Ashley knew that she had done the right thing. Although she missed him with a passion and depth that haunted her most of the time, they both had recognized from the beginning that if their relationship were to flower to its full power and fulfillment, he had to abolish the mantle of failure that he had worn since the publication of his last book.

Ashley was sitting on the terrace having lunch with Kate and Dottie when Joseph Rosetta came down from the mountain.

That morning Ashley had learned of the contents of Nana's will, and they talked about it over lunch. Nana had left remembrances to all her friends, objects that they had admired at one time or another. The house and surrounding land wás left to Ashley. But the mountain cabin, protected by one hundred acres, had been given to Joseph Rosetta.

Nana left Dottie some selected photographs, among which was one of Dottie and Jack that Nana had taken on one of her brief visits to New York when they were all together. The anguish Dottie felt when she saw the picture burned into the heart of her. Until then she had been too deeply ashamed to tell Ashley and Kate what had happened with Jack and Sarah Jacobs. Finally, she had revealed it all to them, and her friends had accepted the story without judging. They knew that Dottie had suffered for the mistake.

To Kate, Nana had left her collection of books on New Mexico archaeology, as well as a number of artifacts to accompany it.

They were both deeply touched by Nana's gestures, and were talking about it when Joseph Rosetta appeared, tall and proud and primitively elegant, on the terrace.

Ashley stood up immediately, feeling slightly awkward. She had told Dottie and Kate about Joseph, about meeting him for the first time as she came down the mountain after scattering Nana's ashes.

Years before, Nana had told him about Ashley's existence. But because of John Van Every's alienation from her, Nana never felt that it was her right to tell Ashley about her brother. It was only when she was dying that she had finally revealed that secret.

And now, confronted with the reality of his presence, Asley could feel his power. And she wondered if he hated her.

Ashley walked over to where Joseph stood. Taking him by the arm, she introduced him.

"These are my friends Kate Griffin and Dottie

Langford," said Ashley with a formal grace. "I'd like you to meet Joseph Rosetta."

He shook hands with them both, his eyes piercing great gaping holes into Kate, who was the epitome of everything that he detested and to whom he found himself unaccountably attracted. Then he turned to Ashley.

"I needed time up there alone to make peace with myself about our grandmother's death. I think now that we can share our sorrow." He paused for a moment, looking straight into her eyes. "We can share it as brother and sister."

Immensely relieved, Ashley moved to him then, and he took her in his arms, surrounding her with his love. He drew her to him as if he had always known her, and she wept for the first time since Nana's death. Wept for her loss. And for his. There was no shame or awkwardness, only the searing and permanent sharing that they could finally permit themselves. He stroked her head, saying nothing, waiting patiently for her tears to reach bottom.

Finally, she said simply, "I'm sorry."

He smiled at her. "There's no need. I shed my tears already."

Stunned, Kate and Dottie sat there and watched. Kate was perfectly silent, awed by the wonder of the moment, and the beauty of the man.

Joseph stayed with them for the remainder of the week. During that time it seemed as if there were at least one important conversation taking place at any given moment.

Both Dottie and Kate felt as if they might be intruding on a new family reunion, and made the offer to return to New York earlier than they had planned. But Ashley and Joseph insisted that they stay, knowing that there would be plenty of time for them.

The only awkwardness that existed during that period was the growing attraction between Kate and Joseph. It had blossomed instantly, like a freeze-frame film that shows the life cycle of a flower in three minutes. Everything existed for them. Everything and nothing.

Kate was drawn to him with a power that she had never before felt. They would walk for hours, talking, exploring, explaining. And he told her the names of the flowers. Sometimes he would look at her, and she would feel that there was nothing about her that he did not already know, that there was nothing she thought or felt that would cause him to turn from her. Because what she experienced with Joseph was total acceptance.

Her feelings moved beyond what she had experienced with Sol. For she felt with Joseph as if he were her oldest friend, as if she had always known him and that she always would.

Two days before she was to leave, Joseph said to Kate, "I am going up to the cabin for two nights. Would you come with me?" He had never touched her. And yet she felt naked before him.

Kate sat at the breakfast table, twisting her wedding band on her finger.

When she did not answer immediately, he said, "It is your choice, Kate. We both know the conditions, and I cannot make the choice for you."

Choice? she thought. How long has it been? My decision, my life, my choice.

"Yes," she said simply. "Yes, I'll come with you."

They rode up the mountain together, Kate sitting in front of Joseph on his horse, with his arms around her holding the reins. For a long while they rode silently. Then he began to tell her the names of the trees and the flowers that they passed.

Kate remembered, then, another man, another time, in which she had also learned the names of the flowers. And she thought how terribly long it had been since she had felt the way she had when Sol touched her face, how long it had been since she experienced this total serenity.

When they reached the cabin, he helped her off the horse, picking her up and placing her gently on the ground. Only then did he kiss her. Soft as a brush of a butterfly's wings. And as beautiful.

He took her face between his hands and said, "It will be lovely." Then he led her into the cabin.

They undressed slowly, each touching the other, exploring, appreciating, finding little need for words; words that could not possibly say what they were expressing with their hands, their lips, their eyes.

Then he picked her up and carried her to the bed, laying her there and standing beside her, looking down at her nakedness with a secret smile on his face. He leaned over and touched her belly, caressed her breasts. Reaching up, she pulled him to her, pulled him to a Kate that she thought had died long ago with a last leap off a bridge.

It was a moment that existed outside time, suspended and golden, as if they had cast their own spell as a lasting gift to themselves. Slowly, slowly they floated together on the enchantment they had created, the magic of their bodies meeting. When finally he entered her, Kate cried out, filled at last. She would not close her eyes, refusing to allow one moment of this beauty to slip past her. She watched the tendons of his neck stretch fierce and strong as he moved above her, his head thrown back. Only then did she close her eyes, close them tight to her coming and his. He watched her, her loveliness and her abandon, understanding instinctively her every need.

As if in slow motion, he fell toward her, floating, free, joyous. And without warning she cried, weeping tears so strong with happiness that she could not even touch the source. He held her in his arms, sharing her emotion fully, a man consumed by the beauty of his own fire.

They stayed together for two days in that country that belonged only to them. Then they bid each other good-bye. There was a sadness in their parting. Yet it, too, was suspended in the glow of their loving.

Kate carried this with her when she left. Just as she wore the tiny silver bird on a chain around her neck.

It was a bird Joseph had created from his own fancy just the week before. And when he gave it to her, he said, "I must have known I was making this for you."

Delicate and graceful and free, it rested above her heart as a talisman, a declaration of her own being, her own uniqueness, her own freedom to choose.

When she was finally alone with Joseph, Ashley feared that an awkwardness might sprout between them, like a weed appearing on a perfectly manicured lawn. But her fears melted away as they opened up their hearts. They learned about each other's lives with an eagerness and interest that consumed them, sometimes staying up until early morning talking and explaining and exploring their pasts.

One day Joseph said simply to Ashley, "I think it is time that I take you to meet my mother."

"Oh . . . Joseph, I don't know about that. It frightens me just thinking about it."

"Don't allow it to. Just be you and she'll love you."

On the way to the Santo Domingo Reservation, Joseph told Ashley about her.

"After I was born, Mother sold jewelry on the streets of Santa Fe. Later at the Palace of the Governors."

"Oh . . . " Ashley's voice cried for her.

"It's too late for that, Ashley. She was proud and she made her own way. Then it was just another way to make a living. In the olden days the Santo Domingans were the possessors of the Cerrittos turquoise mines.

Jewelry was a fine tradition for us. An old one. In the twenties and thirties, unfortunately, the Anglos took over the mines and decimated them. We were left with very little, and we produced an increasingly poor quality of jewelry. All but a few of us . . . my mother among them. My grandfather had no sons. And so, against custom, he taught my mother the old ways, as he had learned his craft from his father. She refused to compromise and consequently made a living. Because she was good."

"Didn't she take money from Nana?"

"For the most part Mother supported us. She used the money that Nana gave her to buy a house and send me to the university. She recognized the necessity and used the money appropriately."

"I'm glad."

"Anyway, by the time I was five years old, I was able to help her. She taught me how to grind and polish the hishi on the same slab of sandstone that had been passed down in her family for generations. We did it the old way. Not on a wheel, but on a fine old piece of stone."

"Did you like it then? When you were so young?"

Joseph smiled indulgently, his eyes on the road. "It had nothing to do with liking it, Ashley. It had to do with survival."

Driving through the property line into the reservation, Ashley was astonished at the barrenness of the place. It was dusty and dry, speaking of a level of poverty that she simply did not expect.

Houses and buildings were scattered about, with the Jemez Mountains as a backdrop. The scarcity of water advertised itself. The land was flat and without relief, and scores of dogs roamed free, their padded paws stirring up dust into little clouds.

As they neared Marcelina's house, Ashley became very nervous. She thought of how she was raised, never wanting, having only to ask in order to receive. As she looked around her, she recognized the harshness of the life her brother had lived, and she was infinitely grateful that he did not harbor any bitterness toward her. She only hoped that his mother would feel the same.

Marcelina Rosetta's house, simply constructed of adobe and timbers, was quite starkly beautiful. Flowers bloomed in the late September sun, flowers she tended carefully and lovingly against a climate that did not favor them.

Joseph took Ashley by the arm, squeezing it in a gesture of confidence, as they entered the house.

At fifty years old, Marcelina Rosetta was still a beautiful woman. Ashley could see even then what must have attracted her father. She was small and delicate and proud, the kind of woman who walked on her own path, compelling others to follow her.

"This is Ashley, Mother," Joseph said simply.

"Welcome," said Marcelina, smiling in an attempt to put her guest at ease.

Unable to do anything except move directly into the awkward feelings that she carried so tenuously with her, Ashley took the hand of this woman who might have been her mother. "Thank you. You're very gracious to welcome me. I'm not certain that I could do the same."

Marcelina nodded in understanding. "It all happened a long time ago, Ashley, and it had nothing to do with you. I've led a good life and I've had a son to love. A son who is your brother. And you will always be welcome in my home."

Six weeks after Kate returned from New Mexico, on an evening when she was certain that Chris would be at the hospital attending a special lecture, Kate invited William to dinner. She had not mentioned Joseph to anyone since she had returned from Santa Fe, but she felt that it was finally time to talk about him.

Neither Joseph nor Kate had written the other a letter. It had been more or less agreed between them that if they were ever to see each other again, it would be Kate's choice. Joseph made it very clear that he would do absolutely nothing to influence her, other than to be there, if Kate were to decide in his favor.

When she told William all this, he was at first unwilling to offer any opinion.

"But you're my brother, Will. I need your advice."

"I suppose so, Kate. But I have no intention of pushing you in one direction or another. All I can tell you is to consider it very carefully."

"God knows I have," she replied.

"Not in that way," he said with a mischievous grin. Then he turned serious. "I know what it's like to live without the person you love, Kate. I've known it for a long time. I have no doubt, of course, that I will meet someone else. But up to now, it's been difficult."

"I've been there, too," said Kate softly.

"Yes, you have," Will agreed. "But you chose to turn your back on it."

"Sol died, Will."

"Now, Kate, if you want me to talk to you like a brother, then you have to accept some pretty harsh judgments from me. That comes in the package deal. Okay?"

She nodded.

"First and foremost, you're dodging the issue, playing games with yourself. It wasn't Sol's death that caused the split between the two of you. It was your decision alone. And don't try to convince yourself otherwise. Lying to yourself can cause a lot of problems. Don't start it."

"A lot of the problem was Mother and Daddy," she ventured.

"There you go again. Trying to blame it on someone else. And, of course, it *was* Mother and Father. But you—and only you, Kate—made the decision. It's about time that you take responsibility for it. Until you do that, there's no way you can make a responsible decision about the rest of your future."

"I'll try, Will. It's hard, that's all."

"Did anyone ever tell you it would be easy?" Kate could hear the annoyance in his voice. She rarely heard Will speak like this and it made her uneasy. It also gained her full attention.

"You turned away from love once," he continued. "And now it's your decision: Will you—can you afford to—do it again?"

"I don't know," she said, bewildered. "I really don't know. The difference in backgrounds, life-styles, all that."

"God knows, it's something that you have to give serious thought to."

"One thing I do know," said Kate. "New Mexico is a great place to study archaeology."

"You still thinking about that?" he asked.

"I never stopped," she said. "I've read almost all of the books that Nana gave me. It started when I found that point. I love it."

"You can also study it here, you know. Right here in the middle of New York City. So don't use that as an excuse to make a move to New Mexico."

Kate smiled. "You're not letting me get away with anything, are you?"

"Those were the conditions, Kate."

"I know." Then she began to giggle.

"What's so funny?"

"I was just thinking of Mother's and Daddy's reaction if I were to chuck everything and move to New Mexico with the children." She paused.

"And?" he asked.

"Once they heard he was an Indian—with just a little Mexican mixed in for good measure—they would plead with me to return to New York in order to find a nice Jew to settle down with."

Her stomach heaved, rebelling at the insult that had just hit it. Joseph held her as she vomited.

"It's all right," he said. "It's to be expected. I told you."

Ashley could not speak, could not say one word in her haste to rid herself of the taste. She did not know which was worse: actually eating the peyote, tasting it like a dry snake crawling over her tongue in an acrid, hideous journey, or the retching afterward. She had never tasted anything like it, these innocent-looking little buttons from cactus. At first, she thought, it was like chewing cardboard soaked in a loathsome substance. But that was only a prelude. When she swallowed it, her stomach reacted with an astounding violence, returning the offending matter immediately.

Joseph had warned Ashley that this would happen, but she was unprepared for the violence of her reaction. She had thought it might be something like swallowing castor oil or being ill with the flu. But that was a piece of cake compared to what was happening to her now.

"It's been a part of my—of our—people for centuries," he had explained. "It will help you to understand yourself and the world in which you live. You will see how we are truly one with the universe."

Ashley had nodded.

"I won't go into all the religious rites involved. But you should know that it is a primary form of communication with God. Or the Spirit. Or Life. It is a way to a kind of knowledge that you have never touched before."

"I never was very religious," Ashley had said doubtfully.

"That's not the point," he replied. "This will open

up worlds to you. Ones that you've never known. But that live inside you. You should know them. Understand them. They are part of you, Ashley, these worlds, these visions. They belong to you."

"Do you think that applies to everyone?"

"I would think so," he answered. "It's a matter of seeing inside yourself. There is great power there. You cannot learn it from me. You have to experience it for yourself. That is the only way. And once you experience it, it is yours forever."

"I don't know if it frightens me or not," she said. "I've never even smoked marijuana."

"It's not the same at all. I promise. And I'll stay with you. I won't leave you."

"All right," she had reluctantly agreed. And now she was very sorry, indeed.

When she finally finished vomiting, Joseph said, "Now eat some more."

Appalled, she looked at him, trying to trust beyond what she had already experienced.

"It's important. I promise."

And so she did it, chewing the buttons as quickly as possible, willing herself not to vomit again.

She did not know how much time elapsed before the fire grew brighter. The colors, vivid in ways she had never known before, almost spoke to her in a flaming insistence that she see. Green, blue, red, the gold of the brightest sunset, the black of a devil's soul. Each color stood out individually, as if it had been cut out and pasted against an undulating background.

The daisies on the table of the cabin shone white like a vision of God. She looked down at her hands and could see the blood coursing through her veins, deep blue, distinct, alive.

Joseph was there. Joseph her brother, her kin. Joseph whose love for her now palpably emanated from him with an increasing strength. She watched in awe as his face changed slowly into that of Alexander's.

Not the one of her nightmares, but the face that expressed how much Alexander loved her, loved the splendor of what they shared. He smiled at her, then touched her face. She could feel the cool burning of his hand, the absolute trust it carried with it. It was a touch of loving and a touch of farewell. In that single gesture he eliminated the last barrier that stood between Ashley and Patrick. It was a touch that freed her for her own future, and she understood the depth of caring that allowed it. Alexander's was now a transcendent love that reached to the farthest corner of her being, engulfing her, liberating her. At peace, she moved beyond him as her field of vision enlarged, as if her peripheral vision had been magically expanded. The pores of her skin were there to take it in; the taste on her lips was new, the touch of a hand profound, the weight of her body diminishing so that she floated in a golden light, the color of lemon, the color of fire, the color of life. The separation between herself and inanimate objects became indistinguishable; everything took on life, movement, color—iridescent, kaleidoscopic, wondrous. A glimpse became a renaissance, a touch became a permanent bonding. There was no more Ashley. No more Joseph, or Alexander, or Patrick, or Nana. Not in the way she had known before. It was all a continuum, her world, each object a part of the other, moving, floating freely in a scheme of its own, before and after life and where she was then. Suspended in between, and a part of it all: birth and death touching, life becoming and being. There were no more boundaries, no parameters to hold her, no walls to stop her. They were all together with her, because they all touched in the time beyond time where a teardrop is as potent as the river into which it flows. It was a spiritual sublimity that floated in the space of her dreams, bathed in a purity of light she had never known, a splendor she had never seen. She was part of it all, and always would be. It was hers now, this vast dominion of vision and understanding. And she knew at last that she would never again be afraid; of the dark or the light, of death or passion or the end of love. She could not be afraid, because it already belonged to her. As she belonged to it. She was a part of it now.

"I received a curious note in the mail today," said Chris casually.

"Oh?" asked Kate, sipping her wine carefully, reading her husband, knowing that he was about to drop one of his little surprise bombs.

"It was about you."

"What about me?" she asked, her antennae now on red alert.

"That you've been having an affair."

Kate's heart crawled to her throat, choking off the air that she tried to breathe so indifferently. She forced a smile onto her paralyzed face. "And who, may I ask, is regaling you with that information?"

"Anonymous."

"Last name?"

"Anonymous again, Kate." He paused, preparing to plunge in one of the minor darts. "Initials A.A.," he said significantly, looking at her glass of wine sitting beside her.

"How delightful . . ."

"Well . . ." he said. "Are you?"

"Am I what? A.A.?"

"Watch it, Kate. You know what I mean."

"Will the prosecutor please rephrase the question."

"One more time, Kate. I asked you—and I want a direct answer—if you are having an affair."

"From my point of view, I really can't see how that would make any difference between us. But, to answer your question, no." Benjamin, the fink, she thought. Ben Hoffer, the goddamn sneaky fink, doing this to me. But, still, I'm holding my own for once in the face of the enemy. Maybe it's because I don't care.

"Then why should anyone send such a note, Kate."

"Beats me," she answered, her fingers stroking the silver bird that she wore around her neck. Then, with an instinct that had lain dormant in her, she turned on the offensive. "I'm surprised, though, that *I* haven't ever received such a note. That's what is really curious." With this tactical maneuver, her voice had taken on an unintentional taunt, one that served to increase Chris's anger, while giving Kate more confidence.

"What are you talking about?"

"I believe you know that as well as I do, Chris. After all, I'm not quite as naive as you've taken me for all these years. Nor as ill-informed," she added with a bluff.

"I haven't taken you for anything, Kate, except for what you are." He was retrenching. She could hear it in his voice, see it in his body language.

"Which is?"

"My wife."

"Fancy that," she said. "You could have fooled me."

"Not that you've always behaved as such," he returned with a volley that slipped a wedge into her fortification.

"No . . . I suppose I haven't," she said, suddenly thoughtful. "We haven't been much good—neither of us—at being husband and wife recently." She was speaking seriously now, believing that it mattered.

Relieved, Chris moved with the change. "What happened to us?"

"I wish I knew."

"If you'd only stop tormenting yourself, Kate. It would help all of us."

"Tormenting?"

"Nothing ever seems to be enough for you. Whatever I do isn't enough," he said accusingly.

"I wasn't aware that it was all up to you," she said,

on the edge of bitterness, losing sight of the reconciliation upon which they had touched.

"You wanted to get married, we get married. You wanted children, and we have two sons. You wanted a larger apartment, and we got one."

"And now we're getting ready to buy a summer place," she chanted, as if it were a new but already tiresome litany.

"That's right."

"Didn't you want any of those things, Chris? Was it all me? Did you not want to marry me? Didn't you, too, want our family to have more living space?"

"Of course," he replied. "But it was done for you."

"Why just me, if it was good for all of us?"

"Because you're the one who initiated it."

"For all of us," Kate said firmly. "For all of us, Chris." All the time she spoke, she was aware of herself standing up to him. She rose from her chair and walked across the room to refill her glass of wine.

"What is it?" he asked. "What do you want?"

"I don't know what I want," she answered with as much honesty as she could muster. "Just something more. I know there's something more." Like Joseph, she added to herself, needing him then.

"More? For Christ's sake. Always more. You *have* more, goddamnit! There are women in this world who would sell their souls for half of what you have. You know that. Don't I provide you with everything, including some incredibly well-used charge cards?" He shot the latter at her without warning.

"It's a way of filling the holes in my life, Chris. At least I recognize the cause," she said with confessional honesty. "Bloomingdale's and all that."

Then he fired off the barrage that turned the tide of the battle. "Looks to me, from the letter I received today, that you have found yet another way to fill your holes."

Her face registered the blow. "That was ugly, Chris.

So ugly. Especially coming from you." After a valiant attempt she began to crumble, not understanding why, only knowing that it had happened. Knowing that she could not stand up indefinitely to the anger that stood before her like an accusing finger, wagging as if it were attached to her father.

Joseph had set her free too soon, had allowed flight before the fledgling was fully ready. The timing had been wrong, she thought bitterly, as she twisted the silver chain around her finger as if it would save her.

"Who else should it come from, Kate?" he asked in a mockery of innocence. "What more can I do? Tell me, and I'll do it."

"I don't know. Just support me for a change."

"In what?" He was driving hard now. "Support you in pottery? In weaving? In shopping?" Then he delivered the coup de grace. "In fucking? Or drinking?"

She looked down in defeat. "Why is it always me?" she whimpered.

"Because I've tried," he replied, strong now. "God knows I've tried."

"Well, so have I, Chris."

"Then why are we living parallel lives?"

"I don't have an answer any more than you do," she said in the form of a plea for mercy, for peace. "I know that our family's important to me. But I feel defeated. Disoriented. I don't know what to do or where to go . . ." She drifted off, no longer knowing in which direction she should be moving.

Once he saw that she had buckled, he softened. "It's important to me, Kate. If you'd just try to be content with what you have, it would help. And what you have is considerable, I might add. If you'd only try, then we might get things going again."

"I'll try, Chris . . . I promise I will."

Even though California made her think of Jack, Dottie still enjoyed her trips to Los Angeles. She experienced an additional sense of power when she was seen in public with Luke Kranz. Her very narrow circle of friends and her work were the only things of value that existed in Dottie's life. The irony was, of course, that she had abused both.

Jack had taken passion with him when he walked out the door that night. With that gone, she poured her energies even more powerfully into her work. It had become her life, her passion, and there was not much she would not do—she had already discovered—to preserve it.

On a bright California morning, the kind of morning that makes West Coast converts out of us all, Dottie arrived at Luke Kranz's office about twenty minutes early. The door was open and the secretary was gone. She intended to knock and walk on in. That was before she heard the conversation taking place behind Luke's office door.

A shrill woman's voice exploded. "What do you mean, he didn't like her? Just look at her. She's a knockout. How should I know he didn't like blondes?"

"Calm down now, Jill. Just calm down. I thought he'd go for it. My mistake," replied Luke Kranz.

"Mistake? Mistake? I take my daughter to meet his holiness himself . . . because you tell me he likes them under fourteen. Well, she *is* under fourteen. You know that. You've known her since she was born, for Christ's sake. She just happens to look older than her age."

"Oh, Mom," said a tiny voice. "Let's go."

"Not yet, Beverley. Not yet. This isn't over."

"It should be, Jill." Luke's voice again. "It definitely should be."

Dottie was mesmerized, unable to pull herself together so that she could walk out.

"Are you telling me that Mel Stewart—*the* Mel Stewart—did not find my daughter pleasing enough even to offer her a . . . Pepsi?"

"He's very nervous at the moment, Jill. We're trying to put together a deal and things are just not working out. Perhaps another time . . ."

"Another time!" she shrieked. "You think I'd put my Beverley into a position so that he could reject her a second time? You got your brains in your balls, Kranz."

"Well, after all, Jill, you're the one who put her in this position in the first place." He paused significantly. "A position, I might add, that has definite elements of sleaziness in it."

The woman's voice turned hard. "No sleazier than pimping for an actor who likes little girls and who's so messed up on cocaine that he can't remember his lines unless they're pasted all over the walls for him to read, Luke. All of America should just know *that,* my friend."

"If you're threatening me, Jill, I think you're barking up the wrong tree. We were both in on it. And I hardly think you can blow the whistle without condemning yourself and your lovely daughter here in the process."

"We'll see about that."

"Let's put it this way, Jill." He spoke with an ominous calm. "If you do anything, anything at all, I'll make certain that you are more than just implicated, Jill. I'll give new meaning to the saying 'like mother like daughter.' And I always keep my promises."

Dottie was ill. Hearing this was out of some foreign nightmare, an ugly eavesdropping, obscene and repulsive. Just as she turned to leave, the door of the office opened. An attractive but shopworn woman stormed through it, a child in tow, a nymphet child, beautiful and innocent and frightened. They rushed past Dottie, mother-harpie dragging child-bride. The woman threw one malevolent glance at Dottie, then departed without a word.

Dottie stood there stunned, too dazed to move. It

has nothing to do with me, she said to herself. Besides, she thought. It's over. And I do have an appointment with Luke Kranz. *The* Luke Kranz.

Pulling herself together, pasting an indifferent expression on her face, Dottie got up and walked to the door of Luke's office.

Knocking softly, she called, "Luke?"

"Yes?"

"It's me. Dottie."

"Well, come right on in," he invited cheerfully. He was mixing a drink when she entered. Turning to her, he put out his arms. "Dottie baby! So glad to see you."

She moved to him and gave him a peck on the cheek. Holding on to her shoulders, he leaned away from her and scrutinized her face. Nodding slowly, he said, "Oh, you heard."

"Yes, Luke. I heard."

"And you're sickened and repelled and shocked."

"That's a close enough approximation."

Luke raised his eyebrows in an expression that resembled a shrug of the shoulders. "That's the way life is, baby. Some like 'em young and some don't."

"I'll grant you that one, Luke," said Dottie as she took hold of herself. "But do *you* have to be involved?"

"Not usually. But this is Mel Stewart. Megabucks, Dottie. That's what he stands for. I make no less than a half a million dollars a year off him. That's a sum that compensates for a lot of sins."

"Perversions," Dottie amended.

Ignoring her remark, he asked, "Can I build you a drink?"

"I could use one. Scotch?"

"Have some wonderful stuff right here. Glenfiddich. Knock you off your ass . . . which, I might add, is looking pretty good these days."

Awed at the cold center of a man who could stand before her and talk like that directly after being involved in such a scene, Dottie just watched him. He handed her the drink. "Neat. Drink it neat. The only way."

"Thank you."

"Sit down, sit down," he invited cordially. "Make yourself at home. This is a big one. And after we complete our business, I'll take you to the best restaurant in town."

"All right, Luke." She was decidedly cool to him and he did not miss it. But for the moment he chose to ignore it. He knew his customers.

"Now . . . the reason that you're here is that I gave Mel Stewart the manuscript of that new book you sent me."

"And?"

"Loved it. Crazy about it. Says he'll do it if I can get Berlini to direct. One phone call was all it took. Big money in this, Dottie. Big clout."

"What's big?"

"Two hundred thousand for your client . . . twenty for you, Dottie. Twenty big ones. And that's just the beginning."

Dottie sat there calmly, but the lure of the numbers he was discussing had struck home.

"Plenty for you, plenty for me. And points for everyone. Even the writer."

"Net or gross?" asked Dottie.

"Net."

"Gross, Luke. If there's that much money involved, it can be gross."

"Dottie, Dottie. You know better than that. Writers never get gross. Just net. You know that."

"And I also know that writers never get any of the profits, because net profits don't exist. The studios never learned how to compute it."

"But your client gets points, Dottie. It *looks* good."

Dottie decided to drop the subject for the time being. "How much are you getting out of this, Luke?"

"We all get a nice piece of the pie, Dottie."

"I have this suspicion that yours is unusually large, Luke."

His voice turned hard. "If it is, it's because I'm the one who's put it together. I'm the only one who can do it. I can get the movie action, the book action, and the talent to go with it."

"Book action? It's still in manuscript form. Nobody's seen it yet."

"I already called Mack Enright at Kluger's. Said they'd take it sight unseen if I put this package together."

Sitting forward in her chair, Dottie objected. "This book deserves something classier, Luke. It's good. Too good for that sleazy house."

"Classy houses won't pay enough money. You know that. That's why I wanted you out here instead of doing all this over the phone. It's a package, Dottie. A package that we put together. And that means the star, the director, the producer, hard- and soft-cover."

"You're forgetting the novel out of which all this grows."

"And the novel," said Luke, nodding his hairy head.

"Let us not forget," pursued Dottie, "that you wouldn't have any of this without that precious manuscript I sent you."

"And let us not forget," he returned, "that you wouldn't have the money you're going to get from it without me. Nor the power you have gained since you've known me," he added, with a dash of remembrance to make the underling properly grateful. "We might be able to make a deal on the screenplay for your client. First draft, anyway. With a step clause."

"I take it, Luke," Dottie said evenly, "that you stand to make three times what I make out of all this."

Kranz sat before her calmly, neither confirming nor denying.

"Which means," continued Dottie, "that if this deal

is acceptable, you get the screenplay for my client." Then she lost her temper. "My God," she said with growing disgust. "If you can get a fourteen-year-old for Mel Stewart, surely you can get a lousy screenplay assignment for my client."

Luke put up his hand. "Wait just a minute here. Slow down. I want to get something straight." His voice was even, hard. "Now you listen to this. It was unfortunate that you overheard the scene that took place in this office. But I won't have you acting high and mighty because of it. You have the option right now of getting up and walking right out of here. You don't have to stay and pass your half-assed judgments. If you don't want to be sullied by doing business with such unsavory characters, then get the hell out." He paused, still a master of timing. "But if you stay, you need to understand that there will not be any more references to it. I don't need you passing judgment on me or my associates. All I have to do is to call your client and tell him about the offer I have and he'll drop you like a nasty habit. Money talks in this world. And I was under the impression that it was carrying on a pretty good conversation with you until a few minutes ago."

Dottie looked straight at him, but said nothing.

"All right," he said. "Which is it? In or out?"

"I'll have to think about it."

"Be my guest."

## CHAPTER 13

"Marry me," whispered Patrick, leaning across the table toward Ashley.

"Not yet."

"Why?"

"The best reason for getting married is having children. And we haven't really discussed that yet."

"Great idea, children," he said.

"What would a child of ours think if its father suddenly took off to Ireland for a year?"

"We'd all go together. As a matter of fact, I saw a house near the sea that I want to buy. I could work and you could work. And we'd be a grand family, Ashley. A grand one."

"We'll see," said Ashley thoughtfully. "Let's wait a little while."

"As long as that little while includes me, I don't mind," he said.

Having finished the first draft of his novel, Patrick had returned to New York just before Christmas. The first thing he had done was call Ashley. She had stayed at Nana's house until then, spending hours working on her photographs, talking with Joseph, riding Troika into the mountains.

It had been a time of growth for Ashley, the kind that can only result from being alone with oneself. And she felt that it was important for her to explore the hidden meanings in the life around her.

She began to see things differently. She began to

understand her surroundings. She was no longer a spectator; she was a part of everything, the heart of a flower or the flight of a hawk. And she knew that she would never feel alone again.

Patrick immediately sensed the change in Ashley. There was a luminosity about her, a new kind of confidence. But it traveled deeper than that, into the soul of her eyes where her serenity reached out to everyone she encountered.

Frequently, people are threatened by those who appear to have found serenity—threatened and drawn to them. But there was no threat in Ashley. She was a woman who dared, who reached toward her own dreams without hesitation in the passage, or fear of the consequences. She had achieved a confidence that was neither bland in its manifestation nor simple in its expression. Filled with fire and light, she shone with a radiance that was bewitching and compelling, a lodestone for those on the other side who sensed that there was something beyond the sunset besides darkness, that there was something in the soul of a fire besides pain. She had lived where others only dreamed of traveling. But the knowledge evoked admiration, not envy.

"I'd like to do a book with you, Patrick."

"On what?"

"On Nana," Ashley replied. "After she died, I went through some of her unpublished photographs. And I also took some pictures of her that I want to be included. One, especially, of her shortly before she died. I took it in the hospital, and for a woman who was terminally ill, there was incredible dignity in her even then." She paused, remembering setting up the camera over Nana's protests. She had waited until the light had come through the window, bathing Nana's face in it. It was a fine photograph. "Will you write the text?"

"You won't believe this," Patrick replied, "but I had

already thought of doing a book about her. And, of course, I'd love to."

"Let's get to work," said Ashley.

It had been another one of those particularly bad days for Kate. A rerun of her low-key but venom-filled times with Chris. When that happened, and such times did with increasing frequency, Kate was at a loss. Except each time the loss appeared to be more severe, the loose ends less attached. She no longer knew in which direction she was going. Or even ought to be. Adrift in a chaotic sea of her own creation, she spent hours thinking about Chris, about Joseph.

Instead of anchoring her now, thoughts of Joseph would spin her into an even greater frenzy of hopelessness. Her desire for him was mitigated by her fear that he would move out of her life before she could ever find the courage to go to him again. She wanted him, but she feared the price she would have to pay to get him.

Like Sol, it would require defiance of her parents. But it would also mean that she would have to stand up to Chris, to withstand the merciless blows of his rage.

Beyond the price, beyond the confusion, Joseph had come to symbolize something for Kate that she knew only in his presence: wholeness and freedom. And yet she was afraid to extend her hand into the darkness and grab hold of it.

All that she had hoped for, all that she had longed for, was now within her grasp. But she could not make that final decision to reach out and get it. She chastised herself for her lack of conviction, her inability to make the most important choice of her life. And all the while she ached at the emptiness of her hands, her heart, knowing now that only Joseph could fill them.

"I had a dream last night," she had told Chris that afternoon.

"Oh?" he asked with an obviously obligatory response.

"I had a party. But I didn't know any of the guests. Except one. I had to keep introducing myself, asking names, finding out who all these strangers were who had come into my life. I had made a pie for dessert. A pecan pie, and it was beautiful." She smiled at the remembrance of it, and at the secret knowledge that the only person she had known in her dream had been Joseph. "But when I took the pie out of the refrigerator to serve it, it had shrunk. And there was a piece missing. I was humiliated because there wouldn't be enough to go around."

Kate sipped her wine thoughtfully. "I was so sad. Desperately sad. Desolately alone in my own home. I walked across the yard—there were Japanese lanterns everywhere—and it was lovely in the dim light. All of that beauty for stangers. I walked across the yard to the corner and Nana was there. She put her arms around me and asked me over and over again what was wrong. 'Tell me, tell me,' she would say. And then I said, 'I am so lonely and so filled with fear that I think I might die of it.' "

"That's it?" asked Chris.

"That's it."

"I don't know what to do about you, Kate," Chris said wearily. "I know you're suffering. God knows, we all know you're suffering."

"What do you think I should do?" asked Kate with a timid hopefulness.

"I don't care, just do something!" Chris exploded like a terrorist's bomb: destructively and without warning. "Do something, anything, for God's sake! Living with you is like living with a perpetual mourner. You bemoan your fate but you don't do anything about it. Look at you, all crumpled up, whining like a two-year-old who didn't get her way. And all over nothing! Do you hear me? Nothing!"

"Nothing?" she said softly, awed by his massive and tyrannical lack of understanding.

Mercifully, the phone rang, and Chris was called to the hospital.

Kate had been drinking all afternoon, but still managed to get the children to sleep early.

She sat huddled in the corner of the sofa, castigating herself for her inability to make one clear choice that would ease her agony. The pain from Chris's attack, from her own screaming inadequacy, had become unbearable. She did not know how the feeling could exist inside her and not explode into pieces, into shards of her former self that bore faint resemblance here and there to the person she had become. This time she could not even wash it all away with the wine. The self-contempt over her own cowardice was stronger than the alcohol, compelling her to stay awake.

She decided to go to bed. It was only eight thirty, but if she could sleep, at least the torment would stop. She poured herself another glass of wine, and went into the bedroom. The carpet, the color of peach champagne, felt soft between her toes. Dropping her clothes in a heap at her feet on the floor, she took her nightgown from a hook in the closet, then closed the mirrored doors. Standing naked before the glass, she looked at her body.

"Not bad," she said aloud. "Not bad for two children." Her flat stomach played a pleasant contrast against the gently rounded curves of her hips. Her breasts were small, but firm and . . . perky, she decided, smiling. Definitely perky. Her face, with a few delicate freckles scattered on her small, straight nose, was pretty. Still unlined, still lovely in the muted light.

"Somebody should want me," she said, speaking to her own image. "Somebody does."

Music flowed into the bedroom from the radio she

had left on. Taking her nightgown, she held it in front of her and began to sway to the rhythm of a Strauss waltz. In perfect time, she held the nightgown like a ghostly dance partner, moving, dancing. One two three, one two three.

The glow from the bedside lamp was caught in the mirrors on the closet, refracting, sparkling, showering light in unexpected places on her body, catching the whiteness of her nightgown, making it whiter.

"What ever happened to the waltz?" she said. "What happened to the waltz?" Dancing around the bed, she spoke to her imaginary partner. "I remember the waltz. I remember the light. All of it in yesterday's dreams. The round glass light at the dances then? What's it called? It shone all over us then. On all of us, on our faces at the last dance. Then it was always 'good night sweetheart . . . till we meet tomorrow . . .' That was always the last dance. So lovely it was then. So sweet. I didn't know it could be so lovely. Remember? How we danced? How we believed? No spoiled dreams then. Just dancing. It was delicious. Delicious so much that I can taste it. Here on my mouth. My mouth made for loving. Can taste it like the spring water at Nana's, all pure and crisp. Someone should want to taste it. Someone does . . . one two three one two three . . . Joseph wants to taste. But I'm afraid. Too afraid. A coward. Remember the light. How it sparkled and shone on us all . . . at the last dance."

Moving into the bathroom, she mumbled to herself, "Got to brush my teeth. Go to sleep."

When she opened the cabinet, the first thing she saw was the bottle of Valium. Her response to it was immediate and sure. That's it, the sleep I need. Forever sleep. No more fights, no more agony. Just sleep. Long, peaceful sleep.

Reaching for the bottle, she took it in her hand and held it up like a priest consecrating the wine.

She stood tall and erect, naked before the cabinet. Very formally, she said, "Here's to Kate. She died of acute cowardice of heart."

At that moment the doorbell rang. Not expecting anyone, she hesitated. Then, out of curiosity, mostly, she grabbed her robe and stumbled to the front door.

Looking through the peephole, she recognized the face of a woman who lived in the building. They were just acquaintances, the kind who smile pleasantly at one another in the elevator.

Kate opened the door. "Yes?" she asked, trying to make herself appear acceptably sober.

"Hi," said the woman cheerfully as she held out a can to Kate. "My name is Gloria, and I'm collecting for mental health."

Laughter cracked from the core of Kate, bursting her open with the blissful irony of the encounter. Gloria stood there dumbfounded, thinking Kate was just the kind of person she was collecting for.

Teetering on the edge of hysteria she was laughing so hard that she could not utter a word. But she held up her hand in a gesture that indicated Gloria should wait right there. Tears streaming down her face, she laughed all the way to the kitchen where she grabbed her change purse and emptied all the contents into her hand.

She returned and dumped the money into the can.

"Thank you very much," said Gloria, backing away.

Kate nodded and closed the door.

She was still laughing intermittently when Chris arrived home.

"What the hell's so funny?" he asked with a strange annoyance that he should find her laughing, instead of broken up over the fight they just had.

His question only served to propel her into new peals of mirth.

"What's so funny?" He repeated.

At last able to speak, Kate answered. "Finally. Finally, I make a decision. A big one. An irrevocable one. I make a choice, Chris . . . and I messed that up, too."

When Dottie weighed integrity against profit, integrity lost. But it was not done without torment, for even Dottie could feel the slime oozing out of her very own life. But it had been perfumed with money, which made it much more bearable.

At least she thought so at the time. When she had called Luke with her decision, he was more than just pleased. He was smug.

"I assumed you'd come to that decision, Dottie. So I went ahead with the deal."

"I see," she said, trying to maintain some dignity in the face of his certainty.

"Well, I'll be talking with you soon, babe." That was all he said.

Knowing she had done something sleazy, she was pleased to have a new book take her mind off it. Ashley and Patrick had presented her with their book entitled *Nana* in the late spring. This project has integrity, she thought to herself. It has meaning.

"Nobody except Dottie would throw a private eleventh reunion party," said Ashley. Her voice was lighthearted and pleased.

Kate giggled on the phone. "I know."

Earlier that day they had both received an invitation from Dottie in the mail that read: "Miss Dottie Langford requests the pleasure of the Troika's company at a high-school reunion in the Catskills, to be held the weekend of June sixth at the Langfords' home. No guests, please."

The idea had come to Dottie suddenly. It was as if she needed to reach back to a past that was kinder. And she could only do it with her friends.

Kate was not able to leave until late on Friday, so

Ashley took the bus with her to meet Dottie, who had driven up earlier in the day.

When they arrived, they were all in a festive mood. Dottie had arranged everything, made all the plans, ordered all the food. All Kate and Ashley had to do was appear.

It was dusk when they arrived. But the outline of the cottage against the trees, the play of dying light on the lake, made them all think back to that other time in their lives when they still held hands with innocence.

"The first thing we do," directed Dottie after they had settled in their various bedrooms, "is to change into our nighties. Here," she said, smiling, holding a box out to each of them.

Opening hers, Kate found a pair of babydoll pajamas, remarkably like those she used to wear. Ashley's were navy blue, flowing, with a sash that tied around her waist. After they were all in their costumes, they went downstairs and built a fire.

"Dinner is simple," Dottie announced. "Popcorn and champagne."

"Oh, God . . . remember the pink champagne we used to drink? We thought we were so sophisticated."

"Well, this time it's Taittinger's. But, you know," said Dottie thoughtfully, "I don't think it could ever taste as good as the sparkling pink."

"No Cokes?" asked Kate. "We must have Cokes."

"Not to worry, it's all here. But I must confess that I stashed some shrimp and lobster alongside the Baby Ruths and Oreos."

"A veritable junk-food feast," said Ashley.

Midway through the evening Kate said, "And now it's time for Ashley to hypnotize Dottie."

"I had forgotten all about that," said Dottie. "Power. That's what I said I wanted."

"I was so afraid your parents were going to come in and discover us," said Kate.

"Well, I got my power," said Dottie.

"And I'm still afraid. Nothing has changed."

"Oh, yes, it has," said Ashley. "We all got our dreams. At least the ones we had then."

Kate said to Ashley, "Dottie got her power and I got my family. But I don't recall you ever really said what you were after."

Surprised, Ashley stopped short. "You know, you're right. I don't think I ever did formulate anything like that in my mind. Later on, I wanted to find something to do, work I loved, but then—"

"Don't forget," interjected Dottie, "that was when you were involved with Alexander."

"And I got him. At least for a while," she added. "Other than that, I don't think I dealt in specifics. I just wanted to live and to feel."

"You've done a good job," said Kate.

"You were smart, Ashley," added Dottie.

"Why?"

"Because both Kate and I have achieved our dreams. And I still don't think it got us what we wanted. It's left a lousy aftertaste."

"I thought you were doing well," said Kate, peering over her fence into the greener grass beyond.

"I am," answered Dottie. "It's just that . . . it gets lonely up at the top. And sometimes pretty sleazy. And it makes me forget that there were times in our lives when we held up Truth and Beauty and Honesty to the light. We believed in them . . . my God, how we believed."

"Once upon a time," said Kate softly.

"Why is it in the past?" asked Ashley. "I still look to those things."

"Really?" asked Dottie. "You really believe in them?"

"I always have," said Ashley. "I never gave it much thought."

"I don't know when it was I lost it," said Dottie.

"Nobody ever does," Kate added. "One day you simply wake up and it's gone. Like a dream you can't remember."

"No, you're wrong," said Ashley. "You choose to give it up."

"There was a choice?"

"Of course, Dottie," answered Ashley in a nonjudgmental tone of voice. "You valued power more, that's all."

"I needed it."

"I know."

"I made the wrong choice, too," said Kate. "And so I stopped making choices altogether."

In the morning Dottie filled two mugs with fresh coffee and went upstairs to awaken her friends.

Sitting up in bed and rubbing her eyes as if she were a child, Kate looked at Dottie. Speaking with a simple gratitude that Dottie did not often hear, she said, "I can't remember the last time when someone did this for me. Thank you."

Dottie realized then how infrequently she made such a simple gesture, as simple as bringing a friend a cup of coffee. Everything in her life was business or preplanned.

When they sat on the beach in the afternoon, it was as if they did not have a care in the world. Three bodies: one delicate, one compact, one long and even powerful. Three women, three friends, celebrating a private reunion in their own lives: a touch in the midst of separations.

Looking at the nearby woods, Kate thought of Sol, of that first morning when he took her for a walk to show her where the Watermelon Baby lived.

Musing about it, she spoke out loud. "I wonder if there ever really has been a choice . . . I don't think so."

Ashley sat up, crossing her legs. She looked at Kate, her arm flung over her eyes to shield them from the sun.

"Do you really mean that?" asked Ashley.

"Yes."

"If you do, you're finished."

"I know."

"Didn't you hear what Joseph was trying to tell you, Katie? Didn't you listen to him at all?" Ashley was not so much angry, as she was impatient. "You are determined to use the shape of your past to predict the form of the future. Haven't you ever questioned that? You don't have to be what you are, Kate. You don't have to do what you do. And you say you haven't made a choice. But you have. You have chosen to deprive yourself of your own freedom. Freedom to choose and freedom to change."

Ashley was propelled to go on; she felt an intense need to get her idea across to Kate. And she didn't care how gentle she was going about it. It had to be done.

"There's an old saying, Kate, a nice vulgar one that applies to you. Shit or get off the pot. Otherwise, don't bother shaking hands with your destiny. Because you've already met."

As the impact of her words tumbled over them, it was met with silence. "I'm sorry," said Ashley, "sorry if I was too rough on you, Katie. I love you, you know."

"I know," replied Kate.

"There's help, if you believe, Katie. I learned from Nana and Joseph that you have to believe in . . . other things."

"Like what?"

"It's hard to find words for it." As she spoke, Ashley was unaware of how beautiful she was. She was regal in her completeness, in the knowledge that she knew where she was going and was satisfied with where she had been. But there was no arrogance in her. Instead, there was the power to feel totally and completely, without intellectual preception or moral judgment. For her things *were*, things *are*. A part of a whole she did not really understand. Instead, she lived it.

"Both of you," she continued to Kate and Dottie, "called the dance from the beginning. And the piper played it. Very obligingly. And now you don't want to pay. But you have to. You can't call for a change in the tune till you've paid for the music."

"Do you really believe you can change it?" asked Kate, like a child talking to Tinker Bell, wanting desperately to believe.

"I really believe it," answered Ashley. "I believe that we are responsible for the choices we make. For instance, I am responsible for the death of Nana. I knew I was doing the right thing, but I suffered greatly for it. Joseph taught me how to take hold of my decisions, to claim them and make them mine. He taught me that there's more power within us than we could possibly learn about. It's not a question of understanding it. Or using it. It's a question of believing and being."

"How?" asked Dottie.

"I don't really know," Ashley answered truthfully. "I wish I could tell you. But I do know that I've paid my dues. It didn't happen overnight. I've crawled deep into dark places."

"Weren't you ever afraid?" asked Kate.

"Of course I was. But that was never really a consideration."

"Why?"

"Because the knowledge was more important than the fear." She paused a moment, thinking. "Do you know what a black hole is?"

"Something theoretical out in space," Dottie answered.

"The theory is that when a large star is spent, when

it burns up its nuclear fuel, it collapses. It collapses in on itself. The gravity of the star is condensed to maybe the size of a golf ball. And it is so dense, so intense, that it sucks up everything around it. Not even light can escape."

"Please continue, Dr. Van Every," said Kate.

"Well, I think some people are like that. Some people take everything and return nothing. They are so turned in on themselves that they no longer reach out. They have nothing, finally, to offer, except theoretical existence. They radiate nothing, touch nothing." Ashley stopped, took a deep breath, and then smiled. "And that, my children, is what happens when you don't make choices. Everything caves inward. Fear becomes a living thing. And knowledge is forgotten. End of lecture."

Dottie put up her hand. "Oh, no, not yet, Professor. The lecture isn't over yet. Kate and I sit here awash in dilemma . . . you're the only one who's gotten to a place where there's peace." Her voice turned serious then. "Why? I want to know why, Ashley."

"What do you mean?"

"I know what she means," said Kate. "I have this feeling that you've known so much more than us. God knows, you've had to bear the grief of five people, considering the number of years you've lived. You've lost more, and yet . . . you're way ahead. Your whole lifetime seems to have been condensed and you've extracted the essence from it. Tell us how. Why?"

Ashley turned serious, her brow furrowing in concentration. "Some of it is genetic, I suppose. And some I've learned. I don't know how. But I've always known—since I was a little girl—that I would have to pack it in, pack it tight. When I was little, I would sit and listen to a symphony on the radio. And the music would take me with it and I knew there was something more. And I wanted to know what it was. I understood that human beings are capable of being transported by beauty. I wanted to be a part of it. Not an onlooker. I wanted to know what was beyond the music. Wicked or splendid, I wanted to know." She paused a moment. "I read something not long ago. Something an old mountain woman said. She was asked what she would do differently if she had it to do over again. And this simple woman answered, 'If I had it to do over again, I would go barefoot earlier in the spring, I would ride more carousels, I would pick more daisies.' I never want to say that at the end of my life."

There was a long silence before Kate finally asked, "Ashley?"

"Umm?"

"Have you learned what it is? Have you seen it? Do you know what's beyond the music?"

"Yes."

## CHAPTER 14

The wash of light upon the mountain, gentled by the wind; the howl of the coyote and the morning greeting of the chipmunk; the silent arc of the red-tailed hawk and the blaze of wildflowers meeting the meadows; the shivering silver sound of the aspens, the crisp air and clean clear night lit by perfect stars; the touch of a hand in loving, the warmth of a body in sleep. All this Patrick and Ashley shared that summer in New Mexico. All.

"Joseph said he might come down tonight for dinner," Ashley said to Patrick at the breakfast table.

Patrick smiled. "You love him a lot, don't you."

"I love him as if I've known him forever. Like a brother."

"Marry me," said Patrick, changing to his well-worn theme. "For the ten-thousandth time, marry me."

Ashley smiled. "All right."

Patrick walked over to her and took her head in his hands. "Do you mean it?"

"Yes. It's time."

"You mean it's about time," he amended.

"No. I mean it's time for babies."

He growled playfully at her, nuzzling her neck. "Then let's go make one. Right now," he invited with a wicked gleam in his eyes, his hand wandering over her body.

"We already have."

"We have?" he asked, half comprehending.

"Yes. I'm three weeks late."

Patrick lifted her from the floor and spun her around in his joy. "A child! A child! We're going to have a baby!"

"Am I to assume, then, that it's all right with you?"

"All right? Did you say all right?" His words were soft, intense, spun from the web of his wild and deep loving of this remarkable woman. "That word is definitely not good enough for the occasion. It deserves a sonnet, at the very least."

"Because it is a special day," said Ashley. "I'm going to take you to the special place where the wood lily blooms."

"I thought you'd never ask," he said.

They rode for several hours, the horses making their leisurely way up the mountain and through the meadow, before they reached the secluded and secret corner of the world where the wood lily grew. Rose-colored and rare, delicate and lovely, they knelt together to examine it.

Nearby moss and fern laid a soft quilt, green and

inviting, for them to rest on. A ruby-throated hummingbird did its gravity-defying act, hovering in midair as it tasted the honey of primrose and bluebell. The music of the creek, flowing over rocks and around fallen branches, surrounded them.

Shining through the spruce and aspen, the sun illuminated the bed where they made love, naked as the nature around them intended them to be. Pure. Without shame. Only with joy and passion and commitment.

Afterward Ashley fell asleep in his arms. Too happy to sleep, Patrick watched, her mouth parted slightly in peaceful breathing, her dark lashes resting on her cheeks. Memorizing her, he thought then what a fortunate man he was that the fates had chosen to smile on him in such a perfect way. He, too, had paid his dues, had wandered in the deserts of his parched imagination and stumbled upon fertile valleys of his own making. But this splendor, this passion beyond anything he had ever known, this quiet loving surpassing anything he had ever conceived, was his treasure. He would not treat it lightly nor forget his gratitude, swearing then to himself never to abuse this trust that had been given them so freely, never to take for granted this quiet serenity that could disappear with the passing of one ill-fated breeze.

When finally she opened her eyes, he was looking at her, committing her to a deeper part of his memory—that sheltered and hidden secret of himself that he could recall at will on a dark stormy night, that he could touch with longing and fulfillment on the distant and solitary journeys that he still was destined to travel.

This, then, was their shining moment, that enchanted sanctuary that rests like the flight of a hummingbird on the wings of time. It belonged to them, all the loving and the living, at that moment. It was theirs: the sky and the water, the deer and the wolf, the blossom and the sun. They were a part of it all, as it was a part of them. And they rested in the comfort of its arms with a joy that only a blessed few have ever known.

Their journey home was silent; they felt no need for words. Their communion was complete.

Disappointed that Joseph was not at the house waiting for them, Ashley said, "I suppose he was too involved in his work to come down tonight."

"We can ride up to the cabin tomorrow and take a bottle of champagne. The advent of a child should be celebrated on a daily basis, anyway," Patrick said smiling.

"Right," she replied, slipping the saddle off Troika and carrying it to the rail. "Steak for dinner?"

"Perfect. I'll charcoal it."

"Steak and salad and champagne."

"I'll drink to that," he said.

Pleasantly tired after their long day, they went to bed early. They built a fire in the fireplace, and the fragrant aroma of piñon perfumed the air in the room.

Patrick fell asleep first, his slow breathing a peaceful companion to Ashley's. She lay happily awake, watching the shadows of the fire dance on the whitewashed walls. Already loving the child she was carrying so fragile and delicate inside her, she leaned over and touched Patrick, his face golden from the light of the fire. "I am so filled with the loving of you," she whispered. "Filled." And she fell finally into a deep and restful sleep.

It was still dark when she awakened. The light from the fire was low, casting a soft glow in the room. At first she thought it was a shadow, hovering there by the wall, just a shadow from the dim light of the fire. But it moved, moved toward her, floating and silent. Then she knew. She had not seen it since Nana died, and its presence awakened all her senses. She was not frightened for herself. She only wondered why it was there. She turned to Patrick. He was sleeping soundly next to her, unaware of the presence that had entered the room. Who then, she thought. Who? And her mind turned to Joseph, alone in his cabin, without any way to communicate if he were in trouble. Suddenly the fact that he did not come home for dinner took on new meaning, and she was deeply frightened for him. Why else would it be here? she thought. If it *is* here. If it is here because of my brother . . .

Slipping soundlessly out of bed, she grabbed her Levi's jeans and went into the bathroom to dress. Pulling on her boots, she stumbled in her haste, catching herself against the wall.

Taking a flashlight with her, she grabbed a heavy jacket off the hook on the wall by the door and walked down to the barn, grateful that there was a full moon to light her way.

"Easy now, Troika, easy now," she said in a soft voice as she slipped the bridle over his head and placed the bit in his mouth. Catching hold of the reins, she climbed the rail on the fence and slipped onto the horse, shunning the time it would take to saddle him.

Riding bareback, she loosened the reins and gave the horse a gentle nudge with her heels. He did not need any further instructions from Ashley. Knowing what it was she wanted, Troika galloped up the road that would take her to Joseph's cabin. Gripping him easily with her strong legs, she leaned close to his neck, her hair flying free behind her.

Let him be all right, she prayed. Let him be safe. Please, God, don't let anything happen to him. Please. No more. I couldn't bear it.

The road changed to a well-worn path as it began its slight incline up the beginning of the mountain. Still she did not slow down her horse, suddenly frantic with her need to see her brother, to cancel out the omen that had visited her room.

The light from the moon and the stars shone on the path before them; the purity of the night stood in direct contrast to the mounting anxiety that was growing inside her.

"Faster," she said to Troika, giving him all of his rein. "Faster."

It was only a roadrunner, common and speckled, long-tailed and funny, that scurried before them on the path. Ashley saw it first. But not soon enough to prevent Troika from shying. Not soon enough to prevent him, his magnificent strong body shining and sinewy, from stopping too suddenly, then rearing in a frantic effort to avoid the threat.

Ashley threw herself forward against the horse's neck. She rose with him as his hooves flailed frantically. Then she flew from his back, tumbling wildly, floating through the air, her hair caught by the wind, her arms outstretched in an awesome and obscene beauty as she fell to the merciless and rocky blanket of earth waiting to meet her.

Kate set the coffee cup down gently on the table beside her. Then she stood up. In the few seconds required to make that simplest of human movements, something snapped inside her. Perhaps it was because she had reached the point of no return and thus had nothing to lose; or perhaps it was because Chris had just loaded the proverbial last straw on her overburdened and underloved back. Mystical or real, whatever it was, something changed in her forever.

"Just last week," she said, her voice clear and even, "you told me that it was all right. You told me that you thought it might be good for me to go back to school. Do you remember, Chris? Those were your very words. That it might be good for me."

"I remember," he mumbled wearily.

"And now that I've enrolled in classes . . . now you tell me that you're having second thoughts."

"Listen to me, Kate," he said in a placating voice. "It's just that it's going to take such a long time. It will be years before you get an advanced degree."

"But I'm beginning now. I don't doubt that it will be years. Because I recognize the fact that I am also responsible to you and the boys, so I can't go back to school full-time. But when I do get the degree, they'll be old enough. Then I can go on a dig. Be involved in my profession."

"But three afternoons a week? And all the studying at night?"

"Yes," she said firmly, taking another sip of her coffee. "Three afternoons a week. And that schedule can differ from semester to semester."

"That's a lot of juggling and changing," he said doubtfully, his voice filled with threats of imaginary consequences.

"What are you trying to say, Chris? That if I want to go to school for fun, just like pottery and weaving, that it's all right? But that if I want to be a real student, be serious about a commitment, that it's unacceptable? Is that why you changed your mind? Because you were afraid of what might happen if I were to dedicate myself to something besides my family? Does that frighten you?"

"Really, Kate," said Chris with an attempt at dismissal of the entire bothersome conversation.

Kate walked over to the window. Standing with her back to him, she thought of herself a long time ago. "Never toady to the Watermelon Baby," Sol had told her then. "If you cower before him, you're his. Enduring is part of the secret." And she remembered Ashley just a few weeks ago telling her that in order to survive, she must assume responsibility for her own choices.

"You know what you remind me of?" asked Kate. Her voice had such a quality of sureness that, had he closed his eyes, Chris might not have known that it was Kate speaking.

"What do I remind you of?" he asked with a languid insolence.

"When I was a little girl, I had lots of ear infections. You know that. Will had them, too. It's hard to believe that there was no penicillin then. But there wasn't." She turned from the window and walked back to sit down. Settled once more, she continued, "The only treatment then was to lance the eardrum. A hideously painful precedure. Daddy allowed us to have a whiff of ether before it happened. But once when the doctor gave it to Will, he stopped breathing for a minute. And after that Daddy didn't allow us to have any more anesthetic. We would just have to bear the pain, he said."

Kate's eyes shone with a fiery brilliance, catching the light of her passion in a trap constructed of years of anxiety. Chris said nothing, just listened intently. "And so . . . we would get another ear infection and mother would take us to this doctor. Dreadful person. He died a couple of years ago and I was glad of his passing. We would go to him and each time I would come away from there the front of my dress—usually one of those little hand-smocked yokes in some pastel color—would be soaked with my tears. God, I can still remember how much it hurt. But that doctor made it hurt even more. And I'll tell you why."

Chris looked at her strangely, then nodded.

"Each time we visited him, he would smile and say, 'Don't worry, Katie. We're just going to look at your ear today. I won't hurt you. I promise.' And each time I would trust him again and I wouldn't object and I would let him look in my ear and all of a sudden, with a scalpel that he had hidden, he would lance it again and I never had any warning because each time he lied to me and told me he wouldn't hurt me, and over and over I believed him." Her mouth tightened, and her eyes flashed with the remembrance. "God, I remember it so well. And looking back on it, I can't believe that I was dumb enough to keep trusting him. But I did. I've never felt pain quite like that again, quite as sharp and piercing and hideous. He made it hurt more because he lied. And every goddamn time he did it I was surprised and he would apologize that he had to do it. And I would scream. With rage as much as pain, I suspect. I would be incensed that I had been gullible enough to fall into the arms of his deceit again. I did it every time . . . he—could—count—on—it."

She stopped then, taking a deep breath, leaning toward Chris with an intensity he had never seen in her. She glowed with it, with the confidence of her conviction. Chris was speechless. Even awed.

Then she continued. "And that's what you remind me of, Chris. That doctor. He would put out his hand and then he would stick it to me again. Just like you, Chris. Every time, all these years, I have believed you when you put out your hand to me. Always, I would believe. And then you would withdraw it and I would fall into a silent rage, soaking my little dress with the tears of your betrayal. And this time, when you said you thought school would be a good thing, I believed you again. I really did, Chris. I thought you meant it. And now, just like that goddamn doctor, you're withdrawing the offer. I have put up my ear for you to examine for the last time, Chris. I trusted you with this one, and now you're holding the scalpel again, waiting to cut me back down to a manageable size. But I'm not going to let you do it this time. Not now. It's gone too far to the other side. I'm strong enough to push it away. Don't ask me why, because I don't know. Something happened, that's all. But it doesn't matter. So I'm taking you at your word, Chris. Your first word. And I'm going back to school. And I am here, sitting right here in front of you, and I am telling you that this is the last time I fall for that. No more, Chris. No more. You withdrew your offer one too many times. And I won't have it. So you can just throw away your scalpel. I won't give you the chance to use it on me anymore. Never never again."

Fully recognizing the enormity of the decision that Kate had made, Chris tried one more time to recoup his losses. "Married people are supposed to make decisions together, Kate. Don't you think—"

"This is what I think, Chris, I think we haven't been really married for a long time. And so I'm telling you. Not asking your permission like the obedient but very angry child I have been for so many years. Good or bad, I'm going to do it. I know that I'm a fledgling," she said, thinking of Joseph as she unconsciously stroked the silver bird she still wore around her neck. "There is a great risk of failure inherent in this decision of mine. And if I try my wings and discover that I can, indeed, fly, then I'll tell you something else I'm going to do, Chris. I'm going to get my life together. And, in the process, I will probably leave you. And there won't be one goddamn thing you can do to stop me. Because once my mind's made up, I'll not allow it. Do you hear? I—will—not—allow—it."

In all her life Kate had never spoken like this, much less experienced the soaring exhilaration that accompanied her words. It was as if she were dressed with a magic that was totally alien, yet one that fitted her perfectly. She could feel its strength, feel the pleasure she derived from it, feel its power, as she made her private declaration of independence. From out of nowhere this mantle of strength was laid on her, and she knew that it would never leave her again. And so she sat quietly and waited. Waited for him to say something.

He did not know how much time passed before he found any words to form with his mouth. In those few moments it had taken her to finish what she had to say, he had watched her transformation into a woman he did not know.

In a voice interlaced with a mosaic of emotions so intricate and obscure that he could not even touch their origin, he spoke. The outrageous and futile irony of his words came to Kate like an enlightening slap in the face. It was emphasized even more by the obvious sincerity of his voice, only serving to magnify the fact that it was, indeed, too late.

"I have never," said Chris, his voice husky from emotion and even desire, "I have never, in all our life together, Kate . . . seen you as beautiful as you are at this very moment."

It was three o'clock in the morning when the phone rang. Unaware of what it was at first, Dottie struggled for enough consciousness to sort out the sounds of her dreams from those happening in reality. On the fifth ring she put out her hand and groped for the receiver. Fumbling, she finally moved it to her ear, her heart beating faster now because of her fear of phone calls at dark hours.

"Hello?"

"Dot?"

"Who is this?" she asked, almost awake.

"Jack."

"Oh," she responded, stunned. Time, she thought. I need a little time to pull myself together. Squinting, she glanced at the clock, its glow eerie in the midst of her confusion. "Do you know what time it is?" she asked in what she hoped was a playful voice.

"Midnight."

"Jack . . . let us not forget that what is midnight for a madman who chooses to live in California is three o'clock in the morning for a New Yorker, sane or not."

"Ah shit. Sorry, Dot. I'll call back tomorrow."

"No!" she said quickly. "I'm awake now."

"And I'm drunk. Stark raving drunk, Dorothy Langford."

"I never would have guessed," she said, reaching over to switch on the lamp beside her bed. "What's the occasion? An extra-special sunset?" She remembered how, when she had visited him, the people who lived on the beach would often come out to watch a sunset, rating it on a scale of one to ten. For a ten, there was always unabashed applause and celebration.

"An extra-special book," he replied. "I just finished it today."

"Congratulations, Shakespeare." Keep it light, she directed herself. Keep it friendly. Keep it. Please.

"The comparison is apt, Dot. To be modest, it's an undisguised work of genius. Splendid. Brilliant."

"As splendid as you are in your cups, I imagine."

"Almost," he said, laughing. "And I want you to handle it, Dot. What's past is forgotten. I want you to be my agent again."

"You know how much I would like that, Jack." Tears of simple gratitude streamed down her face. "I'd like that so much."

"So be it," he said. "But no monkey business . . ."

"I promise, Jack. No monkey business. Ever again." Her hands were shaking with the effort to control her joy. "So when am I going to see this work of genius?"

"Tomorrow?"

"You certainly don't waste any time."

"Thought I'd fly in. You free for the weekend?"

"I am."

"Save it for me."

"I shall. My pleasure."

"Till tomorrow, then," he said.

"Till tomorrow."

Dottie hung up the phone and stared at it as if it were a dear friend. Throwing her arms up in the air, she called out to herself. "Hello, Jack, good-bye, Luke! No more monkey business!" She felt lighter than she had in years, as if a burden had been lifted from her shoulders. A burden whose weight had grown so gradually that she had not been aware of how oppressively heavy it had become. Only the absence of the massive weight could give her what she needed most: freedom. Freedom to choose.

Ashley lay on the path slipping gently in and out of consciousness. Once his wildness had passed, Troika stood quietly next to her, his long neck reaching down, the reins falling from his noble head and coiling on the ground like a benign serpent. He nudged her, but she did not move.

Her eyes opened, fluttering crazily for a moment, and she saw her horse. It took her a moment to discern what had happened. Vaguely remembering the apparition that had appeared in her room, she thought, who then? Was it all the time me?

She had received a serious blow on the back of her head. Her body had landed on the grassy side of the path. But her head had hit a stone. She did not think she had any broken bones, but when she tried to move, she became so dizzy that she lost consciousness. The blood from the gash had dried, forming a congealed dirty mess on the back of her head.

In an injury of this sort the brain is badly bruised. Sometimes, as in the case of Ashley, the blow can be so severe that it causes a rupturing of blood vessels within the brain itself. Called a subdural hematoma, it can be very serious, indeed. Usually, only immediate surgery can aid the victim. The reason is this. The brain itself, a miraculous mass of convoluted nerves and tissue, is protected from harm because it is totally encased in a closed space. The skull protects it from injury. If, however, there is a serious injury inside this region, the result can be hemorrhaging. If the bleeding is minor, the brain can accommodate the very limited accumulation of blood. But if it is a major injury, there is no place for the resulting blood to go. The skull that protects the brain is hard and immovable. It will not expand or contract. Therein lies the problem. As the bleeding continues, there is no space for the blood to pool. Therefore, in a process that first leads to unconsciousness, the brain begins to be displaced by the increasing pressure of the accumulating blood. But there is only one exit for it, only one opening into which it can move in order to make room for this increasing volume of blood. Slowly, the brain is pushed out of the skull. It herniates and is shoved on an inexorable journey down the spinal canal. The next stage is coma. As the brain continues to move, the mass inevitably reaches the nerves that control breathing in the human body. Once these nerves are damaged by the alien presence of brain matter, the result is a loss of the ability to breathe. Then death.

Mercifully, this is a painless process. Once unconsciousness has set in, there is no more feeling.

For an hour or two Ashley slipped in and out of consciousness. She did not feel the chill of the night nor the gentle blessing of morning dew as it covered her like an enchanted blanket.

She lay quiet and unmoving, her sentinel a horse, her requiem a splendid sunrise.

Functioning on levels she had suspected, but never before known, her mind carried her—floating and wispy—to that place where dreams are born.

Beautiful, she thought. Beautiful. But don't want to go now. Soon too soon and my baby needs to grow to live my baby whom I love so much my only pure regret my baby is. Patrick will be alone again and I cannot touch him to ease the pain, so alone he'll be and sorry, Patrick, so sorry to leave you now when it glowed with loving and laughter. Beautiful and delicate and true it is, Patrick. There will be other sunsets for you. I promise. Other secret flowers, other hidden valleys and sanctuaries. Joseph? Are you there? I thought it was you, Joseph, and I'm so glad that it wasn't because I could not bear to mourn again, you shone so brightly in my life. Could not bear it, you shone so, the prism of your love refracting its light in so many ways, teaching me it was possible to see beyond the music. So few. So few left now. Whose love made a difference. Not many in this world. So flawed are we all with the effort of loving. Wanted to show Kate and Dottie. Show them it could be done, that destiny is not so elusive that it cannot be touched. Soon. Too soon. But I'm a part of it now. Part of it all. I've done it all.

Floating now, she rose above her own self, awed by this mystery that had become hers. Floating, she could see her own body. Could see the rising of the sun, its light the purest she had ever known, the whitest, the warmest.

She could see Troika standing beside her, still waiting, his head bent to the earth.

Then Patrick was there. He appeared on his horse, reined it in with a fury, jumping from the saddle before it had stopped. He ran to her then and knelt over her inert body. It's all right, Patrick, she wanted to say. It's all right now. But he did not hear her. Feeling frantically for her pulse, he leaned over her body to see if she were breathing. Patrick, love, it's all right, she called to him silently. I've done it all. Please. His body slumped and he sat down beside her like a marionette whose strings have suddenly been severed. Taking her head in his hands, he pulled her into his lap and held her tighter than she had ever known, his tears washing the stains of dirt from her face. He wept in a final farewell to the beauty and haunting elegance of Ashley's life. He did not know that it was peaceful now. Content. For a long time he held her.

Slowly, disbelieving, he opened his eyes and looked around him. Then, lifting his arm to the sky, he clenched his fist, shaking it in fury at the god who had brought this woman to him, who had blessed him with her child, only to take it away with one capricious wag of his bony finger. He opened his mouth, but no sound came out. It was parched and dry and dead. No sound at all, until finally he screamed, his words echoing off the mountains, the tears spilling onto the dying heart of his love. "NNNNO!" he wailed in an anguished cry at destiny. "Nooooo!" answered the mountains, as if in reply. "AASHLEYYY!"

Then he slumped over her, his arms tight around her body, tight and desperate and despairing. He began to rock her, his body moving back and forth, rocking her as he would have rocked the baby they would never have. The child born out of their forever loving.

That is how Joseph found them. He had heard Patrick's cry long before he arrived on his lonely and spectral journey down the mountain. He heard Patrick's cry. Heard death in it. He already knew, however. He had awakened knowing it. And he had wept on his descent down the mountain.

The light grew brighter for Ashley. The light of a thousand splendid suns. Instead of blinding her, it allowed her to see more, allowed her to see Nana waiting, arms extended in welcome. It's time now, she felt Nana say. It's time to go.

Joseph? Patrick? I must leave now. I must leave you and your loving. Please know it's all right. Please. I promise it's all right. Do you hear me? It's all right. I've done it all. I've heard the music and sung the songs and now it's time. It's time for me to go.